LISA TURNER

A LITTLE DEATH

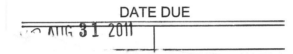

IN DIXIE

Bell Bridge Books

Acknowledgements

I wish to thank the following law enforcement professionals, attorneys, and others for sharing their knowledge and amazing stories. Every one of you should write a book. Any errors should be laid at the author's feet and not theirs.

Assistant Chief Terry L. Leggett, (Ret.) Shelby County Sheriff's Office, Memphis, TN.

Will Heaton, Attorney

Johnnie Walker, Private Investigator (Ret.)

Lieutenant James B. Flatter, (Ret.) Monroe County Sheriff's Office, Key West, FL.

Lieutenant Paul Sheffield, (Ret.) Memphis Police Department

Danny Richardson, Attorney

Glen Bomar, man of the South

Pheobe and Ferd Heckle II, Memphis cotton broker

Thanks to my brilliant and steadfast editors, Debra Dixon and Deborah Smith, for sharing their talent and loving support. DD, you made it happen.

Thanks to my first writing mentor, Michael Finger.

Thanks to wise-woman Linda Kichline for her counsel, expertise and for always believing in this book. You're a true friend.

Most of all, loving appreciation to Rob Sangster for his unwavering patience and good humor throughout this adventure, for sharing his legal and political expertise and for his superior editor's eye.

DEDICATION

For Rob Sangster, a man of wisdom and words,
king of the road and love of my life.

For my mother, sister and many friends who, if they
ever doubted, never showed it.

For my father, who passed away before he could
hold this book in his hands.

Bell Bridge Books
PO BOX 300921
Memphis, TN 38130

ISBN: 978-1-935661-90-0

Bell Bridge Books is an Imprint of BelleBooks, Inc.

We at BelleBooks enjoy hearing from readers. You can contact us at the address above or at BelleBooks@BelleBooks.com

Visit our websites – www.BelleBooks.com and www.BellBridgeBooks.com.

10 9 8 7 6 5 4 3 2

Cover design: Debra Dixon
Interior design: Hank Smith
Photo credits:
river © Avesun | Dreamstime.com
guitar © Dmitry Fetisov | Dreamstime.com

:Le:01:

Detective Billy Able

Cops like me won't admit it out loud, but a lot of us believe murder has its right time and proper reason. Especially in Memphis, where Elvis died and the blues were born out of pride, anger and need. There's a timetable. Shit has its own schedule.

Knifings happen on Friday night. Shootings on Saturday night. The streetlights come up and the shooting begins. Monday mornings? It's road rage if I-240 backs up and people get a chance to look each other in the eye.

Count on multiple killings the week of a full moon or any day the temperature breaks a hundred degrees and air conditioners give out and die. That's when murder happens. The calls come in. The squad responds.

But Saturday morning is different. People shouldn't kill each other on Saturday morning. They should mow their lawns and pick up groceries. Murder ain't your proper Saturday morning activity.

Except in Memphis. In Memphis you can commit murder any Saturday morning you like.

Chapter One

Saturday, 9:30 a.m.

The elderly black man lay crumpled and dead in the marigolds bordering his clapboard house. He lay on his side. The fist-sized gnome that sat beside his head in the flowerbed grinned.

Detective Sergeant Billy Able of the Memphis PD Homicide Squad circled the body then squatted down for a closer look. It was August in Memphis, Tennessee, a city founded on the bluffs above the Mississippi River. Hot, flat, tornado bait. The bluffs were one of the last bunkers on the eastern seaboard before everything flattened toward the Midwest.

Sometimes Billy knew how Memphis felt. Like an outpost on the Southern frontier.

He wiped sweat off the back of his neck and glanced at the blue skies. Too clear to be this humid in the morning. Then he remembered rain would be moving in from Arkansas some time in the evening.

Billy Able was a thirty-two-year-old Mississippi boy, tall and lanky, with the inherited good looks of Southern aristocracy gone to seed. Just that morning his partner had ragged him about his hair. Said he wore it too long for the squad to take him seriously.

Screw that, Billy thought. *What does a haircut have to do with closing a case?*

The Crime Scene Unit had finished with the body. Billy took out his steno pad, noted the blood on the gnome's concrete hat, and shifted the gentleman's face out of the flowers. The neck and jaw had stiffened only slightly, the eyes turned milky behind the lids.

Billy shot his own photos of the body. The camera lens made the old man's whittled-down frame look fragile as a boy's. His legs were contracted into a fetal position as if he'd hit the ground and drawn up. No shirt. One shoe, a scuffed wingtip, no socks. Fly unzipped. Penis exposed. Fingers curled in on themselves like dry leaves.

Billy scanned the side yard for anything out of the ordinary. The neighbor's dog barked at him through the back door screen. Billy sniffed. The air around the body smelled like marigolds and Old Spice. A fly landed on the old man's nose and waded through blood clotting on the upper lip. Billy waved it away, giving the man his dignity.

A shadow passed over him from the porch above. His partner, Lou Nevers, could sneak up on a person, quiet as a bat. But not on Billy. They'd worked together six years, and he knew all of Lou's best moves.

Like this morning when Lou started complaining about Billy's second-hand suit. Lou wanted to get the upper hand because Billy was mad about the overtime shift Lou had lined up. And what the hell, Billy liked his suit, black and summer-weight with a white shirt and black tie, all bought at the St. Vincent DePaul's thrift store off Vance Avenue. Add dark shades and he looked like a Beale Street blues player. He had a reason for not wearing the same polyester crap as the rest of the dickhead detectives. Going against type had its advantages, especially in the interview room.

Lou frowned at him from the porch, saying nothing.

"You get any sleep last night, old man?" Billy said.

"I'll sleep when I'm dead. There's a wingtip up here on the porch."

His partner had lost twenty pounds in the year since his divorce. At sixty-one, the weight loss made him look gaunt, not fit. He wore the same kind of short sleeve shirt as yesterday, the same polyester slacks, and one of two blue striped ties given to him by his ex-wife last Christmas. Lou rarely let himself off the leash where style was concerned.

Since the divorce, Lou had turned into a private man living by his own private rules. That meant, in his dealings with Lou, Billy was shooting in the dark. Best he could do was to try for business as usual.

"Other wingtip's down here with the body," Billy said. "Somebody whopped this old boy in the back of the head. Knocked him out of his shoes. And his fly's open."

Lou came off the porch and ducked under the crime scene tape. Neighbors carrying umbrellas against the sun had gathered across the street. They began to whisper when they saw Lou leave the porch. They didn't trust the police but depended on them anyway, like children with a bad set of parents. Some tilted their umbrellas like shields as a white patrolman moved among them asking questions.

Lou studied the body in the flowerbed for a while, then unwrapped a toothpick and stuck it between his teeth. "Nothing more pitiful than O-M-P."

"What's that?"

Lou pointed at the withered penis. "Old Man Pud."

Billy grinned in spite of himself.

Lou bent and ran his finger over the victim's ribs. Purplish blots under the skin shifted. "Lividity isn't fixed."

"Looks to be about four hours. That puts him in the box around six this morning."

"Maybe he was out all night, came in drunk, fell over the railing," Lou said.

"Nope. I smell Old Spice. He had a morning shave." Billy held back the man's ear to reveal a glob of shaving cream. "Can't say what happened, but the man's business is definitely hanging out of his pants. You find the first officer?"

"In the house with an hysterical witness. Don't want any part of that." Lou squatted down to study the contusion. "Bet I can tell you how he scratched and why, right now, game over, we're out of here before lunch."

"Get out."

"No, really."

"If we're done early, how about you coaching me at the batting cages?" Billy said. He'd been having trouble with his swing and making a fool of himself at the MPD league games. Lou had played shortstop in college and coached Babe Ruth league. He was almost as good a coach as he was a cop. At least part of a Saturday could be salvaged.

"Hell no. If we're done early you're going to buy me a steak sandwich at The Western." Lou's eyes shifted mischievously, like old times.

"You got it."

They stood. Lou's knee popped.

"So what's your call?" Billy said.

The toothpick waggled between Lou's teeth. "The man died peeing off the porch."

"This ain't no heart attack, somebody hit him."

"Trust me. This old boy relieved himself in a natural setting one too many times. Most likely the wife cracked him over the head with whatever was handy."

Billy considered the lump on the back of the man's head, the unzipped fly. Damn. He'd have to stop at an ATM for lunch money. Then he smiled. "You got it half right, pard. I'll go with peeing off the porch, but it wasn't the bang on the head that killed him. What got him was falling face down on a yard elf."

Lou's pager buzzed in his pocket. He carried a department-issued cell phone, but he'd never given up his pager habit. He checked the number and winced. "Pain-in-the-ass . . . I'll get back to him. Go on, I'm listening."

"Adiosis by septumosis. His septum pierced his brain. I had a friend who was fooling around on a neighbor's horse. It reared and smashed the kid's nose bone into his brain. Dead before he hit the ground."

"Hit the ground," Lou murmured. He rubbed the pager's case between his thumb and forefinger, not listening to a word while he stared straight ahead at the squad cars lining the front of the house. He'd been doing that for a couple of weeks, drifting outside himself. Drifting had become Lou's regular thing.

Last week Billy asked a psychologist named Paul Anderson over at Employee Assistance about Lou's trances, his weight loss and his lack of sleep. Off the record, of course. Anderson was a good guy. He offered to talk to Lou, but they both knew it would take handcuffs to get Lou over there.

"Who paged you . . . the Lieutenant?" Billy said.

Lou chewed his toothpick, distracted. "Peeing off the porch. Death by elf. I'm embarrassed to write that one up."

"Did Hollerith page you?"

"Damn it, I heard you the first time."

"Lighten up, man. You said 'pain-in-the-ass'. I assumed—"

Lou shot him a look with crazy heat in his eyes. "How about you get your *got damn* nose out of my *got damn* business."

"Whoa, Lou, Jesus."

Across the street two church ladies cranked up "It Is Well With My Soul". They sang a hymn written by an 1800's lawyer ruined by disaster, bereaved by catastrophe, honored in perpetuity. Heads nodded in the crowd. Hands swayed in the air. The heat went out of Lou's eyes, and his gaze strayed off. He bent down and knocked dried grass out of his cuffs.

"I've had it with this whole damned business," Lou mumbled and started for the porch, leaving Billy standing alone with the body in the bed of orange marigolds.

Chapter Two

Saturday, 10 a.m.

Criminal Court Judge Lamar "Buck" Overton clamped his thighs against the sweat-soaked leather. His back muscles spasmed, but he refused to let up on the bitch, not when he had her pinned. Mistress Colette wrenched her head sideways. Buck saw the panic in her eye, or maybe it was rage. He didn't give a damn. He savored a fight. He wasn't wealthy but he wielded power in Memphis. And power eventually led to money, if played right. The equine urine smell choked the air in the covered arena. Mistress Colette, a four-year-old chestnut Tennessee Walking Horse, churned the sawdust with her teacup hooves and flung clumps of it over the plank barrier enclosing the sides. After battling Overton for an hour, her sweaty coat looked as dark as raw liver.

Buck used his seat to force the mare forward into the bit, sending simultaneous mixed signals, stop and go, to break her will. He used his whole body as leverage. At fifty-seven he still had superior strength. For weeks she'd defied him. Today she would give in or she was dog meat.

Gary Parson, Buck's trainer, snapped his fingers. "Circle and go running walk," he directed from the center of the ring.

Gary was a fastidious man who preferred pink Lacoste polo shirts, custom-tailored khakis and seven hundred dollar alligator loafers. Overton suspected Parson of being light in those loafers, a deviation he barely tolerated, but Parson's clients consistently made it to the winner's circle. That's what mattered.

Developing green horses into champions had made Parson's reputation as a top Walking Horse trainer; however, winning ribbons doesn't always translate into real money for a trainer. Buying and selling horses for clients does.

"She places first at Germantown Charity Horse Show next week or we're shipping her out," Parson called from across the ring.

The mare lunged, ripping the reins from Buck's grip. Her head whipped to the side and flung spittle in his face. He sawed back on the reins. Colette half reared, and he gigged her with his spurs. She hopped forward off her hind legs and settled into an exaggerated, head-bobbing rack.

"Go get yourself a Coke Cola," Buck called as he cut diagonally across the back of the ring. "We're about done." His voice sounded calm, even though the battle infuriated him.

"Better watch it, she's coming into season. A mare can jump goofy on you any time," Parson warned.

"I'll handle her. Go on now."

Parson shrugged and turned away just as Buck felt the mare extend into a full, ribbon-winning running walk. He rocked back on his tailbone in perfect equitation form. He'd won.

"Hey, Parson, look at her go," he yelled. The trainer turned back and applauded.

Halfway around the arena, Buck tightened the rein and gigged Colette with the rowels just for the hell of it, just so she'd remember who was in charge. She grunted and swelled her belly against his leg. He jabbed her again, driving her hard into the bit.

A roar erupted from the delicate mare.

"Better bring her 'round, Judge," Parson said.

Before he could act, she ripped the sweat-soaked reins out of his hands and took off at a dead gallop, blowing and grunting, the flesh quivering on her neck as he scrambled for the reins. Crazed by his shifting weight, Colette pinned her ears and squealed.

"Bail out," Parson shouted.

"Forget it," he yelled back. A kid can jump off a galloping horse and walk away. At his age bailing out meant broken bones. He leaned back and jammed his feet forward in the stirrups.

Colette raced toward the steel gate entrance. The gate was low enough for the enraged mare to try and jump. She'd never make it of course. Too late Buck realized his mistake. He should've bailed.

The gate rushed at them. Colette's haunches bunched. He closed his eyes, expecting her to smash headlong into the barrier. Instead she dipped her shoulder, swerved and catapulted him into the gate. It crashed under his impact. That was the only sensation he remembered as he dropped to the dank sawdust floor.

His next awareness was the ceiling fan winking above him.

"You all right?" Parson said, standing over him.

"I'm okay." A ridiculous statement. He should be dead.

"Don't move. I'll call 911."

He sat up. "I said I'm okay." He stood and brushed sawdust from his slacks. No dizziness. No pain.

Parson shook his head. "You've got some kind of luck."

"I don't believe in luck." He shot a look at the mare who stood at the end of the arena, hot, blowing, her reins trailing in the dirt. "Or losing."

Parson led her over. "It's your call, but I'm done with this bitch. She's on the truck to Florida. We can get two, maybe three thousand for her easy."

"I paid eight. I'm not inclined to take that kind of loss."

"There's a stallion over at Sandy Creek Farms we can pick up for practically nothing. He's big, powerful. A perfect match for you."

Buck liked the sound of the other horse. He took the reins from Parson. "I'll walk her. We both need to cool out."

"Sure you're all right? I think we should get you to a doc."

Buck rubbed the mare's forehead. She dropped her head in submission. "I'm fine. We'll talk about the stallion tomorrow and make plans for this little lady."

He watched Parson disappear through the arena door. The greedy bastard would make a fat commission from both sales. Not this time. Buck would try out the stallion, and if he liked him, dump Parson after the horseshow and buy the horse himself. No more homos snapping their fingers and giving orders. They were a damned pox on the Southern culture he believed in: Walking Horses, dove shoots, debutantes, and membership in secret societies where, during Cotton Carnival, you put on a tuxedo and sip champagne while standing next to a twenty-foot tall, fiberglass sphinx. And then there was his first passion—tournament croquet.

The practice of law had been his vehicle into Memphis' inner circle. He'd moved from a partnership in the old money firm of Broad, Lathin, and Friedman, and later his judgeship led to membership in the exclusive fraternity of power brokers in the city. Everyone agreed he knew the law; not one of his judicial rulings had been overturned. But he had his own sense of right and wrong, even if not everyone would agree with it. He knew a renegade mare and a homophile were wrong. They didn't belong in his world. He knew winners were right and losers were wrong.

He stopped Colette in the middle of the arena and pressed his hand to her chest—still hot but she'd quit blowing and no longer trembled.

For Buck, horses, croquet, and the law were three disciplines in which success depended on assessment of an opponent's skill. He'd misjudged Colette's desire to win. He hoped he hadn't made a similar mistake with a female opponent in a different game. Too much was at stake. Each move had to be weighed against what he would gain, and what he would lose.

The key to his future rested in the hands of one burnt-out cop.

Chapter Three

Saturday, 10:10 a.m.

Extremes mark the face of Memphis: Fortunes made from King Cotton, death from yellow fever, poverty, racism; and music that burns and bleeds from the soul. Sweltering heat cooled by trillions of gallons of sweet water gushing from aquifers beneath the city.

Mr. Tuggle's neat bungalow echoed those extremes, standing out in the decayed, north-Memphis neighborhood that once had been supported by a tire manufacturing plant. The plant closed in 1979. The jobs never came back. Grown men sat on their front steps in the middle of the day with malt liquor bottles dangling between their fingers while their roofs leaked, their porches sagged, and their women lost hope.

In contrast, the victim's house had fresh paint, an edged lawn, and lush beds of hydrangeas spilling over at the front porch. Billy recognized the house was greatly loved and ruled by an iron hand, as he'd witnessed in Mississippi towns where antebellum homes were groomed by their owners as if the pride of the South depended on the health of their azaleas. This house smacked of the same presumption.

Billy called over a patrolman to stand with Tuggle's body and followed Lou to the freshly swept porch with its two aluminum lawn chairs flanking the door. A cardboard fan, picturing a vibrantly colored Jesus cradling a lamb in his arms, lay in one chair seat. Lou's flare-up in the yard puzzled him. Paul Anderson said he should expect bouts of temper from someone as depressed as Lou. The warning helped but not much.

A young cop with his fresh crew cut and shined shoes smoked a cigarette by the front door. He took a last drag, dropped the butt on the porch, mashed it, and reached to open the screen door for Lou. Billy waited for the eruption.

"Don't they teach you any damned thing at that academy?" Lou bellowed. He picked up the cigarette butt. "Never smoke at a crime scene unless you want to be one of the suspects. And who was it raised you to trash other people's property . . . a pack of dogs?"

"Yes, sir. No, sir."

"Pick one, son."

"I forgot about the cigarette. It's my first day. And my dad raised me, sir."

"All right, we got that straight. What's your name?"

"Patrolman Dwight Rad."

"You know what a first officer looks like, Rad?"

8

"Like my partner, Officer Washington."

"Get him."

Patrolman Rad disappeared through the doorway. Moments later a black female officer returned. Officer Byhalia Washington stood close to six feet tall, had biceps like a man and a pair of impressively large but unequally distributed hooters. This imbalance, however, didn't appear to affect her self-confidence. She swaggered toward them with her right hand out to shake Lou's hand, and then informed them of all transpiring events since her arrival. She concluded with a description of their single witness.

"Ida Smith, a female neighbor, found Mr. Tuggle around 8:45 a.m. and called 911 from her own house," Officer Washington said. "She was collecting for The Sickle Cell Anemia Fund and nearly tripped over the body. She's a screamer. I calmed her down and put her in the back den with a patrolman to cool off."

"Has Mrs. Tuggle added anything?" Lou said.

"Not a word. She was sitting at the kitchen table having a cup of tea when we got here. Wouldn't answer the door, so we let ourselves in the back. She's dressed up, wearing her pearls. The house is spotless. I thought it was shock, so I had an EMT check her out. He said her pulse is a little thready, but she's fine."

"Where's Mrs. Tuggle now?" Billy said.

"Her name is Lady Tuggle. *Miz Lady*, they call her. She's in the kitchen with Rad, waiting to talk with you gentlemen."

"We've met young Rad," Lou said.

The screen door slammed. They all looked up to see the rookie standing on the porch.

"What are you doing?" Washington said.

"Mrs. Tuggle had to go to the bathroom," Rad said. "I wanted to check in."

"Oh, good God." Officer Washington barreled past Rad.

Lou beat the six-foot female freight train through the door, and Rad's face blanched as the reality of what he'd done hit him.

"Sit down," Billy said as he followed Washington. "Put your head between your knees."

"And kiss my ass good-bye," Rad said and collapsed on top of the Jesus fan.

Billy hoped Miz Lady hadn't guzzled drain cleaner or hanged herself from the showerhead with her panty hose. He didn't know the woman, but when murder's involved people get desperate. A simple case can turn sour at any time.

The sturdy shoulders of Byhalia Washington blocked his view as he entered the front hall. She stood rooted at a doorway that opened into a dining room. He followed her gaze past the dining table to the buffet on the opposite wall. A gallery light over the buffet illuminated a large sepia-toned photo of a family grouping.

Lou and an elderly black woman stood facing each other near one end of the buffet. Miz Lady's hand had disappeared into an open drawer. In slow motion she withdrew a .38 pistol. Slowly, she placed the barrel in her mouth.

"Hold on now," Lou said.

She cocked the hammer. Officer Washington drew her Glock.

Lou raised his hands, palms forward. "Now, lady . . . I mean Miz Lady, no sense hurting yourself." His voice cracked.

Miz Lady stood erect for a woman her age. Her blue dress hung loose down her thin chest, her nails sparkled pink against the electrician's tape wrapped around the gun's butt. She wore stockings on this hot morning and white heels. From the look of things, Billy figured she'd hit her husband on the back of the head, cleaned the house, bathed and dressed. And now she was ready to meet her Maker.

For a cop, this was as dangerous as it gets.

"Let's put the gun down and talk," Lou said. "I'll hold it for you."

Miz Lady's eyes widened, and the gun trembled as Lou took a step forward. Billy felt Officer Washington tense beside him.

"Okay." Lou began the familiar talk-down. "You keep the gun and I'll stay here."

Resolve glinted in the woman's eyes, but she was listening.

"My name's Lou. Accidents happen. There's no one to blame here, really. Men can be an aggravation. They retire, they get under foot, they spoil a woman's routine. It's understandable."

That's right, Billy thought. *Stay with the program.* He noticed the hammer ease up, and he took a breath.

"Your man wouldn't listen. Sometimes men do the wrong things," Lou said.

Lady Tuggle nodded. The gun barrel slid lower in her mouth.

"Men," Lou said, warming to his subject, "good men do bad things. Especially as they get older. Something weakens inside a man. They let their families down. You understand that don't you, Miz Lady? They disappoint the ones they've promised to look after."

Wherever Lou was going with this, it seemed to be working. The gun barrel slid from Lady Tuggle's mouth. Lou extended his hand. The .38 seemed to hesitate of its own accord, and then she clasped the grip in both hands and leveled it at Lou's chest.

"Uh, ummh," rumbled Byhalia Washington, "that done it."

"I warned him." Miz Lady's voice sounded clear, calm. "He kept on, every morning. Doing his business off the porch. I keep a decent house. My momma didn't raise me to live like trash."

Lou's body stiffened. "You need to put the gun down."

The woman's chin went up. "Preacher Allen said mens are the Devil's fallen creatures. Stealing, murdering, hurting girl chirrun. Far as I'm concerned, all you mens can go to *Hell*."

Lou's head jerked up. "Pull that trigger and see firsthand what God thinks of murders. Go on, shoot!"

"I'll do it. I will."

"*Go on then.*"

Lou's gaze focused on the gun, and his body began to weave. The gun barrel followed. He was provoking her to shoot him. They all knew it.

Washington raised her Glock to shoulder level and trained it on Miz Lady's chest. She had every right, even a duty, to shoot, but it might not save Lou. Washington glanced at Billy. Her expression said, *Do something or I will.*

The dining table stood between Miz Lady and Billy. He'd never get to her before she pulled the trigger. Only option left was to break the spell.

He exhaled, slipped his hands in his pockets and strolled into the room as if he were a guest. He approached the framed photograph on the wall. For a moment he studied the photo, and then stepped back in surprise.

"Isn't this the Caledonia Free Will Baptist Church outside of Pontotoc, Mississippi? Pastor Bean is still in the pulpit after forty years, I believe." He bent forward, looking at the photo. "Miz Lady, is this your wedding party?"

"Leave it," Lou breathed, his voice still heated.

"Is it, Miz Lady?" He could tell she was listening, but he couldn't see Lou's face or the gun.

"That's my wedding day."

"Is your momma in the white hat or is she the lady with the lace collar standing down the steps?"

"Momma's in the hat. Aunt Jet wore the lace collar. She carried my veil down from New York." Her voice warmed with emotion.

"Is that so. Are you wearing your momma's wedding dress?"

Her shoulders stiffened. "Momma didn't have a dress. She saved every cent for school to make a lawyer when she met Daddy. He said he'd pay her way through school if she'd marry him."

"Do I see your daddy here?"

"Next to Walter. My husband." She said the name coldly.

"Where?" Billy assumed the gun was still trained on Lou. If he grabbed her, Lou was sure to take a bullet in the chest. Out the corner of his eye he saw Miz Lady back toward the picture.

"The bald man with the belly. That's Daddy."

Billy angled his head for a better look at the woman. She had turned the revolver on him and was glaring at the photo. The gun quivered in her hand. He should be nervous, but all he could see was this trapped woman making a final grab for self-respect.

"Daddy beat Momma so bad he broke something in her head. She couldn't read after that. She couldn't go to school, so she took in wash.

Momma wanted me to have what she never got. Then Walter starts . . . he wouldn't listen. Damn you, Walter!"

In one motion she swung the gun around and fired.

Chapter Four

Saturday, 11:35 a.m.

The giant A&W Root Beer mug shimmered over the rooftop of a roadside stand. The sign's brown paint, chipped by the weather, left silver patches gleaming in the sun. Broken neon tubing dangled. The mug rocked against sagging guy wires. The sign was a lot like Memphis: seductive, old, with hints of grandeur and an aura of risk.

Mercy Snow made a hard left into the gravel parking lot. Root beer floats were her absolute favorite. If she got a float to go, she would stay on schedule, but if it spilled in the car, she would ruin her new outfit and be late to lunch, not to mention this place was a total dive and a possible health hazard. Handbills glued to the walls flapped in the breeze. Mud peppered the front window. She gripped the steering wheel. Memories of root beer thickened to the freezing point with a scoop of ice cream made her swallow. Oh, why not? She'd lost twenty-seven pounds off her 5'9" frame and had worked hard to change her entire life. She deserved a treat.

This morning she'd dressed in slacks and a sweater the shade of periwinkle her mother once said "Complements your green eyes, and you know, dear, you need all the help you can get." She'd feathered on concealers the way the makeup artist had shown her and parted her blond hair on the side to drape her face and camouflage her left cheek. She'd studied her made-over image. Mercy Snow—award winning pastry chef, bakery owner, and successful entrepreneur who was about to return to the bosom of her family. Unlike Atlanta, where the New outweighed the Old ten to one, family meant everything in returning to Memphis—to her mother, sister and brother-in-law. But home also meant a hurt so deep Mercy couldn't put words to it.

Her scarred face no longer controlled her life. It was about time she acted like it.

Her stomach rumbled. She checked her face in the rearview mirror and arranged her hair. *Screw denial*, she thought, got out of the car and headed for the door.

Stale air hit her in the face. Napkins and straws littered the floor. She took a stool, angling her left side away from the teenage-aged girl behind the counter whose nametag read "Trudy."

"Root beer float, please."

The girl's gaze flattened with boredom. "One or two scoops?"

"One. Two. No, make it one."

Trudy rolled her eyes. She wore the clichéd Goth uniform: black nail polish, heavy black eyeliner, streaks of iridescent eye shadow, and a stud in her nostril. Her root beer-colored uniform strained at her breasts and hips. Trudy's eyes sparked with interest when she picked up on Mercy's scar. Mercy caught the girl's smirk as she turned her back to make the float.

People had two unspoken reactions to the scar: "you poor thing" or "better you than me." She had endured stares and clumsy remarks for eighteen of her twenty-five years, but today Trudy's smirk didn't bother her. Nothing was going to ruin her homecoming.

The girl took a plastic mug off the shelf, blew into it, and wiped the rim with her apron. Deciding it was best to not watch Trudy make the float, Mercy pivoted on the stool to look at the traffic on the highway.

A young woman in a striped halter top and cut-offs sat at a table next to the grimy window. Two little girls in bathing suits and bare feet sat with her. Their wet hair lay plastered against their backs. Mercy wondered if they were cold in the air conditioning. The girls fiddled with their drinks while their mother popped her chewing gum and stared out at the road.

"Drink up," she commanded the girls.

The older child hauled herself up on both elbows to suck on her straw. She tilted the drippy end out of the mug and blew root beer across the table onto her sister.

"Quit that," the mother said and slapped the girl's hand.

The older girl slumped back in her seat, kicking at her sister's chair. Mercy watched the smaller girl eyeing her sister. It could've been her eighteen years ago. She remembered her first substantive lesson in life: big sisters play dirty.

Be careful, little girl.

The older girl scooted closer to her float, filled the straw, lifted the end, and blew root beer in her sister's face. The smaller girl wiped her face with the back of her hand.

"Damn it. Stop that," the mother said.

The smaller girl climbed off her chair, picked up her float with both hands, and dumped it in her sister's lap.

A guilty thrill shot through Mercy.

"That's it," the mother said. "I told you what I'd do if you messed with me today." She stood, yanked the smaller child around and smacked the back of her bare legs. The girl didn't make a sound.

Mercy winced at every blow. *"Stop it,"* she screamed inside.

The spanking went on, a replay of her own childhood.

"Stop it," Mercy said out loud this time.

The mother's head jerked up. "Mind your own business," she snapped, but she let go of the child's arm.

Relief flooded Mercy, and she realized she was close to tears.

"You want your float or what?" Trudy said behind her.

Mercy wheeled around to see the girl's nasty grin.

"Make it to go," she said. She threw money on the counter and grabbed the cup. She didn't want to take the drink with her, but she couldn't look at the child's bewildered face any longer.

At the table the older girl wailed while her mother mopped her lap with napkins. The small girl stared numbly at the floor. Mercy wanted to grab her and run. Instead she escaped to the parking lot, carrying only the root beer float.

The engine cranked, and she pulled onto the highway, aching with a hurt she didn't want to explore. She had to put the child out of her mind and think about this weekend.

The timing was perfect. She'd just signed with a national food chain for her bakery to distribute two of her signature pies. The summons to Memphis had arrived as she'd hit the top of her game.

Her mother and sister expected her at one for luncheon by the pool. That's how her sister, Sophia, had phrased it when they spoke—luncheon by the pool. Sophia's time in rehab had done wonders for her diction. Not a slip. Not a slur. No lapses into hysterical rage. Her sister's invitation had been chillingly normal.

In the car, she flipped her iPod to an old Lyle Lovett album.

Lyle's voice cheered her as her shoulders relaxed, and she steered one-handed while sucking up a chunk of ice cream. Her life had changed. This trip would prove it. She wasn't a little girl to be bullied anymore.

Not a cloud in the sky as Lyle sang about the sun coming up in his coffee cup. Sunlight bounced off the car's hood, almost blinding her. She wedged the drink between her thighs and rummaged through her purse for sunglasses. No luck. She dropped her purse to the floor and felt around the passenger's seat. They had to be there. She glanced down to see the case stuck between the seat and the console.

She crested a hill and looked up to see the dog, a collie, standing in the road forty feet in front of her. Seconds to react, she braked and swerved, but she saw in the dog's dilated eyes that they both understood what was about to happen. She heard a thud and saw a whirl of fur out of the corner of her eye. Gravel pinged against the car's undercarriage as she skidded to a stop. Heart pounding, she looked down. Milky brown root beer soaked her new slacks and sweater.

On the iPod, Lyle sang a song about going home.

Chapter Five

Saturday, 10:49 a.m.

Lady Tuggle's bony hands fought the restraints.

It hurt Billy to watch her struggle as paramedics covered her with a blanket then tightened the gurney straps over her arms and body. Under the oxygen mask, her face looked shrunken. A good thirty minutes had passed since she'd put a bullet through her father's face in the photograph. The smell of cordite still hung in the air.

He would write up the incident as an accidental discharge of the weapon instead of the truth; that Lady Tuggle was done with men, all men, and she wouldn't have minded leaving her mark on a few on her way out.

As a patrolman, he'd learned early that the manner in which an event is presented counts more than the facts.

Miz Lady pointed at a battered cardboard box sitting on a chair next to the wall. Billy looked inside to see a stack of the Jesus fans with an advertisement for Rascal's Appliance Store printed down the wooden handle. He took the top fan, brought it over and laid it on her blanket. She shook her head and pointed at him.

"For me?"

She nodded.

"Thank you, ma'am."

They wheeled her down the front hall that smelled of lemon wax rubbed into old oak floors.

This was the last time Miz Lady would see her house. The stained glass in the door transom sparkled like gemstones. Billy understood what the house meant to a woman like her. She was the same as the women he'd known growing up on the back roads of Mississippi. Hard work. Little money. Poor education. Not a single step in their lives made easy. She wanted a few nice things in her life and some respect. He'd protected women like her all his life. He didn't send them to jail.

The paramedics lifted her through the doorway, their backs blocking his view. He heard the gurney bump the screen door and saw it tip.

"Hey easy," he called out.

The EMT looked back at him with placid disregard. "We got her."

Then they were gone. Not a damned thing had gone right today.

◈

During the search of the scene Officer Washington had found the weapon most likely used to hit Mr. Tuggle on the back of the head—an iron skillet that had been dropped into a galvanized trashcan outside the back door. A single gray hair snagged on a rough edge of the skillet's backside, along with prints on the handle, would tie things up.

Patsy Dwyer, a pot-bellied, black-haired woman of obvious Irish descent, from the Crime Scene Unit, bagged the skillet, the .38, the concrete elf, and the shoe. Autopsy would confirm the cause of Walter Tuggle's death, whether it was the blow to the head, the fall from the porch, or the blow to his face from the elf.

In the yard Byhalia Washington took Billy aside, shaking her head. "Would you explain what just happened?"

"Lou got carried away."

"I saw that. What about you?"

"Me?"

"You, Detective Cool," she said, pointing her finger at him. "Strolling into the line of fire. That woman would've shot you dead except you knew her preacher's name. How does a white man know who pastored a black church?"

"Guess the Lord's looking out for me. I grew up singing in the choir of a black church. We visited Pastor Bean a couple of times a year."

Washington reared back. "You passing?"

"No, I'm white."

"I see. That's why you walked into the middle of that mess instead of giving me the nod to take her down. You love black people."

"Lou's my partner. I did the best thing all the way around. If you took her down, we'd be standing in front of the review board next week."

"Don't try that with me. You've been watching too many cop shows. Playing hero. You saved those two crazy people from being shot."

"Lou's not crazy."

She snorted.

"He got carried away. And by the way, your partner wasn't exactly professional."

Washington rolled her eyes. "Tell me about it."

They agreed, rather than go into detail on their reports, to consider Rad and Lou's more colorful moments to be training for future hostage situations. For the next forty-five minutes Billy ran the traps with the tech team. He didn't want to think about what Lou had done.

Back inside the house the sudden dimness of the front hall made him light-headed. Lou sat in the living room in a tall-back wooden chair staring out the large picture window. A jelly jar of ice water and his cell phone sat on the floor to his right. Sweat made his bald spot shiny. Either he was unaware of Billy's presence or he wanted to ignore him.

Billy wondered if he should bring up the incident in the dining room or turn it into a joke the way he usually did, but he couldn't figure out how. Lou almost got himself shot today, almost got them both killed. Six years they'd worked together, sometimes eighteen hours a day. They made a good team. Billy didn't want anything to happen to that.

Billy's cell rang. At the sound Lou swiveled in the chair.

"Hell of a way you're running this case," Lou said before Billy could answer his phone. "Big fucking mess you got out there."

Lou's lips looked red and wet from the ice water. Something about that angered Billy.

"Hey, Lou. Don't let your mouth start something your head can't handle," he said, about to make the point that any mess out there had been caused by Patrolman Rad, who had an excuse for being stupid. Lou didn't. Then he caught his partner's unfocused gaze and stopped. Lou was trying to push his buttons, just like Anderson had predicted.

His cell rang again, and he ducked into the dining room. The ID showed the call was their boss at the Criminal Justice Center.

"Detective Able," he answered.

"Hollerith, here. Wanted to see how things are adding up."

Lieutenant Kline Hollerith was a by-the-numbers guy. Should've been an actuary instead of law enforcement middle management.

"It's another domestic, an older couple this time. We have the wife in custody, but she developed an arrhythmia so we're transporting her to The Med."

"Things running smoothly otherwise?"

"Smooth enough."

"Any reason another team couldn't take over?"

He glanced across the hallway. Lou held his cell phone up to the sunlight, studying the screen. Maybe getting out of here would be just the thing.

"No problem, sir, what's up?"

"Judge Overton wants Nevers to check into a missing persons at SuperShoppers East. The woman's been AWOL about sixteen hours. Overton insisted Lou head this up. I'd like to accommodate him."

"We're ready to roll."

"Vargas and Nance are heading your way."

He flipped the phone shut and walked into the living room.

Lou turned in his chair. "Guess that was Hollerith on the horn." His eyes shifted under their lids toward Billy.

He knew that look. Lou was wondering if he'd dropped a dime and told Hollerith Lou had almost gotten them shot. *And if I did, you'd deserve it, wouldn't you, my friend?*

"He wants us to move on to a missing person," Billy said. "He's sending over a couple of guys to wrap this one up. You good with that?"

"Got to make a call first."

"I told Hollcrith we had no problems here."

"Yeah? So?" Lou punched a few numbers.

"Thought you'd want to know that."

Lou looked up. "How about some privacy?"

"No problem. Catch you outside."

Lou slumped in the chair, put the phone to his ear and stared out the window as if he were already alone.

Chapter Six

Saturday, 11:17 a.m.

On the second lap around the arena with Colette, Judge Overton's cell rang. He knew who was calling.

"Judge Overton," he answered, using his courtroom voice.

"Ah, yeah, Nevers here."

"I paged you an hour ago. I used the 7-3-7 code. Doesn't that stand for P-D-Q, Pretty Damned Quick?"

"Sorry about that. I'm working a scene."

Lou sounded stressed. Good.

"That problem we discussed before," Buck said, "I'm sure you remember."

"Copy that."

"Can I assume you made a move?"

Silence on the line.

"Hello?" Buck said.

"What the hell you talking about? I ain't moved on nothing."

"Don't play dumb, Lou. The problem's resolved. Your fingerprints are all over it. Hasn't Hollerith reached you?"

"My partner just took the call. Listen, you got it wrong. I made no got-damned move, get it?" Lou was shouting into the phone.

"Are you alone?"

"Hell, yes. You think I'm an idiot?"

"Look, I called to say I'm grateful you've handled my dilemma."

"I didn't handle your dilemma. I'm up to my whacker in my own dilemmas."

Buck stopped in the middle of the arena. This wasn't the reaction he'd expected. Then it came to him. Lou might be a burnt-out cop, but he wasn't a fool. Calls can be recorded. A smart cop would never admit to a crime.

This required a more oblique approach. He started another lap around the arena with Colette. "Let's speak hypothetically. My life has been simplified. Whether or not I thank you for it isn't the issue. Make this go away, understand? Do what you have to, but shut it down fast. Make sure there's nothing the D.A. can hang his hat on."

"Did you talk to somebody else about taking care of your problem?" Lou said.

"No reason for me to do that. You've always resolved difficult matters for me."

"And now I'm done. Get yourself another man."

Buck blinked in disbelief. Damned cops. Damned women. Always a battle. Collette stumbled behind him. He snatched the reins causing the mare's head to fly up. Damned horses, too. He stood in the suffocating heat and tried to get a breath. He had to handle this right.

"Listen closely. You're in this, like it or not. Let's finish and move on."

Silence on the other end.

"I want out," Lou said. "Do what you want. I'm hanging up, Judge. Have a nice life."

Years on the bench had trained Buck to spot a man on the edge. He either had to back off or hit the detective in the gut.

"Don't kid yourself. Remember, you've told me what you've done. You're about to lose your place in West Memphis and everything you love that's in it if you don't follow through."

"What are you talking about?"

Buck knew fear when he heard it, and fear was all over the detective's voice. He'd already won. He led the mare toward the gate.

"I know you were too drunk to remember all you told me the other night, but our agreement stands. Finish cleaning up my mess, and you'll get your money."

The line went dead. It didn't matter. Lou would take care of the scene.

Collette followed him through the gate. He glanced back at the whelps his spurs had left on her flanks. Her head drooped and her eyes were half closed with exhaustion.

Buck didn't believe luck made a man a winner. That took skill and the will to dominate everything and everyone around him. He believed the only true crime a man commits is getting caught. And if you're stupid enough to get caught, the full weight of the law should be applied.

Through the double doors of the arena he saw the sun-bleached gravel yard, white as bone. Not a shadow, only light. He thought about Lou, a man who, up to this point, had been perfectly predictable. Today's behavior puzzled him. He led the mare across the yard toward the stable aisle, dark and cool as a cavern. Since he was a child, his memory for numbers had been unerring. He opened his phone, tapped in the number of his insurance company and pressed "Snd."

Chapter Seven

Billy left Lou and stepped out onto the Tuggle's porch. The heat hit him like a falling wall. Tulip poplar leaves big as the palm of his hand spiraled onto the lawn. The neighbors had given up and gone inside to cool off in front of their air conditioners. Days like this he wished he were one of them, a glass of iced tea in one hand, cable remote in the other, never having to look again into the unfixed eyes of a murder victim.

He breathed in deep. The neighborhood smelled of mown grass and grilling ribs. It calmed him, reminded him of the meat smoker his Uncle Kane kept out back of his roadside restaurant where Billy had worked and lived through his high school years. He thought about the sauce his uncle used on his ribs—Momma's Homebrewed Hot and Spicy, made in an iron pot by a woman living in a dog trot that was over a century old. Remembering his time with his uncle made the knot in his chest loosen.

As a kid he hadn't wanted to be a cop. At seven he'd wanted to be a fireman. At ten, a major-league third baseman. After a year at law school and the senseless murder of the Riley girls—two little black children he'd known from his home church—he decided to be a homicide detective.

He'd dropped out of law school and signed up with the police academy after learning the cops had been racially biased during the kidnapping and murder investigation of the two girls. He decided he'd rather intervene to ensure justice than get involved as a lawyer when all he could do was pick up the pieces.

Billy shook his head. That was the past. Now he had real-time problems with Lou. They needed to head over to the fish camp, kick back and have a talk. Life makes more sense when a man's got a fishing pole in his hand. Maybe it was time to bring up Paul Anderson, the department's psych counselor, after all.

Byhalia Washington stood beside her squad car, talking into the radio hand mike. He should tell her that detectives were on the way, and she needed to stay with the scene. It was a simple case, a grounder. No big deal.

Lou's voice carried to the porch. "Ah, yeah, Nevers here."

Billy listened.

"Sorry about that, I'm working a scene."

Lou sounded nervous.

"Copy that."

An unmarked car pulled up across the street. Vargas and Nance climbed out. Billy pulled out his case notes and started down the walk toward them. Lou's voice followed him, shouting now.

"What the hell you talking about? I ain't moved on nothin'."

He glanced at the house. Lou was really going at it.

"Hey, Able," Nance called out.

He turned back and saw Vargas and Nance start across the lawn. They were the same medium height, same medium build—a pair of white, middle-aged civil servants. Both wore the bored slump and slightly disgusted look veteran cops get when extra paperwork gets dumped in their lap. They'd been ribbing him about his batting slump for weeks.

A breeze picked up and blew leaves across the walk onto his shoes. Vargas and Nance grinned at him.

"Okay, Hot Shot, you're outta here," Nance said to Billy. Nance jerked his thumb over his shoulder like an ump throwing him out of the game. "Take Saturday off. Go hit some practice balls."

Nance's grin widened. That pissed Billy off. Nance could knock the cover off a ball, but he was a smart-ass and a poor excuse for a detective. The guy couldn't find a dead horse in a bathtub. Vargas wasn't much better. Billy looked away and looked back at them.

"Tell you what," he called. "I'll work on my swing; you work on closing a case or two."

Nance held up his hands. "Come on, can't you take a . . . "

He didn't finish. Both men's gazes fixed on the house.

The breeze died. A muffled shout came from behind him.

"What's going on?" Vargas said.

Billy turned as the picture window exploded outward. Glass shards ballooned toward them. At the center, a chair cart-wheeled through the air. The detectives raised their arms against the glass and dropped to the ground. He went down on the walk, saw the chair hit and roll. Everything stopped.

"Freeze!" Washington yelled from the back fender of her squad car. She had her Glock trained on the house.

Vargas and Nance rolled in different directions and came up with their Sigs directed at the window. He followed their focus and saw a figure inside the house step back from the window into the shadowy room.

Lou had been sitting near that window. Was it Lou, or had there been someone else in the house all along?

"Don't shoot, that looks like Nevers," Washington yelled.

"No way," Nance yelled back.

Billy crouched and ran a zigzag pattern toward the porch, hoping the man would be distracted by Washington and Nance.

"Able, you idiot. Get down," Nance shouted.

He ducked behind the bushes along the house. Miz Lady never admitted killing her husband. They assumed she was the guilty one. But old houses have crawl spaces and attics. Maybe the scene wasn't properly secured. She could've been hiding someone—a son, or a jealous boyfriend.

Washington yelled something, but Billy couldn't make it out. He had to get to Lou. He inched forward to the window ledge where he saw the man who had stepped to the window and now stared at the chair in the yard. The sun sparkled off pieces of glass around the frame, making Billy squint. Rage contorted the man's face until he was nearly unrecognizable.

It was Lou.

Chapter Eight

Saturday, 12:27 p.m.

Billy leaned against the wall and watched as uniforms and CSU techs milled around the Tuggle's living room. The sound of a neighbor's piano floated in through the shattered window, reminding him of the afternoons when his mother played, her beautiful hands, pale and limber on the keyboard. He wanted to draw the music inside himself and be anywhere else, instead of in the middle of this chaos, but he couldn't. Not with Lou standing by the broken window, staring at the chair on the lawn like it was road kill.

Lou was his partner, as close to family as he had. He wanted to find a way to cover for Lou, but throwing the chair through the window made no sense. Lou said it was because the phone call was bad news. What bad news would cause a legend like Lou to totally lose his dignity?

Billy had put a call into Paul Anderson, but the department's answering service picked up. Anderson was out of town for the weekend. A woman offered the number of another psychologist, but Billy didn't write it down. He believed Anderson was the only one who could get through to Lou.

Vargas and Nance finished with the techs and went over to talk with Lou about clearing the scene. He answered them reasonably enough, scratched his head, hiked his pants, flipped open the cover of his pad and closed it the same way he always had. No one mentioned the chair in the yard or the glass shards hanging from the window. Both would usually be the source of endless, sick jokes.

Vargas and Nance stood slightly apart from Lou while they talked to him, more than personal space dictated—their only slip, but it betrayed their uneasiness. Both men had worked with Lou for fifteen years, and Lou had pulled their nuts out of the fire more than once. Now he clearly spooked them.

"Sorry about losing it," Lou said after summing up his report. "I was aiming at my partner, not the two of you." He laughed and cut his eyes at Billy.

Vargas punched Lou on the shoulder. "Hey, where I come from chair tossing is a national sport. Forget about it."

Lou relaxed a little. "We'll leave it with you." He looked at Billy. "Let's go, boy."

Billy picked up the fan Lady Tuggle had given him, headed for the door and down the porch steps. Across the street, Byhalia Washington got out of her cruiser to talk about the report she would have to file despite their earlier agreement.

"Tell that woman I'll initial whatever kind of report she wants," Lou said, huffing down the walk behind Billy.

"She's just covering herself."

"Smart move if you can't trust your partner to get your back."

The words struck Billy like a rock thrown at his head. He turned to see Lou ambling toward the fallen chair. "Hey. What the hell's that suppose to mean?"

Lou raised his hand over his head and kept walking.

"Detective Able," Washington called.

He hoped she hadn't heard the exchange. Rad sat in the squad car. His stupid move had put them all at risk and made his partner look incompetent. Maybe Lou's comment about trust was referring to Rad's dumb stunt.

Washington peered at Billy over her wire-rimmed shades. "What's that you got?" She pointed at the fan.

"Mrs. Tuggle wanted me to have this."

"I'd just as soon sit home as fool with you people. Cops begging to be shot. Destroying property. If I write this up the way it happened, I'm a snitch."

"It's okay, Washington. Do what you have to."

"I got two babies. I can't mess around."

"I understand," Billy said.

They watched Lou standing over the chair. He picked up a cottonwood leaf, folded it along its spine and slipped it in his shirt pocket. He scratched his neck. The skin at his throat looked gray.

"What's wrong with that man?" she said.

"He's hit a rough spot. Divorce. Can't seem to get past it."

"Does he drink?"

"Not anymore."

"Kids?"

"No kids."

Washington shook her head. "Kids help. With kids you got a reason to keep it between the lines."

◆

Billy drove down the street to Nana's Grab and Go, where he bought a Big Orange drink and a package of barbecued peanuts for Lou. Lou shook the peanuts into the bottle. After a few swigs, the color came back to Lou's cheeks. They didn't talk. There was too much to say and nothing to be said about it.

They topped the hill on Broad Avenue and saw traffic stacked three lanes across, sitting in front of dropped railroad crossbars. Billy rolled down the windows and shut off the engine. Heat shimmered off the rails. A diesel locomotive heaved into view. Memphis sat on the banks of the mighty

Mississippi, and a large part of the city's wealth depended on distribution and transportation. The endless rail beds crisscrossing the city like broken capillaries had a part in creating that wealth.

"Thirty-five years and I've yet to make this crossing," Lou said. "No, I take it back. Dead of winter in '88 I sneaked under the bars as they came down."

Lou shifted in his seat to get out of the sun. As usual, Lou wasn't wearing his seat belt. Forty-one years he'd driven without one. Said seat belts gave him gas.

"I was driving Ruby to the hospital," Lou continued. "We were at a party out in Fisherville when her water broke—"

"Ruby was pregnant?"

Lou flipped down his visor. "Damn it's hot."

"Thermostat's shot." Billy handed Lou the fan with the picture of Jesus holding the lamb. Lou studied the picture and put it down.

"The baby came early. Back then, babies made it in an incubator or they didn't. We tried again. No luck. That's why Ruby collected Hummel figures and commemorative plates. Those shopping channels nearly put me under."

"You never said a word about losing a child."

"Yeah, there's a lot you don't know," Lou mumbled.

Flat bed cars rocked by. Billy counted them to distract himself, but he kept seeing Lou's face in the shattered window, looking like a stranger. He reached over and tapped Lou's shirt pocket.

"What's the leaf for?"

"You wouldn't understand." The edge in Lou's voice was back.

"There's a lot I don't understand about today."

"I told you I got a call. It was bad news."

"Don't give me that bullshit." Billy revved the engine and clicked the air on high. "Please tell me this craziness is about a woman. We can fix that."

"A woman." Lou chuckled. "You always want an easy answer. If the ball ain't down the middle of the plate, you can't see it coming." Lou yanked the leaf out of his pocket and dropped it out the window. "I never said it before, but you ain't got the goods for this work. You're a lousy cop and an even lousier ballplayer."

Billy cut his eyes over at Lou. Detective work is sport, mental gymnastics. Head games become second nature. Lou was a master at it.

"You're a jerk, you know that?" Bill said, disgusted.

Lou shrugged, as if he were tired of talking to a moron.

"If you won't talk to me," Billy said, "there's a guy at Employee Assist—"

"You're making my point. You think you've got all the answers."

They fell silent and watched the final boxcar rocked past. The crossbars swung up. It had been a tricky conversation. Like walking on ice. Billy regretted not taking down the number for Anderson's substitute.

"You got the specifics on this next case?" Lou said.

"It's a missing persons. A woman. Judge Overton asked Hollerith to put you in charge." Billy decided to make one last try. "How about we take off this afternoon and run a trotline over at the lake? Maybe play some cards."

"Yeah," Lou said. "Great. How about we play Go Fish."

Chapter Nine

Saturday, 1:12 p.m.

If Mercy Snow's daydream came true, her mother and sister would be waving at her from the flagstone terrace as she drove up the driveway. They would pull her from the car and throw their arms around her. Not likely. Beautiful, unpredictable, alcoholic Sophia had been the center of their mother's world, especially after the tragedy. Mercy grew up feeling like an afterthought, in constant competition with her sister for their mother's attention. Sophia always won. Finally, Mercy left for school and never really returned home.

She parked at the foot of the terrace steps, owning up to her unrealistic expectations. Her mother and sister would be inside with drinks in their hands. Or, because she'd left a message on Sophia's machine saying she'd been delayed, they would be off somewhere shopping.

She flipped down the visor to check her makeup. Mascara ringed her eyes and the scar on her cheek looked like a strawberry stitch. She found a tissue to make repairs and brushed her hair. After the accident, she'd been too rattled to stop at a gas station and change clothes. Nothing she could do now about the root beer and bloodstains.

She blew out a breath and looked in the mirror. "I'll leave the motor running and come back for you after I face the dragons," she said to the collie in the back seat.

The stray dog looked sagely down his nose and yawned. He had thirty stitches in his chest and a strip of fur peeled off his hip. The vet said he needed antibiotics and a lot of care, and it would be months before he recovered completely. Sophia might not mind adding a smelly, injured dog to the weekend, but their mother would hit the ceiling.

Sophia's Italian Renaissance house looked as imposing as ever with its terra cotta roof tiles, copper gutters, three fountains and more marble bathrooms than decency allowed. It diminished the *Gone with the Wind* facsimile next door. Everyone thought this was Sophia's dream house, but it was her husband, T. Wayne, who had pushed for an upscale home. He considered the million dollar house an investment in his career with Zelwarc Corp. "Money attracts money," T. Wayne said, and this house looked like real money. He expected Sophia to entertain clients with private dinners and to throw lavish parties several times a year, which she did with the ease of a polished, society hostess. She certainly had the setting for it.

Mercy pulled her bag from the trunk and started up the walk. Only then did she notice that the ten-foot-tall front door was standing wide open.

Maybe Sophia had opened the door, remembered something and went back inside. Mercy glanced around. The walk was freshly swept and the vinegary smell of new mulch overwhelmed her. The gardeners had been by. Nothing looked unusual or out of place.

"Sophia?" she called, peeking through the open door. The drawers of the antique directoire their grandmother had given Sophia as a wedding present hung open. That shook her. She set the bag down and went back to the car.

"Come on, doggie, I need some company," she said, opening the back door. She patted her leg. "Let's go." He moved with decorum, careful of his wounds as he stepped down from the seat. Sir John Gielgud in doggy form.

They walked into the circular entry of the house with its wrought-iron banister staircase that followed the curve of the wall. Light from the glass transoms washed the chilled marble floor. A set of closed doors shut off the entry from the great room.

"Sophia? Hello?" she called.

Maybe Sophia was by the pool, which if she remembered, was off the great room. The doors gave way to a light push. Drawn shades darkened the windows. Her eyes adjusted slowly so the sight in front of her didn't register right away.

Teddy bear eyes stared at her from every angle of the room. Bears of every size sitting on chairs, sofas, the floor. Brown bears, Panda bears, Barrington bears. Bears with hats. Pink, blue, and white bears. Big and small. Bears holding baskets and bears sitting in baskets. Every drawer and cabinet in the place stood wide open.

A noise crawled up the collie's throat.

Her mind scrambled to make sense of it. Someone had broken into the house, rummaged through the drawers and left teddy bears. No. How about Sophia went searching through the drawers, found a bottle of vodka and had a tea party with her bear friends. That didn't explain the bears' presence, but at least it put events in familiar territory. Mercy wove her way through the crowd of bears toward the kitchen. If that room was torn up she was out the door.

Shutters filtered light onto the Mexican tile floor. She smelled bananas, coffee, and the fresh gladiolas in the center of the table. The stovetop gleamed. Not a dish was out of place except for an empty mug by the sink. She looked out the window and saw no one by the pool.

Mercy sighed. Sophia must be in the bedroom, reclining among silk pillows with a cold compress over her eyes and her ears plugged to block out any sound that would make her hangover worse. She'd have an explanation for the door and the bears. Sophia's stunts had always been accepted, even fostered. No homecoming dinner tonight. The dog looked up and solemnly wagged his tail.

"How about if we check the dragon's lair?"

He limped beside her as they went down the carpeted hallway past the gallery of Sophia's photographs and the closed door to the guestroom. Sophia's gamine likeness stared back at Mercy. She looked like a movie star. In contrast, Mercy's reflection floated in a pier mirror at the end of the hall. The scar on Mercy's cheek looked fresh, and the dog's shaved chest looked mangled. She'd worked years to erase the image, yet there she was in the mirror—the damaged one.

"Sophia, it's Mercy," she whispered outside the bedroom door. She peeked around the frame, not wanting to startle her sister.

In place of Sophia's gold leaf French bed, was a walnut sleigh bed covered in navy linens. No mound of silk pillows covering the downy duvet, and no Sophia passed out drunk between the sheets. The room smelled of aftershave and sunlight rather than stale booze and roses.

A pair of crossed rapiers hung on the wall between the windows. An antique broadsword gleamed in its shadowbox frame above the headboard. On the bedside chest were stacks of business journals, a Clancy hardback, and a steel-bladed stiletto. How careless. Before the accident, T. Wayne had collected guns. Now it was archaic knives and swords, and it appeared he was still leaving weapons lying around.

The master bedroom had changed from a frowsy boudoir to an armed camp. The transformation was surprising; the change in sleeping arrangements wasn't.

The dog followed as Mercy walked over to the pair of mounted rapiers and reached out to touch one of the delicately worked pommels. The sword tipped on its hook and clattered to the floor. Startled, the collie ducked behind a chair.

"You're okay," Mercy said, and knelt beside him. His day had been tough enough without almost being skewered. He licked his foreleg as a cover for losing his deportment. "Poor baby," she crooned.

He stopped licking, stared at the door, and cocked his head.

She heard it too, a faint thump down the hallway. There it was again. Footsteps and a clinking sound. The dog growled.

Someone was in the house. Oh God. The front door had been standing wide open. She'd been an idiot to walk in. Now she was trapped.

Even Mercy's kindergarten teacher had taught her—*never, never, never run into a burning house.*

Sophia's house had been burning for years.

Chapter Ten

Saturday, 1:17 p.m.

SuperShoppers. Billy and Lou cruised the jammed parking lot until they found a spot close to the black Acura that had already been cordoned off as the scene. Women bunched along the crime scene tape with their carts full of groceries and their kids running lose.

Lou insisted on checking in with Dispatch. Billy hauled himself out of the car, glad for a couple of minutes of solitary peace. He leaned against the front fender, arms crossed and hands clenched so he wouldn't fidget. Damn. He needed a cigarette. He'd quit ten years ago, but here he was craving a smoke, and it was Lou's fault.

Lou was always some version of a son-of-a-bitch, but at least they had respect between them. Occasionally Lou came down hard on him, but he'd never gone so far as to call Billy a lousy cop. Loyalty between partners was no joke. If Billy found out Lou had been talking trash behind his back that would tear it.

He took a deep breath. The wind blew out of the low hills of Arkansas, down Crowley's Ridge, across the brown water of the Mississippi and straight up the broad, crowded avenue of Poplar, Memphis's main drag. It blew grit in everyone's faces, including the two patrolmen wrestling yellow tape around the Acura sedan. They'd corralled the car by stringing tape through their cruiser's windows and grocery carts. Now the carts wouldn't stay put.

Ray Trit, known as "Wheezer" because of his chronic allergies, stumbled after a cart, yanked out his handkerchief and blew noisily. Onlookers snickered. Billy turned at the sound of Lou slamming his car door, knowing trouble was about to happen. Lou came around, stabbing his finger at Trit and three other cops standing with their hands in their pockets.

"Look at those idiots. I'm working with a bunch of fucking circus clowns. Get the cones out of the back and help those retards. I gotta whiz." Lou stomped toward the grocery store.

"Yeah, well you're the one wanted to work weekends," Billy yelled at Lou's back. He walked to the trunk and flung it open. A stack of orange cones lay beneath a coil of rope. If Lou kept this up, Billy was going to drop him off at a hospital equipped with a booby hatch and let Anderson deal with him.

Everyone in Billy's life was giving him fits—Lou, Hollerith, and as of a couple of weeks ago, his recent ex-girlfriend, Terri Cozi.

Terri was an investigative journalist for *The Memphis Flyer*. Billy had been working a sexy homicide when they broke up. The press was all over it. He knew she was worried about her job and wanted to impress her boss, but he didn't dream she would jeopardize his career to save hers. After catching Terri going through his briefcase in the middle of the night and copying his case notes, he'd moved out.

Last night she'd shown up at his new place, wanting to have make-up sex. He was no idiot, so he went along until he realized she was more interested in getting help on another story than being with him. He'd ended the evening early.

It's a hard lesson to swallow when a man realizes a woman has taken him for a fool once, and then she tries it again.

Lou came back to the car still wearing his badass cop expression. Billy handed off the cones to the patrolmen, took shots of the scene, and then walked over to where Lou was talking to Trit.

Wheezer Trit was as close to useless as a police officer gets. He had a reputation for slow response to a scene, a real foot-dragger who hated doing paperwork generated by a collar.

"We were cruising the area when we got the APB," Trit said. "Spotted the plates right off. Had a hell of a time clearing the area. Couldn't get the women out of the store to move their vehicles. Must be running a special on tampons." He laughed. Phlegm quaked in his throat. He sucked in air and spit.

Lou looked disgusted. "You guys bother to check the vehicle?"

"Ahh, when we got here the driver's door was ajar. There's cleaning hanging up and stuff in the back seat." Trit grinned. "She's probably in with the rest of them, loading up on Kotex."

"So you didn't notice a body in the car, under the car, beside the car. Nothing unusual like that?" Lou said.

"Nooo . . .," Trit said.

"How about the trunk? Body in the trunk? A little trunk music maybe?"

"Nobody said nothin' to me about a body," Trit said.

"I'll check the trunk," Billy said.

He slipped on a glove, opened the driver's door using two fingers on the back edge, and then used a pen to punch the button to release the trunk latch. Inside he found liquefied ice cream, a gallon of hot milk, three chunks of filet mignon past rigor mortis, and a can of Fix-A-Flat. Hollerith said the woman had been missing for sixteen hours. Anything could have happened in that amount of time. Or nothing.

Billy shoved aside the groceries and flipped back the trunk rug covering the tire well. Instead of a spare he looked down at three, one-liter bottles of Absolut.

How many cars had he searched on the street during his sweet year in Vice? Popping trunks yielded all sorts of surprises. Hot stock, balloons of smack, Tennessee hooch, Glad Bags of body parts. More than you'd expect from random searches. But the only time he'd found vodka stored in a tire well was in a vintage, baby blue Mercedes convertible belonging to one Sophia Dupree.

The thought chilled his gut. No. Couldn't be.

He checked the Acura's tag. Tennessee 266-SVL. "Who we dealing with here?" he said to Trit.

"I forget her name. I'll get the report." The cop pushed through onlookers and waddled toward his cruiser.

Lou stood beside the driver's door, jingling his pocket change. The wind whipped his tie around his neck.

Billy stepped from behind the car's trunk. "Judge Overton specifically asked for you to work this scene. Any idea who the woman is?"

Lou shook his head. "Nope."

"Because there's vodka in the tire well. Three liters. Who does that sound like?"

Trit's cruiser door thumped shut.

"You know this ain't Sophia's ride," Lou said, "but I'll check it out." He walked around to the driver's door and grabbed the chrome handle barehanded.

Billy watched through the rear window in disbelief as Lou leaned in, with his left hand on the steering wheel, and popped open the glove compartment. He rifled through the papers.

"Watch your hands," Billy shouted through the glass.

"No registration," Lou said. He grabbed the seat with his right hand and bumped the rearview mirror with his forehead as he backed out. He reached up and adjusted it.

No veteran cop would contaminate those critical points of contact. A rookie might, but not Lou.

"What the hell?" Billy demanded.

Lou's head hit the top of the doorframe as he backed out. "Jesus H. Christ. What're you yelling about?"

"Your prints are all over. The techs will go ballistic." Billy's cell buzzed inside his pocket.

"Answer the damned thing," Lou said, his face glowing with sweat and high blood pressure. He stormed past the car, rubbing the back of his neck like he had something to feel self-righteous about. He'd never interfered with evidence before, even when there was a reason for it. Billy checked his cell's ID. It was Terri Cozi. He answered it to buy some thinking time.

"Sorry to bother you," she said. "Last night was a little weird. Was I dreaming or did you kick me out of your bed?"

Her wounded tone triggered his guilt. A knee-jerk reaction. If he didn't watch it, she'd have *him* apologizing to *her*.

"I can't talk, Terri. I'm on a scene."

"A box of your stuff is at the apartment. How about if I drop it by tonight? We can talk."

"Not a good idea. I'll get my stuff later."

"It'll only take a minute. See you tonight." She hung up.

Trit came up beside him. "The woman's name is Sophia Dupree, missing since yesterday evening."

It didn't make sense. Sophia drove a 280 SL Mercedes convertible, and she was at rehab in Colorado. Billy's knees went weak for a second. Loving a woman as hard as he'd loved Sophia had driven him nuts. Passion, he discovered, has a long shelf life. After a few years the intensity had downgraded to guard-dog status, but the memories still had the power to blindside him. Paul Anderson would probably label his behavior obsession, springing from a classic cop psyche. Cops know about the bad things that happen to women.

"It's supposed to be Sophia we're looking for," he called out to Lou's back, "but I know she's out of town. Lou. Hey, *Lou.*"

Lou didn't react. He appeared to be studying the American flag whipping the pole across the street. Lou was drifting again, silhouetted against the bruised thunderclouds that outlined him. His pants bagged at the seat, and the heels of his shoes were worn down. His shoulders slumped, and his shirt looked sweaty and dingy. From behind, Lou looked like a bum they'd throw into the back of a squad car. Billy quickly dismissed the thought.

Trit flipped a page on his clipboard. "Address, 1219 Wrenworst. The mother called in a report at 10:12 a.m. Director Mosby called a few minutes ago and asked if Nevers had made the scene." Trit raised his voice so Lou could hear. "This woman must be somebody special to have the Director making calls."

Lou pivoted on his heel and swayed toward them. The structure of his face had changed in those few seconds and looked the same way it did when he'd stood in the shattered window. He snatched the clipboard from Trit. "She's somebody, all right. We scrape her out of back alleys and hot sheet motels to deliver her home to hubby. She's a drunk and a bedbug. I wouldn't be surprised if she was selling it out the back seat of her Mercedes."

"Hey, watch your mouth," Billy said, furious with Lou for talking that way about Sophia.

Lou ignored him. "She's never done a lick of time. The letters D-U-I only recently apply to Mrs. Dupree."

Trit grinned. "Sounds like you wouldn't be offended if the bitch disappeared."

Lou lunged for Trit and grabbed him by the shirt. "I got twenty-seven years on the force. What are you? You're nothing. Get your pig-ass out of my face!" The clipboard hit the asphalt.

He shoved Trit, and Billy jumped between them. "Damn it Lou, get a grip."

He turned on Billy. "You're no better than Trit. You're a pile of shit in a cheap suit."

"I'm warning you, pard. Reel it in."

Lou stabbed his finger in Billy's chest. "You been hanging on my coattail like I was your daddy. I'm not your daddy. He ran off, and your drunk-ass momma died doing the same."

A low whistle came from one of the cops standing nearby.

"I should gut you like a cat fish, you know that?" Billy whispered. "You been outta line for months."

"Outta line? I been figuring my next move."

Billy hooted. "You figure to throw another chair through a window? You figure to get us both shot? Stop figuring moves, Lou. You're lousy at it."

Lou's hand came up. "It's hallelujah time. Give me the keys."

"We've got a job to do."

An ugly smile crossed Lou's face. "I get it. You're itching to chase down that society bitch. We all have our needs." Lou eased his revolver from his holster. He pointed the muzzle skyward. "We're burning daylight, son. I'm outta here. Give me the fucking keys."

Every cop in the parking lot froze, eyes locked on Lou's finger resting against the trigger. Billy stepped back, knowing he had to unwind this thing quick and get Lou out of the public eye. He shrugged, trying to keep it casual. "Come on, Lou. What say we swing out of here together? We'll figure the details later."

"You're not handling me like you did that Tuggle woman." Lou lowered the muzzle to Billy's chest. "The keys."

"Cut it out, the guys are watching."

"Last time. Hand 'em over."

Billy shook his head.

The bullet ricocheted off the pavement and slammed into the Acura's door panel behind him. He stumbled backward. A woman screamed. He heard the second bullet clicked into the chamber. No one in the crowd moved. No other guns were drawn either.

"You can leave in a body bag," Lou said. "Or you can give me the keys. It's your call."

He'd seen pain in Lou's eyes. He'd seen despair. They'd never been empty. The look in Lou's eyes was cold as yesterday's grave water. Billy tossed the keys at Lou's feet. "Go on, you crazy bastard. You make me ashamed to be a cop."

"Now you're getting the picture. You thought I wouldn't pull the trigger. You never *could* see what's inside a man. Trust me."

Chapter Eleven

Saturday, 1:57 p.m.

Lou swept up the keys and stomped toward the Ford, his arms and legs pumping like he was a guilty man. A blast of adrenaline hit Billy, flooding his mouth with a bitter taste.

Overhead, the engine of a small plane buzzed. Billy looked up to see a Cessna dragging a banner that read "Dragon House Restaurant". The plane banked over the parking lot. When he looked back, Lou was in the unmarked sedan.

The Ford's engine roared. Lou barreled toward the exit and bolted into traffic without braking, almost sideswiping a van in the middle lane. The crowd watched the plane. The cops watched Lou's crazy driving. Some of the cops watched Billy.

Billy was thinking, *Your hand didn't shake when you pulled the trigger, Lou. You said "trust me" while you pointed a gun at my chest.*

Lou gunned through a yellow light, ripped through the Ford's gears and disappeared over a rise.

Trit let out a low whistle. "Hope he's wearing his seat belt."

"Not a chance," Billy said and tried to inhale, but the air seemed too thick to take into his lungs.

"I never seen nothing like that," Trit said. "I seen cops pull that kind of macho shit in the movies, but I never seen one do it for real . . . pull the trigger, I mean. Jesus Christ."

The plane wagged its wings and veered west. The cops got suddenly busy doing nothing and avoided eye contact with him. The women with their grocery carts moved on. He was too rattled to figure the damage Lou had done to his career. They could both be in hot water. Internal Affairs might say he should've pulled the plug on Lou after he threw a chair out the window at the Tuggle scene.

Damn it, Lou, he thought. *You made idiots out of both of us.*

"You okay, Detective? You're a little green around the gills." Trit pulled out his handkerchief, blew into it and inspected the results. "Damnation, I never seen a cop—"

Billy interrupted, not wanting to hear it. "Forget about Lou. Show me what you've got on Mrs. Dupree."

Trit recited the facts from his clipboard. Billy tried to concentrate.

Sophia's mother had made the initial call. She gave Sophia's address on Wrenworst as her own. Then Judge Overton had contacted Hollerith, requesting Lou as lead detective on the case. Why Lou? And what was the connection between Sophia and Overton? She'd never appeared before the judge and had never mentioned his name.

For years Billy had kept an eye on Sophia, finding her each time she'd disappeared on one of her drinking jags. If she was pulled over, he'd advised her to refuse the sobriety test and give his card to the cop. The cop would then call Billy, wanting to do a favor for an officer higher up the food chain. Usually the cop let her go.

But one time she ran into a hard-ass and got arrested. Lou had stepped in to put on the squeeze. On the day of the trial, the cop who wrote the DUI was conveniently out of town for a training class with the FBI. The case had been reset and then dismissed.

Now she was missing again. At this point Billy was concerned but not worried. The last time she disappeared, she'd abandoned her car downtown and showed up later in a Mississippi motel. That must be her new pattern. If she *had* run into trouble this time, Billy wanted all the bases covered so they wouldn't waste time. But that wasn't going to happen. Lucky stars shined on Sophia.

He looked up to see Harvey Trask swaggering toward him, jingling his keys. Harvey was the East division's patrol squad lieutenant, Trit's boss, and a man whose chain got easily yanked.

Billy spent the next ten minutes briefing the lieutenant and sending patrolmen to canvas the area. Trit verified the Acura's plates with the motor vehicle department. The car was registered to Sophia's husband, T. Wayne Dupree.

"The Dupree home is around the corner," Billy said to Trask. "I want to talk with the mother. I'd appreciate it if you'd take over till I get back."

Trask unwrapped a stick of Juicy Fruit. "Call just came in for a shooting near Poplar Plaza and a dog attack on Park Avenue. I got three cars tied up on your walk-away. I got to roll."

"Timing's crucial on this case."

"Don't talk to me about crucial, Sergeant. I've got ground to cover."

"The exposure in this case is pretty high."

Trask's eyebrows lifted. "Why?"

"Judge Overton has an interest."

"So where's Nevers?"

"Personal emergency, sir," Trit said.

The lieutenant's lips rolled back in a nasty grin. "Personal, huh. Ain't that convenient."

"You want to stay or does Lieutenant Hollerith need to send back up?" Billy said.

Trask hocked a loogie. "I'll stay. Did Nevers really run off with your ride?"

Trit intervened. "I'll drive you over to the lady's house, Detective."

Chapter Twelve

Saturday, 1:32 p.m.

The clinking sound grew louder as it came down the hallway. Mercy recognized it now. Her mother's gold bangle bracelets.

"It's okay, boy," she said to the dog tensing up beside her.

Gloria Snow rushed into the bedroom, her frantic gaze fixed on Mercy. Her elation died when she realized which daughter she faced. Disappointment took its place. Mercy was used to that expression. It said: *You're not Sophia. You never will be.*

Her mother hadn't changed—late fifties, petite, shapely and pretty, blond, over-accessorized. Still unable to mask her true feelings.

"Where's your sister?" Gloria said.

"I don't know. I just got here."

Gloria pointed at the collie. "What's that?"

"My dog."

"Good Lord, it smells." Her mother looked her up and down. "You're a mess. What happened?"

"We had an accident. Would you mind telling me why the front door was standing open when I got here?"

Gloria's chin went up. "Your sister's missing and you bring a filthy dog into her home." A waft of booze and perfume trailed her as she tottered by. The dog rose to his feet and growled. Her mother dove for the bed where she collapsed. "Get that animal out of this house. Don't you have any sense?"

"He's protecting me. We thought you were a burglar."

Gloria jerked her head up, tears in her eyes. "Mercedes, put the dog in the garage and get a grip on yourself. Don't you understand? Your sister's in trouble."

Breaking news, Mercy thought. *Sophia's in trouble again.* Of course her mother didn't ask about the accident even though the dog was obviously hurt and she was a mess.

"I'll bed him down in the laundry room, then we'll talk. Come on, Caesar," she said, a name she grabbed out of the air.

"Hurry up. I'm worried sick."

"All right." But Mercy felt no sense of urgency. Disappearing was Sophia's favorite trick. That and making several liters of vodka disappear with her.

A couple of years ago Mercy had tracked Sophia down at the Confederate Cabanas on Lamar Avenue and found her walking barefoot through the parking lot wearing a black slip, with a carnation clinched between her teeth and a bottle of Absolut tucked under her arm. Sophia didn't always slum. The first time she disappeared she'd registered at the Peabody Hotel under the name Sweet Pickens and ran up a two-thousand dollar tab in liquor and amenities. Everyone assumed she'd been kidnapped. After that, T. Wayne took away her credit cards and put her on a tight cash allowance.

Mercy knew her sister to be an expert at manipulation and head games even before the tragedy that had changed hers and T. Wayne's world. After years of sparring with Sophia, Mercy wondered if she was the only person who appreciated Sophia's true talent in life.

She passed the guest bedroom door, which was open now. The gold-leaf bed stood in the midst of chaos. The bed linens were stripped back, the mattress dislodged, and the dresser drawers hung open. Apparently, Sophia had moved out of the master bedroom, settled into the guest room, and their mother had been searching through her belongings. That explained why the great room had been tossed, but not the open front door.

Mercy found an old woolen blanket in the linen closet, bowls for food and water, and led the newly named Caesar to the laundry room. He sniffed the blanket, circled and lowered himself with a groan. She closed the door.

"I can't believe your nonchalant attitude," Gloria hissed from behind her. "You think more of a dog than your sister. I don't care if he's Rin Tin Tin, you need to take this situation seriously." She stomped down the short hallway to the kitchen, where she stood at the sink.

Mercy followed. "He's a collie. The name would be *Lassie*."

"Don't smart mouth me, young lady." A pot of coffee sat in the coffeemaker. The pot jittered on the edge of her mother's cup as she poured. She put the cup in the microwave and slammed the door. "I was the one who left the front door open. I had an exercise class this morning. I came home and realized Sophia's bed hadn't been slept in." The microwave dinged, she retrieved the cup, and began rummaging through a cabinet. Out came a bottle of Kahlua. She spiked the coffee and sipped. "That's better. I ran out the front door and searched the yard and pool house. Sophia sleeps there when she's having a bad night. I came in through the patio door. The front door must have blown open. I've been on the phone ever since."

Her mother sipped more coffee. The logical recounting of facts, unlike most of her mother's ramblings, unnerved Mercy.

"You live here now?" she said.

"You knew that. I put in a note along with my new address in my Christmas cards."

"I'm not on your Christmas card list."

Her mother blinked. "Oh?"

The last time Mercy had received a card from her mother was in her freshman year at Vanderbilt. A birthday card arrived a month late with a twenty dollar bill inside and was signed, "Best Wishes, Gloria." After that, nothing. Funny how that still hurt.

Mercy heated a cup of coffee for herself and winced at the bitterness. "What time did Sophia leave last night?"

"The evening news was on. Sophia called upstairs, said she had errands to run. The cleaners. SuperShoppers for groceries."

"Did she seem depressed? A little overwhelmed by my visit?"

"She seemed, I don't know, excited."

"She's done this before. Maybe my visit was too much. Maybe she went out for a drink. After a few, she forgot to come home."

"She hasn't done that in years. Well, a year. Last year. Not since that DUI. The judge warned her. She took him very seriously."

"Okay. That's why she didn't come home." Mercy was trying to sound reasonable. "She got drunk and slept somewhere else."

A glint flashed in her mother's eye. "Don't you call your sister a drunk."

"Good God, what do you think all that therapy was about? The accidents, the trips to the ER? A DUI? It's public record."

"Your sister's in trouble and you're criticizing her. Something's happened. I can feel it. Buck has the police looking for her now. He's very upset. I heard it in his voice."

"Who's Buck?"

"You know, Judge Overton."

"The one who let her off the DUI?"

"Not that judge. My friend."

"A judge is your boyfriend?"

Gloria sniffed. "You don't care about your sister, do you? I mean deep down." She pointed at Mercy's ruined clothes. "You show up late, dressed like a rag picker, with a sick dog to look after. Your sister's lost and all you're interested in is the dog and my boyfriend."

"I'm trying to get up to speed. Sophia and I haven't spoken in months."

Her mother's expression turned plaintive. "I know. She wanted you to visit this weekend so the both of you could patch things up."

"There's nothing to patch. We're just not close."

"Your sister loves you. She could've used your support."

"I don't understand what's going on. It's obvious you tore up the house looking for something specific. What's she into now, cocaine?"

Gloria grabbed her wrist. "Don't speak to me like that about your sister."

The phone rang. With a warning look, Gloria released her arm and answered it. Stunned, Mercy rubbed the nail marks on her wrist. With that kind of reaction, her mother must know something about Sophia she didn't want to admit, even to herself.

"Yes," Gloria said into the phone, nodding. "I see. And you'll let us know." She cradled the phone close to her ear. "This means so much. Yes, dear, tonight. Bye now." She hung up. "That was Buck. They found Sophia's car at a grocery store." Tears brimmed in her eyes.

"And?"

"No sign of Sophia."

Chapter Thirteen

Saturday, 2:24 p.m.

Trit drove Billy past the small park with its arched Japanese bridge and koi pond. A bench stood at the edge of the water, tucked between a pair of river willows. How many hours had he sat on that bench ten years ago, hoping Sophia might walk by, drive by? Anything to get a glimpse of her. His passion had changed with time, as had his sense of panic over her alcohol-driven disappearances, which had lately, been more frequent. He would find her, or she would come home on her own as she often did.

Trit dropped him off at the house. In the driveway he noted a blue Toyota with Georgia plates parked at the foot of the steps—a rental, he surmised from the Enterprise logo on the bumper. After jotting down the plate number, he rang the doorbell. A tall young woman with blond hair covering one side of her face opened the door. She gave him a quick glance up and down.

"We're happy with our own church, thanks," she said and closed the door.

She had assumed he was a missionary of some kind. Must be his black suit and white shirt. He took out his badge wallet, flipped open the cover, and knocked. The door opened. This time he noticed a scar beneath her hair running the length of her left cheek.

"Please leave your tract in the mailbox," she said, obviously put out by his persistence.

He flashed his badge. "Is Mr. Dupree home?"

She squinted at the badge. "He's . . . no. May I help you?"

"I need to speak with a family member of Sophia Dupree. Is her mother available?"

"I'm her sister."

"*You* are?" Too late, Billy realized how rude he'd sounded.

The woman's face flushed. "Do you know my sister?"

"We met some time ago." He offered his hand. "I'm Detective Billy Able."

As the woman extended her hand, he noticed brown stains on her sweater and pants. His senses went on alert. He recognized the color of dried blood.

"I'm Mercy Snow."

Her hand was warm, not clammy or tense. The only emotions he detected were embarrassment that turned to shyness, evident in the way she angled her body and moved her hair over her scarred cheek. Still, the possibility of blood on her clothes bothered him. He was alone with no backup.

"I'm looking into Mrs. Dupree's disappearance. Is that your car?" He indicated the Toyota.

"It's a rental. I drove in from Atlanta about an hour ago." She looked past his shoulder down the driveway. "Where's your partner?"

"Why do you ask?"

"I thought all detectives traveled in pairs. Like nuns." She didn't crack a smile, so he couldn't tell if she was kidding him.

"Not always. Is it possible for me to speak to your mother?"

She stepped back to let him in. "Of course, come in. Sorry I slammed the door in your face. You look like a Jehovah's Witness."

"They travel in pairs, too."

"Right." Again, no smile.

"Listen, can you tell me about those stains?" He nodded toward her pants and sweater.

She glanced down at her clothes. "I hit a dog on the highway. He was bleeding when I picked him up. Is there a problem? Do you need to see him?"

"Maybe later. You all right?"

"Yes, thank you for asking." She turned to open a pair of doors leading into a large room. With her back to him, he noticed how her slacks cupped her bottom and that the back of her arms were firm and brown. A good-looking woman, but very different from her sister.

He followed her into the darkened room, wanting to say something reassuring about Sophia. "We're doing everything we can to find Mrs. Dupree. People in these situations often show up on their own."

"That's what I've been telling my mother for the last half hour. She won't listen."

"Have you had any calls?"

"Only one. We were told her Mercedes was at SuperShoppers."

"Acura," he said. "She was driving an Acura."

"That can't be right. Sophia drives a vintage 280 SL Mercedes."

"The Acura is registered to her husband."

The sister went to the window and pulled a cord that exposed the room to full sunlight. Startled, he saw bears around him—bears on the floor, in chairs, on the sofa.

"I know how you feel," she said, reading the surprise on his face. "They had the same effect on me."

The room was chaos. Drawers and cabinet doors in the built-in bookcase hung open. Sophia's fresh lilies looked like they'd been jerked out of their vase and thrown back in. The room had been ransacked, and then an attempt was made to straighten it.

"What do you know about this?" he said, gesturing at the room.

"The bears are Sophia's. Mother made the mess. I haven't figured out what she was looking for."

She busied herself with moving a giant panda off the sofa so he'd have a place to sit, but he wasn't ready to sit. He still had questions about her whereabouts the last twenty-four hours.

"What's the drive from Atlanta, seven, eight hours? You must have been on the road since three this morning."

"Four."

"Traveling alone?"

"Except for the dog the last fifty miles."

"Can someone verify your presence in Atlanta as late as yesterday evening?"

She raised her eyebrows. "I worked with the night crew at my bakery until one this morning." She went to her purse and returned with a business card. "Call this number and ask for Brenda Watson. She's head pastry chef. Now if you'll excuse me, I'll get Mother." She hesitated. "She's pretty agitated. She may be a little combative. Even rude."

"I understand," he said, studying her as she walked away.

He searched for a resemblance. Sophia was pale and delicate with glossy, dark hair cut short. She was sexy, unpredictable. Mercy had the strength and grace of an athlete and was reserved, something Sophia could never pretend to be. They were polar opposites.

He wondered why, after all the years he'd known Sophia, she never mentioned having a sister.

When Mercy didn't return for a good ten minutes, he paced. Finally she came back, with Gloria Snow taking the lead into the room. Gloria had changed little over the years, this time passing off the drink in her hand as coffee instead of orange juice. Apparently, she didn't remember him from the time he'd spent at the hospital with Sophia.

Mercy had switched her bloody clothes for blue jeans and a green polo shirt. She stood next to her mother, looking nervous, with her arms crossed in front of her.

"Afternoon, ma'am," he said to Gloria Snow.

"This is Detective Able, Mother."

She looked him up and down. "Mercy tells me you haven't found my daughter."

"We're doing everything we can to find Sophia. Mind if we sit down and talk?"

Mercy swept bears from a pair of club chairs and Gloria sat, holding her coffee cup with both hands. Billy sat on the sofa, noting that she was upset, but he knew she was tougher than she looked. He opened his steno pad.

"When was the last time you saw your daughter?"

"Yesterday evening just after six. She said she needed to run errands for Mercy's visit—the cleaners, the grocery store, and something else."

He raised his eyebrows, waiting.

"I've got it. The library. I was dressing for a political fundraiser. We left before she came home. The evening ran later than we expected. I never thought to check on her when I came in." She sniffed. "This morning her door was closed. I thought she might be sleeping in. She's worked so hard on these bears for the children's hospital, and then to have company on top of that . . . " She paused, rolled her eyes.

He glanced at Mercy. She looked out the window.

"It was past nine this morning when I peeked into her room and realized her bed hadn't been slept in. I panicked. I called the police, then Buck at his office."

"Buck?" Billy said.

"Yes, Judge Overton." She smiled. "We went to the fundraiser together. He told me he would handle things. But while you're sitting here asking questions, my girl is missing."

"Where's Mr. Dupree?"

"He's out of the country," Mercy said. "I've spoken with his office. They're trying to reach him."

"Unfortunate timing." Billy left the comment open-ended.

"He's a vice president for Zelware Corp. and travels a lot," Gloria said. "He flew to Austin Monday then flew to some place the Russians used to own. U-beck something. They buy frozen chicken from T. Wayne's company."

"Uzbekistan," Mercy filled in. "It'll be hard for him to get a flight out of Samarkand. His office said schedules there are erratic."

Billy scribbled notes and considered his next line of questions. "With her husband out of town a lot, I'm sure Mrs. Dupree finds time on her hands. She must get lonely."

Mrs. Snow straightened in her chair. "My daughter isn't lonely. I'm living here now. And I'm not sure what you're getting at, officer."

"Detective Able may be aware of Sophia's drinking problem," Mercy said.

"That doesn't mean something hasn't happened to her," Gloria snapped.

"That's not what I meant," Mercy said, her voice rising.

Billy held up a hand. "You have every right to be worried; however, your daughter has disappeared before. We need to consider all possibilities."

Gloria's hand went to her throat, bracelets jingling. "She's had trouble in the past, but I want to be very clear. This time is different. Something's happened."

"We don't know that," Mercy said.

Gloria began to weep. "You're not listening to me."

"Take it easy, Mrs. Snow. We'll start by checking hospitals and women's facilities," Billy said. "I'll need her address book, day-timer, and personal diary if she has one. And is there any place she might have gone?"

Mercy stood. "Mother, where's the number for the rehab in Colorado? She may have called them."

"They can't help us. Someone means to harm my daughter."

Billy looked up from his notes. "Someone threatened her?"

"Well, no," Gloria said.

Mercy stared at her. "Did something happen, Mother?"

Gloria raised her cup to her lips, taking her time, ignoring Mercy and studying Billy over the cup's edge. "I have something to show you."

He heard the subtle shift in her tone. She'd spoken to him in confidence, as if they were the only people in the room.

"What is it?" Mercy said.

Gloria rose unsteadily and went to the kitchen. He stood as she returned and took the two small slips of paper she handed him. The first was a Chinese cookie fortune.

"Read it out loud," she said.

"Jealousy rivals love. Therein lies discontent. BEWARE."

"It was in our Chinese take-out," Gloria said. "And this."

The second was a newspaper clipping dated the previous week. He read, "Scorpio (Oct.23-Nov21) Circumstances turn against you. Fast-moving individuals pull a fast one. Focus on security. Expect an unexpected resting place."

"Sophia showed it to me," Gloria said. "It scared her."

Mercy looked at him with a telling gaze. "Mother, why don't you get more coffee while I talk to the detective?"

"How dare you patronize me!" Gloria snatched the bits of papers from him. "You think I'm a joke. Soon as I leave you'll discuss how to handle me."

"That's not true," Mercy began.

Billy cleared his throat. "Ladies, we need to focus—"

"I thought you two were here to help Sophia," Gloria snapped and marched from the room.

Mercy shook her head. "I don't know what to say."

"People strike out when they're upset."

"Upset? She's furious. She'll pour another drink and come back swinging." Mercy shot him a penetrating look. "You know Sophia, don't you? What was it, a DUI or have you pulled her out of some dive for my brother-in-law?"

His cell rang. "Excuse me," he said, relieved he didn't have to answer her. "Detective Able."

"Something's come up at SuperShoppers," Trask said. "A stock boy from yesterday's shift picked up a handbag in the parking lot last night.

Turned it in a few minutes ago. It's Mrs. Dupree's. You want me to send a car?"

Billy kept his tone light so he wouldn't alarm Mercy. "Thanks, I'll walk. It's quicker." He hung up. "Something's come up. Is there a second set of keys to the Acura?"

"What's happened?" Gloria said, returning. She handed him Sophia's calendar and her address book.

"No diary?" he said.

Gloria shook her head.

"I saw extra sets of car keys in the kitchen," Mercy said. "I'll find some for the Acura and drive you to the store."

"That works."

"I heard your phone ringing. Tell me what they found," Gloria said as she followed him to the entry. "Detective, please."

He turned, aware of the anxiety on her face. He didn't feel right putting her off. "Possibly her handbag."

"Oh, God. Sophia never loses her handbag."

Mercy came in from the kitchen. "Let's go."

Chapter Fourteen

Saturday, 3:18 p.m.

Earl Houser, assistant manager of SuperShoppers Grocery, had an office in the middle of the store's second story. An interior catwalk gave him a clear view of the entire warehouse. His exterior window overlooked the store's parking lot. From the office's lived-in appearance, Billy guessed Houser got to work at seven in the morning, ate lunch at his desk, and went home late.

This was a working office with cardboard file boxes stacked up, the desk chair patched with duct tape and a bulletin board loaded with flyers. The board hung across from Houser's desk, next to a poster showing tropical palms and two women in bikinis eating pineapple. Red letters across the top of the poster read "Dole—Sweet and Juicy". It was the only bright spot in the office.

Billy waited in the office for Houser, going over the details he'd gathered, while at the same time, suppressing visions of Sophia in trouble.

Through the interior warehouse window he saw Wheezer Trit and a huge, pear-shaped Chinese boy standing side by side on the catwalk. They leaned back against the railing with their bellies bulging in front of them, the teenager's shirt gapping above his trousers, showing his navel as he rocked back and forth on his heels. In constant motion, he appeared to inhabit a world of his own. The teenager was the one who'd supposedly found Sophia's handbag.

Earl Houser, a fidgety man with thinning hair and a sunken chest, came through the door, profusely apologizing for keeping Billy waiting. He went to his chair, sat, and then sprang to his feet when he realized his visitor had no place to sit. His nerves showed.

In the middle of the desk lay Sophia's expensive black handbag and several plastic bags that contained her wallet, IDs, and personal items. Earl cleared his throat.

"Charles, out there, is one of a group of handicappers we hired under a pilot program for SuperShoppers Inc."

"No problem. We'll take him downtown and find out what he knows."

"That's why I wanted to speak with you first." Earl's lips twitched. "I'm not about to tell you how to do your job, but you'll get more from Charles in my office where he's comfortable."

"Tell me something; is he under-aged?"

"No, but I assume there are rules about interrogating people like him. Should he have his father here?"

"His father can meet him downtown."

Earl cleared his throat again. "Here's my point. People like Charles get confused when you change their routine or put them under pressure."

"Go on."

"Charles relates to what he sees. Talking to him is unproductive; show him and he gets the idea. From here you'd be able to point out the woman's car in the parking lot." Earl fiddled with his tie and swallowed. "There's something else."

"Something you need to clear up about Mrs. Dupree?"

"No, nothing like that. The corporate office is looking for a reason to dump the handicap program. They're concerned about lawsuits down the line. Charles being questioned in the disappearance of a woman customer . . . that's the kind of excuse they're looking for."

Billy turned to watch through the window as the big teenager picked a scab on the back of his elbow. Charles looked up and smiled. Two teeth missing. A mole the size of a dime on his cheek. The boy weighed 275 easy.

"Does this situation affect you personally?" Billy said.

"Actually I like the kid. He's a good worker. I hired him." The tops of Houser's ears flushed. "I'm in charge of the program for this district. I have a review coming up in two weeks."

A woman was missing from Houser's parking lot, and his real concern was his job. It irritated Billy, but he knew that people, in the long run, are interested in themselves and their own livelihood.

He glanced over at Charles. The interview, no matter where he conducted it, would be tricky. The mentally handicapped, foreigners, and teenagers in general made lousy subjects. Charles Chang fit all categories. Billy wasn't even sure how to approach it. The boy's unique point of view would make it hard to put together an accurate picture.

"All right, Mr. Houser, I'll go with you on this. I'll ask a few preliminary questions here. If I get a bad feeling, we'll take him downtown, and his father can meet us there."

"Fair enough," Houser said.

While Houser left to find chairs, Billy looked through the contents of Sophia's wallet. No cash, no credit cards. He palmed her driver's license, then invited Charles in and introduced himself. The boy shook hands, appearing nervous. He wandered around the office, taking only moments to move in on the Dole poster with the women in bikinis.

"You like the beach?" Billy said.

"Nope."

Houser showed up with two dusty folding chairs. Billy set them up near the window, opposite each other, so he and the boy would be facing. He asked Charles to have a seat, and then pointed to the handbag on the desk.

"Charles, did you ever meet the lady whose handbag you found?"

Charles looked puzzled. Billy held up Sophia's photo ID.

"Oh sure, Ms. Sophie. I carry out her groceries." Charles grinned, showing the black gaps between his teeth. "I'm her Superman. She gives me five dollars. Nobody gets five dollars, hardly ever."

"You carried her groceries last night?"

"I did. Yes, I did that."

"Where did she ask you to put them?"

"In the trunk."

"That's good. Now, let's think about last night when you helped Ms. Sophie. What time was it, do you remember?"

Billy knew from a time-stamped receipt what time Sophia had checked out. He wanted to test the boy's memory.

Charles frowned.

"Come on, I hear you're a smart guy."

"The light poles buzz when they come on," Charles said.

"And they were buzzing?"

"Riiiight."

"Great, that's a big help, it sets the time around seven last night. Did you see anyone with Ms. Sophie in the parking lot? Anyone talking to her, watching her?"

"Just me."

"Did she seem happy or sad?"

"Ms. Sophie always smiles."

"Now Charlie, I want you to think hard about this one."

The boy scowled. "My name's not Charlie. Charlie makes me Charlie Chan, like the detective in those old movies."

"Aren't you Chinese?"

The boy's eyes snapped wide. "No, sir, I'm a gawl darn Southerner."

Billy suppressed a smile. "Okay. Let's go over to the window."

They looked out in time to see the impound truck loading the Acura. Mercy stood by the car with her arms crossed. The wind blew her hair off her shoulders. Charles put his hands on the sill and leaned forward, nose touching the glass.

"That's Ms. Sophie's other car," Charles said.

"Ms. Sophie's lost. Do you know where she is?"

Charles didn't answer. He seemed focused on the loading procedure. Billy wondered if the boy understood what he meant by "lost." It didn't seem to register.

"Think now, when you were with Ms. Sophie did she say anything? Did anything happen that surprised you?"

"She gave me five dollars, that's all."

Charles shifted his feet. Billy heard a brushing sound then noticed the boy rubbing his thigh with his thumb. He looked out the window to see Mercy holding back her blowing hair, her back arched, her breasts silhouetted against her shirt.

Billy swallowed before he spoke again, struggling to keep his tone friendly. "You like pretty ladies, don't you?"

Charles nodded.

"You think Ms. Sophie is pretty?"

"My daddy says he'll whoop me if I make sex on a lady."

"But you like Ms. Sophie. She's your special lady friend."

The boy stepped back from the window and smacked his lips. "Mr. Earl needs me now." He turned for the door.

Billy put a firm hand on his shoulder. "Let's sit down. No, come on over here. That's right. Back to Ms. Sophie's car. Tell me what happened after you put the groceries in the car."

"I put the money in my pocket," Charles said. "Took the cart back to the store."

"What about Ms. Sophie, what did she do?"

Confusion clouded the teenager's face. A bell rang in the warehouse. He jumped to his feet. "Got to go to work."

"Sit down and tell me about the handbag."

"Mr. Earl said he'd give me a pizza if I do right with you."

"Sit down and tell me what happened, then we'll talk pizza."

The boy eased into the chair. His leg jiggled and his thick features bunched together in concentration.

"My daddy always says 'don't be late, Dummy.' I miss my bus, Daddy gets mad. He has to drive in traffic to get me. He yells." A round tear broke at the edge of Charles's eye.

"No one's going to yell. What about the handbag?"

"I ran. The purse was by the ditch. I can't miss my bus."

"The handbag was near the culvert?"

Charles nodded.

"You figured you'd turn it in today." Billy leaned in so close their knees touched. "Charles, do you dream about Ms. Sophie . . . at night, I mean?"

"Ms. Sophie is pretty."

He pictured Charles's hands on Sophia's arms, his weight crushing her. He wanted to grab the teenager by the throat and squeeze the truth out of him. Instead, he forced his body to relax.

"Did you hurt Ms. Sophie a little?"

Charles sniffed and looked down, shook his head.

"Did you have sex on Ms. Sophie?"

The bell rang again. Charles put the edge of his thumb in his mouth and chewed. He rocked back and forth. Neither of them spoke. The only sound was the rhythmic squeak of the metal chair.

"Answer me."

Charles stopped rocking. "Not on Ms. Sophie. I'm her Superman."

◈

Mercy walked alongside the rolling impound truck as it prepared to haul off the Acura. It was hard to picture Sophia driving the black sedan after seeing her in the little blue Mercedes all these years. The Acura didn't fit Sophia's image. The crime scene tape didn't fit either. She was getting a bad feeling. Instead of one of her sister's psycho-dramas, this was beginning to look like the real thing.

As soon as they'd arrived, Detective Able had taken the Acura's keys and started the engine. It turned over, which meant Sophia hadn't abandoned the car because of a dead battery. The detective went into the store, accompanied by a sour, officious-looking cop, someone who'd apparently been left in charge. She could tell the cop was giving Able a hard time. She wondered if the detective was experienced enough to handle this case. He didn't look much older than she was.

The wind picked up with a nasty attitude. Thunderheads piled high in the sky. Looked like a storm coming in from the west. She felt lightheaded. She had to pull herself together. Caffeine would help.

Inside the store, she found a kiosk with specialty coffees and ice cream. Behind the counter a pleasant-looking young girl chatted up a male customer.

"Can you make a root beer float?" Mercy said.

"Sorry. How about an iced mocha cappuccino with whipped cream? It's pretty good."

"Fine. Lots of excitement outside. What's up?"

"A lady is missing. Her car's been in the lot since last night."

"Didn't anyone notice a car left overnight?"

"We're open twenty-four hours. No one would notice. One of our guys found her handbag in the parking lot last night, but he didn't turn it in until an hour ago."

"Maybe he knows what happened."

"Maybe. I think she's the lady who tips him five dollars every week. He comes right to me and gets a triple cone of bubblegum ice cream." The girl leaned in. "Charles is an okay guy, but he kind of gives me the creeps. Stares a lot . . . not that he'd do anything."

The girl gestured toward a heavy-set Asian teenager walking along the bay of checkout stands with Able. The detective carried a brown grocery sack and talked as they walked. The boy looked pale, wrung out.

"That's Charles. That's a detective with him. Doesn't look like a cop, does he?"

"It's the suit," Mercy said.

"I'll bet they didn't get much out of Charles. He gets uptight around men. Does better with women."

Mercy took a sip of her iced cappuccino. "Thanks."

She walked to the front of the store. Charles tied on an apron and began sacking groceries. Detective Able handed a patrolman the paper sack. Mercy caught his attention. Able finished with the patrolman and joined her.

"Was that Sophia's handbag in the sack?"

Able took her elbow. "Let's step out of the doorway."

The detective's jaw was set, not tensed, but his expression had a forced calm about it. She knew he was keeping something from her.

They moved to stand in the nearly empty café. "Was it her bag?"

"I don't want you to jump to conclusions."

"How long before that boy found it?"

He frowned. "Who told you that?"

"I pick up on things. She's in trouble, isn't she? Some creep could've pulled up beside her in a van and grabbed her."

Able stared out the door at the parking lot, his profile all angles and planes. "Your mother's right. Your sister, no matter what shape she's in, doesn't lose her handbag. But she's gone missing before, so I'm not inclined to jump to conclusions."

"You really *do* know Sophia."

"All I can tell you now is I don't believe Charlie is involved. Why don't you go home, see if your mother remembers anything else. Here's my card with my cell. When your brother-in-law gets in town, give me a call. In fact, call me anytime."

She shoved the card into her jeans pocket.

Able's expression softened. "I don't want to scare you, but we've put a tap on your phone in case a kidnapper contacts you."

Chapter Fifteen

Saturday, 5:34 p.m.

Billy learned a long time ago that some days are meant to be worse than others. Some days his razor would drag or the garbage bag would rip on the way to the trash. He remembered a day when he stood at the curb with coffee grounds soaking his socks while he watched the neighbor's dog pee on his newspaper.

He considered those days to be divine pop quizzes meant to test his reaction. Then there were days like today, an altogether different category—days to test his soul.

He caught a ride with a patrol car from SuperShoppers to the Criminal Justice Center downtown, asking to swing by Lou's duplex on the way. The beat-up International Harvester pickup Lou used to go fishing sat in the side yard. No Ford in the driveway. No sign of anyone home.

They let him off at the parking garage next to the CJC. The Honda Civic Lou had bought last year at a police auction sat two floors up in its usual parking space.

Earlier he'd been worried about Lou. Now he was thinking what a bastard Lou had been. He'd torn up the Tuggle scene, made a fool of himself, and declared that Billy was the worthless cop. Jerk. Then he took a shot at Billy. Well, not exactly a shot *at*, but close enough to be damned insulting. Drove off and left him stranded with every working cop in the parking lot giving him the fisheye.

Billy took the garage elevator down to street level and crossed to the CJC. Screw Lou. He had work to do.

He spent the next hour at his desk typing reports on the Tuggle investigation to transfer over to Vargas and Nance. He started a file on Sophia. Unfortunately, with her pending DUI, additions to her record could influence a judge's decision in the wrong direction.

He leaned back and laced his fingers behind his head. He needed to think through the facts. Sophia had come home from druggie camp, according to her mother, in good shape. However, he was sure Gloria Snow wasn't the best judge of emotional stability.

The evening before Mercy arrived, Sophia had run errands and did some last minute shopping. There was vodka hidden in the tire well. Was she drunk when she went shopping, and no one had noticed? That didn't surprise him. Sophia could function sober as a nun while testing out at .09 on the breathalyzer. Charles Chan wouldn't know if she were drunk. He'd been too infatuated to notice anything but the chubby he was working on while loading her groceries.

No sign of a struggle in or around the car. No witnesses to a confrontation, not yet anyway. *She takes a taxi, hitches a ride, catches a bus, heads for a favorite hangout where she can get comfortably loaded. But what about the handbag?* Her husband had taken her credit cards so she would need cash to party. Either she took out all her cash and dropped the purse by the culvert or someone dropped it for her. There are sharks in the water trolling for women, especially women like Sophia who drink too much. Women like Sophia and Billy's mother.

When he was a kid, his mother kept telling him his father was away on a business trip and would be home soon. Soon never came. When he'd asked questions, she distracted him with peanut butter cookies or a ride on the hood of the car while she circled the block. After awhile he quit asking. His childhood ended a week before his ninth birthday, when his mother's car left the road at the blind curve in Tayloe's Bend, heading out of town. After the accident, everyone in town scrambled to tell him his no good father had run off, and his mother, even though she was from good stock in Atlanta, was a drunk.

His mother's alcohol problem had been no surprise to him. He'd grown up with her drinking.

Billy looked over his notes, recognizing the traits shared by his mother and Sophia. But Sophia's karma was different. She had a knack for sliding out of tight spots. Tonight he would cover Sophia's favorite bars, talk to the taxi services in town and check in with the hotels. If she'd hitched a ride somewhere he was out of luck. For now, his job was to ask the right questions and touch every base until something new turned up. Tomorrow she'd be home or he would begin to look into T. Wayne Dupree's background, just to see what was up.

Damn, he could use Lou's help about now.

The phone rang. He snatched it up. "Lou?"

"It's Williams in Dispatch. No response from Nevers. What gives? You girls have a spat?"

"Keep at it, will you?" He hung up.

He caught himself staring at the red light on the coffeemaker, feeling saturated by the odor of scorched coffee. He looked around the squad room that was divided by panels for privacy. Sports calendars, newspaper clippings and aged cartoons littered the yellow walls. Lou's desk and empty chair stood next to his.

Maybe Lou was sick. He'd lost weight, hadn't been sleeping and worried a lot about money. The women in Billy's Mississippi church used to talk about the way brain fever changed a man. He wasn't sure what "brain fever" meant, but maybe Lou had a tumor. He'd heard that could cause behavioral changes.

He flipped open the pad and wrote down everything Lou had said and done since the morning. If Lou agreed to see Paul Anderson, a record could be important. Actually it was no longer a matter of if Lou agreed, it was when.

As he wrote, he became aware of a conversation across the room between a younger black man wearing a suit and Rob Carey, the Assistant Attorney General assigned to the homicide squad. As the conversation continued, the man's gaze shifted in Billy's direction, and he nodded then returned his attention to Carey.

"Able," Kline Hollerith said from behind him.

Startled, Billy closed the notepad and swung around. Lieutenant Hollerith, who usually worked in his shirtsleeves, wore a blue blazer with gold buttons and a navy-striped tie. Church clothes, not work clothes.

"Lieutenant," he said.

"The Director's meeting just broke up. A new department is coming online. Stats, data crunching, forecasting. Interesting stuff." Hollerith tugged at the knot in his tie. "Have you made any headway on that missing person?"

"The lady has some bad habits. Couple of times a year she runs off."

"Overton doesn't think she's a walk-away," Hollerith said.

"That opinion comes from the mother. She's pretty hysterical."

Hollerith glanced around the squad room. "The judge wants Nevers to head this up. Where is he?"

"Lou's . . . out."

"Out?"

"He'll be back." Billy fished out a paper clip and bent it open.

"My office. Now," the lieutenant said and strode away.

Billy pitched the paper clip. End to a perfect day. He trailed after Hollerith.

The lieutenant's office had a sterile feel to it, the desktop antiseptically neat. Hollerith sat behind the desk and motioned him to an orange plastic chair in front.

"Give me what've you got," Hollerith said.

"She was last seen at SuperShoppers East yesterday around seven in the evening. No sign of a struggle, no damage to the vehicle. The husband is out of the country. I talked to the mother and sister. Mrs. Dupree is home from a recent dry-out in Colorado, but we found vodka hidden in the trunk."

Hollerith leaned back in his chair. "Oh, boy."

"She has one pending DUI. A few months ago she abandoned her vehicle beside a downtown bar and disappeared for two days. This scene would follow her new pattern except for one thing. Last night a stock boy picked up her handbag near a culvert fifty yards from her car. He didn't turn it in until today."

"You bring the boy in?"

"He's mentally challenged. His supervisor recommended an onsite interview."

"You think the boy's involved?"

"I don't think he has the capacity or the temperament. I may bring him in for a follow-up." He put his hands on his knees and stood. "We'll keep on top of this—"

"What's Lou's take on the case?"

Billy sat down again. "He's concerned about Mrs. Dupree."

"Concerned my ass. Harv Trask called, said he was pulled off supervisory duty to stay with the scene because Nevers was a no-show. Lou's been out sixteen days in the last six months."

"He had a bad day today."

"Bad day?"

"Very bad, sir."

Hollerith squared a stack of memos on his desk. "You're saying he can't work the case?"

"I wouldn't go that far."

"How far would you go?"

Billy shrugged. "I want to check some possibilities on Mrs. Dupree. Chances are good she'll be home before the night's out."

Hollerith looked past him toward the doorway. Billy turned around to see the man who'd been talking to Carey.

"Don't want to interrupt," the man said.

Hollerith stood and stepped from behind his desk. "Hey, no problem, Agent Jones. Come in."

The man held up his hand. "I just came by to introduce myself to the detective." He offered his hand to Billy. "Otis Jones, TBI. You're Detective Able."

"You remember Jones, best running back Vanderbilt ever had," Hollerith said. "This is Otis 'Elevator' Jones."

Jones stood slightly shorter than Billy. Jones' suit coat bulged over the shoulders and chest of a body builder. With that kind of build, the charcoal suit and shirt had to be custom-made. He looked like a player, and not the first to use the Tennessee Bureau of Investigation as a boost for a political career. Hollerith appeared to be impressed. Billy wasn't.

"Thought you looked familiar," Billy said, and shook hands.

"Twenty pounds heavier and twenty seconds slower," Jones said. "Heard about you and Nevers. Highest closure rate in your squad four years running. That's a winning streak."

"Lou carries the ball. I do the blocking."

"Jones starts working Governor Richard's Gang Task Force on Monday," Hollerith said. "The dealer who got popped on Hazel Street was a TBI informant."

"That so?" Billy said. He knew Jones was on the make. He could smell it.

"Your local bangers have racked up an impressive body count," Jones said. "Gang violence is up all over the state, but nothing like here in Memphis."

"Could I get a copy of those stats?" Hollerith said.

"Sure thing," Jones said, never looking away from Billy. "Governor Richards wants a ground level view of the problem. Could you single out some territories?"

"Sure, but they don't call us till the bodies hit the ground. You need to hook up with Sam Waters in Narcotics."

"We'll get that information," Hollerith said. "In the meantime, I'd like your opinion on data collection."

Jones smiled and held out his hand to Hollerith. "Fascinating subject. Let's get together on it sometime."

Hollerith beamed. "How about now?"

"I've got a thing with Senator Noel. Later, okay? Able, I'll get back with you on those contacts."

Chapter Sixteen

Saturday, 5:02 p.m.

Mercy wrestled bags of groceries past the laundry room, where she peeked in on Caesar. No blanket, no dog. She found her mother in the kitchen with rollers in her hair, standing at the sink, peeling potatoes. A pot of boiling water rattled its lid on the stove.

"Is Sophia home?" Mercy said, trying to be casual.

"Not yet." Gloria said.

Mercy put the bags onto the counter. "Where's Caesar?"

Gloria nodded toward a corner behind the breakfast table. The dog yawned and regarded them with clear eyes.

"How ya' doing, boy?" she said.

His tail thumped in response.

While driving home, Mercy had decided she wouldn't mention the tap Detective Able put on their phone line. Anticipating a call from a kidnapper might push her mother into a panic.

"You said you'd call from the store," Gloria said.

"Sorry, I got distracted. Detective Able must have twenty cops out looking for Sophia."

"Buck made that happen, not your detective. He's very concerned about Sophia."

"The detective said all her cash was gone. Are you sure she wouldn't pocket her money and leave her handbag behind during one of her episodes?"

Potato skins flew off the peeler. "If you came home more often, you'd know the answer."

"Mother, I have a business. I work seven days a week."

"If that's your priority . . . "

She sighed. Through the door she saw the great room had been emptied of stuffed toys. "What happened to the bears?"

"I had LeBonheur Hospital send over a truck. We can't fool with that now."

"Good." She stooped to check Caesar's stitches.

"He's a sweet dog," her mother said. "He minds."

Mercy unloaded her baking goods: heavy cream, vanilla beans, three pounds of sweet butter. As a child she'd baked pies on weekends while her mother and Sophia drove all over the state for Little Miss contests and baton competitions. Before long she'd developed her own recipes. She won contests. After college she turned her pastime into a business. The business grew.

Gloria dumped fresh snap beans into a sieve for rinsing.

"The stock boy who carried out Sophia's groceries may have been the last person to see her," Mercy said.

Gloria's eyes widened. "Was he involved?"

"The detective doesn't think so."

"Those police don't know anything. Buck said he's put on the pressure. He's very influential in this town." She pulled out the sprayer and rinsed the beans.

"You've had a hard day. Shouldn't you be off your feet?"

"Cooking calms me," Gloria said.

"Don't go to any trouble for me."

"Sophia and I cook on Saturday nights while the boys have drinks in the library. We use your grandmother's good things. There's so little graciousness left in life."

"You're not planning that for tonight, are you?"

"Tradition is comforting. Surely you know that."

"My life's pretty thin on tradition. Need some help?"

Gloria shook water from her hands. "If you would snap these beans. There's a bowl in the pantry."

Sophia's pantry was stocked with the best ingredients and several rows of classic French and trendy cookbooks. Mercy grabbed a bowl and pulled four cookbooks off the shelf to look through later. It was going to be a long night.

"That pantry is heaven," Mercy said. "Have you flipped through any of the books?"

"Your grandmother's recipes are good enough for me."

She was pretty sure that was meant as a dig, but she wasn't going to get into an argument. She broke the long beans into thirds, the short ones in half. Caesar whimpered, and his road-ragged paws twitched as he dreamed.

"I'm worried about Sophia, too," Mercy said. "It's a miracle this hasn't happened before now."

"If you'd lived through what Sophia has, you'd understand."

Mercy glanced over and saw the knife tremble in her mother's hand. Time to change the subject.

"Have you thought of anything else to tell Detective Able?"

Gloria laid down the knife and gazed out the window. "Not really. Sophia's been under a strain lately but not lost, the way she gets before she runs off."

"Has anyone been bothering her?"

"I covered that with the detective, remember?"

"All right, Momma."

"All right yourself. No one listens to me except Buck. I can't put my finger on it, but I know my girl is in trouble." Gloria wiped her hands and took a highball glass from the cabinet. "I need a drink. Don't you say a word about it either."

Mercy's sister and mother were alcoholics. Addiction ran through both sides of the family. Every born Southerner knows that good cooking, hard drinking, and going half crazy are hardwired traits coursing through the best families' bloodlines.

She watched her mother pour four fingers of vodka over ice. The rollers in Gloria's hair exposed her sagging jaw line, making her look more vulnerable than Mercy remembered.

She put her hand on her mother's shoulder. "I'll bake my chocolate pecan pie. It won 'Best in Region' last year at Chef's Expo in Birmingham."

The ice clicked as Gloria drained her glass, her lips glistening with cold vodka as she smiled. "Buck loves sweets. When Sophia gets home, you can tell us about your little bakery."

A stab of jealousy caught Mercy by surprise. Every experience had to be filtered through Sophia. "We'll have pie, then."

She unpacked the groceries while Gloria laid out the silver chafing dish and meat platter, buffing each piece with a tea towel. "If you use your good silver, you won't have to polish it. Sophia was thrilled last Christmas when I gave Grammy's silver to her. She was just like a child."

Mercy stiffened. She remembered the sterling tea service, Grammy's punch bowl, every type of serving tray, two sets of flatware; family heirlooms from as far back as the Civil War. Every piece had a story.

"This will pass to you one day," her mother had told her many years ago when she'd found Mercy studying the collection in the dining room cabinets. Knowing she would be included in the family's heritage had given Mercy a sense of belonging she hadn't felt since her father died.

Mercy had never forgotten that promise. Apparently her mother had.

She walked into the dining room. Cabinets, like the ones in their mother's dining room, had been installed since her last visit. Grammy's silver winked from behind the glass doors.

She was so tired of playing Cinderella.

She straightened her back and walked into the kitchen, which now smelled of crushed garlic and rosemary. Gloria stood by the sink, stirring up a marinade for roast pork tenderloin, a dish she prepared for special occasions. Tonight was for the judge, not for her.

"Momma, do you remember when Sophia had a date every weekend in high school?"

Her mother glanced over her shoulder, smiling. "She was voted Most Popular."

"Did you know I used to open my bedroom window so I could listen for when she came home?"

"How sweet. Funny what we remember."

"Sophia was usually too loaded to unlock the door. I'd let her in and put her to bed." She ran her fingers over the curve of the chafing dish. "Did you know Sophia was a drunk even in high school?"

Her mother rinsed the dish and turned with the impassive expression of a wounded movie star. "I want you to go upstairs, put on some decent clothes and touch up that scar. Buck will be here soon. Try to make a favorable impression."

Chapter Seventeen

Saturday, 6 p.m.

Billy had a system when he searched for Sophia. First he checked her downtown haunts—not the tourist traps on Beale Street with "Blues Players on Stage Nightly." Sophia hated that slick sound. She preferred it rough and real at the cinderblock joints off Danny Thomas Boulevard—places with tar strip parking lots, metal doors, and security bars on the back windows. Places even the food inspectors, liquor license agents, and fire marshals avoided. Where around midnight, men carried their beat-down box guitars and spit cans onto the blue-lit stage and tore the place up till dawn.

That's where he'd taken Sophia when they were stupid and in love. The blues ran hot in their blood, and a downtown juke joint was the last place she'd be recognized.

She and Billy had been all right then. Nothing touched them.

Funny how Sophia made those places her own. At the Red Velvet Lounge in south Memphis he had watched a falling-down, piss-on-himself drunk hold the door for her like he was a gentleman. Later, when she started flying solo, the club had reserved a table for her and stocked her favorite brand of vodka behind the bar. Sometimes she went home, sometimes to a motel, but she was always all right.

Tonight, after several stops, Billy had learned that no one at the blues joints had seen her in weeks. He circled back to touch base with bell captains at The Peabody and The Madison. Those guys would call him with a room number if she checked in. He called The Med and the drunk tank one more time. At seven he called Lou. Lou's phone was turned off, so Billy paged him. Fifteen minutes went by with no call back. He'd been pissed at Lou, but now his anger was turning into a nagging uneasiness.

Flat rails of storm clouds stacked against the horizon as he headed toward the river, evidence of the rain he'd smelled earlier. A storm would make the search for Sophia that much harder. He needed to keep moving. On Front Street he parked in an alley and looked in on a couple of holes-in-the-wall where the local booze hounds congregated. No one had seen Sophia.

He drove to Midtown and parked behind The Western. Elvis was singing *Don't be Cruel* on the jukebox as he walked through the door. The Western was one of the few local haunts that wasn't full of either roaches or martini drinkers. In the '60's Elvis had staked out a booth in the back. Now the booth was an altar surrounded by black velvet portraits and photographs of the owner with his arm around the King's shoulder.

Billy noted the regulars wearing camos and John Deere caps playing pinball on the old-style machines. No video games here. Some of the lonely-hearts nursed beers at tables by themselves. He took his usual seat at the bar where he could smell the grill at full heat.

He felt dog-tired and washed-out. Nothing he'd done in the last four hours had made a difference. Lou's blowup had emptied him, not to mention the frustration of not finding Sophia. He tore the cellophane off a pack of soda crackers and ate them dry. Crystal came through the swinging door behind the bar just as the jukebox switched to *Lawdy Miss Clawdy.*

"Hey, sweetie, what can I getcha?" Crystal was in her early-twenties, fond of purple tank tops that barely restrained her breasts. She wore her silky blond hair down to her waist.

"Ice water, thanks. Lou been in?"

Crystal hollered through the order window, "Meryle, you seen Lou?"

The older woman's face appeared. "No, hon, he ain't took supper with us in a couple of months. We talked about both ya'll, said, 'Where them boys? They mad at us?'"

Crystal set the water in front of him. "How about some fried pickles to go with it? We can fix you up." She took a swipe at the counter with a rag. "You got your swing back yet?"

Her question caught him off guard. "What?"

"I heard some of the guys talking. They said you were having trouble with your swing."

A perfect end to a perfect day. Billy took pride in his softball stats. She might as well have asked if his dick was broken.

"I'm working on it," he said.

"I play league ball, too. It's hell when you can't hit."

Meryle pushed through the swinging door and put her hands on her hips. "You got to eat something. How about a fried bologna sandwich to go? That's easy to eat in the car."

He remembered Lou saying a couple of nights ago that he'd been catching most of his meals at The Western. Why the hell would Lou lie about something as simple as that?

Meryle came out of the kitchen with a sandwich wrapped in wax paper and a toothpick stuck through the middle. "Here you go. Lou ain't sick or nothing?"

"He's good. We just missed connections."

"That divorce took it right out of him. Change is hard on a man Lou's age."

Change is hard on any man, Billy thought.

◈

A block from The Western stood another of Lou's favorite hangouts, the Satellite Package Store. During the Sputnik era the owner had mounted a large, rotating ball covered in three-foot neon spikes on a two story tall post. Memphis citizens had written letters to the editor, questioning the owner's patriotism. He was glorifying a Russian symbol of success, they said.

The hoopla eventually died down, and now people enjoyed the twisting neon ball for its own sake. The Cold War couldn't trump a sparkling neon liquor store sign. Not in Memphis.

Two sisters bought the store in the seventies. They'd opened the doors every day since, except Sundays. Lou used to buy his booze by the case from them and dropped by on a regular basis to shoot the bull about the American League.

Billy checked the Satellite's parking lot for the Ford. Except for the station wagon the sisters used for deliveries, the lot was empty.

Next he drove south on Bellevue Boulevard for a stop at the parsonage next to the massive St. Paul A.M.E. Church of the Holy Saints. The congregation was mostly black. This had been Billy's church home in Memphis. After his mother died and he'd moved into the trailer with his Uncle Kane, the tiny black church down the road had taken him in, body and soul. He was Mr. Kane's boy, orphaned by liquor and tragedy. The church folks didn't have much, but they had shared everything they had with him.

A non-judging haven of worship, even Lou had dropped by Holy Saints after the divorce.

Reverend Wallace Stokes and his wife, Lucille, who pastored the flock, kept the screened door to the parsonage unlatched. Billy was on the porch before he saw Stokes sitting in the swing in the twilight.

"Come on in, Brother Able. Rest yourself."

"Brother Stokes, good evening."

The chains of the swing strained under his impressive 295 pounds, the reason for his recent announcement from the pulpit that it would be best if the ladies of the church stopped bringing the much-appreciated cakes and pies by the parsonage.

Stokes waved him to a wooden rocker. Through the open door, Billy could hear Lucille running sink water and scraping the supper dishes. He picked up the rhythm of Stokes's swing and rocked at the same pace.

"Had your supper?" Stokes said.

"Thank you, I had a bite."

"Lucille can fix a plate of chops. Lucy!" he called out.

"Don't bother, I'm fine."

A hassock fan threw out a light breeze at their feet and they watched lightning bugs come out of the twilight.

"A storm dumped a bucket of rain on Mississippi. Bet the gamblers at Tunica got their lucky shoes wet," Billy said.

Stokes chuckled. "How can I help you this evening?"

"I wondered if Lou has been by for a visit?"

Stokes frowned. "No, Brother Nevers has been a stranger to us for some time."

"I know he skipped Sunday service the last few months."

"You miss my meaning," Stokes said. "Brother Nevers has changed."

Tree frogs tuned up their rattling voice outside the screen. "Lou's not been himself lately. Tell you the truth, I'm worried he might be sick."

"He's a sick man, but I don't believe it's of the body. Any man who loses his helpmate, his spirit grieves. Sometimes a man grieves so hard he turns from his own trueness. He steps from the path." The reverend closed his eyes, and his lips moved silently. Everyone knew better than to interrupt the reverend when he was communing with the Almighty. "Our brother is lost to us tonight." Stokes patted his heart.

The gesture was subtle, alarming. "Lost?"

"When a man is lost we pray to the Lord. He's our lifeline."

"Sure, we can pray, but Lou might be in trouble. I need to find him."

"Brother Nevers isn't alone. None of us is ever alone. Bow your head, son, and pray. Jesus, our Savior, our Redeemer . . . "

◈

Back in the car, Billy checked for messages. Stokes had shaken him up. *Brother Nevers is lost to us tonight.* He decided to check Lou's duplex again. He considered calling Mercy. He had the feeling she was reliable, unlike her sister.

The rain started as he turned onto Lou's street. His headlights shown on the Ford as he turned into the driveway. The pickup was gone. He left the motor running and ran to the porch as raindrops the size of cherries pelted his back. A piece of paper taped to the front door flipped in the wind. He didn't need a flashlight to read the two-word message. GO FISH.

Damn it, Lou is playing games again. Here Billy was, worrying, and the man had gone fishing. *Screw Lou.* Billy would concentrate on locating Sophia. He backed out of the drive and headed for the Confederate Cabanas.

Chapter Eighteen

Saturday, 7:15 p.m.

Buck Overton hated women who cried. Criers draw attention to themselves, not to the predicament over which they cry, and never to the solution itself. His mother had dealt with problems by crying. She cried for days in her bed, in her bath, over toast and tea. When she was finished crying she would dry her tears and mount a campaign worthy of Napoleon. His mother had been a professional crier. But she had also been a woman of great resolve.

Gloria Snow, on the other hand, had no resolve. Her best decision on any given day involved which shoe to put on first.

He would marry her anyway.

Buck came into the marble-floored entry of Sophia's house carrying his leather croquet mallet case. His mallets were custom-made, irreplaceable in fact, and he never left them in his car. He kissed Gloria's cheek as she snuggled against him.

"I thought I'd go crazy this morning," she said, blinking back tears. "You handled everything."

"We'll find Sophia, don't worry." He patted her hand. "Now tell me what's for supper."

"Pork tenderloin. And I have a surprise. Remember my other daughter, Mercy? Sophia invited her for the weekend. She's here."

Sophia invited her. Why now?

"How nice," he said. "Where is she?"

"Dressing. I want to warn you." Gloria leaned closer. "Mercy was scarred as a child. Oh, here she comes."

A graceful young woman wearing slacks, a cream blouse and a garnet and silver necklace came down the staircase. As Gloria had warned, a raspberry line cut across her left cheek. He laid the mallet case on a bench. How strange for a mother to focus on the scar.

"Judge Overton, it's a pleasure," the young woman said, offering her hand. "I'm Mercy Snow."

He folded her hand between his and looked at Gloria. "Why haven't I met your daughter sooner?"

Mercy answered. "I've been in Atlanta the last three years, starting up a business. A bakery."

"I'd like to hear more about it."

"Certainly." She smiled beneath tired eyes. "May I have my hand back?"

"Forgive me. It's just that I'm intrigued by the differences between Gloria's two daughters."

"The difference right now is that one of us has disappeared."

Her cool self-possession surprised him. She was stronger than Sophia and might prove to be a challenge.

"I could use a scotch," he said. "Let's go into the study and talk there."

Buck poured eighteen-year-old Glenfiddich for himself, Blue Goose for Gloria, and tonic for Mercy. She sat on the sofa next to her mother and told them what she'd seen at SuperShoppers. He kept his questions to a minimum, knowing he would get the details from Lou later. He wanted to ask why Sophia had called her into town, but now wasn't the time.

"T. Wayne will catch the first flight home," Gloria said, sipping her drink. "I'm afraid he's going to fall apart once he gets here."

"He'll be all right," Mercy said. "In all the years he's been married to Sophia, he's always managed to come through for me when I need him."

"Sounds as if you two are pretty close," Buck said.

Lightning flashed, followed by thunder. Mercy stood. "He's been like a big brother. I'll go ahead and put supper on the table."

Buck watched her hips sway and her blond hair swing across her shoulders as she left. An alliance between T. Wayne and Mercy surprised him. He would have to move into T. Wayne's position quickly if he wanted the upper hand in this family. Mercy appeared to be a strong-willed woman and might want a say in her mother's future. He would slip a few questions into the conversation and see if he could uncover her vulnerable spots.

Gloria stared out the window, focused on her private world. They had little to discuss when they were alone, like actors who'd step offstage between acts. Buck preferred it that way. Old Southern society had raised her for this kind of partnership—a marriage of separate parts that made up a whole. The union would give them both what they wanted most—money, power and social standing. If he could bring Mercy under his influence, the marriage would be a success.

He drew Gloria to her feet and draped her hand over his arm. "Let's go in to supper."

The silver flatware and blue and gold Royal Dalton shone in the candlelight. Antique crystal that Sophia and he had discovered in a shop in New Orleans glistened like wet ice. He appreciated fine things and respected Gloria's taste and her Delta aristocracy heritage.

"The table looks beautiful tonight, dear," he said as he seated her. "I know it's been a difficult day for both of you."

"Sophia would want this. And it's Mercy's homecoming."

He studied the young woman's face across the table as they passed the meat platter and vegetables. Both women were masking their anxiety about Sophia's absence. Good. He hated displays of emotions. "I see Mercy has opened a bottle of cabernet for us to toast her arrival." He noted her quick smile and the way she lifted her glass to be filled. Really, she was quite beautiful when she smiled.

Gloria caught a glimpse of the bottle's label. "Oh no, T. Wayne will be furious. He bought that bottle at the Les Passees Auction. He's been saving it to impress a client."

Mercy's smile faded. "I'll replace it in the morning."

"You won't find it in a store," her mother said. "A private cellar donated it."

Buck poured the wine. "Fine wine is for drinking, not hoarding. I'll handle T. Wayne." He lifted his glass. "To Mercy's homecoming and Sophia's safe return."

They clinked glasses. He savored the wine he had coveted since the night of the auction. Gloria took a sip and began sobbing quietly.

Buck tore a dinner roll and buttered it, ignoring her. "Tell me, Mercy, does your bakery have a specialty?"

"Pies. Cakes for special occasions like weddings."

Buck sampled the roll. "This is excellent. What's the bakery's name?"

"I named it Mimi's Hot Pies after Mimi Nickla, an old friend of the family. She taught me how to bake a decent crust when I was ten."

"Mimi never told me," Gloria said between sniffs.

"She dropped by when I was home by myself in the summers. I really loved Mimi."

"You know she died a year ago. Lung cancer," Gloria said.

Mercy's face flushed. "She's not dead to me."

"I'm surprised you got away for a visit," Buck said, distracting her. "New businesses are like babies, you never get time off."

"Sophia called at a good time. August is our slow month."

"Did Sophia say anything that would be a clue to the reason she's disappeared?"

"No, Sophia and I aren't close. I thought she might want a fresh start. But now I'm rethinking some of her other comments."

"What comments?" Gloria reached for her wine and tipped over her glass. "Oh, no," she cried, waving her hands in panic.

"I'll get it," Mercy said and dashed to the kitchen for a towel.

Damn it, Gloria, Buck thought, but said, "Calm down, dear, here's more wine." He refilled the glass. Later he would guide the conversation back to Sophia.

After Mercy sponged up the spill, he cleared his throat to get her attention. "I hate to bring up an unpleasant subject, but I'm sure you know that when a wife goes missing, the husband is the prime suspect. T. Wayne had nothing to do with this, but if Sophia doesn't show up soon, he'll be questioned. I'm prepared to deal with the prosecutor's office to keep things under control."

Mercy stared at him. "T. Wayne was in Uzbekistan Friday night."

"'Out of town' is no alibi in this situation. But don't worry; Lou Nevers is in charge of the investigation. He's one of the city's best detectives. He'll make a reasonable call."

"I met his partner, Billy Able. He said Detective Nevers has a personal situation and wouldn't be handling the case."

"Sorry to contradict you, but I left explicit orders for Nevers to take the lead."

Her eyebrows went up. "You can dictate to the police?"

"I've asked the department to do whatever it takes to get your sister back. Detective Nevers is in charge."

Mercy's chin rose slightly.

Gloria reached over and squeezed his forearm. "Buck has a lot of influence in this city. And he's almost one of the family."

He watched Mercy stare at Gloria's hand on his sleeve. Apparently her mother had failed to mention their plans. He laid his hand on top of Gloria's. "Your mother and I have an understanding."

Gloria nodded. "He's a godsend. He helps me with every decision, even shopping. We just picked out a ten thousand dollar wardrobe at Kittie Kyle."

Mercy turned to him, wide-eyed, "You spent ten thousand dollars on clothes for Mother?"

"I paid for my own clothes, thank you," Gloria said. "Buck helped with the selections. He has an excellent eye."

"It's been years since you've splurged, Mother, but. . ."

"Women have to take care of themselves," Gloria said.

"You don't have that kind of money," Mercy said.

"The attorney who handles your father's estate called a few months ago. Your father owned stock in a company that just went public or some such thing. Explain it to her, Buck. Money talk bores me. Excuse me. I have to go to the little girl's room."

He helped Gloria with her chair, holding her hand longer than necessary to make a point. He was pleased. She'd just handed him all the cards.

After she left the room he sat back down and smiled at her daughter.

"Mother has become quite dependent on you," Mercy said.

"We depend on each other."

"We've never discussed the details of my father's estate. This stock, is it worth anything?"

"Your father traded his consultant services for a block of stock in a privately held medical implement company. The company has developed several new cardiac implant devices. When it went public two weeks ago, your mother's shares suddenly became valuable." He paused, keeping his expression neutral. "They're now worth ten million."

"Good heavens!" Mercy said.

"I've advised her to sell some of her stock and diversify into other sectors. The bank gave her a line of credit, agreeing to hold stock as security. Who can blame her for buying a few new dresses?"

"Mother has wanted to be rich all her life. Not just comfortable or affluent, but rich. I guess dreams do come true. Does Sophia know about the money?"

"T. Wayne and she both know."

"That could be what she wanted to discuss with me." Mercy leaned her elbows on the table and pressed her fingers to her temples. "I didn't want to say anything in front of Mother, but I'm really worried about Sophia. This morning I thought she was pulling another of her stunts. Now I'm frightened. I hate to think of her out in this storm." Thunder rumbled as if in response. Mercy shook her head as if wanting to change the subject. "You mentioned an understanding between you and Mother. What's that about?"

"I've asked for her hand in marriage. She's accepted."

Mercy sat back in her chair. "Isn't this rather sudden?"

"Not really. I'm surprised Sophia didn't tell you."

"Maybe that's why she said things were about to change . . . that I'd be amazed." She frowned. "No, she said I'd be shocked. I thought she was being dramatic. I guess not. Suddenly our mother is very rich and very eligible."

He drained his wine glass. Things had been going well until Mercy found out about the stock money. *Mother is very rich and still very single.* Bitch.

"Your mother's windfall came about after we'd made our plans." A strategic lie, but one she probably wouldn't question.

"I have to be honest with you, Judge Overton."

"Buck, please."

"Mother lives in a fairy tale. For years she's believed her Prince Charming would come. You may be the guy on the white horse, but . . . " She shrugged.

He poured the last of wine, emptying the bottle, and gave Mercy a penetrating look. "I don't need your mother's money; I need your mother."

"Isn't he the loveliest man," Gloria said as she returned. "I'd be so happy, if only Sophia were here." Her voice caught in her throat.

"I told your daughter about our marriage plans."

"Yes, congratulations," Mercy said with little enthusiasm.

"I also explained the upturn in your finances. She concluded I'm marrying you for your money."

"Mercy! Money has nothing to do with our relationship."

Mercy stood. "I'm sure everything will work out. Dessert?"

"She baked one of her prize-winning pies for you, Buck. A chocolate pecan something. Did you say it has coconut?"

"Chocolate liqueur," Mercy said as she cleared the table and left.

He heard her bustling in the kitchen. After her rudeness, the image of her doing menial work pleased him.

"Interesting girl," he said. "Shame about—"

"Her face? I know," Gloria said.

"No, her attitude."

Mercy returned carrying two dessert plates.

"Not having any?" he said.

"I'm not hungry."

"Marvelous looking pie," he said as she placed the plate in front of him. "Could I trouble you to heat mine?"

"It's still warm. Reheating will loosen the filling."

"It's how I'd prefer it. Please."

She gave him a tight smile and returned the plate to the kitchen.

He folded his napkin. "Your daughter has been raised without a man's hand. Maybe I can help her attitude."

"She's always been opinionated," Gloria said.

Mercy returned and set the plate before him.

"Just right. Oh, and may I have ice cream on top? Glory keeps a quart of peach for me in the big freezer."

"Ice cream will overwhelm the flavor of the liqueur."

"I know your mother raised you with better manners."

"Fine." She took the plate and disappeared into the kitchen.

"She'll get used to my hand on the rein," he said. "This is as good a start as any."

"Yes, Buck."

Minutes passed. Gloria shifted in her seat. "The ice cream must be too frozen. I'll start the coffee." She went to the kitchen and returned, wringing her hands. "I don't know what to say. I'm so embarrassed. She threw the pie in the garbage."

"So cut another piece."

"She threw the *entire* pie in the garbage."

"Tell Mercy to come out here. I want to speak with her."

"I can't, Buck. She's gone to bed."

Chapter Nineteen

Saturday, 10:10 p.m.

Billy cruised the dives on Lamar Avenue searching for Sophia—the Confederate Cabanas, Rebel Yell Motel, The Vapors Club, The Princess Club. Phone calls wouldn't get the job done with these establishments. He had to go inside every one to check for himself. Because of recent vice raids, along with liquor license suspensions that had cut into profits and pissed off every owner on the strip, no one would give him a break.

Lou had worked Vice in the '90s. The strip was his beat. His motto was "Give a little, take a little, screw 'em to the wall."

Billy found no cooperation that night. No Sophia, either. It was late and raining hard. Time to find Lou and have that talk. He'd change clothes and hit the road for the fishing camp. Maybe by tomorrow Sophia would show up. This binge would blow her deal on her DUI, possibly even get her thrown into jail. He hated to admit it, but she might need a shock to get serious about dealing with her addiction.

He came off I-240 onto Riverside Drive, where Tennessee and Arkansas bleed together at their borders, and the river is an artery they share. At the cobblestone landing that sloped down to his new home, he turned left.

A couple of weeks after moving out of the apartment he'd shared with Terri, he'd found this place formally known as The Old Man River Bar and Grill. It was a barge tied up next to the *Memphis Queen* paddle wheel, a big tourist attraction on the broad Mississippi. The bar had failed in less than a year. The owner then added a shower and put up a "For Rent" sign. Billy had snapped it up.

As he pulled in, he noticed Terri's red Subaru parked against the barge's gangway. Damn it. He'd forgotten she'd called him earlier.

When they'd moved into the apartment together, they agreed they weren't in love yet but wanted to give the relationship a try. Love never came along, but he considered her a good friend and gave her money for a new car transmission when she was short on cash. She cooked Italian, gave great back rubs, and made him laugh. He was surprised and hurt when he'd caught her going through his notes. Everyone makes mistakes, but disloyalty was a hard one to get past. He'd ended the relationship and walked out.

Now he killed the car lights and watched through the galley windows as she rummaged around in his cabinets. Typical Terri. She must have found his hidden key and let herself in. She wasn't a bad person, and he would miss her athletics in bed, that thing she did with her tongue—most men would chop off a finger before they walked out on that.

She took out a glass and poured a drink. He wanted to confront her about invading his home, but finding Lou and Sophia was more important than raking Terri over the coals. He put the car into reverse and backed out onto Riverside Drive. He crossed the new river bridge, whose "M" shaped superstructure glowed against the black sky, drove into Arkansas, and through the town of West Memphis.

◆

On the highway, the night rolled out in front of Billy, punctuated by billboards, all-night truck stops, and discount motels crowding the interstate. To his right, a halo of lights burned over the West Memphis Dog Track.

Until now he'd avoided an obvious explanation for Lou's behavior. "Suicide by cop" would account for the chair through the window and Lou pulling the trigger on his partner at SuperShoppers with eight cops looking on. It would account for the deadness in Lou's eyes. Was Lou angling for his fellow cops to shoot him?

That's what Billy wanted to talk about. No more head games, just straight answers from Lou.

At Highway 79 he turned south. The rain came down in sheets. He drove until he spotted Petty's Gulf, the place Lou always stopped to buy hoop cheese sandwiches with extra Duke's Mayonnaise and a bucket of shiners for the trotlines. Billy wanted to ask if they'd seen Lou, but the store was closed. The only light came from a phone booth out front. There weren't many phone booths left in the world, except out here, in the middle of nowhere. He switched to high beams. The weather deteriorated.

Rain pounded the windshield with a vengeance for the next twelve miles. He drove until his headlights flashed on a small sign tacked high on a telephone pole. He backed up. "Benton Property—No Hunting." The drive narrowed to a lane flanked by cedar scrub that whipped his car as he inched along. Sleet peppered the roof like buckshot. Tornadoes ripped through Arkansas this time of year, scaring the hell out of everybody. News footage doesn't do justice to a one-on-one encounter with a flatland twister. The way things looked, Billy could be driving into the path of one.

Now that he thought about it, Lou wasn't the kind of guy who would commit suicide. He was too old school. "You got a problem, you run toward it, not away from it," Lou always said. In Lou's book a man who commits suicide is just leaving a mess for other people to clean up. The bastard was probably sitting at a roadside bar somewhere near a lake, picking catfish bones out of his teeth and watching the Cards play the Braves on cable. This trip was probably a waste of time. He'd know soon enough.

Rain gusts pummeled the car. He found the gap in the fence that led onto the gravel apron of an agricultural bridge. Lightning flashed. He saw the normally quiet creek under the bridge churning in a forty-foot-wide flashflood.

The narrow bridge, made of recycled telephone poles, had no guardrails. It was sturdy enough to withstand the torrent but dangerous in these slippery conditions. He lined up his tires with the running boards and rolled forward. The sound of the boards slapping against the support beams made him grip the wheel harder. Halfway across the bridge he caught a glimpse of a dark shape sticking out of the middle of creek. His mind ordered him to concentrate on the bridge in his headlights, but his gut told him to stop. He braked and squinted at what looked like a curved shape. It was an old refrigerator, or maybe an outhouse dragged downstream by the flood.

He forced his door open against the blowing rain and stepped onto the bridge. The powerful beam of his Stealth flashlight hit the object and reflected off glass. Suddenly, the shape made sense.

Lou's International Harvester truck was half submerged in the creek.

Stokes' pronouncement rang in his mind. *"Brother Nevers is lost to us tonight."*

"Lou!" he shouted. He ran along the bridge to the side of the road, fanning the light across the underbrush as he went. He started down the bank, pounded by wind that nearly knocked him over. The ground crumbled beneath him, and he scrambled back. No chance Lou could've climbed up from the water here.

Damn it to hell. He'd known Lou was in trouble, but he'd been too angry to act on it. He should've driven to the fishing camp the minute he'd found Lou's note.

He directed the light at the driver's window. "Lou! Lou!" The current had the truck pinned sideways against an uprooted tree. If the tree broke, the truck would wash away. He grabbed his cell. No signal. He ran back to the bridge and flung open the car trunk, slipped a coil of rope over his shoulder and wedged a hammer under his belt. Both banks dropped fifteen feet into dense buck brush, prime nesting ground for cottonmouths. He fought the impulse to jump off the bridge and swim for it. Without a safety line, they'd both be dead.

Thunder boomed. He picked his way through undergrowth to a hackberry tree with limbs sturdy enough to secure his line and flashlight. The light shot down the rushing water and illuminated the truck. Lou was trapped in there, he knew it.

Hold on buddy, I'm coming.

His hands shook as he knotted the rope around his waist and waded in. The icy flashflood ripped his legs out from under him, knocking him flat. He came up gasping, got his bearings and stroked hard toward the truck. No telling how long Lou had been in the cold water.

Again, Reverend Stokes' words came to him. *"Sometimes a man grieves so hard he turns from his own trueness. He steps from the path."*

By the time the current smashed him against the fender, he was exhausted. He worked his way to Lou's door. A vortex of muddy water boiled over the bottom half of the window.

"Lou!" he shouted. No answer.

He pulled up on the doorframe to look inside. Lou's forehead rested against the steering wheel, eyes closed, his mouth and nose barely above the waterline. Lou could be unconscious. Or he could be dead.

Billy banged his fist on the window, thought he saw Lou's head jerk to the side, but he wasn't sure. The current was so strong, even if he got the door open, the cab would swamp and drown Lou before he could get him out. Limbs blocked the passenger door. The windshield was the only way in.

Teeth chattering, he eased himself on top of the hood, trying to keep his weight from breaking the truck loose. Waves washed over his legs and rocked the truck. He had seconds to get to Lou and only one way to do it. He balanced on his knees, pulled the hammer from his belt and swung hard. The windshield crackled. Water leaked through the opening. He swung again, pulverizing the glass. This time water poured in. He pulled away the net of glass, reached past Lou's head and grabbed his arm. Feet braced against the truck, he hauled back. Lou didn't budge. Water was beginning to rise in the cab.

"Help me," he shouted and hauled back with everything he had. He heard the tree snap. The hood lurched, nearly throwing him off, as the truck swung into the current. Last chance to get it right. He grabbed Lou's wrist with both hands and pulled with all his might. The truck bucked in the current, tilted and rolled like a fish in the black water, carrying them under.

He hadn't expected to die tonight.

"When a man's lost, we offer up prayers to the Lord. He's our best hope."

Water filled Billy's mouth, but he held onto Lou's hand. The truck bumped along the creek bottom, dragging them. His lungs spasmed, wanting air. No air. A light began to burn at the center of his brain. It grew brighter, and he saw the Jesus fan, Jesus holding the lamb. Just before he inhaled water, the line at his waist jerked him to a stop. He burst to the surface, gasping. He turned just as lightning broke across the sky and saw the truck's cab floating away in the dark. He didn't remember letting go of Lou's hand.

"We're never alone. Bow your head, son. Jesus, our savior, our redeemer."

The best he could do now was save himself. He pulled hand over hand on the rope toward the Stealth's light as water and debris crashed down on him. Hypothermia was beginning to take over. His hands and legs would be useless soon. At the bank he reached up for a tree branch and levered himself out of the water. A brown streak whipped across his vision an instant before fangs slammed into his forearm, the cottonmouth's strike propelling him backward into the creek. His head smacked against a rock. Blue lights exploded. Dazed, he floated against the tug of the rope, the water rising to his face. His arm burned. Rain pocked the water around him. Trees groaned overhead in the wind, as if aware of his presence.

His gaze followed the snake gliding through the Stealth's beam and into the dark current. He felt warm, almost comforted. He remembered Lou saying one time that a cottonmouth spends its entire life pissed off.

And he remembered something else Lou had said to him.

"You never could see what's inside a man. Trust me."

◆

"Dispatch, Henderson County Sheriff's Office."

"This is Sergeant Able MPD, badge # 6741. There's been an accident on the Benton property."

"Are you hurt, Sergeant?"

"No . . . yes. Doesn't matter. My partner. He went off a bridge. I found his truck. Oh Jesus, I couldn't get Lou out."

"Hold on, bud. Give me that location again."

"Benton property."

"Can you give me a landmark?"

"It's a bridge. I'm at Petty's Gulf."

"On the way. We'll keep this line open, okay? Sergeant? You there?"

Billy slumped against the booth's door. "Yeah. I'm here."

Chapter Twenty

Sunday, 5:11 a.m.

Arkansas's Henderson County Coroner, Dr. Jimmy Dale Dexter, watched in the pale light of false dawn as the International Harvester pickup was dragged, tailgate first, from the slow-moving creek near Planters Road. It had been hard going for the divers in the creek. A lot of debris. A muddy mess. The deputies said Lou Nevers was inside the truck, a fact Dr. Jimmy would not accept until he saw his friend's body.

Lou and he had been buddies since grade school and raised a lot of hell around the county when they were kids. Lou got away with it. Dr. Jimmy always got caught. Their paths split after he went away to medical school and Lou signed on to the Memphis police force, but they had always stayed in touch.

He dropped his cigarette in the wet grass and crushed it. Lou was his oldest friend still living in this world. Looked like that was no longer true, although Dr. Jimmy wouldn't accept it until he saw the body. Watching that pickup come out of the water was enough to turn him back into a two-pack-a-day man.

He wore his usual clothes: black neoprene boots bought at the hardware store at twenty bucks a pop, a blue, poly/cotton jumpsuit he ordered by the dozen from Sears, and a red, Razorback ball cap. Besides being disposable, the uniform made him instantly recognizable at a crime scene. He carried a crime scene kit and his own camera.

No one in the county took death by unnatural causes as seriously as he did.

After twenty-nine years as Henderson County's coroner, while running a practice as a general physician, his life suited him. He ran a herd of Charolais cattle, had four grown daughters, seven grandkids and the same wife he'd started out with thirty-three years ago. His house, barn and truck were paid for. Most of his hair was gone but his blood pressure remained a steady 125 over 82 and he could still put in a twelve-hour day in the saddle without walking stiff the next morning.

Behind a break of sycamores, the sky flushed orange with the sunrise. Lou's partner should have arrived at the Memphis Med by now. The first responder at Petty's Gulf saw Able was shocky and requested an ambulance. The EMTs radioed from the road that Able was hypothermic, had taken a pretty good rap on the head and was snake bit on his left arm. Lucky for him it appeared to be a dry bite; otherwise, he would never have made it to

Petty's. Mature moccasins, unlike the youngsters, know how to staunch their venom.

The decision to take Able back across the river to Memphis had been a good one. The staff at The Med's ER specialized in trauma.

Dr. Jimmy lit a second Lucky Strike and glanced around in the growing daylight. The twister had knocked the hell out of an equipment shed, and an irrigation dam had broken and drowned a couple of Herefords. Some oaks fell and blocked the highway. An oak tree has no taproot. A storm as forceful as the one last night could bring even the mighty ones down.

It had also brought down Lou Nevers, an unimaginable fact. He sucked in a breath and flexed his hands. Now wasn't the time to fall apart. He had an important job to do.

Able told the first deputy who arrived at Petty's that he and Lou had a blowup yesterday. Able had come to the fishing camp looking to patch things up. If Lou's death turned out to be questionable, Able could be the primary suspect. But Dr. Jimmy didn't believe that, not for a heartbeat. Lou said Able was a hell of a good detective and a good man, almost like his son. Dr. Jimmy missed his own son, dead from bone cancer fifteen years ago this October. He loved his daughters dearly but he understood exactly how much it meant to Lou to have a young man around who thought he'd hung the moon.

On the hill, deputies leaned on their cruiser, drinking coffee out of a Thermos. The night's drama had lost its steam. To them it didn't matter that the best cop in three states, a man who had been Dr. Jimmy's oldest friend, lay dead in that pickup.

To hell with them. They could wait.

It took half an hour to free the pickup from debris and haul it up the bank to level ground. The tow truck fishtailed on the clay-based road, unable to make headway until Reed Johnson showed up with his John Deere and hooked in a second cable.

When it was done, Dr. Jimmy studied the muddy truck while the boys unhooked their cables. Debris had battered the body of the truck, and the windshield was missing.

A deputy tested the door for him. "Locked. You want it jimmied, Doc?"

"Go on," he said. Through the driver's window he could see the side of Lou's face. He pulled out his handkerchief, wiped his eyes and blew his nose.

Able told the deputy he'd smashed the windshield and tried to haul Lou out but couldn't budge him. Then the truck rolled in the water and he'd lost him. Able had believed Lou was alive when he got to him but drowned during the rescue attempt.

The deputy said Able was in pretty rough shape about it.

Dr. Jimmy blew smoke toward the sky and walked over to the pickup. He opened the door. Muddy water poured over the sill and dripped onto his boots as he studied Lou's body, slumped forward, his forehead resting against the steering wheel. He reached inside and smoothed the hair out of Lou's face. The skin felt like iced wax.

"What you got yourself into, son?" he said, noting Lou's opened eyes and milky corneas. The gaping mouth. His heart twisted in his chest and he swallowed, suppressing his emotions. Grief wouldn't serve Lou nearly as well as professionalism.

He lifted Lou's head as best he could. A bruise from striking the steering wheel ran across the forehead. No white foam inside the mouth that he could see, indicating drowning. He scanned the cab. His eyes closed involuntarily. The driver's sun visor was down, ripped. Claw marks of a person trapped in a submerged vehicle. His gaze ran down to Lou's lap. He did a double take.

"Need any help, Doc?" called the sheriff, who'd been on the hill discussing tractor starters with Reed.

"I got it." He rocked Lou's shoulders back, working against the rigor. He looked down, shook his head. "Lou my friend, tell me how I'm going to explain this one?"

Chapter Twenty-One

Sunday, 8:10 a.m.

Mercy woke with a plan.

Dressed in jeans and dark blue canvas Keds, she managed to get out of the house without bumping into her mother. She drove the Toyota around the block, windows rolled down, hot wind blowing her hair.

She couldn't just sit at home. She woke up knowing Sophia was in real trouble and her mother might be in trouble, too. Last night Overton had maneuvered both of them like sheep he planned to shear. Sheesh. If that son-of-a-bitch thought Mercy would ever call him "Buck," he had another thing coming. The judge presented big problems, but for now Sophia remained her focus.

By the time she pulled into the SuperShoppers parking lot, Mercy was wide awake and sure of her plan. At the coffee kiosk in the front entrance, she took a stool.

"Hey, you're back," said the blue-eyed teenager who'd worked the day before.

Mercy ordered an espresso and chatted with the girl between the Sunday morning customers, wondering how to turn the conversation to Charles. No need to worry. The girl did it for her.

"After that lady disappeared, I've kept an eye on Charles. He looks for a reason to touch the women customers when he's bagging groceries. Real slick, you know?"

Mercy nodded behind her cup. "Does he work a regular shift?"

"Today it's seven till one this afternoon. We just switched from the evening shift."

"Must be hard to change hours."

"Not for me. I live three blocks away, but Charles's parents have to drive him in." She pointed across the parking lot toward Poplar. "There's a bus stop in front of the store. He catches the bus home."

Mercy finished her coffee and counted out five singles for a three-dollar coffee. The girl scooped up the bills with a grin and folded two into her shirt pocket.

Mercy hadn't thought her plan was risky, but Charles was a big, young guy who liked women, and who might not know an appropriate way to show it. She would have to be careful.

She called MATA on her cell to check the bus schedule while she cruised the bus route, looking for a spot to leave her car. Then she drove back to the house.

Her mother. The judge. The pie she'd thrown away. True Hell to pay.

T. Wayne Called From Moscow Before His Flight said a note left by her mother on the kitchen counter. Gloria added that she was in bed with a sick headache, her euphemism for a hangover. Mercy knew she'd catch an earful when her mother surfaced for coffee. Throwing the pie in the garbage had been childish. Tantrums weren't Mercy's style. They were, however, her sister's specialty.

Even as a kid she'd known Sophia's screaming fits and destructive tantrums weren't normal. Her rages had worsened after their mother pressured her into taking singing and acting lessons. Gloria excused Sophia's fits, saying beautiful girls were naturally high strung; but Mercy heard her sister crying at night and knew she'd begun sneaking booze out of the liquor cabinet. By the time Sophia was in junior high, their mother was driving her all over the Mid-South for beauty contests and casting calls for car dealership commercials. Sophia won some pageants, but never landed an acting job. Her drinking escalated in high school, and she refused to consider college.

Their mother was visibly relieved when Sophia married T. Wayne. She told friends that a ring on Sophia's finger and a man in her bed would remedy her problems.

In the kitchen, Mercy drank more coffee, then took Caesar out for a walk. She considered calling Detective Able, but knew she'd be tempted to tell him about her plan. She felt sure he wouldn't approve. Better to let him check in with her.

She turned at the sound of her mother shuffling into the kitchen. Smudged makeup made Gloria resemble a bleary raccoon. Her mother stopped and held up a finger. "One question. Just one. Why did you find it necessary to humiliate me in front of Buck last night?"

"I'm sorry, Momma. Really. I'll apologize to Judge Overton. I'll bake another pie for him. I'll bake two. Whatever you want." She had no intention of doing either, but she'd say anything to keep her mother from pitching a hissy fit.

Gloria poured a cup of coffee and glanced at Mercy as she ambled toward the door. "Don't do it again. I'm going back to bed. This is too much."

Mercy changed her mind about not talking to Detective Able. She called his cell.

He didn't call back.

At 12:45 she drove back to SuperShoppers, parked near the bus stop and sat in the car with the motor running. Charles Chan came out of the store, swinging his purple backpack over his shoulder. A MATA bus, wrapped from roof to tires in a big ad for KFC, rolled to a stop. The doors levered open and Charles climbed the steps. The bus swayed a block forward then braked for a red light. Mercy pulled into the traffic behind it.

She had a theory about Charles. It had begun yesterday when the girl at the coffee kiosk commented on his nervousness around the detective. After working for two summers with mentally-challenged kids at a Special Olympics camp, Mercy knew how easily kids like Charles could become frightened and confused by people they didn't know. It was possible Charles knew more about Sophia's whereabouts but was afraid to tell Able. If Mercy could arrange some time alone with Charles, she might be able to learn information the detective had missed.

After two blocks, she pulled ahead of the bus, wheeled into the Best Drugs parking lot, cut the engine and bolted for the stop just as the bus appeared.

Out of breath, she dug in her pocket for quarters and searched the windows for Charles's face as the bus braked to a stop. She hadn't considered that Charles might not be alone; he might be sitting beside someone he knew, a friend who traveled the same route. She climbed the steps and dropped her change in the fare box. The bus heaved forward. Charles sat in the middle of the bus next to a window, arms crossed on his belly, looking out at the traffic. An old man, wearing a bow tie and holding a walking cane, sat beside him. The man's eyes flicked across Mercy's face. He frowned as she passed by; as if he knew she wanted his seat.

The bus engine roared. She sat in the back and tried to remember her questions, but her mind was blank. She studied the back of Charles's head. Bowl-cut black hair, a scratch on his neck. He seemed to be nodding, maybe falling asleep. He looked harmless, even sweet. She would start with something easy, maybe how much she liked his purple backpack. Then she could ask him about work, ease into questions about Sophia from there, explain to him she was looking for new information. Keep it simple.

The old man's cane waggled over Charles's head until it hooked the buzzer cord. The bus stopped, and the old man got off. Mercy moved next to Charles. His bulky thigh and elbow overlapped into her seat. He was awake.

"Hello," she said as the bus pulled forward.

"Hi." He grinned. "You're pretty."

She glanced down. His hands rested on his legs. He had begun to rub his palm up and down, up and down his thigh.

Chapter Twenty-Two

Sunday, 3:15 p.m.

Blue skies, a light breeze, a reprieve from yesterday's storm. An ultra-light hung above the Mississippi like a dragonfly. Two teenagers on Jet Skis jumped in and out of the wake of a towboat and river barge, a dangerous game that had cost the lives of a young couple last spring when their Jet Ski flipped over.

Billy asked the taxi driver to drop him above Tom Lee Park so he could walk the rest of the way to the barge. He wore borrowed scrubs and carried his damp clothes and gun in a plastic hospital bag. The snakebite on his arm burned, his head hurt like hell, and he couldn't get warm, even in the hot sun. He smelled diesel fuel on the water and soured mud down at the waterline. He stopped and watched the river's relentless current roll by.

Lou had been dead for fourteen hours. Billy had never felt so powerless.

Tourists lined up in front of the *Memphis Queen* ticket office for the afternoon tour. Although Billy's home was no longer a bar and grill, the sign advertising burgers and beer remained bolted to the roof. Tourists banged on the door at all hours, hoping for one last round. The barge owner had promised he'd remove the sign next week. The *CLOSED* banner hung in tatters after last night's storm.

Inside the barge, Billy pulled on jeans and a sweatshirt, walked around, picked up stacks of books, then circled back and set them down again. He made coffee and a ham sandwich. The coffee tasted like sulfur, and the sweet smell of the ham made him sick. He pulled money from his wallet and spread it out to dry. His hands shook. Images flashed in his head—the sinking truck, water rising over Lou's head. He remembered the slack-muscled feel of Lou's arm in his hand. Why couldn't he pull Lou from behind the wheel? Maybe the cold had sapped his strength. Maybe fear.

The doctors at The Med had kept him under observation, claiming protocol for a concussion patient, but he suspected they didn't want him to go home alone and see coverage of Lou's death on TV. After years of following up on victims of violence taken to The Med, Lou's professionalism and compassion for their families had won him the respect of the ER staff. He'd been on a first-name basis with most of them. A couple of the nurses had cried when they heard about the accident.

Billy had heard that Dr. Jimmy Dale Dexter would be the coroner in charge of Lou's case. Dexter was Lou's oldest friend and supposed to be the best forensics man in Arkansas. Billy was counting on Dexter to come up with some answers. He'd left a message with Dexter's service, asking him to call as soon as he knew anything.

The message light blinked on the answering machine. Terri had called and so had Hollerith, expressing his condolences, saying that the department was throwing a wake for Lou at The Western tonight.

Billy rubbed the back of his neck and glanced around the barge for something useful to do with his hands. He pulled his Sig-Sauer out of the hospital bag and rummaged through boxes for his cleaning kit. As soon as he clicked the release on the slide an image of the snake's mouth, fangs extended, slashed through his mind. His body jumped involuntarily. *Keep it on track,* he told himself. *Clean the gun, take a shower, go to The Western.* Everyone would expect him. He hoped to talk to Dexter tonight and start fresh in the morning, not dwell on what had happened to Lou in the creek.

He wanted to focus on Sophia, but he felt numb and disconnected. The nurses had taken his cell away after his repeated calls to the squad. He wanted to believe Sophia was out there by her own choice, but every passing hour made that less likely. She was in trouble. *I couldn't save Lou, but by God, maybe I can still save her.*

So what was he doing at home?

The whistle blast from the *Memphis Queen* announced its return. He began to field-strip his gun when he heard footsteps rattle the metal gangway. Probably another tourist wanting to ask what time the grill opened. Ignoring the knock, he soaked a patch in Hoppes No. 9 solvent. The knock turned into banging.

"Out of business," he yelled.

"Detective Able?"

A woman's voice. He didn't want to talk to anyone. He said nothing.

"It's Mercy Snow, Detective. I need to see you."

He laid down the Sig and capped the Hoppes.

"Please," she said. "It's important."

He opened the door to see Mercy standing there, looking overheated and worried, and carrying a rumpled brown paper sack. She wore jeans and one blue tennis shoe. Her left foot was bare.

"I didn't hear from you so I went to the Justice Center," she said. "I overheard two women talking on the elevator. They seemed very concerned about you and said you had moved into what used to be the River Bar and Grill." Mercy frowned at the bandage covering the snakebite. "What happened to your arm?"

Instead of answering, *What happened to your shoe?* he asked, "Is Dupree home yet?"

"Not yet." She held up the paper bag. "Thought you'd want to see this." She studied his face. "You don't look well. Maybe I shouldn't have come."

"No, come in. Sorry about the mess. I just moved in."

She picked her way through the boxes and took a seat on the red leather sofa he'd rescued from a downtown alley. The sack rested on her knees. He pulled up a chair, feeling suddenly spent. He stared at her naked foot.

"This place is something. Lots of potential," she said, looking around.

"What's with the missing shoe?" he said.

"Oh. I traded it for this." She unrolled the sack and pulled out a green sandal. "Mother remembered Sophia was wearing green sandals on Friday. I followed Charles Chan home from work. He had this one in his backpack the whole time."

Billy sat bolt upright in the chair. "You what?"

"I caught the bus he took home from work. We chatted until he got comfortable, then I asked about Sophia. He said he found the shoe next to the handbag, but he was afraid to tell you. I promised he wouldn't get into trouble if he gave it to me."

For a moment, Billy wanted to yell at her for putting herself in the middle of the investigation, for chasing down a witness and a possible suspect—a dangerous move, even if she *had* found evidence he'd missed. But she had a surprised, did-I-screw-up look on her face. He drew in a deep breath and forced himself to relax.

"You took a risk. Charles is big enough to smack you into next week."

"But he's just a scared kid. I've worked with developmentally-challenged people. I hoped, given a chance to go over what happened, he might remember something. You'll back me on my promise, right? He won't get into trouble?"

"I'll do what I can."

"I couldn't just sit home and do nothing." She dropped the shoe in the bag. "I thought this might be important."

"Yeah, it's important." He got to his feet and started pacing. He hoped the sinking feeling in the pit of his stomach didn't show on his face.

"You don't look good," she said. "Have you eaten today?"

"I'm okay. Did Charles say anything else?"

"He remembered a blue van parked next to Sophia's car. It sounded like a utility van."

"Did it have a sliding door?"

Her eyes widened. "Oh my God, I've seen that on TV. I just couldn't accept that it might happen to Sophia. They open the door, haul you in and bang, you're toast."

"I need to make a call." He turned to use the phone and the floor pitched. He closed his eyes and opened them to find her standing in front of him. He smelled cinnamon in her hair.

"You're pale. I'll get some water," she said and disappeared into the galley.

His head was pounding. He heard the refrigerator door open and cabinet doors bang shut. He couldn't understand why she was fussing over a glass of water, but for some reason he liked it.

His equilibrium was returning when he heard a knock on the door. Before he could answer, the doorknob was turning.

"This is a private home," he called as the door swung open.

Terri Cozi came in, carrying a box of his old baseball trophies. She wore a white shirt and a tight black skirt. She ran to him, wrapped her arms around him and snuggled her breasts against his chest. "I heard what happened to Lou. You all right?"

He could hear Mercy rustling around in the galley and untangled Terri's arms. "I'm fine."

"I called a friend at The Med. She told me you have a concussion. Let's go back to the apartment. I'll make you better," she said, her blue eyes warming.

Behind them, Mercy cleared her throat. Terri shot him a murderous look, then peered around his shoulder. "Hi. I'm Terri Cozi. "And you are . . .?"

"I'm pleased to meet you," Mercy said.

She carried a bar tray with a thick sandwich cut in half and a glass of milk. *How had she made a sandwich that quick?* Billy was impressed.

She set the tray on a packing box. "I have a few things to straighten in the kitchen, if you'll excuse me." Still wearing only one shoe, she swayed through the maze of boxes back to the galley.

"Who's that?" Terri demanded.

Irritation shot through him. "That's not your business anymore, Terri."

"Look, I may have blown our relationship, but I'm still your friend. Where's her other shoe?"

"I appreciate your stopping by, but now's not a good time."

They heard sink water running. Her eyes narrowed. "You have to watch out for women. They'll move in on a nice guy like you and try to take advantage."

He nodded, amazed at how ironic that sounded coming from her. "Don't worry, I'll be careful. Thanks for coming by."

"But—"

He shook his head.

Her expression turned contrite. "Okay, I'll go. I am sorry about Lou. I've heard about all the bad guys he's taken off the streets. Lou was a cop's cop."

Billy nodded. "There's a wake at The Western tonight. Try to drop by."

"Wouldn't miss it." She kissed him and closed the door on her way out.

Mercy stuck her head out from the galley. "What's up?"

"A friend, but she tends to be a little territorial."

"Really? I didn't notice. I'm almost finished in here."

He took his cell and went to the bedroom so Mercy wouldn't overhear his conversation with the CJC. When he returned, she was sitting on the sofa with her bare foot tucked under her, looking out the side window at the *Memphis Queen* as she came into her berth. He was impressed with the way Mercy had kept herself together.

The sandwich looked good. Peanut butter and banana. He sat and took a bite, then another. The whole sandwich was gone before Mercy spoke again.

"Yesterday I was convinced Sophia arranged this drama because I was coming to town. Today, mother's church group will be putting up "missing" posters. Part of the reason I wanted to stay busy this morning was to avoid thinking about what all this means. Now I'm getting scared."

"I just called the CJC. There's been no ransom demand, and we're checking every hospital and jail within a 200 mile radius. We've already stepped up the investigation."

"What does the shoe mean?"

"It's troubling. But I'm afraid the possibility of a van parked next to her car is even more disturbing. I need to hold this information back from the media. Keep the shoe and van to yourself. Don't even tell your family. "

She bit her lip. "I have a question. Judge Overton insists your partner is the person I should be talking to, not you."

"This time the judge can't get what he wants. My partner can't help us." Billy had to look away. "Lou died last night."

Chapter Twenty-Three

Sunday, 9 p.m.

Tammy Wynette's *Stand by Your Man* wailed from The Western's jukebox while a hundred of the MPD's finest ate fried cheese and grabbed iced, long-neck Buds out of galvanized tubs on the bar. Everybody had a story about Lou. They all wanted to slap Billy on the back and tell him they knew exactly how he felt. He hated it. Death made people say all the wrong things.

Beside him, Wheezer Tritt blew his nose and folded the handkerchief. "Never known a cop to draw down on his partner then go and drown hisself. Most cops eat their guns. Get it over with." Tritt bent over, sneezed and straightened. "Sorry, smoke's getting to me."

"You need to get this straight," Billy shouted at Tritt over the music. "It was an accident. Lou's truck slid off a bridge."

"Right. Hell of a way to go. Wonder what made him do it?"

Billy considered popping Tritt in the mouth just for the hell of it, but the man was too drunk for it to be much fun. Instead he fished a beer out of the tub. His head was killing him.

The squad had rented The Western and hired the staff to keep the beer and T-bones coming. Everyone threw thirty bucks in the pot. A tremendous horseshoe of red carnations showed up with a banner reading, "See You in September." No one knew where it came from or what it meant. Lou would have appreciated this kind of send-off—his buddies hanging out, telling stories, getting stewed. No regrets.

Billy dug another beer out of the ice. Nobody discussed the weird crap Lou had pulled on Saturday. Nobody looked him in the eye, either. Only Tritt seemed interested in carrying on a conversation, and that was about as helpful as a hobo in a ball gown. Everyone told Billy he looked great, and they'd get together with him later over a beer, but one glance in the mirror behind the bar told him they were lying like dogs. Not only did he look like a corpse, he wasn't going to gain new drinking buddies because Lou had died.

Crystal carried a platter of sizzling T-bones and Texas toast through the kitchen's swinging door. He grabbed a plate and looked around for a seat.

At a table beneath a print of a matador and charging bull he spotted Sam Waters, one of Lou's old partners in Vice. Sam had that Clint Eastwood intensity and a habit of being too candid around the brass. His cocky attitude had not only hurt his career but also his dealings with other cops.

Lou told great stories about the two of them on the job but never talked about the situation that had stirred up bad blood between them. Lou transferred from Vice to Homicide. Waters moved on to Narcotics. Billy had only a nodding acquaintance with Sam Waters but figured tonight he wouldn't mind sitting down with another man who had partnered with Lou.

Sam looked up as Billy reached his table and signaled for him to have a seat. "Good to see you, Able. Not too crazy about the circumstances."

Two whiskies and a beer-back sat in front of Sam. He didn't have a drinker's reputation, but he was working on one tonight.

Billy put his plate down and sat. "I keep thinking Lou's going to bust through the door any minute and holler, 'Hey guys, I scammed ya.'"

"Hard to believe the man's taking the dirt nap. Want to talk about it?"

That was exactly what Billy wanted to do. Talk. "I'm still trying to figure out what happened. One minute Lou's sweet-talking a gun away from an old woman, the next he's daring her to shoot him. That was for openers. Then he throws a chair through her picture window."

"Whoa, hold on. I'm talking about the accident. He ran off a bridge in Arkansas, right?"

"He was driving to the fishing camp."

"In that storm?"

"Yeah, that's the kind of Grade A decision he's made lately. Half the scumbags he's arrested threatened to slit his throat, and what takes him out? A damned farm bridge."

Billy swigged more beer. The room had taken on a fuzzy glow, and he finally felt warm. At The Med, they'd told him to stay away from alcohol. Screw 'em. And screw Sam. Billy wanted to talk about Lou, not about the accident that killed him.

He changed the subject. "Lou was a hero. Even at the academy we heard the stories," he said. "Remember when the mayor was getting death threats? Lou was with him when they walked into mayor's office in the middle of the day, and the lights were out. Lou stopped him from flipping the switch. Some nut in maintenance had rigged an overhead light bulb with gun power and shrapnel. They both would've burned alive. Lou never worked the bomb squad. He just knew shit. He knew people. You can't replace a man like that."

Sam knocked back a whiskey. "Time was, I believed that bullshit too. Life sucks when you find out Superman's a jerk."

Between the headache and the beer it took a second for Sam's words to sink in. Billy stared at him. "What the hell are you talking about?"

"Sorry. A man's wake isn't the time to tell the truth about him."

"Lou was a righteous cop. Fifty guys will say the same."

In the dim light he saw the older cop's indulgent smile.

"When I signed on with Lou I was like a kid meeting a rodeo star," Sam said. "He taught me what strings to pull to get the job done. We had three good years in Narcotics. Lou moved to Vice, and I followed a year later. God, what a time." Sam's smile faded. "Lou made some underhanded choices. I couldn't stand by them. You think he had a bad day yesterday? He had a whole string of them when we worked Vice."

Anger shot through Billy. "Bullshit. You're the cop with the bad rep."

"No one but myself to blame for my mistakes. Lou was the best I ever worked with, but he was also one erratic son-of-a-bitch. Now I wish we'd patched things up. I could paper this room with regrets where Lou Nevers is concerned." He shrugged, but held Billy's gaze.

Billy made an allowance for the booze Sam had consumed, and the fact that grief makes people say crazy things. Besides, Billy had a lot of questions about Lou. Sam might have some answers.

"Did Lou ever lose it with you?" Billy said.

Sam snorted. "All the time. I tried to gauge his tantrums by cycles of the moon. Couldn't make sense of it."

"I mean really lose it. Pull a gun on you."

"He chased me around the cruiser with a broken beer bottle one time. Lou had a nasty edge to him." Sam knocked back the last whiskey. "How about you cutting the crap and tell me what happened last night? You need to tell it and I need to hear it. It's closure."

Across the room, Meryle struggled through the crowd, carrying a tray of empties. She was crying. *What the hell,* Billy thought. There was enough hurt to go around, and Waters probably deserved to share in it.

"Bottom line, the truck went off the bridge. I went in the water and found Lou unconscious behind the wheel. I had one shot at getting him out. I blew it."

"From what you've said tonight, and the rumors circulating about Saturday, Lou was in big trouble before his truck went in the water. I gotta say, it sounds like suicide."

Billy's fingers tightened around the neck of his beer. "It was an accident. End of story."

"I don't know. Suicide fits the scenario."

"Lou never walked away from a fight in his life."

"You were his last partner. You'd know what was going on in his head." Waters shrugged as if it was an offhanded remark, but his gaze stayed on Billy.

"That's right. I should've known. But here's what *you* should know. You remember when that rookie Lewis walked into a domestic fifteen years ago and got shot and died?"

"I remember."

"You knew his kid had cerebral palsy, right? Lou set up a private fund that's saved that family from all kinds of hell." He shoved his plate away. "I know because I ran into Lewis' wife, and she told me. Lou never told a soul. So. Good to have this talk with you, Detective. Let's not do it again."

Sam held up a hand. "Hold on, I know Lou had his good side. Go on, finish your steak, I'm heading to the house."

Before Sam could stand, Terri Cozi swayed her way through the crowd to their table. Her mink-black hair glistened, and her perfume drifted across the table to Billy as she slid into the chair next to Sam. Billy caught the intimate glance that passed between them. It said they'd had sex recently and were planning to do it again soon. Terri and Sam. His ex-girlfriend and Lou's ex-partner.

She reached over to squeeze his hand. "You okay, baby?"

Her hand felt like sun-warmed velvet. Terri was the most dangerous kind of female: sweet, sexy and totally without scruples. She let go of Billy's hand and took a sip of Sam's beer.

"I'm good. You two know each other pretty well?" Billy said.

Sam bumped Terri's shoulder with his. "I'm helping her with a series on drug runners using the I-40 corridor. We're about to wind things up."

"A series," Billy said. "You must've spent a hell of a lot of time together over the last few months while I was at work."

Terri looked startled, then put on her bulletproof smile. "Don't be jealous, sweetie. It was just business."

Sam shifted in his chair. "Hey man, you know how it is."

"No skin off my back, but let me give you a heads up. When she sleeps over, put a lock on your briefcase. She likes to dig around for late-night reading material. Take my advice. Hide your notes. Could save you from getting hauled up before the review board."

Terri's mouth opened, then it closed, and she looked away. She couldn't defend herself. It was the truth.

Sam stood. "You better watch your damned mouth."

Billy started to rise then felt a hand on his shoulder. Kline Hollerith leaned in, unaware that he'd stopped a fistfight. "I see you got my message. How are you holding up?"

"I'll be in tomorrow."

"We'll see." Hollerith shook hands with Sam, nodded to Terri. "Ms. Cozi, thanks for coming. Someone wants to speak with Able. Mind if I borrow him?"

"Not one damned bit," Terri snapped.

Billy was glad to have a reason to leave the table. He didn't have the emotional juice to handle Terri and Sam right now.

In the back of The Western stood a landmark known to Memphis locals as *the Elvis Booth*. Covered in tufted black Naugahyde and surrounded by photos and memorabilia bolted to the wall, the booth had often sheltered The King in the '60's and '70's. Elvis would drop by The Western when he was in the mood for a cheeseburger and some privacy.

Judge Lamar Overton sat in the booth now, a man Billy admired for his efficient court, his consistent fairness, and his farsighted rulings.

"Judge Overton cancelled a meeting to come by tonight," Hollerith said as they walked over. "Lou and he go way back."

Overton half stood and shook Billy's hand. "It's a sad day for us to meet. Lou's told me a lot about you. Have a seat."

"Thank you, sir. I didn't realize you and Lou had that kind of relationship." He noticed the judge had left Hollerith standing in the aisle. The lieutenant took the hint and left.

"We go back to my first years on the bench," Overton said. "We've kept in touch. I understand how difficult this is for you, so I hope you won't mind if I ask a few questions."

"Don't know if I'll have the answers."

Overton looked down at his hands. "I want to be sure that Lou's death, particularly because it occurred out of our jurisdiction, is properly handled. You understand?"

"I appreciate your concern."

"You were first on the scene."

"That's right. When I reached the bridge, his truck was already partially submerged." Billy swallowed. "I swam to the truck and tried to pull Lou out, but the current got us." For a moment he was back in the water with the truck rolling under him.

The judge was speaking to him.

"Sir?"

"I asked if Lou was coherent when you found him. Did he say anything?"

"No, sir."

"Was there any indication of foul play?"

Billy frowned. He'd been considering the same possibility. "What makes you ask?"

Overton gave him a solicitous smile. "I have no reason to believe it was anything but an accident. However, we have a dead police officer who sent a lot of people to prison. I'm not comfortable crossing jurisdictional lines to insert myself into the investigation, but I am concerned. I wonder if you'd keep me updated?"

"I have a call into Dexter for the autopsy results. I'll be sure to raise the question."

"Good." Overton leaned back. "Dexter interned at Johns Hopkins. He could've gone anywhere; instead, he's looking after poor people, handing out death certificates and raising those damned white cows."

The music change to a country ballad. Out of the corner of his eye, Billy saw Terri and Sam walk to the dance floor. Terri pressed herself against Sam. His fingers caressed the small of her back as they swayed. Billy's gut tightened, a stupid caveman reaction. He looked away when he realized Overton was studying him.

"I noticed you were talking with Waters," the judge said.

"Sam and Lou were partners. But I guess you know that."

"Some bad blood passed between them. Waters tried to have Lou brought up on charges."

"Yeah, I heard, but Lou never discussed it," Billy said.

"I'm not surprised. There's some misplaced bitterness on Waters' part."

He wanted to know more, but the judge lifted his glass and took a drink.

"Judge Overton, about the Dupree case. I know you have a personal interest. I've already done some legwork, and I want to assure you I'll be back at my desk tomorrow. I'll do everything possible to find Mrs. Dupree."

"That's good to know, but do what's best for yourself, first."

"What's best for me is to get back to work. The last time Mrs. Dupree went off on a lost weekend, she abandoned her car and called home a day later from a motel in Mississippi."

"I'm aware the woman has emotional problems."

"I was expecting her to show up on her own again, but now I don't see it happening that way. I'm stepping up the investigation."

Anger flashed over the judge's features. Billy made a mental note as the judge tried to cover it by taking another drink of water.

"What changed your mind?" Overton said.

"It's been over forty-eight hours. When Mrs. Dupree goes off on a binge, she's usually home by now." The combination of the purse, the shoe and the possibility of a van parked next to Sophia's car was the real reason for his alarm, but he wasn't giving out that information, even to a judge. "I'll know more tomorrow."

"Forgive me for asking, but with Lou gone, do you think you can handle the Dupree case?"

Billy inwardly bristled at the implication that he wasn't experienced enough. "I'll do everything in my power to find her. I promise you that."

Overton slid across the booth. "You look tired, son. You've been through a lot."

"I'm fine, sir."

"I have to say, I can't believe Lou's gone. Old P-D-Q. Mr. Pretty Damned Quick. He'll be missed." The judge stood. "I'll just slip out the back."

Billy watched Overton go out the back door. It had been an odd conversation. First of all, Lou had never mentioned knowing Overton, much less being his friend. Second, why did the judge lose his cool when he mentioned stepping up the investigation?

He went to the bathroom, splashed water on his face and looked in the mirror. One too many beers was making it hard for him to concentrate. He needed to get out of here but didn't want to have to squeeze past Sam and Terri on the dance floor. Overton had the right idea about using the back entrance. He took the judge's exit route.

Outside, SUVs and pickups packed the parking lot. Streetlights barely illuminated the back steps. He smelled rain-soaked cardboard and rotting garbage from the Dumpster. The night, a cool one for August, was a gift of last night's storm.

Waters had put his finger on it; Billy told himself he should've seen this train wreck coming. He'd known Lou was in trouble yesterday, but he'd been too pissed off to do anything about it.

Down the street, the neon Sputnik ball rotated over the liquor store. It reminded Billy of the tilt-a-whirl ride in the carnivals that came through town when he was a child.

He watched a Cadillac back out of its parking space into the alley. Judge Overton was the driver. The taillights dipped as he pulled out onto the street.

The world looked the same tonight as it did every night. Except tonight Lou Nevers was no longer in it.

Chapter Twenty-Four

Dr. Jimmy had changed from his jumpsuit into slacks for Lou's wake; a fresh white shirt and the Stetson he'd managed to keep in pretty good shape over the past twenty years. He considered adding his turquoise bolo tie out of deference to the occasion but decided against it. The tie would cause questions from his wife, Evie. There was a lot of respect for each other's privacy in their marriage, but sometimes she pushed it. Tomorrow he'd be able to talk to her about Lou. Discussing it with her now would make the loss too real.

It was Sunday evening. He was driving to Lou's wake, and he was dog-tired. His hands on the steering wheel ached with arthritis that was cutting into his knuckles like baling wire. A few years ago he could put in a day at the clinic, followed by a couple of autopsies, and never skip a beat. Not true anymore, especially after a day like today.

Holding the dead heart of his oldest friend in his hand had taken its toll.

August twenty-eighth would be his last day as Henderson County's coroner. His friends warned him he'd regret walking away, but Evie's health wasn't good, and she'd always talked about taking an Alaskan cruise. Last week he'd put a Canadian-bred Charolais bull in the field to see if he could get a prize-winning calf for next year's Mid-South Fair. That was all the challenge he needed now, matchmaking for the bull and heifers.

Besides, retirement made sense. He'd witnessed enough stupidity and meanness to last ten lifetimes.

He crossed the long river bridge into Memphis and spotted the rotating Sputnik ball, candy-colored against the black sky, his guidepost to The Western. Odds were good Able would be at the wake. He wanted to talk to him face to face.

In the alley flanking The Western, a tall, lean figure stood outside the back door, left hand in his jeans pocket, a gauze bandage poking out of his cuff. Dr. Jimmy rolled down his window. "Evening. Are you Billy Able?"

The young man stooped to look in the window. "You a friend of Lou's?"

"Lou ever tell you about the time he seeded the sheriff's yard with cow pies?"

"Nope."

"The sheriff didn't watch where he was stepping. Smelled like shit all day."

Able grinned. "Story he told me was on an old boy named Dexter. Almost got kicked out of medical school for working on a cadaver with cow shit under his fingernails."

Dr. Jimmy laughed. "That's about right. Lou could tell it."

They shook hands through the window. Despite his grin, Able looked exhausted. His dilated pupils reflected the streetlight, and he swayed, reeking of beer and grief, an odor Dr. Jimmy knew well. He started to mention that alcohol and a concussion don't mix, but a few drinks under the belt might make what he had to say to this young man go down easier.

"I got your message and headed over." He pointed at Able's bandage. "I heard you got pretty banged up."

"Nothing a case of BC Powder won't cure."

"You're lucky. Those young snakes can't staunch their venom. Must've been a granddaddy that hit you."

"Old as Methuselah. Big too," Able said.

"I figured after what you've been through, some answers would be your best medicine. You got time to talk?"

Able stared into the darkness. "All I've got tonight is time."

"Hop in."

Dr. Jimmy parked and turned the radio down so he could still hear his gospel station while they talked. He pulled out the single cigarette he carried in his shirt pocket and lit it. Smoking calmed him. In the early days he'd used the smell of tobacco and the taste of whiskey to clear his sinuses of the stench of putrefied flesh. After he'd married Evie, a hard-shell Baptist, the whiskey went down the drain. He'd pretty well kicked the tobacco habit until yesterday.

A stream of smoke curled out the window. "I've cut down to a single smoke after supper. That's the extent of my sins these days."

"Sin is in the eye of whoever wants to pin something on you," Able said.

"You said a mouthful. A while back, Lou and I were a couple of wildcats. Used to tear up the honkytonks till morning, sleep a couple of hours and head for our jobs at seven. Weekends we'd see the sun rise over the bare breasts of the willing ladies of Henderson County. Lou was one live son-of-a-buck. I hate how it's ended."

"How *did* it end?" Able said.

Dr. Jimmy took a moment to consider where to begin. "I drove over so I could put your mind at ease. I was told you thought Lou drowned when the truck got away from you. That you blame yourself for not getting him out. I'm here to tell you he was in the water a while, but he didn't drown."

"What killed him?"

"A bad decision, probably a whole string of them put him in the water, but it was a heart attack that got him. It's easy for an old man to get off in the high weeds and lose himself."

Mahalia Jackson belted out *Peace in the Valley* on the radio. He watched Able's eyes close, probably picturing Lou's panic as the water rose and the pain seized his chest.

"I suppose he suffered," Able said.

"Not for long. The shock of the cold, the alcohol poisoning—"

Able's head jerked toward him. "Lou quit drinking last March."

"Maybe so, but last night he was Dixie-fried. His level tested .22, high enough to trigger a heart attack in a young man much less a salty dog like Lou. I saw two empty fifths of Jack on the truck's floorboard."

"You're telling me Lou got drunk, swerved off the bridge, and had a heart attack."

The statement hung between them. Dr. Jimmy could let it go at that, and they'd both sleep easier. Or he could tell the rest of it.

Able must have read the uncertainty on his face.

"Tell me exactly what happened, Doc. Don't sugarcoat it."

He blew out a slow stream of smoke. "I found items in that truck I couldn't explain until I started adding things up."

"Like what?"

"First off, Lou was wearing his seatbelt."

Billy shook his head. "No way. Lou considered it his constitutional right to go through the windshield."

"I unbuckled it myself. That's why you couldn't get him out of the truck. And I found these."

Dr. Jimmy reached down and pulled three chrome handles—two door and one window—out of the paper bag resting on the console between them. He turned over a door handle in the dim light so Able could see the bent rim above the crank. "They were all popped off. The fourth must have washed out of the pickup. I had these checked for prints. Nothing but Lou's."

"You're telling me Lou couldn't get out of the truck?"

"He locked himself in so he couldn't change his mind. He got drunk then drove off the bridge. It was no accident."

Able looked at him like he was crazy. "Just one damned minute. You're saying it was suicide."

"'Self-execution' would be more accurate."

Able shifted in his seat, then shook his head. "No. If Lou had a tumor making him act irrational, maybe I could buy your theory. Otherwise, Lou was no suicide."

"His brain looked normal. I can run tests for a degenerative condition, but I don't think I'll find anything."

"Run them anyway," Able said quietly.

The door to The Western banged open. Two guys stumbled out, spilling light into the parking lot, so that Dr. Jimmy caught a glimpse of Able's stark profile and sunken cheeks. He'd made the decision to drive over, knowing it wouldn't be easy to convince Able of his findings. No cop lets his partner's death go with a simplistic explanation, even if it was the truth.

The door closed, and they sat in darkness again.

"Homicide is way more likely than suicide," Able said.

"But there were no tire tracks other than yours and Lou's, no cigarette butts to show another person on the scene. Between the storm and the crew recovering Lou's body, you'd be hard pressed to find much evidence on the ground. I can't even tell you what triggered Lou's heart attack—fear, the alcohol, the exposure. But I got a funny feeling when I opened the truck door and saw the seatbelt."

"What feeling?"

"Like Lou had killed himself. Like he did it because he hated himself."

"That's bullshit," Able said.

He shrugged. "I don't know, son. Maybe he confronted something he couldn't live with." He crushed out his cigarette. "I'll run those tests, see what comes up."

He was feeling guilty about hedging. He knew of one possible reason for Lou to hate himself, but it was only an outside hunch. Bringing it up without proof was reckless, not to mention betraying an old friend with groundless accusations.

"Someone could have forced the whiskey down Lou, strapped him in and busted off the handles," Able said. "So why do the facts add up to suicide instead of homicide?"

Dr. Jimmy pulled a walnut nightstick from the bag and handed it to Able. "Recognize this?"

Able inspected it. "It's one of Lou's. He has three."

He clicked on the overhead light. "Look it over."

Able held the stick to the light. "Fresh dents in the finish."

"Dents that match the rims on the door handles. Check it yourself."

Able turned a handle so the crimp in the rim lay against one of the dents. He studied the handle and the nightstick a while longer, then slipped the handle back into the bag. "You know where Lou keeps his nightstick?" Dr. Jimmy said.

"Between the car door and seat."

"Of his pickup?"

"No."

"Ever see it in his pickup?"

"No."

"I found it wedged beside the seat of Lou's truck."

"This could've been stolen out of his car or house. It proves nothing," Able said.

"You're working hard for an explanation, when the simple one always works best."

They sat in the dark while the jukebox inside The Western throbbed. They had reached a stalemate. Able spoke first.

"Have you made out the death certificate?"

"I ruled natural causes."

"Then you falsified the report."

"Not at all. He died from myocardial infarction complicated by atherosclerotic heart disease and alcohol poisoning. Technically there was no suicide because his attempt failed. Lou was a walking hero. I can't come up with a good reason to change that. He chose that bridge because he knew I'd be the one to handle the scene. Lou expected me to cover for him, and that's what I'm going to do."

The door clicked open. Able got out, shut the door and walked around to Dr. Jimmy's half-opened window. "I don't know a single reason Lou had to commit suicide, but I do know some bad people out there will be happy to know he's dead. Any one of them could have killed him."

"I understand your reasoning, son; I just don't agree."

"I'm going to find out why my partner died. I'd appreciate it if you'd get back to me with those test results."

Chapter Twenty-Five

Sunday, 11:45 p.m.

The entrance to the twenty-four hour Crosstown Mart blazed with enough candlepower to simulate high noon in July. Buck Overton grabbed a shopping basket from the rack inside the door and strolled past the lone female cashier checking out the purchases of two hulking, teen-aged boys. He passed a Day-Glo beach ball display. After the velvety darkness of the Elvis Booth at The Western, the store's cellophane glare assaulted his sensibilities. He hated discount stores, but the coupons in his pocket were good only at this Crosstown Mart.

His bailiff periodically warned him against late-night stops in the Crosstown area. Seven percent of the city's crime occurred there; however, the Mart was the only store close to Midtown and still open at this hour, where he could pick up what he needed. He overlooked the nastiness of the place, feeling almost jaunty, buoyed by the prospect of equilibrium returning to his life.

The last two days of stress had peaked when he saw Detective Able talking to Sam Waters. The two men knew Lou Nevers best. Between them, they held the majority of the puzzle pieces that could reveal what had happened. Buck noticed their truculent expressions and stiff body language when the girl had shown up; they were like two fighting cocks about to spar over the plump piece of ass who'd seated herself at their table. Neither man had the gumption to concentrate on the death of a partner and friend.

How predictable—sex had scuttled the best of intentions.

Fortunately, Able and Waters worked in different squads and functioned at different levels of command. That left little chance they'd bump into each other, and Buck believed he had successfully dissuaded Able from contacting Waters by creating doubt in his mind about the other man's motives.

He felt a surge of satisfaction as he turned down the toiletries aisle. Able was vulnerable without Lou, his mentor. Lou had been unable to make a last-minute confession revealing either his or Buck's roles in Sophia's disappearance. That was critical. Also, Buck had counted on Lou to shut down the investigation. When Able mentioned stepping it up, Buck nearly lost his temper. He wondered if Able had noticed. Probably not.

For the most part, people only see what they expect to see, even a detective.

As a kid, after being caught at small mischiefs, Buck had become adept at covering his deeds with an innocent poker face. When a neighbor's cat was found strangled in the garden or a potting shed caught fire, he could appear completely blameless, often shifting culpability elsewhere. His mother, his greatest teacher, was a master of easy lies and manipulations. Remorse had never once entered her mind. By example, she'd taught him to operate within societal bounds to get what he wanted.

And what he wanted were the finer things in life.

He craved success and social position. He wanted control of his life and power over the lives of others. Becoming a prominent judge had provided all he desired except for great wealth. If nothing else, Gloria had that to offer.

There was, however, one niggling loose end involving Lou that, if left unresolved, could bring his plans to a halt. Able could help him or hurt him with that situation. Thanks to the investigation, Buck could stay in touch with the detective and learn anything he'd dug up about Lou without appearing suspicious. Yes, his plans were unfolding nicely, but there were still challenges ahead.

His attention turned back to his shopping. He scanned the shelves for brands matching coupons in his pocket from the store's mail-out flyer. He detested using coupons, but two forces were compelling him to do it. First, he was operating on cash because his credit cards were over their limits. His mother had drilled the other reason into him.

Despite her pretensions of grandeur, she'd taught him to pinch money hard enough to bend a dime. She never bought without coupons, never bought until the second markdown. She was witty, beautiful—everyone said so—but also totally selfish and demanding. She wouldn't waste money on comic books and ball games for him or even electricity, at times. Countless nights he'd sat in the dark and the cold, waiting for his mother to come home from her dates.

He'd known, even then, that his mother was a society whore, although she never would have seen herself in that light. She had an illustrious Tennessee family name; she was educated but too class bound to work a menial job in an office or shop. By the time he was seven, he suspected that the wealthy men who escorted her almost nightly were receiving her sexual favors in return for money or gifts she would later hock. She kept some of the small appliances. They had two toasters and the first Waring blender on the market.

A tiny trust fund left by her father paid their rent. But the rest—food, clothing, Buck's school tuition—were paid for with money she earned from the men she fucked—most of them married.

He understood perfectly well why his mother had never married. She enjoyed her power over men far too much to give up her freedom.

He'd developed a cynical worldview because of his mother and a need to manipulate and control everyone and everything around him. Sophia had tried to use sex to gain an edge on him, but he kept her in line by getting inside her head and playing games until she didn't know which way was up.

Unfortunately, in the end, he was forced to dispose of her.

But everything else was falling into place. He would buy a car as a wedding gift for Gloria. Something classic, simple, with good resale value. American cars were reasonably priced these days, and he could pick up a deal; but on the other hand he didn't want anything cheap around him. No, maybe a Lexus would be better. He felt a pleasurable tingle in his groin, thinking about the power Gloria's millions would give him. In a matter of days, he would have control over everything—Gloria, the money, and his future.

At the check-out, the clerk, flipping through a magazine and drinking a Coke, didn't look up. She'd spent a tremendous amount of time braiding and lacquering her hair into a complicated structure on top of her head. A canned version of hip-hop flowed through the store speakers.

"I have coupons for everything in the basket," Buck said, and put the coupons on the belt in front of her.

"Uh huh," the clerk said and continued to flip pages.

"Look here," he began.

She took a sip of Coke and adjusted a hair decoration. "Welcome to Crosstown Mart," she said, and began waving the items over the scanner. The phone rang. She took the call, laughed, and then hung up. Still chuckling, she bagged his selections and rang up the total.

"Forty-seven fifty-eight," she said.

He had already tallied a rough total in his head. "You forgot to subtract the coupons."

"Ain't no good." She handed them back to him.

"They're your coupons. How can they not be good?"

"Expired. Look it." She pointed to the date.

"That's today."

"Yesterday." She nodded toward a clock over the door. It read 12:07. "Now it's tomorrow."

"Young lady—"

"My register's got a clock in it. It won't read past due coupons. Ain't nothing I can do about it, happens umpteen times a day with them blessed coupons." Her hands went on her hips. "Nothing I can do. No."

A line had formed behind him. One woman held a screaming infant in a plastic carrier. Buck's good mood evaporated.

"Then call the manager," he said in a firm tone.

"She'll be back in twenty minutes."

"I'm not waiting twenty minutes."

"You want to fuss about coupons, you can wait over there." She flung a manicured fingernail toward a chair by the door. "I got customers."

"Young woman, do you know who you're talking to?" he said, trying to control his voice but failing.

"Yeah. One of them mens who thinks hollering gets him what he wants."

She raised the Coke can to her lips. He snatched it from her and threw it across the row of empty check-out stations, Coke splattering into the aisle.

"Check me out now," he shouted. "Don't think about it. Just do it, bitch."

Her cheeks puffed with anger. "Who you calling bitch? I ain't yo' bitch. I'll bust you one, Mr. Just Do It. I got me a 911 button under this counter. My brother is a police. He'll haul yo' ass out of here."

Everyone in the line fell silent, all eyes on him. The last thing he needed was an incident. He threw down a fifty dollar bill and yanked up the bags.

"Hold on Mr. Nike Man, you got change coming."

"Buy another Coke with it. I hope you choke."

"Don't bring your badass attitude back in my store, you hear me?" she yelled.

He heard laughter, and the people in the line applauded as the automatic doors hissed closed behind him.

Chapter Twenty-Six

Monday, 8:27 a.m.

Damn, Billy thought as he walked into the lieutenant's empty office. *Hollerith will go nuts when he sees this mess.*

An AC condensate line above the desk had rusted through and soaked the ceiling tiles. During the night, the tiles had collapsed and crashed onto the desktop. Hollerith, obsessed with neatness and punctuality, was already twenty-seven minutes late for work. He would show up in a foul mood and see his desk. Not a great time to ask a man for his cooperation.

After last night's wake, Billy had gone home, put on a pot of coffee and made notes about his take on Lou's death. He also detailed Dexter's information, ending with their conflicting conclusions. On one point they'd agreed. It was no simple accident.

He made a second list of facts surrounding Sophia's disappearance, including the information Mercy had brought him about the van and shoe. He wondered what clues he might have overlooked by assuming Sophia was off on another binge. At most crime scenes, detectives walk up to a guy standing over a body and say, "You want to tell us about it?" And the guy does. Case over. With Sophia, doubts about what he might've missed had made Billy uneasy all night.

He rubbed the back of his neck. The doc at The Med had told him to expect headaches, but he didn't mention these damned jitters. Billy shoved his hands in his pockets and paced in front of the window. He had to get his head on straight if he wanted Hollerith's approval to investigate Lou's death. Without it, he wouldn't be able to face Lou's empty chair. Hollerith strode in, rubbing at a brown stain on his shirt with his handkerchief. "Damn it to hell," he grumbled.

"Morning, sir. Sky's falling." Billy pointed toward the ceiling.

Hollerith looked up, then down at the debris on his desk. "My God. What happened?"

"An AC condensate line plugged up overnight. They've called Maintenance."

Hollerith's eyes widened. "My notes! I'm leading a statistics panel in twenty minutes." He scrabbled through the wet tiles then jerked open a drawer and ran his fingers across the tabs until he pulled a file. "I backed into a pole at the gas station and spilled coffee on my shirt. Now my office looks like a dumpsite. Ever have a day when you can't make a right move?"

Billy studied his shoes. "Saturday wasn't my best."

Hollerith's face reddened with embarrassment. "Guess my priorities are out of line. Did the doctor give you clearance to work?"

"I'm ready to roll. Just some facts we need to cover first."

"Of course. Then I'd like for you to check in with Paul Anderson over at Employee Assistance. You've been through some real trauma. I'll line that up."

"After the funeral, maybe," Billy mumbled.

Hollerith didn't seem to notice. He used his thumb to push a clump of insulation off the frame of his wife's photo. "Haven't had a conversation with Lou in weeks. I was too busy . . . " He shrugged and shook his head.

Billy sensed real remorse in the lieutenant. Now was the time to push for an investigation. "Dexter tracked me down last night, filled me in on the details of Lou's—"

"Accident."

Billy shook his head. "Lou's death was no accident. I want to open a file."

"I talked with Dr. Dexter. He didn't give all the details, but he did say alcohol was involved." He glanced up. "You did everything you could, you know. No reason to feel guilty."

Hollerith's appeasing tone stung. "Did Dexter say I had a problem with his ruling on Lou's death?"

"Your name came up. Smart move to request tests to check for any hidden physical problems. That would explain a lot about Lou's recent behavior."

"Lou's blood alcohol level was .22," Billy said. "Dexter found two empty whiskey bottles in the pickup."

"He said cause of death was a heart attack brought on by the accident and/or alcohol poisoning."

"Alcohol poisoning? You know as well as I do that Lou kicked his binge drinking six months ago."

"I *don't* know that. People fall off the wagon all the time. Lou's been seriously unhinged for a year. The squad knows it; Director Mosby knows it. Lou was fine one day and slinging a chair through a window the next."

The image of Lou's face glowering through the broken window flashed in Billy's mind. Hollerith was overstating Lou's past behavior, but he was right about Saturday. Convincing him this wasn't an accident was going to be tough.

"Something happened to Lou on Saturday," he said. "That's where I want to start."

"I read Washington's report. She says Lou jeopardized everyone in the room. Then he went to SuperShoppers, discharged his weapon in the parking lot, and left the scene. That's completely irrational. Listen to Dexter; Lou got drunk and ran off a bridge. Leave it at that."

Twice now, Billy had been told to turn his back on Lou's death. *Like Hell.* "I'd sign off on the doc's explanation, but Lou put a lot of bad guys in the state slammer. Hard time. Any one of them could've done this."

Hollerith exhaled. "Give me a name. Connect it to a threat. Bring me something legitimate, and you can open an investigation."

Billy *had* evidence: the seatbelt, the handles, the nightstick, even the two empty bottles of whiskey. But the same evidence could point to suicide, a possibility only he and Dexter knew about. Neither one would let that be Lou's epitaph.

"I'll get the evidence if you'll back me up," he said.

The lieutenant flicked the muck from his fingers. "I understand your feelings, but your revenge theory is horseshit. The sheriff's team worked the scene for hours looking for signs of foul play. The best forensics man in this area went over Lou's body with a magnifying glass. He's Lou's oldest friend. If Dexter or the sheriff had the smallest doubt about the cause, they would have said so. End of discussion."

"Lou made this department's reputation. You owe him more than a farewell beer bust. He was your man. It's your responsibility."

Hollerith picked up a pad and began to write. "I'm shutting you down. Here's Anderson's number. Counseling is a condition of your return to duty." He ripped the paper from his pad and held it out.

Billy grabbed it, balled it up and fired it across the room. "Damn it, I don't need counseling, I need answers," he shouted.

Hollerith's face stiffened. A passing secretary glanced in the door then scurried past.

Billy knew he'd just crossed the line between negotiating and getting slapped with a suspension. He pulled back quickly.

"I apologize, Lieutenant, but there's more to Lou's death than binge drinking and bad luck. I'll work the case off the clock. In the meantime, I'm familiar with Sophia Dupree's past behavior. No one in the squad can clear that case as quickly as I can. We'll close that investigation, then I promise I'll see Anderson."

Hollerith looked out the window and sighed. "Five women have been assaulted, abducted, or murdered in public places this year. Sophia Dupree could make it six. We were short two investigators before this, and now we've lost Lou. City elections are in six weeks, and the mayor's opponent is beating him up on crime. This case could be a tipping point. We're talking panic among women. The League of Women Voters will turn out every woman in the city to vote against the mayor if we don't handle this right. Best thing you've said is that you can close the case quickly."

"Absolutely."

"All right. I'm bringing in Agent Jones."

Billy stared at him in disbelief. "That ex-football player?"

"He offered to handle some case details while you were out yesterday. TBI headquarters has agreed to temporarily assign someone else to lead the gang task force so he can fill in here."

The idea of a Bureau agent hanging around made Billy nervous. He wouldn't be able to investigate Lou's death or Sophia's disappearance the way he saw fit.

"We don't need TBI horning in. We can take care of our own shop. I'll have answers on Sophia Dupree in the next forty-eight hours. And I can work Lou's investigation on my own, no sweat."

Hollerith's expression hardened. "All right. Jones will take over the Dupree case. I'm putting you on leave, and you won't come back until Anderson clears you." He picked up the file and flipped through it. "We're done."

Hollerith was bluffing. He'd already shown his cards. For political reasons he needed the Dupree investigation shut down, and he needed Billy to make that happen.

"Hold on. My guess is Jones doesn't have enough homicide experience to handle this. If he screws up, he'll leave town, and our department gets the black eye. Especially you."

Hollerith regarded him. "The mayor is nervous about this case. When the mayor gets nervous, our boss gets nervous. Mosby is banking on being reappointed next term. If this goes big in the media and we don't close it quickly, someone's going to get an "F" on his fitness report. That kind of grade will stop a career. And it's *not* going to be mine."

It's not going to be mine, either, you jackass, Billy thought. But this time he kept his mouth shut. "I'll work the Dupree case with Jones, like you said."

"I'm not sanctioning a file on Lou. And I don't want any surprises. Got that?"

Billy shrugged. "I understand your position one-hundred percent."

Chapter Twenty-Seven

Monday, 9:02 a.m.

Screw Hollerith, Billy thought as he stomped out of the office. The man had no concept of loyalty.

He realized he'd been spoiling for a fight, but picking one with the lieutenant was a zero-sum game. With tracks going cold and twenty-four hours shot while he recuperated, he couldn't let himself be sucked in by Hollerith's ass-covering agenda.

He'd start with Lou's old case files—every bad actor Lou sent away in the last ten years. No, wait. He needed to check on the canvas reports from SuperShoppers and anything back from the lab. And what about the forensics on Lou's truck? Damn. He slowed as he neared the squad room. Who was he kidding? He needed help.

Jones seemed like a sharp guy and had good resources out of Nashville, but Jones had also stepped up to the plate mighty quick. Billy couldn't figure how working a case on a missing woman would benefit a TBI agent.

The other day Jones had dropped U.S. Senator Noel's name as if they were friends. Maybe Overton asked the senator to get more firepower assigned to Sophia's case. Jones would be Noel's obvious choice. If that were true, Overton should have brought it up last night.

But now was not the time to worry about who was calling the shots behind the scenes. He'd go along with Hollerith and give Jones a chance. Besides, taking Jones on would keep Hollerith off his back while he worked Lou's case.

Work Lou's case.

The phrase hit him hard. Lou wouldn't be at his desk reading the obits and classifieds this morning. He wasn't at the courthouse. He wasn't on vacation. He was dead.

Billy swallowed hard. Breaking down in front of the other detectives, dickheads like Vargas and Nance, wasn't an option. He had two choices— turn left and spend the day at the bar around the corner. Or turn right and go to work.

He turned right and walked into the squad room. Jones was sitting at Lou's desk, sleeves rolled up, shadow of a beard and a half eaten package of Lance crackers in front of him. Lou's Braves coffee mug and the Webster's Dictionary that Ruby had given him when he made sergeant grade lay on the floor. Heat flashed up the back of Billy's neck and his blood pressure hit the roof. He couldn't get his breath as he walked up to the desk.

Jones glanced up. "Oh, hey, glad you're on your feet. I was about to drop these reports by your house but this is better. We can go over . . . " The corners of his mouth drooped. "What?"

Billy snatched the mug off the floor. "The *fuck* you doing sitting in Lou's chair?"

Jones looked confused. Every cop in the vicinity ducked behind his computer screen.

"The guys on nightshift said I should sit here. I didn't mean any disrespect," Jones said.

"Nobody messes with Lou's stuff."

Jones eased out of the chair. "My mistake." He bent to pick up the dictionary.

"Leave it. I'll handle it," Billy hollered.

"Whatever, man. Just calm down."

"What's that paperwork all over the desk?"

"Preliminaries on the Dupree car, the hospitals and morgues I've covered, canvas reports coming in." He handed the reports to Billy.

Billy flipped through them, glancing at Jones, trying not to let his suspicion show. Jones must have pulled an all-nighter. This much information would make up for the twenty-four hours he'd lost.

"Hollerith said you want this assignment. That true?"

Jones looked sheepish. "I've been the governor's errand boy for two years. I've never worked homicide, and the direction my career's taking, I'll never get another chance. I saw an opportunity to work with you, so I suggested to Hollerith that I sign on for the short run." He yawned. "Excuse me, I need coffee."

Billy picked up the mug. Lou's knuckles had worn off the "B" in Braves. No telling how many cups of coffee Lou had drunk sitting across from him. He'd trusted Lou. But there was no reason he should trust Jones.

Jones was watching him. "I'm going across the street for some real coffee. Think about the direction you want to take this. You can let me know when I get back."

After Jones left, Billy sat and picked up a stack of mail. Phones rang around him, keyboards clicked. No one had the balls to speak to him after his blowup with Jones, and they were right, he wasn't in the mood for condolences. He fanned through the letters. One envelope caught his eye, addressed in Sophia's flowery cursive and postmarked the day she'd disappeared. A ticking began in his head. He pulled on latex gloves and slipped a letter opener along the flap. A business card fell out—*his* business card.

He'd written a note on the back: *Officer, call me at this number day or night— Detective Billy Able.*

Last year Sophia had waved the card under the nose of a couple of patrolmen who had pulled her over. The card convinced them to let Sophia go with a warning. For Sophia the card would have been gold, especially if she'd gone off on a lost weekend.

She wouldn't have let go of it. Unless someone forced her to. Panic hit. Billy sprang to his feet. The clicking of keyboards stopped, and several pairs of eyes watched him. He eased back in his chair, trying to look casual.

If anyone learned of his affair with Sophia, he'd be booted off the investigation, no questions asked. Only Lou knew that story, and he'd sworn to carry it to his grave. Billy slipped the card into the envelope, bagged it and put it in a drawer.

He was still thinking when Jones came in and handed him a cup of fresh coffee. The decision about Jones was moot.

"Are we on?" Jones said.

"We're on."

❖

Jones summarized the reports. Two store employees recognized Sophia's picture, but none remembered her shopping on Friday. The techs lifted only Sophia's and Lou's prints from the car and found no blood or cordite residue. The lab was analyzing debris vacuumed from the interior.

Jones put Sophia's record in front of Billy, including her current DUI. "She's gone missing in the past. All reports were resolved within a couple of days. Your name came up on a few of the earlier ones."

Billy focused on the pages in front of him, trying to keep his tension under control. "I see you know about the shoe and the blue van."

"Mercy Snow called and briefed me last night. Do you have any reason to believe she's involved?"

Billy shook his head. "We need to verify the time Mercy left Atlanta, but I'm not inclined to consider her a suspect. I dropped the shoe at the lab on my way in."

Jones cut his eyes over. "Sounds like you know this Dupree woman pretty well."

"Hmm," Billy said, shutting down that line of questions.

"Chan's information about the van sounds promising."

"He's not a reliable source. He's mentally handicapped, and he'd tell a beautiful woman anything to keep her talking. Mercy brought up the scenario of a van snatch at the first interview. She might have unconsciously planted the idea."

"Happens."

"I want to hold back the van and shoe information," Billy said. "I asked Mercy to do the same. We need to get Charles Chan in here and push him on the van. A bad lead can waste a lot of time. I've chased broken-down vans into every trailer park around here for nothing."

Jones made some notes. "I'll get hold of Charles' parents and tell them we want to bring him in." He looked up. "So you think Sophia Dupree's a possible walk-away? I don't mean she's off on a drunk; could this be a 'wifey's-had-enough' disappearance?"

Billy shrugged. "This woman isn't a planner. And with that much vodka in the car I'm inclined to believe she was drunk on Friday night, which would lower the odds even farther."

"Her sister mentioned that Dupree used to live in the New Orleans area. I have a friend at the Attorney General's office there. I gave him a call." Jones handed over some papers. "This came an hour ago."

Billy studied the paperwork. The report covered a no-contest plea by T. Wayne Dupree to domestic assault against Caroline Dupree, his first wife. He broke her arm, broke ribs, punctured a lung. Their divorce was final a year later. While Dupree was a student at Tulane and again while working as a car salesman in Baton Rouge, he'd been arrested for disorderly conduct and public drunkenness. None of the charges had brought jail time. An assault and battery charge for a country club brawl was later dropped.

Billy closed it and noticed his hand was shaking. The possibility that it had been Dupree hitting Sophia made him crazy. He should have gotten her away from the bastard a long time ago.

"I found nothing local on Dupree. That doesn't mean he's changed his ways," Jones said. "He could've been knocking the shit out of his second wife for years. She got fed up and hit the road."

Billy stood and walked to the window to stare down at the morning traffic. Yesterday's cool spell had already dissolved into a narcotic-like heat. Even the sun appeared to be dragging itself through the hazy sky.

Sophia had never mentioned she was Dupree's second wife. She probably didn't know he'd beat the hell out of his first one. Billy thought about the split lip and broken wrist she'd blamed on a fall down the stairs. Last year she'd ended up in the hospital with a couple of broken ribs. Said she'd tripped over a lawn chair. Six months ago it was a black eye. He'd accepted her explanations without question because she was an alcoholic. He should have known better.

He turned back to Jones. "I just don't see her as a walk-away. Stranger-danger is a possibility, but I'm betting on Dupree. He's got a big ego. He's in a high profile position at Zelware Corp. and connected with the power brokers in this city. The Dupree's are a constant on the society page. Somehow, his wife held up her role as corporate wife for years. This recent DUI is a sure sign her drinking is hurting her husband's image."

"Keeping her on the society page and off the DUI list must have cost some bucks," Jones said as he gathered the reports. "I'll start on Dupree's financials, phone bills and insurance."

"He should be back in town later today. I'd like another shot at the mother and sister before he gets home."

If Billy was going to pretend Sophia was just another missing woman, and if he wanted to look into Lou's death, he had to get a grip. "Jones. About your sitting in Lou's chair. Sorry I blew up."

Jones nodded. "Not a problem."

Chapter Twenty-Eight

Monday, 1 p.m.

Cool hands, warm heart.

Afternoon light softened the kitchen. Mercy dripped ice water around the bowl's rim and pushed flour toward the center with a fork. She placed her palm over the lump of dough. Cool and moist, just as it should be. Hot-handed people can't make a decent piecrust to save their lives. They work against the dough, toughen it. Cool hands and a light touch work the fat into the flour and trap moisture to make steam. Steam makes a flaky crust. Nobody wants a tough crust.

Nobody with brains wants a warm heart. A warm heart leads to a broken heart. That had been Mercy's experience.

She felt numb. She'd be happy to curl up in the corner with Caesar and sleep, except she knew sleep wouldn't come. For two nights she had agonized over Sophia and the never-ending conflict between them. Her sister was talented, beautiful and loved, yet she had no peace, especially after her son Casey had died. We all have our demons, but in the end, Sophia's demons had gotten the upper hand.

Maybe by concentrating on baking pies, she wouldn't dwell on the alarm she'd seen on Detective Able's face when she handed him the shoe. She almost regretted following Charles. Each piece of information seemed to lessen Sophia's chances.

Mercy wrapped the dough, put it in the refrigerator, and threw a fistful of flour on the board. A *Commercial Appeal* article about Detective Nevers' accident reported that Able had been injured while attempting to rescue his partner. She remembered his bandaged arm, and that his girlfriend, or ex-girlfriend, had mentioned a concussion. Mercy worried that Able wasn't up to handling Sophia's case while dealing with his partner's death.

She heard her mother running the vacuum cleaner in the great room. Assorted bumps and thumps confirmed she was banging into the furniture. Gloria had been popping pills at night and starting off her mornings with screwdrivers. Vodka and pills might temporarily get her through this ordeal, but as soon as they found Sophia, Mercy would insist her mother seek treatment.

The doorbell rang and the vacuum shut down. Friends had been dropping by all day to pick up stacks of the "Missing: Have You Seen Sophia Dupree?" posters. Mercy smoothed her hair and took off her apron to go to the door one more time. She hesitated. No, maybe she would let Gloria answer it. A minute passed. The vacuum started up again.

Relieved, Mercy picked up a knife to level off a cup of flour.

"Something smells delicious," Detective Able said, causing her to start. He stood inside the doorway, giving her a polite but tired smile, wearing another rumpled suit, needing a haircut, his hands looking too big at the ends of his sleeves. She was so glad to see him it surprised her.

"I'm baking."

He glanced at the cooling racks. "I can see that."

Suddenly she realized the probable reason he'd come. Her hand flew to her chest. "My God, is Sophia dead?" Her knees buckled.

Instantly he was next to her, cupping her elbow as she righted herself. He stood so close she could see the hollowness beneath his cheeks.

"No, nothing like that," he said quickly.

The warmth in his voice steadied her. "I can't sleep. I keep thinking about the horrible things that happen to women who've been abducted." She shuddered. "It's weird that I'm in here baking, but I have to stay busy or . . . "

"Understandable." Able motioned toward the pie shells. "I was raised to never pester a busy cook, but I have some questions. Can you take a break?"

"Sure. Have a seat. I'll get coffee."

He hung his jacket on the back of a chair. He looked so diligent, sitting with the sun on his arms, flipping through his notebook. She wondered why he'd become a cop. A hum started inside her, that pleased little hum she hadn't felt in a while . . . oh, crap. This guy could get under her defenses even when she was worried that her sister had been abducted. *Get a grip.*

She poured the coffee and took a chair across from him.

"The monitoring report said you've had no unusual calls," he said.

"Just a couple of reporters. I put them off."

"Good. Remember, don't discuss the van or shoe with anyone, even your mother. We always hold back a few case details."

"I won't." This was easy so far. She relaxed a little.

"Have you thought of anyone who might be angry with Sophia? Family, friends?"

"I don't know Sophia's friends. As for family, there's only Mother, T. Wayne, and me."

Able's pen scratched across the paper. "Tell me more about Mr. Dupree."

She wrapped her hand around her cup. His leading question was intended to make her fill in the blanks. *Listen for the question behind the question,* she reminded herself.

"T. called last night. They've routed him through Amsterdam. Should be here anytime."

"Do you get along with your brother-in-law?"

"Sure. He helped me choose a college, remembers my birthday. Things like that."

"Like a big brother," he said, smiling.

There it was again, the smile she shouldn't trust. "T. has always been there for me."

"Have you noticed a change in him? Any problems? Depression, health, money?"

"Shouldn't we discuss Sophia's problems?"

"It's related. What about your sister's private life—for instance, their marriage. Has she ever mentioned any kind of abuse?"

"Abuse?" she said, insulted by his question. "Let me clear up something. Sophia is the aggressive one with her drinking and screaming rages. From what I've seen T. Wayne has never raised his voice to her, much less his hand. He must love Sophia, or he'd have left years ago."

"Maybe he was on his best behavior when you're around. A lot of what goes on behind closed doors has very little to do with love. I'm sure you know they were having problems."

His smile was gone. Now he sounded like a cop. For some absurd reason, that hurt. Her own tone went cold when she answered. "For twenty-five years I've watched Sophia throw tantrums and T. Wayne cope. He isn't the one capable of violence."

"Your sister's been to the emergency room four times in the last two years."

"Sophia gets drunk. She falls down. Don't blame T. for her accidents."

"I stopped to talk with The Med's staff on my way here. They recognized Sophia from her picture. They said she comes to the ER with injuries consistent with abuse."

This information rattled Mercy. She looked out the window, catching her breath as she pretended to study the sunlight on the pool. She looked back. "Then why hasn't the staff filed an abuse report?"

"She uses a false name. Pays cash. The next time she comes in with bruising and broken bones, they'll call social services."

Mercy's chest tightened. Either T. Wayne had been lying about Sophia's injuries or Detective Able was wrong. She didn't know which. Nerves pushed her to her feet. "If you'll excuse me, I need to put a pie in the oven."

Caesar woke up from his nap. He limped over and shoved his nose under Able's hand. "Hi, pardner," Able said, scratching the dog's head. "You're one lucky puppy."

"If getting hit by a car makes you lucky, then I guess he *is*," Mercy said over her shoulder. She jerked open the oven door, frustrated. Able's questions had upset her.

"Sometimes bad turns out to be good," Able said. "I'd say he's made a pretty soft landing, haven't you boy?"

She felt his eyes on her back as she slid the pie into the oven. He came over with his cup.

"I'd love more coffee if it isn't too much trouble." He used that warm tone, adding a half smile.

She didn't know how to respond. His attempt at manipulation had disappointed her.

"You think bad can be good?" She poured the coffee and shoved the cup in his hand. "We both know bad can be really bad. Being murdered is bad. Being chopped up and buried in the woods is bad. I guess you believe T. Wayne had a hand in this, but it's just as possible a sicko, driving a van, snatched her. If that's true, what are her chances?"

Able took a long sip of the coffee. "This case would normally be stuck on a desk in Missing Persons. But because Judge Overton lit a firecracker under the department, you've got me and another ace detective working overtime." He told her about the TBI agent, Jones. He was the man she'd spoken with on the phone.

He patted her arm. "It'll all work out."

"Don't patronize me. You're trying to trick me into helping you build a case against T. Wayne."

Billy looked as if she'd slapped him, then his gaze hardened. "If something bad has happened to your sister, I'll find out who did it. *She's* my priority, not your brother-in-law, unless he's responsible. If he is, I'll put him *under* the jailhouse."

Mercy released a shaky breath. Against her better judgment, she believed him. She instinctively knew he was right. This wasn't about her opinion of him or even about T. Wayne. Able would do everything he could to find Sophia.

"Let's start over," she said. "How about a piece of pie to go with that coffee?"

❖

Billy cut into the rhubarb pie. The crust flaked against his fork, then gave under pressure to expose the rich, creamy custard beneath. He slid the bite into his mouth. Tangy, sweet, rich. After everything that had happened: Lou, Sophia. To be eating pie and enjoying it. This should be wrong, but it felt . . . sane. Comfortable.

Mercy sat across from him, studying his reaction. She had flour on her chin and a perfect white handprint on her chest.

A moment ago he'd lost her trust by trying to mollify her, a successful strategy with the families of most victims, because they wanted assurance. Mercy wanted the truth.

"Delicious," he said.

"I'm experimenting with rhubarb. A woman named Greeta Watson shared her recipe. It isn't classically Southern."

"I baked pies at my uncle's roadside canteen in Mississippi. Our crowd went for sweet potato."

"Did you use cream or condensed milk?"

"Buttermilk worked for me."

She cut a piece for herself. "A chef detective. Who would've guessed?"

He liked watching the way she poked her fork into the filling, checking its consistency. She looked up. Her eyes were a deep gray-green.

"You worked with your uncle?" she said.

"Yeah, and I lived with him. I lost my folks early. I remember my dad's big hands picking me up. That's about it. My mom died in a car accident when I was nine."

"Dad died when I was four. I found a bottle of his aftershave. I've kept it. I take a sniff now and then. It makes me feel like he's still around. What about your uncle? Who bakes the pies now that you're a big city detective?"

Billy hesitated, concerned that talk of violence would upset her, but he found he wanted to tell Mercy things he shouldn't. "My uncle was shot dead behind his cash register five years ago. The shooter was a kid. Showed up with a gun, trying to be a big man. He got scared. The gun went off. There was only fifty bucks in the till."

She reached across the table and touched his hand. "You've had a lot of loss. Was your uncle's death the reason you became a detective?"

"No, it was something that happened earlier."

"I'd like to hear about it," she said with that steady gaze he'd seen before.

He took another sip of coffee. "Uncle Kane had his heart set on my becoming a lawyer. I was in my first year of law school when two little black girls, the Riley sisters, disappeared. Their parents were members of my church. The police never questioned a man in the neighborhood who was a businessman with some pull in the community—a white man with friends on the force."

Billy went silent. She leaned forward. "It's okay to tell me the rest."

"He kept the girls in his basement for weeks."

"You mean . . . "

"Yeah. The man had a heart attack and died in his sleep. Days later, the housekeeper found him and the bodies of the girls. They died, waiting to be rescued."

"Oh, no."

"Early on, the Riley's church had asked members to help look for the girls. If I'd come home and helped with the search, I might have made a difference. After I saw the grief on the parents' face, I quit law school and came to Memphis to be a cop. Looking back, I made the right choice."

"Your uncle must have been proud of your decision."

"Just the opposite. He was devastated. He cut me off. A few years later, he died."

"You shouldn't blame yourself . . . "

"Let's just say that I understand, first-hand, what a victim's family goes through." He took a bite of pie so he wouldn't say any more. He should have kept his own sad stories to himself. Mercy couldn't help but compare her sister's situation to the Riley girls. He studied her, worrying.

It was a good lesson to remember if he felt tempted to tell her about his relationship with Sophia.

She laid her fork down. "How can I help you find my sister?"

He wanted to say, *See your jerk brother-in-law for who he really is, because, chances are, he killed her.* But Billy understood how hard that conclusion would be for her.

"You've already done a lot. What we need is a break."

Caesar whined from under the table.

Mercy looked down at him. "What's the matter, boy?" The dog gagged and threw up, splattering Mercy's tennis shoes. She jumped up. "Oh, geez, it must be the antibiotic."

The kitchen door swung open. Gloria walked in wearing too much makeup, her hair over sprayed, carrying a tumbler of diluted orange juice. Her nails gleamed cherry red against the glass. Billy caught the scent of alcohol. He knew a screwdriver when he smelled one.

"Heavens, Mercedes, where are your manners? You're entertaining this gentleman in the kitchen with that nasty dog!"

"Entertaining?" Mercy echoed. "We're talking about Sophia . . . you know, the investigation."

Her mother marched over and clamped her hand on Billy's arm. "Come with me, Detective. Mercy, clean up that mess and knock that flour off your shirt. You look ridiculous."

Chapter Twenty-Nine

Monday, 1:20 p.m.

Billy left the kitchen with Gloria's hand clamped on his arm and Mercy's hurt expression stamped in his brain. He hated hearing her mother talk down to Mercy like that, but there wasn't much he could do about it. He had the person closest to Sophia alone. He wondered if he could get Gloria to admit, even to herself, what was really going on in this house. She leaned on his arm and blinked her puffy eyelids at him.

"That girl will never have Sophia's polish," she said in a voice husky with alcohol. "It's a shame. Mercy took after her father's side—common, not fine-boned like Sophia and me. And that face. A woman doesn't have a chance with a face like hers." Gloria peered at him. "Did you hear what I said? *A woman doesn't have a chance.*" She gripped his arm. "You have to find Sophia."

Gloria was drunk and should be put to bed before she hurt herself. He'd done the same for his mother when he would find her asleep on the sofa, an empty bottle on the floor beside her.

He squeezed Gloria's hand and steered her toward a hallway. "Does this lead to Sophia's bedroom?"

She nodded, made a little two-step. "She loves to dance, you know, Sophia does."

Photos of Sophia lined the hallway. They passed one from a newspaper society page—Sophia in a black gown, shoulders bare, and the hollows of her collarbones exposed, descending the steps of the Memphis Brooks Museum of Art. She had glanced away and the photographer caught her in profile. A copy of the same photo had lain in Billy's desk drawer for five years. Last year he realized he was hanging onto a painful memory and threw it away.

Gloria stopped at a snapshot of Sophia as a child on stage, wearing a tiara and a satin banner across her chest that read "Little Miss Channel Five." The child's head tilted coyly, her hand waving.

Gloria stood with her head tilted the same as her daughter's in the picture. "Sophia won her first time out. Mercedes never even made the finals."

He heard the worst message a parent can give a child—*you'll never be good enough.* So this was how Mercy had grown up. He focused on the photograph. Losing his temper wasn't an option.

"Sophia looks like a happy little girl," he said.

"Never a cloudy day when Sophia was growing up. The problem started later, after the tragedy."

"I'm aware she lost her son."

"She's a fragile soul. Breaks my heart. They say that animals sense an earthquake coming. I've noticed there's been a tension, like a vibration, around this house for weeks. Sophia disappeared, and now the tension is gone. It's like the calm after the tremors have stopped."

"So she was tense, jumpy?"

"No, the vibration didn't come from Sophia." Gloria frowned. "I can't explain it."

They reached Sophia's bedroom. The heavy drapes were closed so only lamplight washed the rose-colored walls and gold-leaf bed. The thick carpet and tapestry bedcover gave the room a sequestered feeling. Nothing appeared to be out of place, down to the vacuum strokes in the carpet.

He knew Sophia to be a perpetual mess in motion, never picking up anything she put down. "Is this the master bedroom?"

"T. Wayne snores. She moved out of the master temporarily. She needs her rest."

No books, no personal items on the dresser except a photograph of her son, Casey, splashing in the pool. "Mind if I look around?"

"If you think it will help." Gloria sat on the edge of the bed to finish her drink.

He opened drawers and found Sophia's sweaters, her lingerie. His fingers brushed the cool mounds of silk. Everything in the drawers appeared to have been placed there by a perfectionist. "Any of her clothes missing?"

"Only what she wore Friday."

A jewelry box held costume pieces and a charm bracelet. In a corner of the room, he saw bolts of fabrics standing on end. "She must have picked up a new project."

"More charity work. I told her not to wear herself out, but she wouldn't listen."

He pointed to the walk-in closet. "I'd like to take a look."

"Just don't disturb anything."

In the closet, surrounded by her wardrobe, Sophia's scent pressed in on him. All he had to do was close his eyes and she'd be in his arms again, her face close to his, her lips on his. From the day they'd first met, she'd possessed him. But he couldn't fall apart because he got a whiff of perfume.

"It's as if she's with us," Gloria whispered, stepping in beside him.

He flipped on the light and began opening shoeboxes and shopping bags of clothes, finding most still had the tags attached.

While he searched, Gloria's hand traced the row of garments, and she pulled out the black dress Sophia had worn in the photo—the dress that had fed his fantasies after she'd left. Black sequins shimmered over the skirt. Gloria gathered it to her face and breathed in. "She's a living dream in this one." She sobbed. "I can't take this, I need a drink."

The woman's grief touched his. He guided her out of the closet. "We need to focus. Let's begin with this room. It's very neat for a person with a drinking problem."

"She keeps her room this way," Gloria said stiffly.

"I don't believe that."

She looked guilty. "I vacuumed, picked up a few things." She inched toward the corner of the bed.

He noticed the mattress sat askew on the box spring. "You've searched under the mattress and straightened your daughter's room. Hiding evidence won't help her, Mrs. Snow."

Gloria pulled a prescription bottle of a heavy-duty tranquilizer from her pocket. "I found this. T. Wayne keeps the rest of her meds locked up. I don't know where she got it."

"Is this all you found?"

"Gardenias pressed under the mattress, and a swizzle stick from Commander's Palace in New Orleans. I didn't know she took a trip to New Orleans. And I didn't know gardenias had a special meaning for her. White roses do. I've searched for a diary. I believe she was keeping one, but I haven't found it."

He was surprised. He hadn't known about the New Orleans trip or the possibility of a diary. Both could be important.

"This isn't like the other times when she's gone off to drink," she said. "There's a pattern before she slips. She sleeps all day, gets angry over nothing. She seemed all right after she came back from rehab in Colorado. But then she got that warning in the Chinese fortune cookie. Do you people have a psychic on staff?"

"No, but we'll look into that if we need to." His next question wouldn't be so easy. "Was she seeing another man?"

"I wondered when you'd get to that. Believe me, I'd know if Sophia were running around." She hugged herself, avoiding his gaze. "I really need that drink."

He was losing her. "We'll get you a drink in a minute. Has her husband been depressed?"

She cut her eyes away from him. "T. Wayne will be home soon. You can talk to him."

"You know what goes on in this house. You need to tell me."

"There's one thing I'm sure about." She went to the dresser, opened the jewelry box and held up a bracelet. "I gave her this gold Mercedes charm for her sixteenth birthday. It's a bond between us. She'd never leave it on purpose."

"I understand that you're devoted to your daughter." He didn't say "daughters," and she didn't correct him. "But what about Sophia's husband? How do you feel about him?"

"T. Wayne has been good to both of us."

She fumbled the bracelet between her fingers and looked down, avoiding confrontation. If he pushed too hard, she'd shut down.

"You have to choose," he said. "I know you want to support your son-in-law, but you can't protect him at the price of your daughter's life."

Her gaze shifted, her loyalties swaying. "Last year Sophia drank too much at a party his boss gave for clients. She insulted an important guest. Shortly after that, T. Wayne's boss passed him over for a promotion. He blamed Sophia. They had a terrible fight. After that he started spending a lot of time out of town. Down in Texas. Austin."

"We found vodka bottles in the Acura's tire well. Did you know she was drinking again?"

"It doesn't take much for her to start. T. Wayne sold her Mercedes while she was away at rehab. It's a collector's car, very valuable. I thought she'd never stop crying."

"She was crazy about that car," Billy said.

"T. bought the Acura. She hates it. She's been driving his BMW. For some reason he took the BMW to the airport, so she had to drive the Acura for the last few days."

Her face took on a dreamy quality, and she wandered over to the bed, fluffed pillows and smoothed the bedcover. "But then T. Wayne sent roses with the sweetest card the day he left the country. He booked a two-week cruise in the Greek Islands for their twenty-fifth anniversary." She traced her finger over the headboard. "I thought this was the perfect marriage. It hasn't turned out that way."

"Has your son-in-law abused your daughter?"

Her dreamy look melted. "I've wondered. She's had so many accidents. Sophia's not clumsy and hasn't fallen once since I've moved in. T. seems restless, like his mind is somewhere else. Sometimes I get up for a late snack, and he'll be on the phone in his study." She gave him a sly glance. "He keeps his knife collection in there. I don't like weapons of any kind, not since the accident with Casey."

This was the most honest she'd been since they had left the kitchen, and the best excuse he'd heard to get into Dupree's study. With Gloria along, he wouldn't need a court order to look around.

"He's a collector?" he said.

"It was guns before. Now it's knives and swords."

"I'm a collector myself. Can I take a look?"

❖

Mercy was nowhere to be seen as Billy followed her mother through the house. He wondered if Mercy unconsciously sensed Gloria would spill more information if left alone with him, a man. Women like Gloria tended to operate that way: ignoring or even competing with their daughters for any man's attention. Gloria picked up a stack of mail from the entry table and led him upstairs to Dupree's classic English study. A carved desk sat in front of a display cabinet. Billy walked over and flipped on the interior light. The case held bowie knives, stilettos, even a broadsword.

"This stuff is ancient," he said, stooping down. "That dagger must be fifteenth century."

"T. spends hours looking things up on the computer before he buys them."

Billy stood and noticed the stack of bills on the desk. Wanting a closer look, he said, "I should check in with my office. Is this phone all right?" Before she could answer, he sat, picked up the receiver, and pretended to dial, scanning the stack of papers at the same time: a travel itinerary, an envelope from SilverSpring Mortgage Co., and a bank statement from National Trust.

"Agent Jones, did you reach Mr. Chan?" He said into the dead receiver. While Gloria shuffled through the mail, he rifled the stacks in front of him, then took a blank sheet of paper from Dupree's printer and laid it next to the itinerary. "Hang on, let me get that down." Still pretending to listen, he copied the travel information, bank account numbers and the mortgage information.

Gloria waved an envelope with a cruise ship logo in the left hand corner.

"Thanks," he said and hung up.

"Cruise tickets," she beamed and tore open the envelope. As she read the single sheet of paper, her expression changed. She held up the letter with the word "Cancelled" stamped across the bottom and frowned. "I don't understand."

"May I see it?"

A credit card slip fell out of the envelope. Billy read the letter and inspected the slip. "He cancelled the cruise two weeks ago. Got his full deposit refunded. Four thousand dollars."

"That bastard." Gloria took the letter back. "He cancelled the trip behind her back, the same way he got rid of her Mercedes."

Chapter Thirty

"Mercy Pie!" T. Wayne called out as he strode into the kitchen, a broad-shouldered, handsome man in his mid-fifties who, for years, had convinced Mercy everything in life was going to be okay.

"T.!" She threw her arms around his neck, suppressing her surprise that he looked so much older than he had the last time she'd seen him, two years ago. And he had a new scar, a white line running across his forehead. She hugged him again. Now that he was home, responsibility for managing her mother could shift to him.

"God, I'm glad you're here," he said, his voice cracking with exhaustion. "Tell me Sophia is home, sleeping it off."

Mercy shook her head. "She went shopping Friday night and disappeared."

He blew out his breath. She caught a whiff of scotch.

"I caught the first plane out. I've spoken with Buck a couple of times. I know they found Sophia's car in a parking lot, and later some guy turned in her purse. Do the cops know anything else?"

"You can talk with Detective Able when he finishes interviewing Momma. I'll get you some pie and coffee."

T. Wayne swallowed as if he had a throat full of sandpaper. "There's a detective in this house alone with your mother?"

"Well, yes."

He slammed his fist on the counter. "Damn it, Buck warned me the cops would put the screws to me as soon as I landed." He scowled at her. "What's wrong with you? I thought you were smarter than to let a detective get hold of your mother."

"Don't be ridiculous; I can't control who he talks to." T. Wayne's words felt like a slap.

"You don't get it. He'll pump your mother for something he can use against me."

"It's his job to ask questions. He was questioning me up until a few minutes ago."

"You? What did you tell him?"

"Nothing. There's nothing to tell."

T. Wayne stomped into the entry. Mercy followed, her mind churning with excuses for his angry attitude. He was worried about Sophia, certainly. He'd raced across continents to get back to Memphis, fighting with airlines and crossing time zones to get home. On top of that, the judge's warning must have really shaken him.

"I'm sorry, Mercy, but I don't like being blind-sided in my own house." He stopped, listening. "You hear that? You *hear* that? They're upstairs in my office," he said as he raced up the steps.

She ran after him, praying Able wasn't in T. Wayne's study. At the landing T. Wayne paused and rotated his shoulders as if adjusting his attitude. As they neared the study, Mercy heard her mother's voice through the half-closed door.

"That bastard," Gloria said. "He cancelled the trip behind her back, the same way he got rid of her Mercedes."

T. Wayne pushed through the door. Mercy followed and saw Detective Able, sitting behind the desk, writing on a sheet of paper. He looked up as T. Wayne came in. Able's features became a neutral mask as he folded the paper, slipped it into his jacket and stood.

"I'm Detective Able. I'm investigating your wife's disappearance."

T. Wayne extended his hand but stood far enough away to make Able come from behind the desk to shake it. Able came around and gripped T. Wayne's hand. Both men gave a small, tug-of-war pull before dropping the handshake.

T. Wayne nodded toward his desk. "Is that what you were doing? Looking for my wife?"

Able shrugged. "I can take a closer look, if you want."

"You need a warrant to go through a man's desk," T. Wayne said, his voice rising.

"Hold on. I wasn't searching your desk. And aren't we working the same side here?"

Mercy's throat tightened when she saw predatory amusement lighting Able's eyes. This wasn't going well.

Gloria pushed between them. "T., I told the detective he could use your phone, but let's forget about that and talk about this." She shook a piece of paper in his face. "You cancelled Sophia's anniversary cruise. I want to know why."

T. Wayne snatched the paper out of her hand. "You opened an envelope addressed to me?"

"I don't need a court order to look at a letter in this house. I thought these were the tickets. I told the detective you were taking Sophia on a fancy cruise. You lied. You *cancelled* the cruise."

He scanned the letter. "For God's sakes, this says I've cancelled the *Pisces*. But I've booked another ship, the *Pacific Dawn*. What the hell's wrong with that?"

Gloria's eyes went wide. "Oh, sweetie, I saw the word 'cancelled' and went crazy."

Mercy noticed Able studying T. Wayne, who was already red-faced and fuming. What in the world was wrong with T. Wayne?

Everyone knows the cops believe an innocent man worries about his wife. A guilty one worries about his rights. She needed to turn the subject to Sophia before T. Wayne made things worse.

"We should be talking about Sophia, not cruise tickets," she said.

"Shut up, Mercy," T. Wayne snapped. "I still want to know why this man's in my study."

Mercy stared up at him. *Shut up. Shut up!* No man spoke to her that way. T. Wayne had never done it before. She caught a slight movement from the corner of her eye. Detective Able had shifted into a tighter stance. His stare was ice cold.

"There's a perfectly good reason," Gloria said. "I told the detective about your knife collection. He collects too, and wanted to see what you have."

"So you're a collector," T. Wayne sneered. "What's your specialty, jailhouse shivs?"

"Got some good ones," Able said, his voice soft and lethal. "Then again, I don't get to see fine collectibles like your left-handed Spanish dagger here. But like Mercy said, we should be talking about your wife. So why the hell are you trying to bust my balls about your desk and your knives when it's your wife you should be worried about?"

T. Wayne drew himself up. "Don't you lecture me. I flew halfway around the world to get here, and I want to know about every damned lead you have. You're familiar with Judge Lamar Overton?"

"I discussed the case with him last night."

"The judge intends to keep an eye on this investigation until we get some answers." T. Wayne's shoulders slouched. Apparently, he was running out of steam. He rubbed his eyes. "Look, I need some coffee. Let's go downstairs. You can tell me what you know."

"I'll give you the important details now, but I'll need to talk to you tomorrow when you're fresh. Ten in the morning at the Criminal Justice Center."

T. Wayne nodded. "I want to hear if anything breaks. You got it?"

The men left the study without so much as a *You first, ladies,* of standard Memphis manners. Mercy felt like she'd been tossed in the middle of a dogfight. The last thing she'd expected out of T. Wayne and Able was a pissing contest. She understood why T. Wayne didn't trust Able, but he'd always been the sensible one in the family, not a hothead foolish enough to try and bully a cop. Instead of taking the pressure off, T. Wayne had made things worse.

Gloria perched on the study's sofa and began smoothing her hair as if she were a bird with ruffled feathers. "Well! I never. T. Wayne acted just terrible."

"He's worried about Sophia. Plus the judge must have scared the daylights out of him. Able didn't help matters, either."

"I've seen T. Wayne act huffy before. He considers himself to be a swinging dick, but he's not."

"Mother! Where did you hear that phrase?"

"From Buck. Now *there's* a man. By the way, Detective Able didn't pick up anything but a piece of paper. I watched him the whole time."

"That's good, Momma."

"I asked him if the Memphis police have a psychic on staff."

"You didn't."

"I'll hire one myself if they don't find Sophia soon. I'll hire a team of psychics. God knows I have the money."

Mercy chewed her lip and decided to say nothing. Consulting a psychic would give her mother a mission. In the meantime, Mercy was going to have to keep an eye on T. Wayne. His behavior worried her. If this was an example of his co-operation . . .

"There's something I don't understand," her mother said.

Mercy gave an internal sigh. "What's that, Momma?"

"How did that detective know Sophia was so crazy about her little blue Mercedes?"

Chapter Thirty-One

Monday, 4:00 p.m.

In 1967, cotton baron Pinky Hanson and his wife, Ruth, donated five acres of their wooded estate adjacent to the River City Club in Midtown. They requested two acres be reserved for nine-wicket croquet courts and a formal garden be established with Ruth's own heritage roses. They also stipulated that the croquet courts be bordered by as many of the century-old oaks as could be saved. Croquet fanatics paid for the leveling, sod and top-dressing of the lawns, while rose enthusiasts designed the gardens. The resulting courts rivaled the finest installations: Florida's Palm Beach Polo and Country Club, the Meadows Club of Southampton, Long Island or the BonVivant Country Club in Illinois.

The club's serious players purchased their mallets from England's John Jaques and Son, Ltd. That hadn't been good enough for Buck. His mallets were custom-made of mahogany and hickory, with solid gold ring fittings for the shafts.

The River City Club required players to follow rules of courtesy. Players wore formal whites—long after tennis had forgone the tradition—white Sea Island cotton shirts, white flannel trousers and pristine white tennis shoes for the greensward. However, committee rules didn't require a player to share his umbrella with an opponent during a rainstorm.

The controlled aggression of tournament croquet topped the list of Buck's passions. That, and wagering on the games. To Buck, croquet represented civilized victory.

Buck played doubles twice a week without fail. His regular partner was Lee Church, a tall athletic man who was senior partner of a venerable Memphis firm that specialized in real estate law. The opposing team was Lester Schutt, a cigar smoking, fist of a man who was a successful real estate developer. And Hamlin Hull, son of a Mississippi planter—rich in Delta farmland, old money, and the traditions of the plantation South. The foursome had played croquet at the club on Monday and Thursday afternoons for the last seventeen summers.

The sheltering oaks turned out to be a blessing, shading the court from the brutal August sun. Buck made a *roquet* on Schutt's yellow ball, and then took his croquet shot, sending Schutt's ball past the wicket. His next stroke would be a simple, direct shot. He aimed at the sixth wicket, breathed deeply, and took an easy swing. The ball thumped the uprights, trapping itself in the jaws of the wicket, leaving him stranded.

"Been a while since I've seen you stuff a wicket," Hamlin Hull said as he squatted on the court boundary. "You must have a touch of the wedding jitters." He grinned at Buck. His belly protruded like a pillow between his spread knees. People thought Hull was just another wealthy good old boy who'd never worked a day in his life. But he was more than that.

Hull knew how to play the game.

Buck made the rover wicket with a series of well-planned breaks. Lee Church took a drive shot, made a *roquet*, took a beautiful short split shot, ran the wicket and set up for his next *roquet* on Schutt's ball. Then he broke down and turned the play over to Schutt. Schutt had positioned himself perfectly. He made a long *roquet*, took croquet, cleared a wicket and made a second *roquet*, executing one maneuver after another until he drove his ball into the stake with a solid *whack*.

"Peg out," Schutt hollered and took out the red scorebook. He recorded everything, charting their wins and losses.

Buck made a mock bow to Schutt and Hull. "Drinks on me this evening, gentlemen."

Although Buck's strategy remained sound, he'd been losing to Schutt for months.

Today's loss made the total fifteen thousand, money he wouldn't have until he could tap into Gloria's account. Buck looked good on paper, but actual greenbacks were harder to come by.

Schutt looked up from the book. "Hope you remembered your checkbook, Judge."

"You think this heat will warp the shafts?" Hull said, interrupting Schutt.

"Just don't leave them in a hot car. I carry mine inside, everywhere I go," Church said.

Buck noticed the way Church and Hull had given each other a quick look as they wiped down their mallets and stowed them in their leather cases. They didn't want Schutt's big mouth to blow their deal with Buck.

Four months ago all three had come to Buck with a proposition. They had connections in Washington. President Terry Leggett's Chief of Staff had asked Senator Noel, as Chairman of the Judiciary Committee, to submit a candidate's name the Senate could confirm without objection. For five hundred thousand dollars, wired to Senator Noel's Cayman account, Buck could be the next appointee to the 6th Circuit Court of Appeals, located in Cincinnati, Ohio.

During Noel's twenty years in office, Schutt, Church, and Hull had been the senator's biggest contributors. As campaign finance laws tightened, they had become "bundlers"—supporters with the ability to collect the maximum donations from hundreds of individuals and package them as PAC contributions. As trusted supporters with the ability to sniff out cash, they were asked by Noel to come up with an appeals court nominee who would also be willing to pay for the seat. The three men took a risk by coming to Buck with Noel's offer, but they knew his holy grail was to serve on the Federal Court of Appeals, and that Buck would realize, as they had, that this opportunity would be his one sure chance at a seat.

He was qualified, respected by his peers, and had published in several law reviews and ABA journals. None of his articles would send up red flags to the Judiciary Committee. His taxes were current, his reputation exemplary.

Buck had accepted their deal on the spot, shaking hands and breaking out his oldest single malt scotch. Only later did he face the fact that his lifestyle had left him with a second mortgage, maxed-out credit cards and no cash of his own with which to buy the appointment.

Only one avenue had been open to him. Gloria Snow.

◈

After the game, they took their usual table on the side porch off the club's dining room. Four debutantes played doubles on the tennis court in front of them.

This was Buck's domain. The club occupied the most desirable, pristine acreage inside the city limits. It was limited to an exclusive membership based either on legacy or sponsorship. The ten-man nominating committee reserved the right to discriminate on whatever basis it chose.

Buck had worked hard for inclusion in this society, beginning with his scholarship to Princeton and his law degree from Harvard. His prestigious law practice followed, then his election to the bench as a Shelby County Criminal Court Judge. His nomination to join The River City Club, where traditions of the old South remained intact, completed his campaign. His mother's old Southern name had gotten him a seat at the table, but he'd done the rest.

Now he wanted more.

Except for the elderly black waiter in a white jacket, arriving at the table with old-fashioned glasses, a pitcher of branch water, and a fifth of Glenfiddich, the porch was deserted. The men had laid their mallet cases flat on an empty table top rather than leaning them against their chairs. A serious player goes to great lengths to protect his mallet from warping. Harpo Marx built an air-conditioned room out in California, for the sole use of storing his equipment. Buck was just as fanatical.

He watched on the tennis court as one of the club's young female members served aces over the net. She stopped and waved at him. Recently, her father, a fellow croquet fanatic, had asked him for help with the girl's ex-boyfriend, who was stalking her. Buck had promised to handle it. He'd called Lou, who then confronted the boy while he sat in his car outside the girl's condo. Lou had intimidated the kid so badly, he left the boy with a wet spot on his khakis.

Over the years, Lou Nevers had handled a number of such annoyances for Buck. Buck and Lou weren't friends, but their alliance had worked for both of them. In some ways, Buck would miss Lou. Damned shame the way he'd died. But it was certainly convenient.

When the server left, Church drummed his fingers on the table to get Buck's attention. "I prefer to not discuss business while I'm at the club, but I had a call from our Washington D.C. friend. He's an impatient man. He brought up your overdue payment."

"Is this your way of saying you're pulling your support?"

"We're one hundred percent behind you," Church said, "but we need some assurance about the money. Your referral should be in front of the Chief of Staff no later than five weeks from now. After that, things will move quickly based on the background check. Our Washington friend let me know he wants his money now."

"Noel's got a couple of expensive women to keep up," Schutt said.

"No names." Church gestured toward the server approaching with a bowl of macadamia nuts.

The man set down the bowl and swept a practiced gaze over the drinks. The group paid him a yearly bonus to keep the side porch clear of other members when they were present.

"Thank you, Taylor," Hull said. The waiter nodded and retreated.

Schutt picked up the conversation. "Like Church said, we're one hundred percent behind you unless you don't have the money. You know we have alternatives in mind. The stakes are too damned high to let this deal fall through."

Ceiling fans swished overhead, and the tennis ball tocked back and forth between the beauties on the court.

These men had the ear of a U.S. Senator. Now they wanted influence with a judge on the Federal Circuit Court of Appeals, knowing that, in time, some aspect of their business or their political interests would fall within his jurisdiction. On the federal appeals court bench, Buck would have real power, a place where 'black-letter law' was laid down. From there, the next step up for him, a nearly impossible dream but one he'd secretly held his entire career, would be the Supreme Court.

Buck finished his scotch and topped off everyone's glass. These men were wealthy enough to pay Noel themselves, but paying someone else's tab isn't how rich people stay rich. And if Buck paid, they'd feel they had a bargaining chip to hold over him. Now they wanted to hear details of his plan to pay off the senator with Gloria's money. He decided to deal with the problem straight up.

"I'll give you a status report. The IPO was fully subscribed and went like clockwork, but the brokerage firm handling it screwed up. It's a week late in transferring the proceeds. They swear the money will move to Gloria's account on Thursday. From there I'll parcel it out into investments."

"How much are we talking about?" Church said.

"Ten million."

"Jesus, and you haven't married the woman yet?" Schutt said. Hull elbowed him, and Schutt shrugged. "What? He's got to marry her to get his hands on the cash."

"Unfortunately, we had a complication," Buck said.

"We know her daughter is missing," Church said.

"Then you may also know that she has a habit of disappearing. I have people handling the situation."

"We have people too," Schutt said. "Our sources say the lady is more than missing. If she's found dead . . . " Schutt shrugged.

Church put his hand on Buck's arm. "Understand, we don't mean to sound callous."

"Absolutely," Schutt said. "But if the media finds a way to turn her disappearance into a scandal, you can kiss the nomination and your money goodbye."

Buck waved a hand. "Gloria relies on me. The situation with her daughter makes her even more dependent. I've arranged a civil ceremony on Thursday. Monday I'll pull out half a million from Gloria's funds. Tuesday at the latest." He smiled until he saw the concern on Church's face.

"Maybe," Church said, "but our Washington friend says he's been contacted by a judge in Nashville who mentioned a sizable campaign contribution. If we give them enough time to think about it, this guy could ace you out."

Buck gazed down through a stand of darkening trees. Sons-of-bitches thought they could squeeze him. Bunch of amateurs. "You're too late to back another horse. Unless you want to put up the money yourselves, you'd better get off my back."

Schutt grunted and grabbed a handful of nuts.

Hull chuckled, enjoying Buck's power play. "That's right, Your Honor. Nobody treats you like a fool. Least not for long."

"Sophia will come home," Buck said. "If she doesn't, the odds are good she'll stay missing. That's what happens in these cases. Either way, the issue will be resolved."

"And your fiancée, is she a problem?" Church said.

"Like any good wife, she'll be eager to invest in her husband's political career, even if she doesn't know about it."

"Just remember, you're not the only horse in the running," Schutt growled. "Make sure your lady says 'I do' on Thursday."

"I've drafted a general power of attorney. Once Gloria signs, I'll move things along."

"I had a New York cousin pull that power-of-attorney crap on his great aunt," Schutt said. "He thought she wouldn't know the difference. She prosecuted his ass right into prison." He laughed and signaled for Taylor to bring more nuts.

Chapter Thirty-Two

Monday, 1:30 p.m.

Billy took the steps down to his car two at a time, eager to make a few more notes and get back to the CJC. Even before today he'd had good reason to detest Dupree.

Years ago, Billy had been first officer on the scene after Sophia's five-year-old son, Casey, had taken a loaded Glock from the unlocked cabinet in Dupree's office and accidentally shot himself in the head. Billy arrived even before the medics. He found Sophia kneeling beside her son with his shattered skull cupped in her hands.

"Help me," she'd whispered, her eyes locking onto him.

Casey was the first child he'd seen torn apart like that—brain tissue speckling the desk and Oriental rug. The sight nearly took him down. He slowed the bleeding and kept the boy breathing until the EMTs came.

Dupree showed up at the hospital while his son lay in a coma. Sophia had stood pale as marble while her husband screamed at her, saying she might as well have handed the gun to the boy. Billy never forgot or forgave that.

Dupree never took responsibility for leaving a loaded gun in an unlocked case where his son could find it. His only gesture was to sell the guns and collect a different deadly toy.

If T. Wayne Dupree had a hand in Sophia's disappearance, he was one stupid fuck. His melodramatic reaction when he walked into that study had been worth the price of a ticket; and his preoccupation with his rights rather than his wife's whereabouts was a classic perp performance. Dupree's bullying tactic might sell chicken in Uzbeckistan, but it sure as hell didn't work with a cop.

Billy felt good about the information he'd learned from Gloria and everything he'd picked up from Dupree's desk. But he felt bad about Mercy being trapped in the middle of that dysfunctional family, especially with her sister missing. No wonder she'd moved to Atlanta. Alaska would have made more sense.

At least she got a glimpse of Dupree's natural meanness. He was probably giving her and Gloria hell for letting a cop into the house. Or he was locked in his study, drinking himself blind, because he didn't know what else to do.

◆

At the CJC, Billy took a chair across from Jones's desk.

"What's up?" Jones said.

"That bastard's going down." Billy ground his finger on the desk to make his point.

"I take it Dupree showed up."

"First thing he did was drop Overton's name as if the judge would cover for him. If Overton gets a whiff of what I smelled, he'll haul Dupree down to the courthouse himself."

"What is it about the man that ticks you off so bad?"

"Besides being a wife-beater? His kid shot himself in the head with a gun Dupree left in an unlocked cabinet. He blamed his wife."

"Oh, man."

"It's why Sophia Dupree binge drinks. The man's a lightweight, a hairdo. He walked into the house today making all the noises of a guilty man."

Jones pitched a printout to him. "Take a look at this."

Billy flipped the cover page on twelve months of Dupree's long-distance phone records. "Quick work."

"Hackers. The bureau has exposed me to a lot of talent. If we want to use the stuff, we can get the subpoena later. I'm working the man's cell carrier now."

Scanning the pages, Billy saw midnight calls to Dubai, Kuwait, and a number of calls to Texas. "You see those two-in-the-morning calls to Austin?"

"Couldn't miss them," Jones said.

"I copied information off his desk. He has a mortgage with SilverSpring Mortgage in Austin. He booked a cruise for their anniversary then cancelled it. Said he rebooked on a ship called *Pacific Dawn*, but the way he talked, I didn't buy it."

"I'll look into it," Jones said.

"Dupree is coming in tomorrow morning at ten. It may be our only shot before he lawyers up."

"We'll have plenty to work with by then. If he's guilty, we'll catch the son-of-a-bitch."

"You hook him, I'll cook him," Billy said. They both grinned. Despite the concussion headache, it was the best he'd felt in days.

He made a fresh pot of coffee and settled in to go over the notes he'd made at the house. The gardenias and swizzle stick under the mattress intrigued him. He thought he knew Sophia, but these items, which must be precious to her, baffled him. If there was a diary, Sophia's private thoughts might give him insight, but it also might reveal their affair. He'd have to deal with that if it came up.

He moved on to the canvass reports and Sophia's address book. Nothing of use there. No ransom demand by phone, mail, or computer. The business card remained a mystery.

After a couple of hours, he switched to Lou's old case files, still determined to find some clue that said Lou had been murdered. But every conviction had held up, and the felons currently out on parole didn't have the brains or the grit to ambush and murder a cop.

Lou, dead. And Sophia, missing.

He closed his eyes. Case details generally sifted through his mind like numerical possibilities. The propensities of human nature—anger, jealousy, lust, greed, even stupidity—made easy predictors. He knew Lou's and Sophia's behaviors as well as a parent knows his child's favorite hiding place, but he wasn't getting a clear picture on either.

At four o'clock, Jones stood and stretched. "It's the last day of an airline ticket sale, and the travel agent won't return my call. I'm going to her office before it closes. I'll be back."

After Jones left, Billy went to Lou's desk and slid open the pencil drawer. A second set of car keys lay taped to the back.

A few minutes later, he crossed the alley behind the Justice Center and took the elevator to the garage's fifth floor. Lou's Honda Civic was parked in the rear corner, his usual spot, with a CSU van parked one space over. On the Honda's passenger's side, CSU tech, Patsy Dwyer, knelt, dusting the door handle.

"I owe you one for this," Billy said.

"Lou was the best." She blew on the carbon powder and laid tape across the handle. "Not much here. Maybe one clear print."

Patsy had started her career wearing oxford-cloth shirts and men's work pants, so she wouldn't be stereotyped as a delicate female. She took her job seriously, and there was good reason for it—a husband with multiple sclerosis and three boys to put through school. It hadn't taken long before the detectives began to ask for Patsy, especially for mysteries.

"I'll bag the interior." He snapped on gloves and checked between the doorframes and the seat. No nightstick. Its absence proved nothing. He found a receipt from Sputnick Liquor dated May fifth. Not good. Lou had begun drinking again. He bagged the receipt and popped the glove compartment. Inside were maps, a roll of electrician's tape made gummy by the heat, and a half-empty pint of Jack Daniels.

Patsy tapped on the window. "Find anything?"

He shoved the bottle back in the compartment. "Nope."

On the backseat he found a Big Orange bottle, a James Lee Burke paperback and Lou's *Rawlings* pitcher's mitt. Add up the odds and ends of a person's life, and they tell a story the same as broken pottery and campfire remnants at an archeological dig.

He opened the trunk. Lou piled his real junk there: a cardboard box of rusty tools, a tackle box, and a blue suitcase.

Patsy came around to the back of the Honda. "I'll vacuum inside; see what I can suck up." She stared at the suitcase a moment then frowned. "Looks like Lou was planning a trip."

"He didn't need a suitcase where he was going."

Patsy made a face. "Sorry. I wasn't trying to be funny."

"Lou would have loved the irony."

"No, Lou loved his Ruby and bass fishing in that order. And you. He loved you like you were his own."

Billy looked at Patsy's earnest face and found he couldn't speak. He didn't want her to see, so he fumbled with the suitcase latches.

"You want me to pop those?" she said.

The thought hit him that he should quit digging into Lou's life, but he knew that idea came from Dexter and the reverend hinting he would find more than he'd bargained for.

"Go ahead," he said.

She opened the suitcase and left him to sort through it. He found underwear, a *Sports Illustrated*, no shaving kit. Maybe Lou had a woman stashed somewhere, after all. At the bottom of the suitcase, he found a DVD disc case. It was black plastic and had four silver, metallic star-shaped stickers running up the spine.

"Anything in there you want printed?" Patsy said.

He tucked the case into his jacket. "No, it's just clothes."

"I'll have the latents by tomorrow afternoon. If there's anything pertinent, I'll leave a message."

◆

Back at his desk he pulled out the disc case, remembering that Lou had bought a camcorder and used it at a few league games. The stick-on stars were an odd detail, not something he'd expect to find on Lou's belongings.

He went to the conference room, inserted the disc into the DVD player and hit PLAY. Images popped onto the screen. He recognized a squad softball game that had been played a month ago. Lou's voice came over the speaker in a low mumble of curses while he adjusted the focus. A wave of loss hit Billy at the sound. The camera swung right, and he watched himself walk to home plate, turn to the camera and touch the bill of his cap.

"Yeah, yeah, pretty boy," Lou hollered. "Hey Smitty, throw inside. He can't touch it."

Lou loved to harass batters at the plate. Billy watched himself crouch, the bat high off his right shoulder, feet a little too close together. The squad jeered in the background.

Then Lou began talking to himself.

"If it ain't down the middle, you can't see it, can you boy? Come on, dickhead, strike out."

The venom in Lou's voice startled him. He watched himself settle over the plate and frown at the pitcher. He swung, missing by inches. The umpire called strike one.

"Atta boy, fuck up some more. I got it all on tape."

What the hell was that about? He turned up the volume.

This time Lou shouted, "Come on, Billy boy, get a hit."

Smitty fired one low and inside. Billy took a long stride and swung. He heard the crack of the bat and watched the foul rip toward the camera lens. Lou grunted in surprise. The picture tilted sideways, shooting grass. The squad razzed Lou. Billy saw the toes of his own Nikes running into the tilted frame.

"You okay?"

"You ain't hitting the ball hard enough to dent a doughnut," Lou grumbled. "And you *ain't* getting a new partner that easy."

Billy heard himself laugh. The camera came up off the grass, and Billy saw himself back at the plate, bat cocked, eyes on the pitcher.

"Strike two, asshole," Lou *growled under his breath.* *"You're on your way out."*

Billy hit STOP on the player. He'd heard enough. Lou's contempt stunned him.

If the ball ain't down the middle of the plate, you can't see it coming. Lou had said those exact words on Saturday. He'd recorded this game weeks ago. He must have been stewing all this time. Why was Lou so angry?

When Billy was a kid, a neighbor's dog bit him on the leg. Jumped off the porch and really tore into him. Wouldn't let go. There was no reason for it. He and the dog had always gotten along. Yet suddenly he'd seen hate in the dog's eyes.

A sound behind him made him turn.

"Hey." Jones stuck his hands in his pockets. "I heard the game and came to check it out. Didn't realize it was personal."

"How long you been standing there?"

"Long enough. Who was the jerk with the camera?"

Silence spread between them.

"Lou."

Jones looked startled. "Lou, your partner?"

"Yeah. Guess we got a dose of what Lou thought of my ball playing."

Jones raised his hands, laughing. "No way, man. That was the beer talking. Some guys . . . you know? We all get out of line."

"Lou was sober."

"Come on, he was your partner. He didn't mean it."

"Sure he did. He meant every word."

Chapter Thirty-Three

Monday, 9:30 p.m.

Supper was a nightmare.

It began with T. Wayne and the judge shutting themselves in the library to watch news coverage of Sophia's disappearance. Mercy had bought a hen for herb-roasted chicken, but Gloria insisted on cutting it up and frying it, because Overton preferred his chicken fried. Mercy let the grease get too hot. The chicken was too wet. It spattered and burned her mother's hand. While they iced Gloria's hand, the rolls burned.

By the time the men came to the table with their drinks, everything was cold.

Mercy had no appetite for chicken. After two days of worrying and calming her mother's hysterics, she only wanted iced tea with mint and a wedge of lemon, the way she drank it at her own kitchen table, where she had some degree of control. She brought a pitcher to the table and settled in to listen.

"I want the best for this family," Overton said. "That means a low profile—no spontaneous comments to the media. T. Wayne has powerful friends in this city. That's to his advantage, as long as things don't get out of hand."

"I like your idea of getting ahead of the problem by offering a reward," T. Wayne said. "The D.A. won't be so quick to point a finger at me if I put up a significant amount, say fifty thousand."

"That's low," Buck said. "One hundred thousand and an emotional appeal to the public to help find your wife will put some pressure on the D.A.. Even with that I'll have to do some arm twisting."

"More potatoes?" Gloria offered the bowl around, as if unaware Sophia's fate was being decided. Mercy sat there feeling helpless and worse, relegated to silent female status.

"I got a heads-up from Ted Newski at corporate," T. Wayne said. "I'm the negotiator on a big contract with a Saudi prince. Saudis hate publicity, especially when a man's wife is involved. They keep up with the wire services, even the CNN crawler. I may be pulled off the team if this thing gets sensationalized."

"The mayor called me," Overton said. "If the department doesn't handle this right, it could make him look bad enough to lose the election."

T. Wayne shook his head. "We could all come out losers."

Mercy banged her glass down on the table. "Finding Sophia is more important than Saudi opinions or the mayor's reelection."

T. Wayne's cheeks reddened. "That's not what I meant."

"You should ask Detective Able how to handle a reward offer," she said. "What you say on TV could make a difference in the investigation."

"I'll take Buck's opinion over that idiot's any day. And don't question my priorities. You don't have the right."

"Let's calm down, eat our supper," Overton said. "Gloria, I believe I'll have another piece of your good fried chicken."

"Yes, Buck." Her mother passed the chicken and handed the tea pitcher to Mercy, her eyes icy with warning. "Pour yourself another glass, dear. You must be dehydrated. You don't seem to be thinking clearly tonight."

The judge raised his wine glass and waggled it. "Looks like Miss Mercy isn't the only one with an empty glass."

Mercy watched T. Wayne pour more wine, still frowning at her comments. Overton had won loyalty points with her family while she appeared to be thoughtless.

The interminable supper went on. Gloria told her favorite story about Sophia's baton twirling mishap at the Mid-South Fair. Overton recommended that T. Wayne meet with Able at the CJC without his lawyer present, to continue the appearance of cooperation. T. Wayne sank into a boozy haze while Overton told horrific tales of innocent men being prosecuted for the deaths of their wives.

No one asked for Mercy's opinion. She was dismissed from the conversation as if she were a child. She stared at the judge. Overton was playing to everyone's weaknesses. He was in charge, and he wanted her to know it. He caught her eye and grinned at her like a satisfied cat.

In the kitchen, she shoved dishes into the sink. T. Wayne and the judge had spent more time strategizing damage control than figuring out ways to find Sophia. T. showed no signs of grief or any sense of urgency.

Truth be told, Mercy wondered how she would feel if Sophia walked through the door at that very moment. More angry than relieved? She wasn't sure.

More than anything, she felt sickened by what she was learning about her family. Momma was more childish than ever. T. Wayne had a petty, sinister side he'd keep hidden all these years. Or had she not wanted to see the dark side of the only person she ever counted on?

Mercy wiped down the counters and headed outdoors with Caesar following behind. On a rise behind the turquoise-lit swimming pool shimmering in the dark, behind the lattice-covered cabana and the curving beds of bone-meal-fed roses, she found some sanctuary—a painted metal swing, a glide that creaked and sagged as she lowered herself until it swung smoothly back. She breathed in the night air, closed her eyes, and just rocked.

◈

Her mother's hand on her arm woke her. "Buck's gone home. I can't keep apologizing when you disappear from the table."

"Sorry, Momma. I needed to think."

"That'll get you into trouble." She patted Mercy's knee. "Scoot over, sugar, I have something to tell you."

She settled in beside Mercy as if it was the most natural thing, a mother and daughter enjoying an evening chat. Through the window they could see the TV blinking fluorescent greens and blues. T. Wayne slept in a club chair, dead to the world.

"How's your hand?" Mercy said.

"Never mind that, we have to talk about T. Wayne. You know he's a good man, but he's not strong."

"Now, Momma."

"Sophia is the strong one in a crisis. T. Wayne is worthless. I've seen this kind of behavior before."

"You mean with Casey?"

"He fell apart. You were at that boarding school studying for finals when it happened. I didn't tell you how badly Casey was hurt, because I was afraid you'd rush home and not take your tests. Then you wouldn't have gotten that Vanderbilt scholarship."

The truth is, you sent me to boarding school to get me out of the way, Mercy thought. *Then you downplayed Casey's injuries.*

"Casey was my nephew. You should've let me make the decision about coming home," Mercy said.

"But there was nothing you could do. And besides, I was so shook up, I didn't have good sense."

"Even after I came home for the funeral, none of you would tell me the details of what happened."

Gloria shook her head. "You don't understand. It was horrible. T. Wayne refused to come to the hospital after the first day. That baby laid in ICU for days. Sophia never left the hospital. She was crazy with grief. I thought we might lose them both."

Blaming Mother won't change things, she thought. *And now isn't the time to go into it.*

"I can't imagine T. letting Sophia and Casey down," Mercy said. "He worshipped that child."

"Men are funny. He talked tonight as if that Saudi deal means everything. He's in denial about Sophia. He can't face what's happening."

"I don't care. Sophia's in danger."

Her mother sighed. "We all handle heartbreak in our own way. I have to tell you though, this is almost too much for me."

"I'm here, Momma." She touched her mother's shoulder.

"Your life is in Atlanta. You've always hated coming home. I understand more than you realize."

In spite of the wine, her mother sounded sober, even thoughtful. "You said you had something to tell me."

"Buck asked me to marry him. I said yes. We're getting married on Thursday."

Mercy froze. A knot formed in her stomach. "Please tell me you're joking."

"He says we need each other now, more than ever. We want something simple. He has arranged for a civil ceremony at noon and a family luncheon at Powell's afterward."

A wedding in the middle of this crisis. The word *repulsive* sprang to Mercy's mind, along with a few others. She tried to sound calm. "How long have you known Judge Overton?"

"Your sister has known him for . . . I don't know, a long time. She introduced us five months ago at a party. We played a few hands of bridge. We were good partners."

"Five months. That's not long."

"Your father proposed after three. I was pregnant with Sophia a month after the wedding."

"But your families knew each other. There was never a question of background."

"Background! Your father grew up the son of a Mississippi cotton farmer. Buck is quality. His father was an Episcopalian scholar. His mother was D.A.R."

"His father was *what* kind of scholar?"

Her mother glared at her. "That's right, make fun. Buck has a wonderful reputation, and he's welcomed everywhere in Memphis. After your father died everyone who counts in this city forgot I existed. I raised you girls alone. It's my turn to have a life."

Mercy understood what it was like to be lonely, to feel excluded and invisible. But for Momma to marry a man she barely knew . . .

"Judge Overton claimed he's financially comfortable. Is that true?"

"Mercy! Nice people don't talk about money. Buck is a judge. He drives a new Cadillac and lives at the best address in Midtown. He loves me. That's all I need to know."

"So why would a man like that give up his independence?"

Gloria arched an eyebrow. "You're asking why a man like Buck would marry an old woman like me unless it's for money?"

"That's not fair."

"You should thank your lucky stars he's willing to have me."

"I don't want to see you hurt, Momma."

Her mother's pained expression was clear even in the darkness. "What if Sophia is dead? The light of my life will be stolen away. How could I be hurt any more than that?"

The light of her life. Sophia. "I hate to press the point, but I'm not sure this man's being honest with you."

Gloria heaved herself out of the swing. "If you want honest, I'll give you honest. You're upsetting me. If you'd stayed in Atlanta, I'd be talking to Sophia tonight instead of you. And let me tell you something. She'd be *happy* to know I'm marrying Buck."

Chapter Thirty-Four

Tuesday, 6:25 a.m.

The nightmares were killers. Snakes circling him, Lou screaming for help. Billy woke up, tangled in sweaty sheets, Lou's sarcasm buzzing in his head. When his mom drank, she'd say terrible things to him. The dream had been like that . . . a punch in the gut coming out of nowhere.

He dragged the pillow over his head. A week ago his biggest worry had been getting his swing back. Now Lou was dead. God, how many clues had he missed? How many bean balls had Lou thrown at his head, trying to get his attention?

A towboat blasted its horn. He rolled out of bed. Last night, to get his mind off the video of Lou, he and Jones had gone to The Rendezvous, a restaurant famous for its ribs. Jones distracted him with stories of TBI operations and screw-ups at the governor's mansion. They ate three orders of dry ribs, drank two pitchers of beer then switched to shots of whiskey. It seemed like a good idea at the time.

He stumbled barefoot through the galley onto the afterdeck. Humidity lay thick on the water, and the sun turned the shoreline platinum. A speedboat slapped past. The sound hurt his head. He hosed down the deck and swept it with a push broom. Then he swept it again. By the time he'd finished, his hangover had diminished.

The truth was, Lou's body was lying in a cold drawer at the morgue, and Billy no longer believed Sophia was coming home on her own. He had to find out what had happened to both of them.

◆

The back elevator doors slid open at the twelfth floor of the CJC. Billy stepped out and headed for his desk, noticing the place had a weird stillness about it. As he rounded the corner, he heard Lou's growl break the silence. *"Atta boy, fuck up some more. I got it all on tape."* His insides went cold. He'd left the disc in the player last night.

In the conference room, five people with coffee cups stood in a semi-circle around the screen. Lou yelled, *"Come on, come on, Billy boy, get a hit."* The camera panned to Smitty winding up for a pitch. Billy watched himself swing and heard Lou grunt as the foul clipped him.

"This oughtta be on YouTube," a uniformed cop hooted. He elbowed the guy next to him.

"Shut it off," Billy yelled. He pushed through the group to rip the disc from the player.

Having Jones see the video was bad enough. With these guys, he'd never hear the end of the jokes. Or worse, he'd never hear the jokes at all.

"Shit, man, we didn't know what it was," Barry from Maintenance said, grinning.

"Lou could be a real son-of-a-bitch," Smitty said. "Everybody knows it."

"Fuck you, Smitty," Billy said.

"Fuck you, Able," Smitty shot back. "Hey, maybe Lou was right. Maybe what you need is a good ass- kicking."

"Come on then," Billy said.

"Knock it off," a loud voice said. The group jerked around to see Director Mosby standing in the doorway. "We got felons loose on the streets. Go out and catch some."

Billy squinted at Smitty. "Later."

◆

It was a simple room, eight by eight with no windows, a beat-up metal table and three chairs, one with handcuffs dangling from the arm. A giant map of the city hung on the wall. On the door, the flip sign read "Interview in Progress."

Jones dropped a pile of reports on the table and sat opposite Billy. He didn't bring up last night's multiple shots of Jack, and he sure as hell didn't mention Lou's video. Jones was all about the job. Billy appreciated that. He scanned the canvass reports and saw nothing new until he got to the bottom of the pile. Jones had come up with a pertinent name and address.

"Miss Courtney Burdine," Jones said, "is a resident of Childress Place, a high-rise condo in Austin, Texas, financed by the SilverSpring Mortgage Company. Miss Burdine is single, early-thirties and a looker, according to the guard at the desk. The property is listed as a second residence for Mr. Dupree, not a rental." Jones grinned.

"Jackpot, we got us a bimbo hidden in the tall grass," Billy said. "Good work. A few more facts on the table and we'll nail the skunk with this later." He stretched, rubbed his face and noticed Jones studying him. "What?"

"You get decent sleep on that floating tub you call home?"

"Ol' Man River rocks me all night long."

"Looks like Ol' Man River kicked you in the head. You sure you're up for this interview with Dupree?"

"Like a kid at Christmas."

"All right, then." Jones flipped through the reports. "I see we've got a lot on paper, but it's all circumstantial. I'm wondering how hard we should push the man's buttons at this point."

"You know what this guy does?" Billy said.

"Senior V.P. at Zelware Corp. based in Austin. Closes big deals on food products shipped to the Balkans, Central Asia and the Middle East."

"He's a glorified salesman. You ever meet a salesman who could keep his mouth shut? Poke him with a stick; he'll give us what we want. Besides, he's used to running with the big dogs. Yesterday he acted like I was too stupid to live. Two cops in cheap suits won't look like much of a threat."

"Talk about your own bad jacket, leave mine out it." Jones shoved another stack of papers forward. "Here's Dupree's Louisiana record. It's compelling, but not easily admissible. He lied about booking a cruise on the *Pacific Dawn*. There's no ship registered under that name. Mrs. Dupree's visits to the ER could be considered spousal abuse or a good defense attorney could say she's a drunk who falls down a lot. I'm wondering; if we avoid bringing up the girlfriend in Texas, where's our leverage?"

Jones had proven he was a great researcher, Billy thought, *but he hadn't spent much time in an interview room.*

"Dupree's a weak man. He's done a bad thing. He knows it. *That's* our leverage."

Jones rolled his pen between his thumb and index finger. "So we're going to assume—"

"Assume nothing in this room. Know your facts when you walk in or you'll lose the upper hand. Here are some facts: Dupree is a foul-tempered son-of-a-bitch who beat his first wife so bad he could have gone to jail for it. He's responsible for the accident that killed his son, but he put the blame on his wife. He lied about the cruise, and he'll lie about hitting Sophia."

"The man was out of the country. And men buying hits on their wives are rare."

"There's a hot younger woman waiting for him in his Texas condo. That's reason enough for a lot of guys to do crazy things."

I don't know, man. I got a funny feeling about this."

"Funny feeling?"

"Yeah." Jones looked down at the reports on the desk.

A rap came at the door. Billy ignored it. "You going to help me knock the strut out of Dupree's walk?"

The rap was louder this time. Jones looked him in the eye. He nodded. "Let's do it."

The door opened, and Hollerith put his head in. His hair had been styled, and he wore a charcoal suit and a red tie that made him look more like a politician than middle management. "Dupree is upstairs shaking hands with the director. Tread lightly until we know where we're going with this one."

"Come again, sir?' Billy said.

Hollerith stepped into the room and gave Billy that look you give a kid who's about to act up in front of company. "Unless you have material evidence, I want you to interview Dupree as a family member of the victim, not a suspect." He looked around. "Maybe you should move out of this room. It sets a negative tone."

"We could take him to brunch and beat a confession out of him over eggs benedict," Billy said.

Jones bent forward as if organizing reports. "Ease up," he said under his breath.

"You're not hearing me," Hollerith said. "I want material evidence on this case."

"Yesterday you wanted the case closed," Billy said. "Now you're tying our hands."

"The Dupree woman has disappeared before. She could be a walk-away."

"I've covered hospitals, jails, her regular hangouts. This isn't her usual pattern."

"What about a random abduction? You look at that?"

"We're working that angle, sir," Jones said.

Hollerith switched to Jones. "I want you to act as liaison with Media Relations. Dupree will offer a reward of a hundred thousand dollars on tonight's six o'clock news. That kind of incentive may catch us a break. Since neither of you has worked as lead on a big case before, I want you to clear your moves with me."

Jones nodded.

"I don't work on a leash," Billy said.

Jones stared at him like he was crazy. Hollerith straightened his tie in the door's two-way glass panel. "Listen up, Able. Play it like I say it or you're out." He glanced down the hall. "Dupree's on his way here."

Hollerith ushered Dupree into the room. Billy noted the man's thousand-dollar suit and high-dollar alligator shoes. He wanted to send a message: *I've got the bucks, boys. You don't.*

"This is Detective Able and Agent Jones with the Tennessee Bureau of Investigation," Hollerith said. "They're collaborating on solving your wife's disappearance."

Dupree looked at Billy, ignoring Jones. "We've met."

"Can I get you anything? Coffee, a cold drink?" Hollerith said.

"Coffee, thanks," Dupree said and stepped to the city map on the wall, turning his back on everyone.

"I'll let you gentlemen get to work," Hollerith said.

Jones angled up beside Dupree and extended his hand. "Sorry we're meeting under such tough circumstances. Please, have a seat."

Jones gave Dupree the chair next to his, elbow to elbow. Billy sat across from them. He let Dupree make the first move.

"We had a misunderstanding yesterday, Officer Able." Dupree put his hands on the table.

"It's Detective Sergeant Able."

"Right. It's just that I was surprised . . . you in my house, sitting at my desk."

"I understand," Billy said, taking full measure of the man sitting in front of him. The scar he'd noticed on Dupree's forehead yesterday was more visible under the interview room's bright lights. Whatever happened had required stitches. He'd established a baseline on Dupree's eye movements the day before. Now he checked Dupree's breathing. The man appeared to be calm.

"I looked into your department's national ranking," Dupree said. "Top five for homicide case clearance seven years in a row."

"We do all right."

"Mercy told me about the death of your partner. Sorry to hear it."

Dupree's condolence surprised him. "Lou Nevers was the best cop in the city."

"Judge Overton agrees." Dupree paused. "So if he was the talent, won't his absence cripple this investigation?"

Billy smiled. All right, no surprise, Dupree was a bully. He pushed only when he thought the other person wouldn't push back. "I wouldn't worry about that, Mr. Dupree. Jones and I are very good at our jobs."

Dupree nodded. Wet his lips. Looked away.

"So let's get started," Jones said. "We'll appreciate anything you can tell us."

Dupree sat back, glancing around as if just noticing he was in a dingy interview room. "Whatever I can do to help out."

"First off," Billy said, "what do you know about your wife's disappearance?"

"What do I know? Not much. I was out of the country. You verified that with the airline, right? And I'm sure you're aware . . . well, Sophia has a drinking problem. She's done this sort of thing before."

Billy flipped through papers. "But her behavior doesn't follow her usual pattern. Your wife was expecting her sister's weekend visit. Her mother described Sophia as being organized, in good spirits. She ran a couple of errands and had a trunk-load of groceries . . . " He looked up at Dupree, raised his eyebrows.

"I heard a bag boy found her purse. You think he's involved?" Dupree said.

Typical perp move. Fishing for other suspects.

"We're not ruling out anyone," Jones said. He frowned, as if a question had just occurred to him. "Has your wife seemed upset or worried lately?"

"Are you asking if somebody was harassing her?"

Jones shrugged. "Was anyone?"

"Not that I know of, but something was up. She's been a real mess lately. Anxious, bitchy, worse than usual. Then she got the DUI. Actually, the trip to rehab turned out to be the best thing that's happened." He brightened. "Maybe her therapists have some answers."

"We called. They had nothing to add," Billy said, shutting down that avenue.

"All I know is she came home from rehab, talking about plans to redecorate," Dupree said. "She bought rolls of fabrics, drew up designs. I've been encouraging her to try new things. Thought this project would get her mind off the bottle."

Billy didn't buy it. Gloria Snow said the rolls of fabric were for a charity project. Her live-in mother would know if Sophia had plans to re-do the house. "You've got the decorator's name?"

"She wanted to deal directly with the wholesale workrooms. Said we'd save money if we cut out the middle man, especially if we paid cash. I gave her the deposit money the day I left."

"Yeah," Billy said. "I've heard those decorators are pretty expensive. Sounds like you made a smart move. But considering her past, I'm surprised you gave your wife that much cash."

"This was different. I thought the project was, you know, healthy, so I agreed."

"How much did you give her?"

Dupree's gaze shifted. One side of his mouth lifted. "I don't recall. I'll have to check my records."

"How about receipts or the names of the businesses she dealt with?" Jones said.

"She was just getting started when I left town," Dupree said.

Billy sat back, wondering why Dupree had brought up the fictitious decorating on his own, a stupid thing to do, unless Sophia had lied to him. Or he could be trying to establish a reason for a large amount of cash leaving his account?

"Would your wife come to you if she were in trouble?" Billy said.

"Honestly, I don't know anymore. Our marriage is . . . challenging."

"I guess the anniversary cruise was meant to patch things up."

Dupree ran his thumb down his jaw line. "I want to clear that up."

"You said you rebooked on the *Pacific Dawn*."

"No, I upgraded."

Jones flipped through his note pad. "I talked to your travel agent. She said there's no ship registered under the name *Pacific Dawn*, and that you told her you didn't plan to rebook."

"You talked to my travel agent?" Dupree blinked. "That's illegal . . . I mean, I changed agencies when I looked into rebooking."

"Could you give us that agent's name?" Jones's pen hovered over his notepad.

Dupree bristled. "I don't have to give you that information."

Billy stood, giving himself the advantage of height. "Your mother-in-law wants to find her daughter. Your sister-in-law wants to find her sister. We assume you want to find your wife . . . or were you tired of her, the way you got tired of your first wife?"

Dupree's head jerked back. "What?"

The door to the interview room swung open. A receptionist, new at the job and not realizing she shouldn't disrupt an interview, waltzed in carrying a Styrofoam cup of coffee. "For Mr. Dupree." She set the cup down, flashing Jones a big smile before she walked out.

The interruption gave Dupree enough time to get his feet under him. "Those records were sealed. Besides, that situation has nothing to do with Sophia's current . . . predicament."

Billy gave a short laugh. "You call your wife's disappearance a 'predicament'?"

Jones tapped his pen. "I think we should go back to—"

Billy continued, "I guess you want us to ignore those drunk and disorderly charges against you in Louisiana. And the assault charges brought by your buddies at the club. You must be pretty good with your fists. That explains your wife's four visits to the ER in the last two years."

Dupree glared at him. "My wife's a full-blown alcoholic. She gets drunk. She hurts herself."

"A broken arm. Admitted with cracked ribs and a punctured lung. She embarrassed you at a dinner party, ruined your promotion. So I'll just throw out a scenario. You're tired of dealing with an incurable drunk, but you know the court will be sympathetic toward a woman with your wife's history. Last thing you want is to give her a pile of cash. You make a few calls. You take a trip. She goes missing."

Dupree was red-faced and breathing hard. Billy hoped he would fold right there. Instead Dupree came out of the chair. He flattened his hands on the table.

"Something has bothered me since yesterday," Dupree said. "Now I know what it was. I remember you from ten years ago. You were in the hallway at ICU the day my son was admitted."

"You got it, buster. I was the first officer on the scene when your son accidentally shot himself."

"That boy's safety was Sophia's responsibility."

Billy leaned across the table into Dupree's face. He smelled liquor and saw the yellowing of liver damage creeping into Dupree's eyes. It was a mistake to take the interview in this direction, but he couldn't stop himself.

"You were responsible for leaving a loaded Glock where your son could reach it."

Jones cleared his throat. "We're off track, gentlemen."

Dupree rolled his shoulders back, seeming to regroup. "I remember something else. Gloria told me a young cop spent a lot of time hanging around my wife at the hospital." He pointed at Billy. "That was *you*."

Billy's focus telescoped down to Dupree's finger. He could snap it. He could lunge across the table and pound this guy pretty good before Jones could stop him. He'd get a lot of satisfaction out of that, but then he'd be in a cell instead of Dupree. He looked down at the full cup of coffee between them. He picked up a file and brushed it against the cup. Coffee flooded over the edge of the table onto Dupree's alligator shoes.

Dupree jumped back. "The fuck—you did that on purpose."

"Ah, Jesus," Jones said, and buried his head in his hands.

Billy slammed his fist down on the table. "Casey's death was your fault, but you put all the blame on your wife."

Dupree drew himself up. "Let me tell you something. It was my job to provide for my family. *I was doing my job* the day Casey died. And I was doing my job last Friday when Sophia disappeared. My wife's a sick woman. An uncontrollable woman. If I'd been there ten years ago or four days ago, it wouldn't have made a damned bit of difference."

He turned and walked out.

Chapter Thirty-Five

Tuesday, 11:20 a.m.

At breakfast, T. Wayne had asked Mercy to dress like money. He explained that his campaign contributions had wired him in politically, and that in Memphis, who you know and how you are perceived is what counts, especially when you're in trouble. He wanted her to look especially good for the TV cameras today. He said it was important. It was for Sophia.

His hand shook when he'd poured his coffee. Despite his rather self-aggrandizing explanation, she wondered if maybe she'd misjudged his sincerity the night before.

So she'd dressed like money. Her power suit. She knew the pencil skirt made her legs look long. The cut of the jacket revealed the right amount of cleavage to be sexy and still allowed her to be taken seriously. Mercy had bought the Carolina Herrera suit as an asset for her negotiations with a major food distributor over the licensing of her holiday pumpkin and chess pies. Wearing that suit had helped her close the deal she wanted: a three-year contract with the unilateral termination working in her direction.

She'd packed the suit on the chance Sophia was planning a special evening out. It gave her confidence.

Now she sat in the reception area of the downtown CJC, overdressed, flipping through old *Reader's Digests*. She wondered what was taking so long in the interview between T. Wayne and Detective Able. Overton had assured them the meeting would be brief and friendly. Then they were supposed to join the judge at noon for lunch to discuss the details of the reward offer.

Tired of waiting, she walked down a corridor and turned a corner. Two cops were coming toward her, hauling a foot-dragging Charles Chan between them. His thighs bulged out of polyester shorts, and the front of his Spiderman T shirt strained to contain his belly.

Charles spotted her. His features contorted. "Miz Mercy, I hurt myself," he blubbered, pointing to a red welt on his knee.

"You let him go," she called out to the cops.

Charles lunged toward her. "I wanna go home!"

"He's just scared, ma'am," one of the cops said. "Bumped his knee getting out of the car. We didn't cuff him or nothing."

The corridor turned hectic as a group of police academy recruits spilled out of the elevator, laughing and joking. In the midst of the confusion, T. Wayne banged out of a doorway and stalked toward her, his mouth pressed in a tight line.

"We're out of here." He stabbed his finger at the elevator.

"Don't leave me, Miz Mercy," Charles wailed, refusing to take another step.

"Where's Detective Able?" she said to T. Wayne over the noise. "I need to take care of Charles."

"Forget that asshole." T. stomped to the elevator and pushed buttons. From the whipped look on his face it was clear the interview had gone sour. Able must have gotten the upper hand.

She turned to see Able striding toward her. "What's Charles doing here?" she said.

"He's a material witness. Nice suit, by the way."

"Never mind my suit; we had an agreement. You promised he'd be okay."

"I said I'd do what I could. Besides, he's not in trouble." Able gave Charles the once over. "You're all right, aren't you, son? Look at me."

Charles cut his eyes at Able then threw out his chest, his manhood suddenly called into play. "Yeah, I'm okay."

"See?" Able said. "Officer Bob, take him down the hall. Buy him a Coke."

"Can Miz Mercy have a Coke too?" Charles snuffled.

"Maybe later. Go with Officer Bob. Get him to buy you a Snickers bar while he's at it."

"I'm calling a lawyer for him," Mercy said, controlling her voice.

"Can't imagine why."

"He's a child."

"He's not a child, and I brought him in here to confirm important information." He gave her a pointed look.

T. Wayne gestured at Charles' retreating backside. "You mean my wife's chances hinge on what some *moron* knows?"

Able smirked. "Depends on which moron you're talking about."

T. Wayne's face flushed with anger.

"Detective, if you want more information from Charles, you've blown it," Mercy said. "He's too upset to tell you anything."

Able smiled. "I'm not worried." He pointed at Dupree's forehead. "By the way, where did you get that scar?"

Dupree glowered. "That's none of your business." He stepped into the elevator. "I'm leaving," he said to Mercy. "If you want to help your sister instead of wasting time with this jacked-up yokel, you're leaving too." Mercy gave Able a troubled nod as she followed T. Wayne into the elevator.

◆

Mercy and T. Wayne walked the two blocks to Powell's, a landmark restaurant located next to the trolley line. Overton had told them to ask for

George—a jockey-sized man of indeterminate age with artful hands and an eye for tracking every server delivering a plate.

Powell's had large windows, deep booths, white tablecloths and fresh daisies on the table. The lunch menu included gumbo, fried chicken, chops and steaks, southern-cooked vegetables, and yeast rolls the size of small grapefruits served with pats of iced butter. For dessert you could order Mississippi mud pie, banana pudding, coconut cake or pound cake with homemade pecan ice cream and fudge sauce.

George seated them at the best table in the room, regularly reserved by Judge Overton at noon.

"Judge Overton will come through that door in one minute," George said. "He runs his court by the clock."

T. Wayne bumped the flat of his hand on the table. "I need a scotch on the rocks. Now."

"Remember, you have to make the reward offer," Mercy said.

"Afternoon, George." Overton slipped into his chair and smiled, meeting both their gazes.

He wore a seersucker suit and a sky blue shirt that set off his blue eyes. He appeared fit, certainly handsome. No wonder her mother tripped over herself to satisfy him.

"You won't believe what I've been through," T. Wayne grumbled. "Worst day of my life."

Overton ignored the comment and looked over the menu. "I'll order for us."

She glanced up, surprised by his presumption. "I'm sure I can find something."

"How about that scotch," T. Wayne said to George. The server remained motionless at the judge's side.

"Bring the gentleman a glass of chardonnay," Overton said. "And a mimosa with shaved ice and two cherries for the lady."

"Iced tea is fine for me, thanks," she said, keeping her tone pleasant, but she caught T. Wayne's warning look.

Overton spread his napkin on his lap before he spoke. "Son, you're on TV in a couple of hours. You need to keep a clear head."

"I need a drink," T. Wayne said.

The trolley rattled by the big picture windows. Downtown hadn't changed much since Mercy's move to Atlanta, but T. Wayne had. He'd become a heavy drinker.

She leveled a cool gaze at Overton. "T. told me you arranged the reward offer with Channel Seven and an interview with the *Commercial Appeal.* Last night you suggested we keep a low profile. What changed?"

"If your mother were missing, I'd do everything in my power to find her. I realized this isn't the time for a subtle strategy. T. Wayne should do what his heart tells him."

She couldn't tell if he was being honest. He didn't appear to love her mother, but he seemed to appreciate her. He enjoyed terrorizing T. Wayne, but was willing to go out on a limb to help him. He was manipulative, complex, and worst of all, he was about to become her stepfather.

George arrived with drinks and a basket of fragrant rolls.

"We'll have two New York strips, bloody, Caesar salads, fried okra, and chicken salad on wheat toast with extra mayonnaise on the side," Overton said. "And Annie's Mississippi Mud Pie all around."

Mercy had no appetite, and it angered her that Overton was taking charge. She said nothing.

"Speaking of pie, I'm looking forward to sampling your desserts," Overton said. "Your mother pitched a fit when you tossed out my serving."

Mercy focused on her hands resting on the table. "I don't serve that pie with ice cream."

"You're an artist in the kitchen, and I should have deferred." He laid his broad hand over hers.

"It was a difficult day for all of us." She slipped her hand out and took a roll.

"I thought that son-of-a-bitch Able was supposed to go easy today," T. Wayne broke in. "Didn't your guy talk to him?"

Irritation flicked across Overton's face. "What happened?"

"They questioned my travel agent. Can they do that without a warrant?"

"A detective's badge opens doors. Even ones it shouldn't."

"Able tried to bust my balls. He spilled coffee on my shoes, pretended it was an accident."

Overton suppressed a smile. "Did he mention other leads?"

"Hell, no. He brought up Sophia's trips to The Med. I can't figure out how he knew about the hospital visits; she always used a fake name and paid cash."

"The staff identified Sophia from a photograph," Mercy said. "They plan to call social services the next time she comes in with injuries."

"How do you know that?" Overton said.

"Detective Able said he talked to The Med staff yesterday."

"You should have mentioned it at dinner," Overton said.

"I wasn't included in the conversation," she shot back. "Able knows Sophia drinks and has accidents. I made it clear to him that I back T. Wayne one hundred percent." She said the words, but T. Wayne's behavior was beginning to cause serious doubt to creep in.

T. Wayne waved at George and held up his glass. A second glass of wine appeared. "Able was the first cop at Casey's accident. I didn't recognize him until this morning."

"Really," Overton frowned. "That's a problem. It means Able is already biased against you. Ah, here's the food. No, George, the chicken salad goes to the gentleman. The lady is having the steak."

"But . . . " she said.

"You haven't finished a plate of food in two days. You need your strength to help get your mother through this."

Mercy took a deep breath and picked up her fork, keeping in mind this was about Sophia, not food.

"He's biased?" T. Wayne stared at his sandwich. "Holy God, I'm done for. I need more wine. Bring the bottle, George."

"No more wine," Overton said. "Let me explain the nature of cops. The death of any child offends their moral code, but especially when firearms are involved. I guarantee your son's accident left a mark on Able. We have to factor that into our strategy." He cut his steak.

"But this is about Sophia, not Casey," Mercy said.

"Doesn't matter. Able will go after T. Wayne's past and anything else he can get his hands on to prove he's responsible for her disappearance. This situation is trickier than I realized."

T. Wayne took a bite of sandwich and glanced away.

"What do you mean by T. Wayne's past?" she said.

Overton shook his head. "Let's stay focused on the issues. Able was injured last weekend trying to rescue his partner. How did he appear during the interview?"

"Like a mean son-of-a-bitch," T. said. "Mercy, you've talked to him. What's your take?"

She shrugged. "He has a concussion. The side effects can be pretty severe."

The judge nodded. "That works in our favor. Given the right circumstances, he could be replaced, but I'd need time to work it out. My docket is overloaded and my private life is . . . unsettled."

Mercy put down her fork. "By private life, do you mean your sudden plans to marry my mother?"

"It's hard to protect your family while I'm outside of it. The sooner we're married, the more effective I'll be."

"You've only known each other five months."

Overton folded his napkin, radiating disapproval. "We had hoped for your blessing."

"I don't know, Buck. You think Gloria is up to a wedding in the middle of all this?"

Overton smiled. "She says if there was ever a time she needs me, it's now."

The statement jarred Mercy. "Mother told me that's what you said to *her*, not the other way around."

T. Wayne sighed loudly. "Who gives a damn. If they want to get married, and if adding Buck to our family helps put an end to this persecution, I say fine. As long as the cops focus on me, the real criminal is getting away." He turned back to Overton. "Can you sidetrack Able?"

"We're about to find out." Overton rose from his chair.

Able came to the table and extended his hand to Overton. "Saw you across the room, Your Honor. Ms. Snow, Mr. Dupree."

T. Wayne grunted.

"Pull up a chair," Overton said. "George, get the gentleman a glass of whatever he needs."

"Thanks, but I can't stay. I wanted to know if you'd like to say a few words at Lou's service tomorrow morning."

"I'm sorry, I have a case in summation, but I'd planned to send a representative. Mercy, would you be my stand-in?"

His casual toss stunned her. "I . . . excuse me? I really hate to leave Mother alone."

"I'll be at home tomorrow," T. Wayne mumbled. "I'll look after Gloria."

"So it's settled," Overton said. "By the way. Detective, I understand you gave my boy, here, a real going over this morning."

Able shrugged. "Routine questions. No big deal, right Mr. Dupree?"

Mercy rose. "Detective Able, may I have a word with you?" He was enjoying crowding T. Wayne, and she'd had her fill of pushy men today.

Able nodded. He led her to a side room. A platter with a double cheeseburger, home fries, an iced tea, and a chocolate shake covered the small tabletop. Apparently the detective's appetite had returned.

"Have a seat," he said.

"No thank you. I just want to know what happened to Charles."

Able picked up the iced tea. "Nothing *happened* to Charles."

"I promised him that if he gave me the shoe he'd be okay."

"He's fine, except for Dupree calling him a moron."

She felt herself flush. "I'm not in the mood to apologize for my brother-in-law. But he *was* upset."

"He needs to be upset. By the way, was Sophia planning to redecorate?"

"I don't know, and don't change the subject. There was a van parked beside her car on Friday night. You need to find those guys before you hang T. Wayne out to dry."

"We're covering every angle, but let me be clear, if Dupree hurt your sister, I'll get him."

"He's got his problems, but there's no way I'll believe he had anything to do with her disappearance. You're a mean man, Detective. You've been through a lot in the past couple of days. Maybe you shouldn't be handling this case."

"Well, this 'mean man' needs for you to step aside so Mr. Chan can sit and eat his cheeseburger."

She looked over her shoulder. Charles stood behind her, grinning and wearing a patrolman's hat.

Chapter Thirty-Six

Tuesday, 2:41 p.m.

Billy knew the best part of being on the team is getting to wear the hat. After Officer Bob had taken Charles to the break room to get a Coke, Billy rummaged through storage, looking for an old patrolman's hat. His idea had worked. Eating a Snickers bar and feeling like a member of the force, Charles quickly verified the information he'd given Mercy, even recalling Mississippi tags on the blue van. New details made the van lead more plausible.

After lunch he drove the kid home in a patrol car. When they turned onto his street, Charles rolled down the window and banged his hand on the door, hollering at his neighbors so they could see him in the front seat, riding in style.

I should have given Dupree a hat. Billy thought. *Maybe he'd have confessed.*

Truth be told, Dupree hadn't interviewed like a guilty man. For sure he acted guilty as hell about beating up Sophia, but his underlying frankness about her disappearance was surprising. The man had a bad attitude, didn't have his story straight, and had walked into every trap. He hadn't figured the angles.

Back at his desk, Billy considered whether the van Charles saw could have been used for a hired hit or a creep grabbing women out of parking lots. On the other hand, the van could've belonged to some guy picking up his Friday-night six pack.

He put Dupree and the van information in the back of his mind to percolate and picked up a note from Jones. It said Jones had put more lines in the water, and another batch of information should come in after five.

He checked his watch. Just enough time to take a look around Lou's house.

◈

Thunderheads were piled high behind the dilapidated duplex Lou had called home. When Lou bought the place after the divorce, it sounded like a step in the right direction, until Billy saw it. Lou had lived with Ruby in their spotless brick ranch for twenty years—not a leaf on the lawn, not a window that didn't sparkle. Lou's bachelor duplex had cheap siding, a dirt yard, and chain link fence. Lou had the balls to refer to it as an investment, a sign that even then his thinking was becoming skewed.

The porch steps creaked under Billy's weight. The same note he'd read two nights ago hung on the door. *Go Fish.* He opened his kit and folded the note into a paper bag.

The door key turned easily. The living room swam in cool air, empty except for a lawn chair, a TV, and a lamp made from a bronzed figure of a nude woman with a clock in her belly. The lamp sat on a cardboard liquor box in the corner of the room. He switched it on and traced his finger through dust on the woman's bosom. Nothing about this place seemed like Lou.

The window air conditioner clicked on. Cool air brushed his face. Suddenly, all he wanted to do was relax in the chair and forget about digging for answers he wasn't sure he wanted in the first place.

He shook off his lethargy and photographed the room. Then he moved to the kitchen.

The refrigerator contained Wonder Bread, Velveeta, and eggs past their expiration date. In the freezer he found two boxes of grape Popsicles. Under the sink were two bottles of Jack Daniels. Billy's first impulse was to hide the booze, but that was pointless. So far, no one had been shocked to learn Lou had been drinking again but him.

A *Memphis Chicks* mug stuffed with pencils sat on the kitchen table along with three textbooks: *Spelling and Grammar, Arithmetic and You,* and *History of Our World.* Inside, each book had been stamped *Property of Le Bonheur Hospital.*

Why Popsicles? Why school books? Maybe Lou had been tutoring a neighbor's kid, or could he have had a girlfriend with children? That would explain his absences, even on rainy weekends, when he claimed to be at the fishing camp. But why would Lou keep a girlfriend a secret? A woman with children would've been a good thing in Lou's life. Living alone in this place wasn't.

In the bathroom, the medicine cabinet held nothing of interest but a bottle of blue fingernail polish and prescription sleeping meds. He bagged both and moved on to the bedroom.

He opened the door, darkened by blackout drapes. The room had a creepy feel to it. He'd opened other bedroom doors to find bodies with their arms flung out in full rigor, blood blackened around a gunshot or knife wound, eyes glazed, tongue protruding. He flipped on the light to see a neatly made bed and a pile of clothes in a laundry basket. He walked an abbreviated grid around the bed and found nothing on the floor.

Lou's phone had disappeared, but his pager sat on the dresser. Billy scrolled through the calls. Many were unfamiliar numbers. One had the 7-3-7 tag, signaling the call was urgent. He remembered Lou had checked a page at the Tuggle's house and made a call—right before he threw the chair through the window. Billy wrote down that number.

In the closet he found Lou's service revolver wrapped in cloth. A lot of the older guys had never moved up to semi-automatics. He smelled Hoppes

No. 9 solvent. Lou must have taken the time to clean the gun on Saturday and then left it behind.

The bedside table held a phone, a notepad, and a book about Marilyn Monroe opened to a picture of her as a child posing in a bubble bath. Lou had a thing for Marilyn. On the pad, Lou had written Thursday's date, the number *662*, followed by the letter *L* then the letters *VS* stacked below it. Underneath the *VS*, he'd written something like "pig out" or "peg out." Six-six-two was a Mississippi area code. The letters looked like an abbreviation for Elvis. "LVS."

Billy sat down on the edge of the bed, thinking. Knowing Lou the way he did, putting together clues from this scene should've been a snap, but the crazy feel of this house and Lou's sarcasm on the video—it was like getting a lungful of bad air without knowing the source. He looked around. The camcorder was missing.

A knock at the front door startled him. He grabbed his kit and went to the living room. Reverend Stokes was waiting on the porch, looking shaky on his feet.

"Come in out of the heat," Billy said. "You look like you could use something cool to drink."

Stokes coughed. "Tap water's fine. I need to take a pill."

When Billy brought the water and a straight-backed chair from the kitchen, he noticed the way Stokes eyed the lamp of the nude woman and clock. "Did you ask the judge if he wanted to speak at the funeral?"

"Judge Overton can't attend. He has a case in summation tomorrow."

"No matter. Plenty of folks want to stand up for Brother Nevers. Had thirteen men offer to carry him to his resting place. Two are regulars at the jailhouse. Brother Nevers treated them with respect. They remember."

The air conditioner hummed, blanketing them in cool air.

"I came to look around . . . see where Lou had been living," Billy said.

Stokes heard the subtext. "Find what you came for?"

"No, sir. It's turning out to be a real mystery."

"I stopped by a number of evenings to check on Lou. Our brother was never at home. The Lord laid him on my heart, night after night. Sometimes I'd wake up so burdened I couldn't pray."

"Lou started drinking again. I found his stash."

Stokes pointed at the box under the lamp. "And there's that case of Cold Duck."

"It's a packing box. He never drank that sweet stuff."

"Box has a rip on the side. I can see the bottles."

Billy moved the lamp and popped open the flaps. Six bottles of Cold Duck sparkled in the low light. Less and less in this house made sense.

"Whiskey's not the devil here." Stokes frowned. "Brother Nevers' sorrows are over, but I worry about you picking up the sad trail he left behind."

Billy went over to squat in front of Stokes. "If you know something about Lou, it's important you tell me."

"I can only say this is a crime no man can put right." Stokes' mouth trembled. He looked down into the empty glass. "The Lord troubles me with dreams. Last night I found myself in a field of tall red stones. They seemed to be alive. I wondered where such a place was on Earth. The stones surrounded me, and I heard the moaning of the unrighteous from their graves. Their misery tore my heart and I fell to my knees." Stokes whispered, "I realized I was standing on defiled ground. Then a sword flew out of nowhere, and a voice said, 'Holy is Thy Name. Thy Name is holy.' I saw Brother Nevers running across the field, that sword chasing him. He threw up his hands, and quick as that, the sword cut off his head and hands. His head rolled until it came up against a stone. His mouth moved, and I heard the words. 'Forgive my degradation upon this Earth. Loose my soul.' And then Brother Nevers' eyes closed, and his hands melted like snow."

Tears streamed down the reverend's face. "I didn't sleep no more last night. No, sir."

Chapter Thirty-Seven

Tuesday, 4:18 p.m.

T. Wayne wheeled his BMW into the Sonic Drive-In and ordered root beer floats for himself and Mercy over the speaker box. A breeze had picked up while they were at the TV studio, so the heat was bearable. They got out of the car and waited for the floats under the covered patio. Except for a carload of teenagers who placed their order and left, they had the drive-in to themselves.

Mercy relaxed a little. She loved drive-ins. In high school she'd fantasized about cruising through the parking lot with a guy in a convertible, his arm around her shoulders. They would order root beer floats and she'd flirt. He would kiss her, not seeing the scar, only her. Except for a few uncomfortable dates with a football player named Judd, that fantasy made up the sum total of her high school love life, and was possibly the source of her craving for root beer.

T. Wayne took out a quarter and began flipping it over his knuckles, a trick he'd taught her when she was a kid. Focused on his own thoughts most of the day, he'd been oblivious to her silent fuming.

An hour earlier, they had taped the appeal for Sophia's return and offered the reward. When the cameras stopped, the reporter had asked some personal questions and T. Wayne went into a rage.

The entire day, T. Wayne had been borderline berserk. Mercy worried his temper would hurt Sophia's chances if he alienated the wrong people. They needed cooperation from everyone. Unfortunately, it was going to be her job to confront him.

A dreamy look came over T.'s face as he glanced up from the coin balanced between his knuckles. "When I was a kid in Baton Rouge, Tucker Stans and I hung out at a drive-in called Little Pigs. We watched the girls in their mini skirts flash their panties as they climbed out of their cars. Drove us nuts. Best double bacon cheeseburger. Best root beer ever." He sat quietly, his gaze following the traffic. "Tuck and me, we had it all. Now look at me."

My God, he's feeling sorry for himself, Mercy thought.

"Okay, T. You've got to get a grip," she said. "Alienating the media and police won't help find Sophia. We need everyone on our side."

His cheeks puffed out with anger, but then his face went slack. "I know I'm acting like a jerk, but when I was in front of that TV camera, it suddenly hit me. Sophia is dead, and I'm the most likely suspect. This is just the beginning of pressure from the police. It could go on for months."

Mercy's skin chilled. "Don't say that. Sophia's alive. We have to believe that. The reward will move the story to the front page. By tomorrow this will be big news."

A car horn blared. Three kids on skateboards shot across the street, hit the parking lot, and raced around the other side. He straightened. "You think CNN might run it? Because the people at Zelware keep up with CNN. I could have a problem."

She nearly exploded. "Forget your job. We're fighting for Sophia's life. I hope CNN *is* on our front step in the morning. We have to stay calm."

"I'm calm. I can handle it."

Oh right, she thought. *Like the way you handled it at the TV station.* "Able said we have to protect the investigation."

He threw her a heated look. "I'm not taking orders from Able. That son-of-a-bitch bent me over today."

"You want to talk about it?"

He shook his head. The carhop came with the drinks, beaming at T. Wayne as she set the cups on the table.

"Thanks, sweetheart," he said, and over-tipped her.

Mercy punched the ice cream down into the root beer. "At lunch, Overton mentioned your past. What *past?* You both avoided my question about it."

"Nothing to discuss. Buck enjoys playing games. By the way, I got in touch with my lawyer. I won't talk to Able again without him in the room."

Mercy wanted to shake him. "Stay with me on this. Can Able use something from your past against you?"

His jaw tightened. "I was pretty rowdy at college. I took a swing at a golfing buddy once. It wasn't my fault. He dropped the charges."

"Buck made it sound worse than that."

He slapped the table. "Stop needling me. They'll use anything. My wife is missing. That makes me ground zero for an investigation."

The kids on skateboards zipped through the patio. One grabbed a half-eaten burger off a nearby table.

"Hey, get out of here!" T. Wayne half stood and sloshed his float on the table. "Damn coons." He pivoted toward Mercy. "Put your handbag under the table; they might come back."

Mercy looked up at him, shocked. "I've never heard you talk like that before. What's wrong with you?"

He scowled at her. "Don't be naïve. They'll grab anything that's not nailed down. *Including my wife.*"

"You don't know that."

"You don't know either. Last January, a wanna-be gang-banger shot a woman in the head while she sat in her car in a department store parking lot. Murdered her for points. Two teenagers car-jacked another woman and her dog from an ice cream stand. They shot the dog, took the woman to a field, beat her and ran over her. Both boys were out on early release. What makes you think gangbangers didn't grab Sophia?"

"They could have . . . but the police are looking at you. If you have nothing to hide, you shouldn't be worried."

"You think I killed your sister?" His voice cracked.

"I know that you love Sophia. Otherwise, you would've divorced her years ago."

"Well, thanks for that."

"And you loved Casey."

His gaze grew distant. "More than my life."

"So I don't understand. Why would Detective Able be biased against you because of Casey's death?"

T. Wayne took a slow, deliberate drink. "You know what happened, right?"

"Momma and I talked about it last night, but I've never heard all the details. I guess I was in denial at the funeral. I should have pushed harder for answers. I'd like to know now."

He blew out a breath. "Casey found a gun in my study. He played with it and accidentally shot himself. The doctors said he'd never regain consciousness. I was pretty rough on Sophia. I accused her of drinking and letting him find the gun. A lot of people heard me. Able was probably one of them. I couldn't just stand around a hospital waiting for my son die, so I left and didn't come back."

"How could you put all the blame on Sophia?"

T. gave her a pained look. "Are you asking if it was my fault?"

"It's a reasonable question."

"I left the cabinet unlocked, and yes, the Glock was loaded. But that doesn't change the fact that Sophia was the one in charge. She was drunk. Must have been. She never admitted it."

"You're saying you were unaware she was drinking."

He looked at her a long moment. "I didn't know. I thought she was happy. I'd just started working for Zelware, and I was so caught up with the job I didn't paying enough attention to my family. Like Overton said, my gun, my fault."

Out of nowhere, the kids swooped by again. One circled the BMW, thumped the hood with his hand and raced off laughing. T. Wayne jumped to his feet. "Come back, you little shit!"

The waitress came running. "Go on now," she yelled after the boys, who were already disappearing into the traffic. "Sorry about that. They're not bad kids; they just get a little wild."

"They could be killers," T. snarled.

The waitress gaped at him. "What?"

"Let's go, Mercy Pie."

The day had been too long, and she'd seen too much. He jerked the car door open for her, but she stood there, not wanting to get in.

"Mercy, they're trying to lynch me for Sophia's disappearance. I need your support."

"I don't know what to think at this point."

"I've always been there for you. Remember that Christmas your freshman year at Vanderbilt? It snowed five inches in two hours. You thought you wouldn't make it home."

She nodded. "You drove six hours to get me."

"They closed the road behind us the whole way. You wanted to quit school. You couldn't admit you were having trouble dealing with all those new people. I told you I'd almost quit my freshman year for the same reason. You told me you felt better after that."

She wondered why he thought it was necessary to ask for her support. It made him seem guilty. "You've always been there for me. So what makes you think I won't be in your corner now?"

He looked down. "If they actually accuse me of being involved in your sister's disappearance, it might change how you feel."

"Look. If you tell the truth, we can deal with whatever comes next."

"What about your mother?"

"Overton is her future. She'll vote with him. Stay on his good side, and she'll be with you."

They got in the car. T. Wayne looked contrite, but calmer than she'd seen him all day.

"Just remember," she said. "You owe me big time. I ate that bloody steak at lunch for *you*."

He patted her hand, started the engine, and pulled out into traffic.

God, she thought. *I sure hope I'm right.*

Chapter Thirty-Eight

Tuesday, 5:10 p.m.

Billy left Lou's house, shaken by Stokes' dream. He understood how it felt to be haunted in your sleep. A couple of times a year he'd wake up in a cold sweat, tortured by memories of the worst night of his childhood—the night his mother died.

He remembered being asleep in his old bed at his mother's house. He could still hear her voice, low and angry, talking with his Uncle Kane in the next room. He remembered how he'd pulled the covers over his head to ward off the sound of her desperation. A child knows when his survival is at stake.

"Walk out on your boy, it'll rip your heart out," Kane had said.

"He's better off with you," Billy's mother had answered.

"Lila, please."

The door had slammed, and he heard their steps on the porch. He got out of bed by the light of the moon, after two days of freezing rain. He saw his mother walking toward the car, her body tilted under the weight of her suitcase. Her dark hair swung over the back of her coat, and she wore tight, shiny pants that were no good against the cold. He hit the window with his fist to make her turn around, but she kept walking and got behind the steering wheel without looking up. His uncle stood on the walk in his shirtsleeves and watched as the car backed out on the highway. He stood there long after she was gone, his arms hanging loose at his sides.

His uncle came back in and stood in the hall outside of Billy's room, the crack in the doorway showing him in a band of light. Billy knew his uncle was in love with his mother. Kane was still a young man then and shy, glancing at her only when her back was turned so she couldn't see the intensity on his face. But Lila was his brother's wife, and she'd never filed for divorce.

His uncle had stood at Billy's door a long time. Then he ran his hand over his hair and left. Billy remembered turning over in the cold sheets and crying himself to sleep.

It was still night when the banging on the front door woke him. Red lights in the front yard flashed across his bedroom walls. He pulled on his jeans and went into the living room, where his uncle stood at the door talking to a deputy. The deputy wore a black leather jacket and a gun. He held a pair of sheepskin gloves and switched them from hand to hand as he spoke. They stopped talking when Billy came into the room.

"Back to bed," his uncle said. "I'll handle this."

The next morning Billy found his uncle sitting at the kitchen table. Kane ran his hand over the stubble on his chin and nodded for Billy to take the chair across the table.

His uncle began to talk about black ice. He said no one could drive on it, especially not women. There'd been ice on the road outside of town last night. His mother had missed the curve and hit a tree head on. Kane looked away at the stove, then he looked out the window.

"Where's Momma?"

"Lila's gone."

Billy stared at the square of gray morning light on the floor and felt the emptiness of the house. He knew about death. His mother was in a place he couldn't go. He didn't know why she'd left or where she'd been going in the middle of the night.

After that, Billy never counted up the number of people who had walked out on him. He never asked himself why they did it, because he had no way of knowing. His father, his mother—they owed him the minimum of what a parent owes a child, and yet his father had disappeared without a word, as easily as transferring jobs, and his mother had driven off with no explanation. His uncle disowned him. Sophia walked back into a destructive marriage.

And Lou . . . what had Lou done?

◆

He'd been too wired to eat after Dupree's interview; in fact he felt like he hadn't eaten in days, so on the way back to the CJC he speed-dialed Domino's and picked up two pepperoni pizzas. He was carrying them down the hall when Hollerith stepped out of the washroom, drying his hands with a paper towel. He wondered if Hollerith had asked Jones about the Dupree interview. He'd counted on giving it his own spin, but Jones knew how to cover. He was a pro.

"How did it go with Dupree this morning?" Hollerith's voice gave nothing away.

"No problem."

The lieutenant's expression hardened. "I got a call. There *was* a damned problem. I've seen you put a rapist at ease by offering him a smoke and asking about his momma just to get him talking. But not with Dupree. You had to bust his balls."

"Not really."

"I say you did."

"If I did, he deserved it. We were catching him in lies."

"I gave you specific orders to go easy. On top of that, I'm told you have a history with these people."

He shrugged. He was expecting this. "My first day in uniform I was called to a scene. It was Dupree's son. He'd accidentally shot himself. What's your point?"

"It's simple. I want a photograph of Dupree with a smoking gun in his hand before we go for an indictment."

He knew where Hollerith was going with this. He wanted his departmental ass covered in every direction.

"I believe Dupree arranged a hit. To give you what you want, I'll have to find the guy he hired. That'll take time."

"You don't get it. Pressure is coming at me from all sides. I told you we need a quick arrest, and it needs to be solid." Hollerith took off his glasses, rubbed his eyes.

Something was wrong. A good investigator plugs information in as he goes along. That wasn't what Hollerith was asking him to do.

"Who called and complained about the investigation?" Billy said.

"None of your damned business, but I'll tell you somebody who *did* call—a reporter putting together a story claiming this department can't keep women safe in this town. If we screw up, that one issue could blow the mayor's re-election." Hollerith stabbed the top of the pizza boxes with his forefinger, almost knocking them to the floor. "If the mayor loses, I won't get what I want."

"What do you want?" he said.

"I want you doing your job. Not delivering pizza."

◆

Jones fished copies of Dupree's cell-phone bill from a stack of reports and handed them to Billy. "Most calls to his condo are on his cell. He talked to Courtney in Austin several times a day, sometimes in the middle of the night. The bill goes to the office. And look at these." Jones pointed out three highlighted numbers. "The first number is Jazzy's. It's on our Gang Task Force list."

"Dupree called that joint on State Street?"

"We've got a tap on Jazzy's. I'll have the tapes checked for Dupree. The other two calls are to The Lava Café in Baton Rouge. I smelled mob connections so I had a friend look into it. Theo Stans owned the place. He was a real piece of work, too smart and too well-connected to be indicted. He died a year ago and his son, Tucker, took over. He's following in daddy's footsteps."

"You're better than the FBI."

Jones grinned. "Dupree has accounts at three different banks, one in Austin. He's made two, ten thousand dollar cash withdrawals in the last two weeks. By the way, this guy is floating in cash."

Billy took a bite of pizza. "Not surprising. Sophia's Mercedes was worth sixty thousand, easy."

"I ran up some blind alleys on the life insurance until I realized he'd changed companies. He used an Austin account to pay one credit card and his insurance premium."

"Great work. I appreciate the way you've stepped up."

Jones nodded. "I'd like to wrap this up before the Bureau yanks me out of here. By the way, a guy driving a van made a try for a woman behind the Dixie Theatre. Grabbed her by the arm. She hit him with her purse."

"You get a description on the perp or the van?"

"It was too dark. The woman said she thought he was drunk."

Jones had put a lot of time in on the case. Billy felt bad about not being totally straight with him, but Jones was better off not knowing about his relationship with Sophia.

"Carson turned in his report on the bus drivers," Jones said. "He passed around Mrs. Dupree's picture. He came up with nothing."

Billy flipped through the rest of the paperwork. "What about this report on a van in Mississippi?"

"Besides Dupree, it's one of our strongest leads. Sheriff's office in Holly Springs reported a woman being dragged from her car at Duff's Dollar Store. A guy tried to yank her into his van through the cargo door. An army recruiter with a table set up in the parking lot broke it up."

"Anyone get plates or a description?"

"White guy, forty-something, no tags. The van was green."

"You think Charles could confuse green with blue?"

Jones took a swig of Dr. Pepper. "Your guess is better than mine. I'll stay with it, make it a priority. Maybe get you off Hollerith's shit list."

That was the difference between Jones and him—Billy didn't give a damn about Hollerith's opinion. Jones, on the other hand, always had his eye on the rear view mirror.

He glanced down at Patsy's inconclusive fingerprint report on Sophia's business card. They had a lot of information coming from a bunch of sources but nothing pointed in any one direction. There wasn't much he could do but go with his gut.

"By the way, did you talk with Hollerith about the Dupree interview?" Billy said.

Jones spewed his Dr. Pepper. "Oh *hell*, no. If I did that, I'd have to tell him the truth. Then we'd really be screwed."

Chapter Thirty-Nine

Tuesday, 7:58 p.m.

Billy unlocked the barge door, grabbed a beer from the fridge, turned on Channel Seven, and sat down on the sofa just as a photo of Sophia took over the screen. Her short, dark hair framed her delicate oval face, and her smile lit up the screen. The anchorman opened with details of her disappearance while the camera panned across the front of the swanky Dupree home. He described the couple's community involvement and ended with a stock shot of Zelware's headquarters in Austin.

Sex, money, power, and mystery. The story was a media bonanza for a slow week in August.

The camera switched back to the studio. Dupree, with Mercy standing beside him, gave a strong pitch for Sophia's return, almost convincing in its sincerity. Mercy looked steadily into the camera, giving Dupree a credibility he could never have achieved on his own. Toward the end, he slipped his arm around her shoulders in a gesture of solidarity. He closed his appeal with an offer of one hundred thousand dollars for information leading to the safe return of his wife.

The pair made media gold. Their sympathetic image could sway public opinion. And from the smug look on Dupree's face, he knew it.

As Hollerith predicted, the mayor made a statement following the report, condemning violence against women and promising stepped-up police action.

Billy clicked off the TV. So far, Media Relations had controlled leaks, but Mercy might be tempted to confide case details to her idiot brother-in-law. She hadn't spent a lot of time in Memphis since she'd grown up, so she probably had only seen him on his best behavior. She didn't know he would do anything, including divulge information, to get out from under scrutiny.

Feeling jittery, needing a task, Billy dug out his DVD player and connected it to the TV. He'd brought Lou's video of the baseball game home to watch in private. The meaning of the silver stars running down the spine of the case still eluded him. Maybe it was Lou's coding system. He loaded the disc but didn't hit Play. The last thing he wanted to hear tonight was Lou's voice. Tomorrow, after the funeral, he might have the heart to watch it.

He moved furniture and unpacked a few more boxes. By the time he'd finished, the light outside had faded, and the river looked satin brown and curved like the calf of a woman's leg. His new Jet Ski waited, gassed up and tied astern. He needed to run the river for a few minutes. Get his head straight. He dug into a bowl of loose change and rubber bands where he'd tossed the keys. Halfway out the door, the phone rang. The machine picked up.

"Detective Able, this is Judge Overton's office returning your call. He asks that you come by his home at eleven this evening. The Judge apologizes for the late hour."

Overton's quick response to his call surprised him. Billy threw the keys back in the bowl and picked up his notes about Lou. He wanted to work back from their face-off in the parking lot to Lou's first cup of coffee that morning. And he wanted to ask Overton why his phone number had been on Lou's pager.

Billy had questions. He hoped Judge Overton had answers.

◆

The neighborhood association of Belvedere Boulevard, an upscale area in Midtown Memphis, quiet and lined with large trees, had petitioned the city to keep their old-style street lamps rather than replace them with high pressure sodium lights. Billy parked in the soft pool of light in front of the judge's home. The two-story stone house, with its granite steps and deep porch, looked intimidating. A whiff of mossy bricks came to him as he rang the bell. Beveled glass panels flanked the door and allowed him to see the elderly woman in a loose housedress coming down the hall to peer at him. It was nearly eleven o'clock at night. He wondered why someone her age was up so late.

She opened the door a crack. "Yes?"

"Sorry for the late hour. I'm Detective Able. I have an appointment with the judge."

She frowned. "His Honor needs his rest."

"Yes, ma'am. This was his idea."

She pursed her lips, but stepped back to let him in. She wore an apron over the housedress and pink leather slippers with the side cut out of the right one to accommodate a bunion.

"Wait here. And don't touch anything." She waddled down the hall, carpeted in Oriental runners that silenced her steps.

A door to Billy's right opened into a study with a carved desk sitting in front of a wall of leather-bound law books. He stepped in to examine photographs on the mantel—pictures of Overton in Washington D.C. shaking hands with the Vice President, another of him seated at a forum with two past governors and Overton in a horseshow winner's circle sitting astride a Tennessee Walking Horse, holding a silver trophy.

He eased back into the entry. On a chest, fresh gardenias floated in a crystal bowl. Beside it was a sterling tray for collecting visitors' calling cards. This was a respectable home of the old South. It smelled of rubbed mahogany, flowers and integrity—not the usual aromas a cop runs into this time of night. His questions for the judge seemed out of place, which somehow made the answers even more important.

The woman returned and led him through a tiled solarium and French doors to a garden with a pool and a shadowy, open-air cabana. Judge Overton waited in a fan-backed chair, wrapped in a dark robe, his hair wet and slicked back. A Siamese cat was sitting on the ottoman beside his bare feet. A ceiling fan swirled the faint aromas of mildew and tobacco.

Overton took a slow draw on a cigarette. "Welcome to my retreat, Detective."

"Evening, Judge."

Overton removed his feet from the ottoman. "Have a seat. Just push the cat on the floor. Get down, Taboo. Bad cat."

Billy didn't want to sit at the judge's feet. He angled the ottoman away to create space then sat. "I appreciate you seeing me so quickly."

"So tell me, what's on your mind?"

"Something I need to clear up."

Overton held up a hand. "No apology necessary. Hollerith said you'd go easy on Dupree unless the situation gave you a reason to pressure him."

"I'm not here to apologize."

The judge drew on the cigarette and blew the smoke toward the ceiling. "Cigarette?"

"No thanks. Sir. It's about Lou. I went to his house—"

Overton interrupted by pointing to the housekeeper hovering in the doorway. "What'll you have, Detective? Scotch, maybe a beer?"

"Nothing, thanks, ma'am."

"Some of Mary's good lemonade? I insist."

In the dim light Billy couldn't read Overton's expression. The judge was doing everything possible to control the conversation. Billy decided to play along. "All right, lemonade."

Overton dismissed her with a wave. "Now, Detective, you were saying?"

"I went to his house and found his pager. I scrolled through the memory and saw your number listed on last Thursday and a second page on Saturday."

"And?" The judge flicked ashes into an ashtray balanced on the chair's arm.

"I'm curious about your conversations."

"Are you now?" The judge inhaled deeply. "Gardenias. Nothing like their fragrance on a summer night. There's an Arabic proverb, let me see if I can quote it . . . 'If two loaves of bread are all you possess, sell one loaf and buy flowers to feed your soul.' How do you think Lou's soul is doing tonight?"

Billy shrugged, irritated. *Pretentious prick was ducking the question.* "I don't know. Sir."

"Lou was a troubled man. I bumped into him at the courthouse last week. He looked exhausted. I was concerned, so I called him. By the way, did you find anything else of interest at his house?"

Distracted, Billy shook his head. "I've been thinking over our conversation at The Western. You said you and Lou go way back. I wondered how you became tight with a flatfoot like Lou."

"Interesting story. But excuse me a moment." Overton got up from his chair, went to a bank of switches, and flipped on the pool lights. "No reason for us to sit in the dark." He picked the cat up and settled back in the chair.

"If Lou has told you this story, indulge me. When I was with the D.A.'s office, I prosecuted a man named Paley for robbery. The evidence was circumstantial, but I convinced the jury. Paley was convicted. Later, another man confessed. That's the way it breaks, sometimes.

"After Paley was released he showed up at the courthouse one day. Lou happened to be testifying in a fraud case. Lou spotted the guy. Didn't like his looks. He followed him into my courtroom, grabbed him twenty feet from my bench. No metal detectors back then. Anyone could walk into the courtroom with a weapon. Paley had a grenade."

"Jesus," Billy said.

"I owe Lou my life. It's a longstanding debt. I called him Thursday night because I suspected he was drinking again, and I wanted to encourage him to get help. He denied it, of course."

Mary returned with the lemonade. Billy accepted the glass and took a long drink. "You used the 7-3-7 code on his pager last Saturday."

"Gloria was hysterical when she phoned about Sophia's disappearance. Naturally, I wanted Lou to take over. He's the best. I spoke with Hollerith, and then paged Lou using the code. He called back, started yelling then hung up. Hollerith called and said Lou would be handling the case. The next morning I learned about the accident." Overton frowned and stroked the cat's head. "I should've called Lou back. I'll always regret that I didn't."

Billy let the silence stretch. "After you talked with Lou he threw a chair through a plate glass window. He told me your call was bad news. That doesn't square with your version."

"Let's get something straight. I called Lou, because I needed his help. I don't know why he blew up."

"No bad news?"

Overton stubbed out his cigarette, his voice taking on a nasty edge. "I'm told Lou took a shot at you in a parking lot. Sounds to me like *you* were the bad news."

"In twelve hours, Lou went from depressed, to demented, to dead. Your call triggered some part of that. I'm going to figure out why, no matter who I piss off."

The night was still. Overton lit another cigarette.

"Son, Lou drove off a bridge in a storm. You nearly died trying to save him. There's nothing you can do about that."

"Lou was my responsibility. A man named Paley came after you with a grenade. Maybe somebody came after Lou."

"Are you trying to open a file?"

Billy hesitated, wondering how candid he should be with the judge. "I'm doing the legwork, but Hollerith won't back it."

"Not surprising. Dexter listed heart attack as cause of death. Besides, Lou drank enough that night to kill a mule."

"His heart may have killed him, but I believe someone else put the truck in the water." A chill hit Billy. He closed his eyes. He was in the water again, trying to hold onto Lou's arm.

"Able. You okay?"

He opened his eyes. "I was angry with Lou. If I'd gone after him sooner, I might have saved him."

Overton wet his lips. "That's guilt talking, son. Let it go. I understand your wanting to look into Lou's death, but there's a missing woman out there now who needs your help."

"I know. This is about priorities. And from what I've seen, the evidence will lead us right back to her husband."

"You have what you need to hand the case over to the D.A.?"

"We're getting there." He drained the glass, set it on the tiled floor, and stood. His head was throbbing and his snake-bit arm burned, making it hard to think. Maybe some of that cottonmouth venom had gotten into his bloodstream after all.

Overton stood and put his hand on Billy's shoulder. "Just keep your perspective. I trust you to do the right thing."

Billy shook his head. "You may be the only one."

◈

After the detective left, Buck finished his cigarette and shut off the pool lights. Mary's bedroom light was out so he dropped his robe, walked naked around the pool and into the house, where he poured himself three fingers of a good, single malt scotch. Upstairs he found she'd remade the bed with fresh, eight-hundred-count Egyptian cotton sheets and turned back the covers. He slipped in and exhaled.

The meeting had gone pretty much as he'd planned, except for the moment he had to pull that grenade story out of the air. Able's question about his connection to Lou had caught him off-guard. At least the story backed up his phony sense of obligation to Lou. If Able were smart, he'd look into it, but that wasn't going to happen. The story reinforced his hero worship of Lou. And Able was too busy investigating Dupree to check it out.

Buck took a swallow of scotch in the soft light of his beside lamp and replayed his last phone conversation with Lou. Damned shame Able overheard part of it, but then the boy made up for it by showing his cards. Able had searched Lou's house and found nothing of interest except the pager. Good to know. All Buck had to do now was play smart defense. That Mississippi peckerwood wasn't cunning enough to sandbag him. Able's face had gone white when Buck brought up Lou's truck going into the water.

Able felt guilty for not saving Lou. Guilt would make him damned easy to manipulate.

Buck tossed back the last of the scotch, hardly tasting it. Curious that Able thought he had his teeth into some kind of evidence against Dupree. A couple of months ago, Sophia had confided she thought Dupree was having an affair and hiding assets with divorce in mind. Buck would love to see Able pin Dupree with Sophia's death, but, unfortunately, he had to get the idiot out of the detective's crosshairs instead. Having his new wife's son-in-law tried for murder could be a big problem in Buck's confirmation process. No senator would bring it up in public, but they might use it to vote against him.

Bottom line? He had to get Able off the Dupree case and away from Gloria and Mercy. He'd do it, and the boy would never see it coming.

◆

Billy left the judge's house too keyed up to go back to the barge. He cruised Riverside Drive with the windows down while he played the conversation back in his head.

Overton had a serious line of bullshit going, a hustler of the first water. The grenade story seemed manufactured and at the same time believable. But spotting the guy at the courthouse and grabbing him from behind—that sounded like something Lou would do. Lou had never mentioned the incident, but then he'd never said anything about Ruby losing a baby either.

Overton hadn't cleared up the question about the pages or the phone calls.

Billy might have let the question slide, but he'd picked up on Overton's mind racing the entire time they'd talked. The judge probably thought he wouldn't notice. Men like Overton assume everybody else is a nitwit. Yep, there was something going on with the judge. Overton had tried to control the tone of Dupree's interview and had probably been the one who called to complain about it being too aggressive. Then tonight he'd offered his personal backing for the investigation into Dupree's involvement. Overton was playing both sides. Eventually, his motives would surface.

Billy took Highway 61 and followed the river across the state line into Mississippi. He drove to the Twinkle Town Airport, a tiny airstrip. It was closed. He parked on the darkened field, climbed out and leaned against the car, the highway behind him empty of traffic. The Delta lay flat as a river rock and ran three hundred miles to Natchez. The glow from Memphis lit the horizon, curving around him in a giant arc.

He tried to picture Christ in his heaven and wondered if life would really balance out in the end. He'd heard that sentiment repeated by people who were desperate for comfort while they struggled to reconcile a loss, but he didn't buy their cosmic scale of justice. Not after all he'd seen as a cop and the loss he'd endured in his own life. The only justice he knew required facing the truth.

Herefords bustled in a pen across the road. He smelled their dung and the gasoline from the crop-dusters tied down in the field. He wasn't alone. The quiet night stood by his shoulder.

The fact was, Lou had been his responsibility. What the judge said about guilt didn't matter. Lou died because Billy didn't have the backbone to stop him in the parking lot. He handed the keys to Lou, something he would never have done if Lou had been drunk. He didn't stop Lou, and he chose to put off driving to the fishing camp to check on him. That hour would have made all the difference.

Starlight reflected off the wings of the small planes around him. He knew he'd made the decision out of pride and anger. He could never take it back. Now Lou's funeral was tomorrow.

Billy fell to his knees.

The night sky above him seemed to roll on forever.

Chapter Forty

Wednesday, 7:52 a.m.

Dr. Jimmy Dale Dexter got up before sunrise, fed the Charolais and showered. His sweet Evie had spent the last two days at their daughter's house, nursing the grandkids, all of them down with the chicken pox at the same time. Her bedroom door was closed, which meant she was still sleeping. Evie wasn't in the best shape. A woman with congestive heart failure can only do so much.

He ate eggs and cantaloupe for breakfast and checked with the clinic. Then he went upstairs to put on his jacket, his best Stetson hat, and the belt with the buckle Evie had commissioned for their twentieth anniversary.

She'd carried a photograph of a mammoth oak tree to a jeweler in Little Rock and asked him to cast a likeness in gold, adding the word "Forever" on the back. They named their farm Oak Hill after the lone tree that had stood for years on a rise at the front of the property. The tree had been a symbol of their future. Evie was the love of his life. That buckle was his favorite possession in the world.

He got in his truck and headed out Highway 40 with the windows rolled down and the air blowing off the soybean fields. He was driving to his oldest friend's funeral, a man he'd assumed would outlive them all.

He had one stop to make before the service.

◈

The young man sitting behind the counter at the Child Services reception desk wore a yellow, short sleeve shirt, a bow tie, and his brown hair parted down the center and tucked behind his ears. The skin on his arms was as white and smooth as a woman's. The young man studied Dr. Jimmy's coroner's ID and clinic license through glasses with rhinestones in the corners of their black frames.

"She's six," Dr. Jimmy continued, "lots of curly blond hair, green eyes. A beautiful child. Rebecca Jane is her given name. I don't have her family name or contact information."

"Your clinic doesn't have a file on her?"

"A friend brought her in the week of that E. coli outbreak. I worked her in-between patients. Never had any paperwork on her. Point is, I want to follow up and make sure she's okay."

"So call your friend."

"Can't do it. He died unexpectedly."

"What about your friend's family? They don't know how to find a relative?"

He took off his Stetson. "My friend and the child weren't related. It's complicated."

The young man waggled his pen in the air. "Do you want to file an abuse complaint?"

"I'm not saying she was abused, but I need to find her. I hoped she was in one of your programs and a caseworker could identify her." Dr. Jimmy wasn't about to discuss his real concern. He had no proof, just a feeling.

The young man handed back the ID. "Speak to Sammie in records. She'll schedule an appointment, although she's on break right now. She'll be back in thirty minutes."

"I'm under some time pressure," he began.

The phone rang. The young man answered and pointed down the hall, indicating their conversation was over.

The nameplate on the counter read *Stuart Wright*. Dr. Jimmy wanted to give ol' Stu a lesson in manners, but that wouldn't get him anywhere. He waited until the phone conversation ended. "I'd like to speak with a caseworker now."

Stuart took a swig of Mountain Dew. "They're in a staff meeting. You'll need an appointment."

"You're not listening. She came in with a bad respiratory infection. She could relapse without anyone noticing."

"A quarter of the kids in this city are poor and a lot of them are sick. All you have is someone who might get sick. With our caseload, that's not going to get immediate attention."

"And what *would* get your attention?" he said.

"Sexual abuse or beatings. That's why I asked you about abuse."

The phone rang. This time Dr. Jimmy grabbed up the receiver and held it. "This child's parents don't give a damn about her. I'll do the legwork to find the girl, but I need help getting started."

Stuart reached up and took the receiver. "Call back, please." He hung up and punched all the lines on hold. "Dr. Dexter, I've been in this business a long time. People come here with all kinds of stories. They don't necessarily have a child's best interest at heart, if you know what I mean."

"That's not my problem. I'm a doctor and I'm looking for a patient. Now are you going to help me?"

Stuart leaned back in his chair. "You think she's indigent?"

"All her life."

"Was she ever hospitalized?"

"At some point she had pneumonia."

"People with no resources carry their kids to Le Bonheur when they get sick. Deb Moore signs off on those admissions. You should start with her."

Dr. Jimmy checked his watch. Just enough time to make the funeral. "I'll give Ms. Moore a call this afternoon."

"She's leaving town at noon. If you want to see her, I'll call and tell her you're on your way."

◆

Deb Moore, Special Needs Coordinator for Le Bonheur, sat waiting for him in the lobby of the hospital with the strap of her garment bag looped over her shoulder.

She looked fragile and tired. Fighting for needy people is exhausting work. She rose to her feet as he approached.

"Dr. Dexter, it's an honor. I'm familiar with your clinic. I wish more doctors would put themselves on the battle line. Stuart gave me some background on the girl you're looking for."

"He's very protective of the kids in the system."

"He has the unique perspective of having been one of them. He knows what can happen." She pulled out a folder. "I searched our files and came up with the name Rebecca Jane Belleflower. Here's her picture."

The photo showed a very sick Rebecca. "That's the girl."

"Her parents brought her in. Karen and Fred Belleflower. She was dirty, slightly undernourished. No overt signs of abuse. We treated her for pneumonia. Here's the address they gave. It's probably not current."

"You have amazing recall, Ms. Moore."

"She was an unforgettable child. Tons of charisma. A child that pretty should be in the movies."

◆

Billy woke up late, showered, buffed his shoes and put on his best suit. He could see in the mirror that he still looked like hell. He didn't eat. He didn't want to think. On the gangway he picked up the paper and glanced at the headline:

SENATOR NOEL LEADS COALITION ON GANG VIOLENCE

He threw the paper on the passenger's seat. So far he felt pretty calm for a man heading to his best friend's funeral.

He watched the hearse pull to the back of The Holy Saints in Christ Our Redeemer Church which was downtown off Beale Street. They unloaded the casket and wheeled it into the sanctuary crowded with American flags and mourners. He saw rows of cops in blue, politicians, family members of victims for whom Lou had won justice, hookers, retired strippers, and cleaned-up addicts who had come to show their respect. Mosby and Hollerith, in full-dress uniform, sat with as many members of the squad as could be spared. He saw Mercy Snow come in and sit in the back.

Ruby held a seat for him. She looked shrunken and sad, sitting in the pew. She and Lou had been married a long time. Billy clasped her hand and looked around. Dexter, Lou's oldest friend, was a no-show. What the hell was that about?

The other night at The Western, Dexter had insisted Lou felt guilty about something, even hated himself. What a bunch of psychobabble. Lou was guilty of being a cranky old fart and drinking too much. He was guilty of acting like a crazed bull for the last year, but Lou had never felt guilty about one damned thing his whole life. Dexter's fixation on suicide had offended Billy to the bone. On top of that, his coroner's ruling had made talking Hollerith into an investigation impossible. That had really pissed Billy off.

The service opened with the thirty-member choir, decked out in purple robes trimmed in gold, singing *Rock of Ages*. Reverend Stokes preached on the mercy and grace of Jesus. People took the pulpit and spoke on behalf of Lou's life. Some cried, a few told funny stories. Then the choir swayed down the aisle behind the casket singing, *It Is Well with My Soul*.

Billy took a deep breath and joined the other pallbearers.

◆

The aroma of Southern funeral food pulled Billy through Ruby Nevers' front door: pineapple casserole, smoked ham with hot pepper jelly and cheese biscuits, bing cherry Coca-Cola salad, barbequed turkey, fried chicken, tomato aspic, deviled eggs made with mustard and onions, homemade pimiento cheese, six different kinds of pies, and a triple layer coconut cake. The food covered the dining table, a sideboard and two card tables. Someone shoved a cup of punch in Billy's hand. He realized he was hungry. Just as he settled on the sofa with a plate, he saw Dexter at the door, kissing Ruby on the cheek.

I'll be damned, he thought. *The guy shows up late wearing a cowboy hat. What kind of show of respect is that?* He set his plate on the coffee table. Ruby pointed in his direction and he stood as they approached.

Dexter extended his hand. Billy ignored it. "Mind if we step out on the porch?" Billy said.

"Ruby, I'll get with you in a minute," Dexter said. "Save a piece of that sweet potato pie for me."

Outside, Billy got right to the point. "Nice of you to show up for the food. Too bad you skipped the funeral."

"I had a reason," Dexter said.

"I don't give a damn. A miss is a miss."

Dexter leaned back against the railing. "I was a good friend to Lou, including best man at his wedding, so get off my case."

"Then be a friend and don't repeat your suicide theory to Ruby. This day is hard enough without shaking her faith in Lou."

Dexter's eyes narrowed. "What kind of rock do you think I crawled out from under? I'm not here to upset the woman. You're the one upsetting her, calling me out here with that murdering look on your face. What's she going to think?"

"She thinks her ex-husband died in an accident. I want it to stay that way."

"Ruby knew Lou was in bad shape. She's peeking through the curtains at us right now. Put a smile on your face."

They both put on frozen grins and waved at Ruby. Billy turned his back to the window so Ruby couldn't see him. He wasn't finished with Dexter.

"Have you gotten results from Lou's tests?"

"Nothing conclusive."

"The other night you hinted there was something in Lou's life he couldn't live with. What was that about?"

Dexter squinted off the porch. "Make it what you want. Lou downed a fifth of whiskey, popped off the door handles and hit the gas pedal. He had his reasons."

"And you're willing to let it go at that."

"Son, Lou was capable of mistakes just like the rest of us. If you don't see that now, you probably never will."

"That's bullshit."

Ruby opened the screen door. "Jimmy, Aunt Bertha brought her apricot pound cake. Come get a plate."

Dexter drew her out onto the porch. "Thanks, but I need to get back to the clinic. I wanted to come by and offer my respects. I loved Lou like a brother. They broke the mold when they made him. I'll stop by for coffee some time this week, I promise." He started down the steps then looked over his shoulder. "Able, I hope you find some peace."

Ruby put her hands on her hips and watched him go. "Billy, I'm surprised. That's not like you to use profanity. Jimmy was white as a sheet. What did you say to him?"

"Doc and I have a running disagreement."

"Over Lou?"

"Something like that."

"I know all about Lou. Come with me."

Ruby grabbed a glass of wine as she led him to her bedroom at the back of the house, the only place people hadn't settled with a plate of food. In her wedding photos, Ruby had been a brunette stunner. The years had dulled her hair and put inches on her hips, but the showgirl walk was still there.

In the bedroom, display cases stuffed with booty from the Home Shopping Network lined the walls. Lou said one time, that her shopping nearly broke him: porcelain baby dolls, Hummel figurines, handmade baby quilts, tatted infant clothing. He must have worshiped Ruby to pay for all of it.

Ruby offered Billy a chair, took a seat on the bed and tossed back half the glass of wine. "I have a question for you. Were you angry with your momma for dying?"

"I never thought about it. Why?"

"I'm so mad at Lou I could kill him." She punched the mattress, and tears glittered in her eyes. "Look at me. Look at this house. We're both falling apart. I didn't want the divorce, but he couldn't forgive me."

Billy stared at her, baffled. "You?"

"I met a salesman at Carpet World when we put that wall-to-wall plush in the living room. We had an affair. Lou caught us. It broke his heart." She sobbed. "I could just strangle him."

"I'm not following you."

"For dying, leaving me broke. I got the house and a little alimony. Lou got the insurance. He cashed it in. It's all gone, and I don't have a claim on his pension." She wiped her eyes. "This place needs a new furnace and I need a tummy tuck. I can't make it without Lou's check. Mom's having a second childhood. She's taking rumba lessons. My inheritance won't come through for years."

"Lou was always careful with money," he said, remembering the overtime Lou had insisted they put in. "That duplex he bought was cheap. How could he be broke?"

"My girlfriend at the credit union ran a check. He charged up to his limit on three cards and was behind two mortgage payments on that slum he was living in. I drove by the other night, feeling lonely. You think he had a girlfriend?" She pressed her fingers to her lips. "Sorry. I shouldn't ask."

"He never mentioned anyone."

She nodded. "I thought he was running around when he worked with Sam. I'd had a disappointment. I spent money, ran up some big bills. Lou told me he was working overtime, but Sam would call looking for him. They always worked together."

"Maybe Lou took a second job."

"I asked, but he would just cut me off. Lou was a complex man."

Laughter rolled down the hall, followed by the clink of glasses. A toast to Lou. Billy had questions, but everything he wanted to know would upset Ruby.

"I'm still looking into what happened Saturday night," he said in a neutral voice.

"I see." She took a breath. "That's why you and Jimmy were fighting on the porch."

She went to the mirror over the dresser and watched him while she ran a brush through her hair. "Jimmy believes Lou committed suicide."

"He told you that?"

"He didn't have to. We both knew Lou had a shadow inside. He worked hard to hide it, especially from you."

Billy stood, feeling like a traitor for talking about Lou when they'd just put him in the ground an hour earlier. "Lou never let me down. If you know anything about his death, you need to tell me."

She leaned against the dresser, studying his face. "Cops are smart about criminals, but they don't see the truth about the people they love. None of us really knew Lou."

"I can't accept that."

She came over, put her hand on his cheek. It smelled like mint. "Lou's things are coming to me. If there's anything you want, you let me know."

Gently, he removed her hand. "Lou had a camcorder. It's not in his car or at the house. I wondered if you picked it up."

"I haven't seen it, but if I run across it, it's yours."

That wasn't the reason for his question, but he left it at that.

"I am curious about something else. Did Lou come by on Saturday to talk to you?"

"On Saturdays he visited Tutwiler Jackson at Grimes Nursing Home. Do you know Tut?"

Billy shook his head.

"Old court bailiff. Pal of Lou's. I called Tut about the funeral. He couldn't make it. If Lou talked to anyone last Saturday, it would've been Tut."

Billy hugged Ruby, said good-bye to the reverend and headed for his car. He got behind the steering wheel and dialed Jones.

"Everything all right?" Jones said.

"Yeah, nice turn out. Thought I should check in."

"You had a chance to look at today's paper?"

"Just the front page. Did something happen?"

"There's been a leak. Check out the editorial page. Sorry, my man."

◆

Memphis Women Living In Fear

The editorial piece focused on the growing number of missing and murdered women in the city, and the inability of the police department to stop the crime wave. After several paragraphs of the editor's sweeping condemnation of city government, he narrowed down to his case in point—the details of Sophia's disappearance.

The last section contained the bomb Jones was talking about. "Sources report that the Memphis Police Department is focusing on a blue van that was parked beside the victim's car around the time of her disappearance. Police suspect the van's driver may have been involved in violence against other women. Although proof that a van is being used to prey on women has yet to be confirmed, detectives in charge of this investigation refuse to comment. Their reticence shows a lack of regard for public safety . . . "

Billy balled up the paper and slammed it against the dash. Lack of regard? The son-of-a-bitch was scaring women to sell papers. The van could be irrelevant. It could be a figment of Charles's imagination. If it did figure into Sophia's disappearance, it was transportation for Dupree's hit man, not the getaway vehicle for a stranger preying on women.

Who was the leak? Mercy could have talked to the press or told Dupree. Jones knew about the van, but had a lot to lose with a bungled case. A squad member could have compromised the file as a favor to the journalist. That happened, but not often.

Mercy or Dupree were the obvious answer. He thought Mercy had understood the importance of holding back case details from the public, but her loyalty to her brother-in-law may have overridden her good judgment. Now he'd have to be on guard with her. What a shame. Just seeing Mercy at the funeral had made him feel less alone. He couldn't help wondering what might have happened between them if they'd met under better circumstances.

He shook his head. *You're dreaming, buddy.* He started the car and drove toward Whitehaven. Maybe he'd find some answers there.

Chapter Forty-One

Wednesday, 4:00 p.m.

Buck was amazed as, wicket after wicket, he set up shots and cleared. Today he was going for a four-ball break using jump balls, pass rolls and stop shots. Brilliant play, if he said so himself. Classic strategy. Nothing like a croquet match to settle the nerves.

The lawn swam in the late afternoon heat. Hull, Church and Schutt complained about sweating through their whites; however, Buck remained cool. Today he was magic. The bank had contacted his office to say Gloria's money would transfer by two this afternoon. Account signature cards already bore his name. Monday he would transfer the money that guaranteed his seat on the Federal Sixth Circuit Court of Appeals. His vote to uphold or overturn lower court decisions could have a far-reaching social impact. With his stellar credentials and Senator Noel's support, he had a shot at the U.S. Supreme Court.

But it would be a mistake to look too far ahead. He was a week past the agreed payoff date with Noel. He had to assure his match partners and the senator that he was good for the money and the right man for the job.

The day's case before his bench had wrapped up early, so he'd contacted his croquet partners for an impromptu match. No reason to risk their switching horses midstream, not when all the news was good. In croquet, if you shoot your ball perfectly every time, you're virtually unbeatable.

Focused on the game, he gripped the shaft of his mallet and lined up his next shot. Everything stilled. He drew back.

"Noel called me last night," Schutt said, breaking Buck's concentration. "He's worried about the negative publicity over the Dupree woman's disappearance and how it might affect your confirmation."

He glared at Schutt, a crude man, the type who wipes his nose on his cuff

"Quiet," Church admonished.

"Hell, this is important. The senator hinted he may shift the nomination to that mule-faced judge in Nashville."

"Walsh?" Church said. "That idiot can barely find the courthouse."

"But he can sure find the bank. His friends have deep pockets." Schutt scratched himself through his trousers. "They offered to wire money to the senator's account tomorrow."

Buck pointed to his ball. "How about some consideration here."

He settled over his mallet, executed a perfect stop shot on Hull's croqueted ball and sent it rolling out of bounds. Church let out a whoop and gave Buck a thumbs up.

Schutt leaned over to pick a weed out of the path of his next shot. He looked up, eyes narrowed at Buck. "You got your hands on that money yet?"

"Let the man finish his play," Hull said. "We'll talk business at the club house."

"I want to know now." Schutt bumped the ground with his mallet for emphasis.

Although The Croquet Association manual recommends that a player never swing his or her mallet at another player, Buck was tempted to brain Schutt. If this was a sample of what to expect from these guys he'd be setting the record straight, but only after securing his seat on the bench.

"All right, gentlemen," he said and began toweling down his mallet. "Let's step into the grove for some privacy. We'll cool off, get this cleared up."

They followed a trail through an elegant avenue of trees. Schutt sat on a bench and fanned his face with a towel. Hull and Church focused on Buck, smart enough to appear contrite.

"You'll be happy to know that ten million dollars transferred to Gloria's account today," Buck told them. "She'll sign a power of attorney in the morning. Judge Will Heaton will marry us at noon. I'll wire Noel's money to his numbered account on Monday."

"What's wrong with tomorrow?" Schutt said.

"I want Gloria in my house, under my control, first. I don't want trouble down the road from her younger daughter."

"Noel plans to meet with Walsh this weekend," Hull said.

"The senator should focus on who's the best man for the job," Buck said. "Walsh will embarrass him."

"We could stall with a bonus, of say twenty thousand," Church said.

"Whose pocket will that come out of? Damn it, tell him I'll wire the amount we agreed to on Monday," Buck said.

Church shrugged. "All right, I'll make the call."

"And what about the cash you owe me?" Schutt said.

"Christ, don't pressure me over chump change," Buck said.

"I'll be a chump all day long for fifteen grand," Schutt said.

Schutt is a lowbrow bully, Buck thought. *Time to make the jerk sweat.* "Okay chump, double or nothing on this last break . . . if you've got the guts to go for it."

The solid click of a croquet ball being struck came from the greensward. They all turned in that direction.

"What the hell, someone's playing our court," Hull said.

"Son-of-a-bitch," Buck said, leading the way to the greensward.

A small Asian man in a filthy lab coat stood by the rover hoop with a golf club in his hand. He appeared to be talking to himself until Buck noticed a cur dog lying in the grass near the south flag. The man swung the club, sending Buck's ball down the green. He spoke to the dog. It quivered with happiness.

"Hey! Hey, buddy," Church yelled.

"I'll handle this," Buck said, clutching his mallet and striding toward the bum. "This is private property. Take your mutt and get out."

The dog rose to its feet and snarled. The man whacked Church's ball, still cooing at the dog.

"Stop that!" Buck advanced, furious someone so insignificant would ignore him.

Head slung low, teeth bared, the dog raced straight at him. It leapt, and he whipped his mallet in an arc that brought the head squarely into the dog's ribs. The dog yelped and collapsed at his feet. He raised the mallet to smash the dog's head, but caught himself when he saw Hull's stunned expression.

"Self-defense, gentlemen. It's every man's right under the law." He lowered his mallet. "Now let's get the balls back in place and get on with our match. And you there," he said to the bum. "Get your dog, and get the hell off this property."

Chapter Forty-Two

Wednesday, 3:00 p.m.

Mercy punched the CJC number into her cell.

"Homicide, Agent Jones."

"This is Mercy Snow. I saw Detective Able this morning at the funeral, but we didn't have a chance to speak. His cell is turned off. I need to reach him."

"Something new about your sister's investigation?"

"Do you know if he read the editorial in the newspaper?"

"Yes, he has."

"He'll think I leaked the van information. I didn't."

"Yes, ma'am."

"I didn't do it. Please tell him that."

Mercy hung up, feeling better. Able couldn't lose trust in her, not just for the sake of the investigation, but for some reason, she wanted his respect, for him to trust her. She walked through the library's lobby to the research desk, where she checked out microfilm for the *Commercial Appeal* covering the last twenty years. She wanted information about her future stepfather. She'd left Memphis years ago and couldn't rely on her mother's friends to be discreet about her questions. The wedding was tomorrow. She had to know more about Overton.

Scrolling through, she found an interview written after his first judicial election. The article revealed that he had graduated in the top ten percent of his Harvard law class, and that his ultimate goal was a federal judgeship. She scanned more articles and came across photos of Overton shaking hands with presidential candidates. He appeared to be successful and comfortable running with the big dogs. She found shots of him holding up trophies at croquet tournaments and also listings of his bridge tournament wins. His name appeared on lists for charity events along with photos of the ladies he had escorted. They were beautiful women, considerably younger than he.

Overton was getting older, but he was still an eligible bachelor. Yet he'd chosen her mother for marriage. Mercy still believed money was his motivator; however, they also seemed to compliment each other's worlds. Her mother needed a strong influence in her life, and her money would buy any future they wanted.

She switched to the Internet and read more of the same. As she began to wrap it up, a boy and girl charged through the lobby, where they ran circles around a big-hipped woman who spoke sweetly to them with absolutely no result. The woman shrugged as the kids broke away for another lap through the Memphis Room. The woman stared blankly at Mercy, then brightened and waved.

Oh, good God, Mercy thought. *Julia Fontaine Tice.* The kids ran to their mother, whooping when she pulled out chocolate bars. They settled on the floor and ripped open the candy. Julia made a beeline for Mercy.

She'd put twenty pounds on her hips and wore the classic Ladies Exchange lime green skirt with pink embroidered frogs. She looked like an aging cheerleader on steroids.

"Mercy Snow, I can't believe my eyes, it *is* you. I wouldn't have recognized you except for the. . ." She blinked. "You just look wonderful."

"Julia, how nice," she said, ignoring the woman's back-handed compliment. In high school Julia had been homecoming queen and Mercy, the disfigured loner.

"We missed you at the reunion," Julia hummed.

"I'm in Atlanta now."

"Judd mentioned that. He travels there twice a year and saw an article about your little bakery in the paper."

Mercy already knew Julia's husband traveled to Atlanta. He had dropped by Mimi's Hot Pies and suggested they go out for a drink and talk about old times. After two martinis, he tried to run his hand up her skirt.

"He was so pleased your life turned out." Julia's Kewpie Doll eyes narrowed. "You knew Judd and I were married."

Mercy nodded toward the children. "Yes, looks like you've been busy."

"Judd is such a lamb. I do hope our marriage wasn't upsetting for you. I know how you felt about him."

"That was high school, Julia. We're all grown up now."

"Oh. Well, listen. I'm so sorry to hear about Sophia. Do the police know anything?"

"They're working several leads."

"I read the article in today's paper. Sounds like that detective dropped the ball."

"The reporter didn't get his facts straight. I'm afraid the article may have hurt Sophia's chances."

Julia tilted her head to one side. "You poor thing. The way your mother lives and breathes for your sister . . . I bump into them occasionally at the salon." The children ran up and smeared their chocolate covered hands down the back of their mother's skirt. If she noticed she didn't let on.

"I'll tell Mother we spoke," Mercy said. "I'm afraid my life in Atlanta has put me out of touch."

"Families are always difficult to handle, especially from another city. Judd plays golf with T. Wayne. They talk. Poor T. Wayne seemed at his wit's end with Sophia's problems. Even hinted to Judd about another woman." Her hand flew to her mouth. "Oh, I shouldn't have said that, but you know how men are. And maybe Judd read too much into T. Wayne's comments."

She grabbed the whining children by their hands. "Give me a call, we'll have coffee."

Julia walked away with chocolate handprints on her rump. She didn't have a clue about the realities of her own marriage, or if she did, she hid it well. Her comments about T. Wayne were either a vicious dig or a thoughtless slip. Hard to tell which, with a Southern belle like Julia.

◆

Billy left Ruby's house and drove to the Grimes Nursing Home to speak with Tutwiler Jackson. Maybe the old court bailiff could give him some insight into Lou's state of mind on Saturday. Instead he learned that Mr. Jackson had been taken for dental work and wouldn't be back before supper. He gave the nurse his card and asked her to tell Mr. Jackson that he would try to stop by tomorrow.

He left the nursing home to drive by places that reminded him of better times with Lou. Every telephone pole seemed to have a poster with Sophia's smiling face. The sun was setting when he stopped at a florist's shop just before it closed. Then he headed to his final appointment of the day.

Color was fading off the horizon, and lightning bugs floated under a grove of cedars in the tiny, ancient cemetery where Sophia's son was buried. Billy located the marker and bent to trace his finger over the sleeping angel carved in the marble. He was surprised to see a bouquet of roses had already been laid on Casey's headstone. Wilted white roses.

He had visited the grave every year on the anniversary of the boy's death. Sophia never knew. She brought white roses at dawn; he brought white roses at sunset. He was three days late this year. The anniversary had fallen on Sunday, two days after Sophia's disappearance. Seeing the other bouquet of roses might have sparked hope in him that Sophia was the one who'd brought the flowers. But there was a more realistic explanation.

Gloria Snow must have known about the ritual and brought the roses in her daughter's place.

This morning they'd buried Lou. Ten years ago they'd buried Casey. Billy wondered how long it would be before they found Sophia's body and buried her too.

He stared down at the grave, thinking back to the days after the boy's funeral when Sophia had packed a bag and left her house. Dupree never made a move to stop her. He'd driven to Baton Rouge as if he didn't have a grieving wife who needed him. Billy had tracked Sophia down. He found her drunk and crying in a downtown bar. That was the real beginning for them.

He'd taken leave from work, and they rented a room by the week at a motel on Summer Avenue. It had a double bed, a kitchenette and a broken TV. They lay naked in each other's arms and listened to the radio for hours. They closed down the clubs on the strip. Days, they drove the flat roads of the Mississippi Delta listening to the blues, drinking vodka, drinking beer. Drinking, not talking. They didn't talk, they didn't eat, they didn't cry.

He held Sophia through the nights. He did everything in his power to convince her that Casey's life had ended, but not her own. After making love one morning, she told him she was going back to T. Wayne. He'd fought, pleaded, promised they would get through her grief. She left him anyway.

Billy came to realize that Sophia's suffering had taken her down into the grave with her little boy. She'd never really come out.

His cell broke the cemetery silence.

"Able," he answered, still staring at the grave.

"Judge Overton, here. I'm calling to see how you're holding up after the funeral."

"I'm fine, sir."

"Lou was a friend. I guess he was like a father to you."

"That's right." He ignored the tightness in his throat.

"I thought about our conversation last night. I wondered if you have anything new on Lou's accident?"

"Not much. There's one thing I forgot to mention the other night. I found a note by the phone at his house. It was like a code: the numbers 662 with the letters LVS written under it, and then the words 'pig out.' He dated it the same night you had that talk. Does it relate to your conversation?"

Silence on the line.

"Judge, you there?"

"I don't recognize any of it. LVS could be shorthand for Elvis. *Pig out.* Maybe Lou ordered an Elvis cookbook by phone." He laughed, cleared his throat. "Sorry, bad joke. Was there anything else of interest you didn't mention?"

"No, I gave the place a good search. It looked like he didn't even live there."

"Well, I know you're running all the traps. Say, I saw the editorial in the paper. The mayor must be furious. Makes him and the whole investigation look bad. And you."

Billy stared straight ahead. Bad enough someone leaked confidential information; now the judge was needling him.

"The editorial mentioned a maniac in a van snatching women," Overton said. "If that's true, it's good news for Dupree. It lets him off the hook."

"It's bullshit. The information was leaked. In fact, the van may not even exist."

"Sorry to hear that. Have you found the leak?"

"I'll look into it first thing tomorrow." He had no intention of telling the judge the leak might be Mercy or Dupree. "Someone left flowers on the grave of Sophia's son a couple of days ago. White roses. Any idea who might have done that?"

"Why are you interested in Casey's grave?" Overton said.

"Tying up loose ends. The boy died ten years ago Sunday. It's a date I happen to remember."

"How do you know there are flowers?"

Billy didn't want to explain the reason he was standing next to Casey's grave. "I'd appreciate your asking Dupree and Mrs. Snow about it."

"You're getting off track, son. Chasing ghosts. Get focused."

They hung up.

◆

A smoky harvest moon hung above the horizon as Billy drove to the CJC. In the office, he pulled Sophia's file and spread the paperwork in front of him. With his new resolve about the past, and with Lou's funeral behind him, he felt like a weight had been lifted off his shoulders. He could concentrate, now.

Jones had done a great job fielding calls triggered by the reward offer. Most were crackpot calls; a few sounded like leads but had quickly turned bogus. Bottom line, no one had seen Sophia after she left the grocery store. She'd simply vanished.

After an hour studying the file, he had four possible theories. One, she was a walk-away. Two, someone she knew set out to kill her. Three, she'd been a victim of random violence. Four?

Dupree had paid to get rid of her.

Billy no longer hoped Sophia was off on a drunk or believed she was capable of pulling off some kind of ruse. She had no motivation unless she'd learned about Courtney Burdine. They say the wife always knows. Probably not this time. Sophia was too self-absorbed to notice her husband having an affair.

Around midnight he discovered new information Jones had added to the back of the file—Dupree's credit card statement and the life insurance policy paid for through his Austin bank account. Over the last nine months Dupree had paid off thousands of dollars in charges at Neiman Marcus, Nordstrom's and several expensive Austin restaurants. He might claim they were for business and personal use, but Billy knew better. Courtney had been burning a hole through Dupree's Austin credit card. The next revelation in Jones's notes sealed it.

Courtney Burdine was now the sole beneficiary of Dupree's life insurance policy.

The rat bastard had started replacing Sophia with Courtney months ago.

Anger galvanized Billy's thoughts. Maybe Ms. Burdine was unaware Sophia was missing. She might not even know Dupree was married. Or she could know everything. He needed those answers from Courtney, but it would have to be face-to-face.

In a perfect world, he would turn Courtney into a witness against Dupree. If she balked, he could scare her, charge her with accessory to murder, but to accomplish any of it, he had to get to her fast. The moment Dupree realized his girlfriend might be questioned, he'd make her unavailable. Billy had to get to Austin before that happened. Getting Courtney Burdine to flip on Dupree would be a guaranteed shortcut to pulling together a solid case quickly.

He locked the file in his desk drawer and dialed Terri Cozi. He had loose ends to tie up in all directions. If anyone could get hold of the information he needed, it was Terri.

Chapter Forty-Three

Thursday, 7:30 a.m.

It was a gold Mercedes-Benz S65 AMG sedan with espresso leather interior and natural maple wood trim, 604 horse power—the most powerful, hideously expensive car Mercedes-Benz makes. More than transportation, the car was a measure of wealth and personal power.

Gloria had phoned Buck to say that he should come over at once. He thought she was calling about Sophia. He cut himself shaving and ran a red light to get there.

The fact that her call had been about a car infuriated him.

He slammed his car door and stalked around the yacht-sized Mercedes. Gloria had gone behind his back. Bought the thing without his permission. He traced his finger across the lacquered, gold-bar finish, gripped the handle and pulled. Locked.

She thought she was in charge. He would fix that.

The front door opened. "Buck!" Gloria squealed. She minced down the steps, holding her yellow silk robe together with one hand, the other held up, swaying lightly. "Isn't it beautiful? I've waited all my life for this car."

The sun revealed every line in her face, reminding him that at noon he'd be marrying an aging woman. She pressed her body against him and rubbed her cheek on his sleeve like a cat. He wanted to pull away. Instead he put his hand over hers and lightly squeezed it.

"When was it delivered?" he said.

"Seven this morning. The salesman was as excited as me."

"As I," he corrected.

"Excited as I. He brought a Thermos of coffee and a wicker basket packed with croissants and Brie. Wasn't that sweet? How about if we drive to the lake and have a wedding breakfast in my new car."

"Did you give them a deposit?"

Her lips, that had been hastily outlined in coral, pursed. "What's wrong? Oh, you're worried the bank won't cover the check. No, silly, I paid in full with a check post-dated for today."

He closed his eyes, willing himself to remain calm. "We don't have checks for that account."

"The manager at the dealership knows Mr. Quinn at the bank. They agreed I could use a counter check. Don't you love the color? It's special order."

She batted her lashes, matted with sleep and yesterday's mascara, and reached over to stroke the fender. Her robe slipped open, exposing the sagging flesh on her neck and breast. A smell like iodine and stale perfume rose from her cleavage.

She is so foolish, he thought. *So old.* But punishing her would be a bad strategy. This was their wedding day.

He realized Gloria was still prattling away. "And the computer on the dash runs everything. Isn't it marvelous?"

She searched his face with childlike trust. No reason to be cruel to her. A federal judge needs an appropriate wife, and without Gloria's money there would be no judgeship.

"Don't worry, dear. We'll stop payment on the check."

"Why should I?"

"You don't need a two hundred thousand dollar car."

"It's two hundred and twenty thousand when you add the fee to get it here four weeks sooner."

"My God, you paid sticker price?"

"It didn't come with a sticker. I told Chad what I wanted, and he told me what it cost."

He felt his face flush. "I'll be damned if you'll throw money away after we're married."

Her adoring expression evaporated. "I raised two girls on no money and nothing extra for me. I only wanted Sophia's happiness and to one day drive a golden Mercedes. Foolish, I know, but that was my dream. Now Sophia is missing. She's probably dead. Only one part of my dream can come true." Gloria gathered her robes at her throat. "You've ruined everything, including our wedding. I'm going inside."

"No, no, you don't understand," he said, hating the sound of panic in his voice. "It's my job to protect you."

"You don't fool me. You're angry because I went out and bought a car. And with my own money."

"I'm angry because you trusted a car salesman, and he took advantage of you. You didn't let me do my job. But if I'd known what the car means to you, I would've kept my own counsel."

"Oh, really," she snapped.

"People will try to cheat a sweet lady like you. Don't get me wrong, the car's a beauty."

Her mouth quivered in the tiniest smile. "You think so?"

"Of course. I love it."

"You really love it?"

He nodded and grinned like an idiot for her.

"You're not angry because I spent the money?"

"Oh, sweetheart."

"Well, no one likes to be taken advantage of," she said, stroking the fender and pouting.

"I can change that if you'll let me."

"How?"

"I'll make a few calls, then go by the dealership. First, you have to sign some papers. I planned to discuss them with you tonight, but we should take care of this right now. I have them with me in the car."

She crossed her arms in front of her. "Papers? I don't know."

"Let's get this business out of the way and go for that picnic. Celebrate our first fight. It'll be fun. Besides, I haven't had my coffee yet." He smiled, hoping for boyish charm.

"Poor baby," she said in a neutral tone, but she didn't move.

The sprinkler system erupted across the lawn. He needed a new tactic. He turned off the smile and brushed his hand down her arm. "I want to take care of you. I can't stand to see you unhappy. I love you."

She gazed across the rainbow mist from the sprinklers. "It's been so long since a man said those words to me."

Ha. He had her.

Buck's eyes settled on the arched iron doors of the porch. Sophia had loved those doors. She had explained to him once, as he lay naked on top of her, sucking her exquisite left nipple, that the doors had been custom-designed in Portugal for this house. They'd spent many evenings discussing architecture. He would miss that. He missed fucking her. Warmth spread in his groin. His eye traced the patterned ironwork in the door, helping his anger to subside.

A door slammed. Mercy emerged from the back of the house with that scruffy collie of hers on a leash. Running shorts showed off her well-shaped legs, and her tank top revealed firm breasts and the taut biceps of an athlete, so different from Sophia's slender figure.

"Mercy, come here dear," Gloria called.

Buck smiled.

◈

Mercy inhaled fresh air, feeling like a run for the first time since Friday. A kind of bleak humor ran through her. The gossip at the library had stuck in her mind. Did T. Wayne have a girlfriend? And now this: her mother said Mercy couldn't see the car until after the judge had come and gone. Gloria's incessant dream of a golden Mercedes had haunted Mercy's childhood. But now that the car was a reality, she wasn't invited to the party.

For God's sakes, I was named for that car.

She walked Caesar down the opposite side of the drive from where Gloria and the judge stood. He was looming over her mother, like a hawk over a pigeon, while they had an intense discussion. Mercy gave a small wave and averted her gaze. It bothered her to see them together.

"Mercy," Gloria called. "Come here, dear."

She held up her hand. "Don't mind me, Caesar needs some exercise."

Buck waved her over. "Your mother sprang this surprise on me this morning. Come see the car."

Her mother smiled. Mercy recognized the smile. It was her mother's trick smile.

"I need your advice, Mercy. Buck wants me to sign some papers concerning money. What do you think?"

"What kind of papers?"

The judge patted Gloria's hand. "Just some documents that allow me to look after your mother's interests."

"Something like a power of attorney?" Mercy said, knowing full well that's what he was after.

His jaw tightened. "Well, yes. There are several types of powers of attorney."

She nodded. "I understand. Mother, this is really none of my business. It's your money."

"It's your father's money, and you're a smart business woman. I want your opinion."

"All right," she said, even though she felt the trap closing. "To be sure you're both protected, I'd recommend you discuss the matter with your own attorney before you sign."

Gloria's smile continued. "Buck *is* my lawyer. He wants me to sign now."

"Okay, let's go inside, read through the papers, and the judge can answer any questions we may have." She thought she had offered a diplomatic solution until she caught the flash of anger on Overton's face.

"I have a meeting this morning with the Director of Police Services to discuss your sister's case. Of course I could cancel." He stared pointedly at Mercy.

You son-of-a-bitch. You are *up to something,* she thought.

"Don't you dare cancel," her mother said. "That was thoughtless of you, Mercy. Buck's time is too important to waste explaining papers. Buck, sweetie, if you have a pen, I'll sign those papers now. You need some coffee, and my mouth's watering for a taste of that Brie."

Chapter Forty-Four

Thursday, 7:49 a.m.

Billy was pumped for the early meeting he'd book with Hollerith. He pulled out his best suit, buffed his oxfords, and gave himself a close shave. He needed the lieutenant on his side today, figured if he suited up instead of showing up in his usual Blues Alley, sax-player-hand-me-downs, he'd have a better chance of getting what he wanted from Hollerith. He straightened his tie and checked the mirror. Hollows under his cheekbones. Bloodshot eyes. Not the look he was going for. He'd been up half the night going over Sophia's file, and then, for the third night in a row, he couldn't sleep.

But this was the first morning he'd felt steady on his feet, no headache, no edginess. His case against Dupree was shaping up, one he could hand over to Carey, the assistant D.A., by tomorrow if Hollerith agreed to send him to Austin today.

He grabbed his keys and opened the door to see Mercy walking up the ramp with Caesar on a leash. She wore running shorts and a tank top. Her face was tight with anxiety.

"What's happened?" he said.

"I can't deal with my mom and that damned judge. And T. Wayne is . . . " She pressed her palm to her cheek. "Oh, God, I really need to talk. I didn't know where else to go."

She was catching it from every direction. He wanted to put his arms around her but fought the urge, knowing his history with Sophia was between them.

He led her around to the afterdeck, called the office to delay his meeting with Hollerith, and then joined her at the railing with two cups of coffee. She relaxed a little. They drank coffee and watched a towboat jockey a line of barges between the bridge supports until she was ready to talk.

"Overton pushed my mother into this spur-of-the-moment wedding, then showed up with a power of attorney this morning," she said.

"Is it a general power of attorney or limited to specific acts?"

"He wasn't giving out those kinds of details."

"If it's a general power, he could use her money to buy a car, sell stocks. If it's limited, he can do only the specific things listed. Did she sign under duress?"

Mercy gave a short laugh. "Of course. He dangled a wedding ring in front of her nose."

"Very funny. Sounds like she's made up her mind to trust Overton with her money, and she doesn't need your approval to do that. The good news is your mother can revoke it at any time. Get your hands on a copy and see what it says."

"I tried. Mother acted like I was a villain for suggesting we read it." She sipped her coffee. "I'm trying to be rational about this. I've met the judge under extreme circumstances so maybe I'm overreacting, but we're constantly crossing swords. He's so manipulative."

"He's a respected judge, a good man to have on your family's side."

"He's also a son-of-a-bitch."

Billy smiled to himself. Mercy must be giving Overton fits. The judge wouldn't appreciate a strong woman questioning his actions. "Can you talk to your mom at all?"

She rolled her eyes. "Mother only listens to Sophia. I'm more like a possession than a daughter. She named me after a car, for God's sakes. After the accident, she stopped calling me Mercedes and switched to Mercy. Talk about a fall from grace."

He watched the bright chop bounce off the side of a passing cabin cruiser. Another shining example of the damage mothers inflict on their children. At least Mercy had escaped. Sophia had been doomed from the start. He swallowed some coffee, wanting to keep the anger out of his voice. "Mind telling me about the accident?"

"I was carrying a big fish bowl. I tripped. The bowl shattered and I fell into the glass. Slashed my cheek to the bone. The intern who sewed me up botched the job. This was the best repair a plastic surgeon could do." She studied the bridge. "Mother can't seem to stop blaming me for ruining my face."

"Let's get something straight. You're beautiful, a total knock out." *And to hell with your mother*, he thought. "By the way, I prefer the name Mercy. It suits you."

She shrugged, staring at the water. "It's certainly less to live up to."

"I know you're worried about the power of attorney, but Overton has a reputation to protect. He's not going to do something stupid. And I've had a couple of talks with him. He seemed sincere about helping your family."

She straightened off the railing, suddenly angry. "He's playing you too. He wants to get you kicked off the case. He says you're going after T. Wayne because of the way Casey died."

That's bullshit, Billy thought. "How about you? Do you think I'm biased?"

Her gaze shifted away from him. "I don't know."

Now he was angry. "You *should* know. Dupree left a loaded gun where his son could find it then blamed your sister for his death. He might as well have shot her too."

"I believe you're making Overton's point."

She was right, and it pissed him off. "Like hell I am. I make the best case I can against a suspect no matter who it is, and Overton knows that."

"Overton doesn't want his wife's son-in-law indicted for murder. Everything he does is for his own benefit, not for T. Wayne and certainly not for my mother." She passed her cup back and forth between her hands, looking uncomfortable. "The other day at lunch, he brought up T. Wayne's past as if it mattered. I couldn't tell if he was baiting me. I asked T. about it, and he downplayed the issue." She glanced at him. "Is there a problem?"

"Do you know about Dupree's first marriage?"

Her mouth dropped open. "*What?* When?"

"Right out of university. About a year into the marriage, he beat her up. Broke her arm, cheekbone, ribs. He pled No Contest to domestic assault, and she divorced him. He has a history of getting drunk, getting violent."

She put a hand on the railing to steady herself. "You're sure?"

"It's a matter of record. Look, I worked several hours last night going over Sophia's case. I hope to have some definitive answers by tomorrow."

She swayed, still holding onto the rail. "It's all happening so fast. I don't know what to believe or who to trust. It's really hitting me now. *My sister may be dead.*" She stared across the water.

Then she looked over at him. Her eyes begged him to say that Sophia was okay. He couldn't do that. No matter what happened over the next few days, Mercy was going to be hurt the most. He could give her part of the truth now, or he could give her all of it. He decided to get it over with.

"I think your brother-in-law paid to have your sister murdered. I think he hired a pro, which means we may never find her body. It's harder to get a conviction without a body, but that doesn't make him less guilty."

She shook her head, stunned. "I don't believe it. I can't. You have actual proof?"

"I'm sorry, I can't discuss the details."

"Because you think I leaked the van information?"

"No, the leak came from inside my department."

"Who would do that?"

"A lot of people had access to the file. The real question is why. This case is making a lot of important people look bad. With the election in six weeks, they want it out of the headlines." He tossed the last of his coffee into the river. "I'm sorry, Mercy, I have to go. I have a meeting with my lieutenant. I have to move fast on information I got last night."

"Wait a minute, you can't drop a bomb like this and leave. What if someone else grabbed her? That article said bad things are happening to women all over this city." She blinked. "You can't even prove she's dead."

"Bottom line, just so we're clear: I'm ninety-eight percent certain that Dupree is responsible for your sister's disappearance. If I can put him behind bars, I will. Thanks for the heads-up about the judge. I'll keep my eye on him. I'm sorry, but I don't have a choice."

With that, he left, forcing himself not to look back.

◈

Billy ducked under the tape blocking the door of Hollerith's office. The place smelled like used gym socks. Maintenance workers on ladders were ripping down soggy ceiling tiles covered with black mold. The carpet, the furniture, Hollerith's framed commendations—everything had been trashed by the condensate leak.

He found the lieutenant down the hall, sitting at the conference table with a laptop and a stack of paperwork in front of him. His jacket hung over the back of his chair and he had his sleeves rolled up, something Billy had never seen before.

Hollerith glanced up when Billy walked in. "Nice suit, Able, but you still look like crap. Have a seat and tell me how you're doing."

Billy laid his file on the table and took a chair opposite the lieutenant. "I'm good. The headaches are history. Listen, we need to—"

Hollerith held up a hand. "I got a call from Paul Anderson at Employee Assistance. He said I should've placed you on medical deferment last week. He put me on notice. If you blowup, your body parts will fall on me."

Billy started to laugh, then held back because he realized Hollerith was serious. He cleared his throat. "I'm not planning to blowup, sir."

"I saw the forensic report you ordered on Lou's car. Patsy Dwyer could be censured for your unauthorized wash. She's got kids in college. She risked her job for you. You think about that?"

"I'll apologize. But come on, Lieutenant, give me a break. You knew I'd go after the facts on Lou, even if we didn't open a file."

Hollerith looked at him over the top of his reading glasses. "You disregard my orders again, I'll do what I have to do. Got that?"

"Yes, sir." He'd seen the lieutenant have a bad day. This was off the charts.

Hollerith pulled two articles out of his pile. "You see today's paper?"

"Not yet."

He handed them over. "Yesterday's editorial was bad enough. Today the mayor said the department is all but incompetent. And just when I'm counting on you to wrap up this case, Anderson warns me you can't handle the pressure."

"All due respect, I haven't even talked with Anderson, so he's full of shit. As to the case, that's why I asked to meet with you. I've got it all laid out here." He pushed the file across the table. Hollerith began to flip through while Billy talked.

"First, Dupree's marriage was already in trouble when his wife moved her alcoholic mother in on them. He and Sophia Dupree were sleeping in separate bedrooms. Second, the victim's public drunkenness was hurting Dupree's career. He assaulted his first wife and it appears he was doing the same to Sophia. Third, Dupree has a girlfriend living in his condo in Austin who is now the beneficiary of his life insurance. Fourth, Dupree recently withdrew twenty thousand in cash and says he gave it to his alcoholic wife to redecorate their house."

Hollerith leaned back, crossed his arms. "Go on."

"I have an idea where the cash went. He made calls to Jazzy's here in Memphis and the Lava Café in Baton Rouge. One is a hangout for gangbangers, the other for the Louisiana mob. I believe he was shopping for a hit on his wife. Jones said TBI has a wiretap on Jazzy's, so we may get the taped conversation. Dupree's buddy owns the Lava Café. I don't know if we can get him to flip, but it's worth a shot."

"A contract hit seems out of bounds for Dupree."

"His wife had no job skills and a history of mental instability. In a divorce she'd get a lot of sympathy from the court and end up costing Dupree a fortune. A hit was his cheapest way out."

Hollerith closed the file. "Interesting premise. Unfortunately, everything you've got here is circumstantial."

"Switching out your wife for your girlfriend on your life insurance is pretty damned suspicious."

"It's persuasive, but not enough to take to Rob Carey."

Billy expected some resistance, but Hollerith was being a jackass. Billy sucked it up and continued.

"All right. You're not persuaded. That's why I need to go to Texas today. Dupree's girlfriend may be in the dark about his wife's disappearance. Or she could have helped him plan it. I'll get a clearer picture when I talk to her face-to-face. I've checked into flights to Austin. A direct flight out of Memphis will get me there by one. If she knows anything about the disappearance, I want to convince her to testify against Dupree at a grand jury. Or maybe we can use her statement to pressure his buddy in Baton Rouge. All I need is some outside corroboration to make Dupree fold. I need your authorization for the ticket to get things moving."

"Slow down. My budget won't allow for a bus ticket much less a plane ticket." Hollerith pulled out a sheaf of papers. "According to FBI stats, Dupree is only a twenty-four percent match for a second domestic violence incident. He profiled out at two percent as murder for hire. In fact, his wife works out at fifty-eight percent as a walk-away. These numbers say your conclusions are flawed."

"Let me have a look." Billy shuffled through the papers, wondering what kind of chump information the lieutenant was throwing around. None of it made sense. Important aspects of the case were missing.

"The cash and the girlfriend don't show up in this data," Billy said.

"Dupree said the money went to a decorator's workroom."

He stared at Hollerith. "What decorator? What workroom? Dupree wouldn't hand his wife a roll of hundred dollar bills when he barely trusted her with fifty bucks to buy groceries."

Hollerith shrugged. "It was a cash deal. Even rich people can't resist a discount."

"And the girlfriend?"

"We don't have enough data to include her."

"That's bullshit. If that's what you believe, you should be willing to buy the plane ticket yourself so I can talk to her."

Hollerith's chair skittered back as he stood. "*Damn it*, what about the guy who's grabbing women in Holly Springs?"

"Jones is already on it."

"Has he come up with anything?"

"It's secondary to—"

He jabbed his finger at Billy, forcing the point. "Answer the question!"

"I talked to Jones this morning, but we didn't discuss the van," Billy said calmly.

"You didn't discuss it." Hollerith sneered. "What about the attempted abduction behind The Dixie?"

"That was a drunk trying to get some action."

"You don't know that. When you add the van and the other kidnapping attempts, it's a pretty sure bet that Mrs. Dupree was abducted. I want you to go to Holly Springs. I have contacts there who'll help you sort through what they've got. After that we'll discuss a trip to Texas."

Billy stood and flattened his palms on the table. "The quickest way to close this case is to get a confession," he said. "Send me to Texas. The girlfriend will cooperate, or I'll threaten her with an accessory to murder charge. If there's something there, I'll get it."

Hollerith picked up the phone and barked, "Get Jones in here." He banged down the receiver, his face flushed with resentment. "Overton called me at home last night. He knows you were on the scene when Dupree's son was shot. He believes your investigation is biased and wants you off the case. He even hinted that you've been involved with this woman. That you interfered with patrolmen who've pulled her over for drunk driving. Is that true?"

Billy shrugged. "I felt sorry for her. I gave her my card. I made a few calls."

"Damn it, Able, Overton scheduled a meeting with Director Mosby this morning. You've exposed me to a lot of questions I can't answer."

Mercy had been right about Overton. Somehow the judge knew he had a relationship with Sophia and was using it to get Hollerith to dump him off the case.

"Overton's hands aren't exactly clean," Billy said. "He arranged a quickie marriage to Dupree's mother-in-law, who just came into a big pot of money. The judge is ambitious. The last thing he wants connected to his name is scandal. He'll do what it takes to keep Dupree from being indicted."

"You don't get it. Overton isn't the problem. *You* are."

"I work for you, not Overton. I'm a straight cop. I want to do my job. Send me to Texas."

Hollerith jammed his hands in his pockets. The words he spoke sounded rehearsed. "I've overlooked your insubordination out of respect for what you've been through, but I can't continue. You're to have no contact with Dupree's family. Go to Holly Springs. Check out the van. Fax your findings, e-mail them, do what-the-hell-ever you want. But stay out of my sight until I get in touch with you."

Jones strolled in as Hollerith leaned into those last words. The room went quiet. Billy was at the dividing line. Play it smart or stick to what he believed. He thought about Sophia and Mercy. He had only one choice.

"You hear that, Jones?" he said, unable to keep the smart-ass out of his voice. "We could wrap this case tomorrow, but the lieutenant wants to play politics."

"You're skating on thin ice," Hollerith growled.

Jones held up his hands. "How about if we work the van angle, see what turns up?"

"Let me explain how this detective thing works," Billy said. "You pick your suspect. You turn over every rock until you're done collecting evidence. Charge the guy if he's guilty. If he's not, you move to your next suspect. The next rock I plan to turn over lives in Texas."

"If you go, you'll leave me no choice," Hollerith said.

"Do what you have to do, sir." Billy headed for the door.

Jones caught up with him striding down the hall. "What in hell were you doing back there?"

"You taking his side?"

"This shit's too deep to be talking sides. You've been selling Dupree hard on circumstance. Take a couple of days. Check out the van angle. Then you can make your Texas run with Hollerith's backing."

"Naw." Billy swatted his hand through the air. "I have to get to Courtney Burdine before Dupree shuts her up or ships her off. It *has* to be today." He sat at his desk and went online with Jones standing in front of him. "There's a cheap, Southwest flight out of Little Rock in three hours. I'll buy the ticket myself."

"Listen, man. We're treading in deep water. It's one thing to solve a case. It's another to survive it. If we don't, we're going to lose. *I'm* going to lose."

He heard the edge in Jones' voice and looked up. A soured investigation would go against Jones's record—a risk he hadn't signed up for.

"Hollerith showed me stats he'd worked up on the case. I saw the change of beneficiaries in Dupree's insurance in his notes. Did you give him that information?"

"No."

"Then Hollerith's been in the file. He's the leak."

"Why would he do that?" Jones said.

"Because people will justify any damned thing to get what they want."

Jones nodded. "Yeah, somebody's always trying to get ahead. Hollerith, Overton, the mayor, Senator Noel—from the way things have been handled, I'd say every one of them has something on the line. All I know is guys like us . . . best we can do is outlive the politics and move on."

Chapter Forty-Five

Thursday, 10:17 a.m.

Buck rarely entered the Criminal Justice Center through the main entrance. The lobby crawled with the dregs of Memphis showing up for their day in court. He walked through the center of the atrium, where the skylights made the atmosphere tolerable. This situation wouldn't exist except for Sophia's stubbornness. If she'd seen the wisdom of his plan to marry her mother, she'd be alive and none of this . . . this unpleasantness . . . would've been necessary.

Nothing between Sophia and him would have changed. He'd even promised never to have sex with her mother. Why would he want to? After his appointment, Sophia could have left Dupree and lived with Gloria and him when they moved to Cincinnati. Gloria would have been thrilled, and the marriage would've provided a perfect cover.

Crazy bitch. Sophia had no vision.

She'd thrown jealous tantrums about the marriage for weeks. After every one, he'd taken her wherever she stood, over the backstairs railing, on the kitchen table. He'd forced her, used her until she cried, either from emotional dramatics or physical pain, he didn't cared which. He knew she liked it.

Actually, he relished her possessiveness. No woman had ever put up that kind of fight for him. One minute she was clingy, the next she turned vicious and threatened to go to the media with nasty details of their affair.

There was the rub. The FBI would conduct a background check. Agents would talk to everyone, down to his boyhood Sunday school teacher. If they found an alcoholic mistress willing to spill the details of his kinky sex life to the press, the appointment would evaporate.

Following a particularly ugly fight, he'd come to the certainty that Sophia would eventually ruin him. Instead of understanding the brilliance of his plan, her threats had forced his hand.

A week after that, Lou had called in the middle of the night, drunk as hell, and said he wanted to propose a money-making proposition similar to the one they'd run with Tutwiler Jackson. When Buck said he wasn't interested, Lou broke down, babbling about being desperate, and blurted out the reason why. Disgusted, Buck had hung up. But the call reminded him of his past business arrangement with Nevers and Jackson, a weakness FBI agents might ferret out.

In the past Lou had headed up the Memphis P.D. division that raided topless clubs, busting owners for serving minors and for permitting dancers to strip naked and play touchy-feely with the customers. A guilty verdict resulted in a suspended liquor license, which translated into thousands of dollars of lost profits for the club.

Buck's relationship with Lou had begun when Lou saw an opportunity for them both to benefit. Lou could give owners a heads-up when undercover cops would be trolling their clubs. When a bust went down outside of Lou's control, Lou wanted to provide insurance against a guilty finding for a stiff price.

Lou had approached his old friend, Tutwiler Jackson, with a plan. Jackson was the General Sessions criminal court bailiff for Buck at the time. Nevers proposed that he'd provide protection for the clubs at his level. If a case got through, Buck would dismiss it at the preliminary hearing. Club owners would pay Lou. Prosecutors, too busy to track a few slime-ball cases, would let them fall through the cracks. The risk of exposure would be nearly nonexistent.

Lou, Tut and the Judge set up shop. After each case, Buck found an envelope stuffed with cash that had been left in a desk drawer by Jackson. The money had allowed Buck to make important social connections that later led to political influence. Benefits kept rolling in until Sam Waters entered the picture, started snooping around and they were forced to shut down. The back-scratching relationship between Buck and Lou had remained, however. After Jackson retired, Buck had called on Lou to handle any sticky situation his friends and croquet buddies got into.

After Lou's recent drunken plea for help, Buck had realized he needed Lou's expertise again. And the more he thought about Lou's situation, the more he knew Lou would do whatever he was told. Lou had a secret. He'd given enough details for Buck to know it was very nasty, and therefore big leverage.

The next day he'd called Lou and said he had a solution to Lou's financial squeeze. Lou interrupted and confessed he couldn't remember what he'd said. He'd sounded anxious, his voice thick and uncertain with a hangover.

Buck said he wanted Sophia removed from his life, and he wanted Lou to make it happen. He offered Lou forty thousand dollars the day after Sophia disappeared. Lou said he wasn't a hit man and to fuck off. That's when Buck reminded Lou of their conversation and what Lou had said about needing money in connection with The Aviary Condominiums. Buck added that it would be a shame if that situation were exposed.

"Don't threaten me, Judge," Lou had said. "I'll bring down your whole house. I kept notes on those titty club owners and how much they paid you."

Buck had cleared his throat, trying to regroup. "Really, there's no need for threats. You handle my problem, and the forty thousand will solve your problem."

He'd given Lou the Acura's plate number and told him Sophia was driving that car instead of the Mercedes.

She disappeared the next evening.

But in Buck's conversation with Lou on Saturday, Lou had denied being involved. He'd blown up. He died that night either by accident or out of guilt. Buck would never know which one for certain.

Every aspect of Buck's plan had fallen into place until Able found Lou's pager with Buck's number on it and the note on his nightstand. Lou had written the Acura's license number backward, maybe because he was drunk, or out of a quirky habit, but lucky for Buck, Able hadn't deciphered the number.

Last night Buck had nearly dropped the phone when Able asked if he knew what the note meant.

Why the hell had Lou written "peg out"? Buck didn't remember saying that. Thank God Lou had poor handwriting so Able couldn't translate it. The croquet term was a flimsy connection to him, but he still felt he'd dodged a bullet. Able might stumble into reversing the numbers, and that would link Lou with Sophia.

After talking with Able, Buck felt sure the graft payments notes weren't at Lou's house. That left only one place they could be. Buck would have to take the risk of going there. Now he had two good reasons to take down the detective.

Yesterday he'd begun the process by calling Paul Anderson to warn that Able's psychological state could jeopardize the department. He'd followed that up with a late-night call to fluster Hollerith. Finally, the meeting he'd arranged with Mosby this morning should do the job of undermining Able enough to get him off the case.

Buck checked his watch as he crossed the atrium. An elevator door slid open. Lawyers with their clients bustled into the lobby. Detective Able was the last man out.

"Able . . . over here," he called. He watched the detective's eyes sweep the lobby. Able hesitated, crossed the atrium and stopped with too much distance between them to shake hands. He looked like hell. The concussion and heavy workload were telling on him. It pleased Buck to see his opponent so compromised.

"Judge," Able said with a nod.

"Good to see you, son. You've been on my mind."

"I'm late for an appointment, Judge."

"I followed up on our conversation about the flowers left at Casey's grave."

"Yes?"

Buck paused. He made Able wait, right up to the point the detective's eyes narrowed, then he answered. "Gloria knew nothing about it."

"How about Dupree?"

"I haven't seen him to ask."

Able thought it over, shrugged. "It's probably not important. A friend might have left the flowers. Could've been anyone."

An obese couple pushed past them, shouting at each other. Buck wanted to escape the chaos of the very public lobby, but keeping tabs on Able's state of mind was important. He switched his tone to sound more agreeable. "Wish me well. Gloria and I are getting married today."

"Mercy told me this morning."

The bitch probably complained about me wanting power of attorney, too. Buck managed a smile. "I'm sure she told you she's not totally on board. It's awkward timing for a wedding, but I want Gloria to feel secure in case the worst happens."

Able's eyebrows went up. "You mean in case we arrest Dupree?"

"Of course not. I meant if Sophia turns up dead. But Dupree's arrest would also be horrible for Gloria. He's been like a son to her."

Able leaned toward him. "So what do you think, is he guilty?"

Arrogant jerk. Buck let the moment stretch. "Your opinion matters more than mine."

Able's jaw flexed. "I'd say your opinion carries a lot of weight. Hollerith jumped down my throat this morning, because you told him I'm biased against Dupree."

"Have I given you that impression?"

"The other night you said you trusted me to do the right thing. That you'd back me. Hollerith set me straight on that and a few other things."

Ah. Hollerith had finally nailed Able about the drunk driving stops Able had handled for Sophia. Good. One night when Sophia had been into her second bottle of *Veuve Clicquot*, she'd bragged about her affair with the hot young detective and how he'd protected her from DUIs. She'd made Buck crazy jealous. He'd turned the noxious information to his advantage.

"I also suggested you keep your perspective," Buck said. "Anderson says you need counseling. I agree."

"You called Anderson?"

Able had picked up on his slip. "No, I believe Hollerith brought up his name the last time we spoke. A lot of good people in the department are concerned about you."

"Looks like you're calling the shots in this case," Able said, unable to mask his sarcasm.

"This case is personal with me. You understand that."

"Right. No judge wants an in-law charged with murder."

He didn't like Able's aggressive tone. No matter. The meeting with Mosby would neutralize him soon enough. He stuck out his hand.

"You said you have an appointment, Detective. It's been a pleasure."

Able gave him an angular smile. "Give the director my regards when you see him. And Judge, that power of attorney Mercy was concerned about this morning? I told her that her mother can have it revoked at any time."

◈

The last person Billy had wanted to see when he got off the elevator was Overton. He wanted to tell the judge off, but he'd held his temper. It paid off.

It was clear Overton had a bigger agenda than protecting Dupree; the judge had a personal stake in this case, important enough for him to try to influence members on the force. *Try,* hell. He'd intruded to the point of obstructing justice. Anderson had fallen into line after one call from Overton, and Hollerith seemed nearly desperate to accommodate him. Billy wondered how Director Mosby would handle the pressure. With the mayor's possible defeat, even Mosby's job was on the line. Like Jones said, they all had something at stake.

If he had any sense of self-preservation, he'd listen to Jones and go to Holly Springs. But he was as hardheaded as his Uncle Kane, a man who never learned to back up or back down. Billy was going to Texas even if it meant his job.

He'd booked the flight to Austin with an early morning return. To make it on time, he had to drive home, grab a clean shirt and get across the river by noon.

As he came up the barge's gangplank he saw Terri stretched out in a chair on the afterdeck, wearing shades, her skirt drawn up to her panty line so she could grab a little sun on her legs. Terri's body ran a close second on her list of priorities. He knew from experience that her career came first.

He pointed at the paddlewheel docked beside the barge. "Ms. Cozi, you're driving those guys on the top deck nuts."

She took off her glasses and waved them at the three young men gawking at her over the rail. "We all deserve a little sunshine in our lives." She shimmied her skirt down and stood. "I have a ray of sunshine to share with you, too."

"I'd love to hear about it, but I'm on the run."

"Hold on, mister. This is for your benefit, not mine. I ran into some juicy gossip about Judge Overton."

◈

". . . so after the second time she caught Larry trying on her underwear, Pam dumped him and got a job in Nashville as an assistant in Senator Noel's in-state office. We've kept in touch." Terri lay draped across his bed, flipping through a magazine while he dug into packing boxes for a clean shirt.

"So much for lost love," he said. "Now what about Overton?"

"The senator asked Pam to prepare drafts for two different documents. The first is Noel's recommendation of Judge Walsh for the next seat on the 6th Circuit Court of Appeals in Cincinnati. The second draft recommends Judge Lamar Overton."

He stopped digging. *Overton was campaigning for a seat on a federal appellate bench?*

"I'm sure you know the senator heads the Judiciary Committee," she said. "Either nominee will be a shoo-in, unless something ugly shows up in their pasts."

"Or their present."

"Exactly," she said. "So from that angle, Overton pushing to marry into this Dupree melodrama doesn't make sense. Is it possible he doesn't know about the nomination?"

"Oh, he knows. And the marriage is about money, not love. Mercy had him pegged from the start."

Terri closed the magazine. "That's a pretty cozy reference to the woman I caught hiding in your kitchen."

"Who's cooking in my kitchen isn't your business anymore."

"Is that what you call it now . . . *cooking?*" Terri rolled over onto her stomach and pouted. "I've missed you, baby."

"Really."

"I have. We were good together."

"How's Sam been treating you?"

"Now, don't be jealous." She scooted forward to show her cleavage at its best advantage. "Sam and I are buddies."

Terri fished with delicious bait, but Billy was no longer interested in biting. He had another woman on his mind.

He stopped in the doorway with his bag on his shoulder. "You're a good friend, Terri."

"Uh oh, the 'F' word."

"Overton's been playing me, and he's got Hollerith on the line too. I'm going to find out why."

"If it's juicy, I want an exclusive." She grinned. "Does this mean all is forgiven?"

Terri was a lot like Sophia—selfish, beautiful and brilliant at getting what she wanted.

"If I have a job when I get back, the story is yours. And yes, we're all square."

Chapter Forty-Six

Thursday, Noon

The wedding ceremony took place in Judge Will Heaton's chambers. Gloria cried the moment she said "I do" and continued crying during the limousine ride to the wedding luncheon. Neither did she stop including Sophia's name in every other sentence. Mercy felt as if a ghost were floating in and out of the limousine.

Surely, she thought, *its bad luck to focus on tragedy the day of your wedding.*

Overton had arranged a sumptuous luncheon in the elegance of Powell's private dining room, handling everything with great style as only a Southern gentleman could. Lavender orchids graced the table along with a hand-scripted menu of Gloria's favorite dishes.

His attention to detail impressed Mercy, as did the orange-cream wedding cake ordered from Commander's Palace in New Orleans, except that the gesture was also an affront. Overton hadn't bothered to consult her about the cake, either assuming her bakery incapable of producing a fine wedding cake or still punishing her for throwing out his pie the night they met. As the photographer snapped pictures of T. Wayne, posing beside the smiling couple, Mercy's head throbbed with the bizarreness of it all: *Sophia is probably dead. T. Wayne may have killed her. Mother doesn't seem to notice and no one else is saying a word.*

After lunch, the limousine took the wedding party back to T. Wayne's house, and Overton left to prepare his Walking Horse mare for the Germantown Charity Horse Show scheduled for that evening. Ever the steel magnolia, Gloria insisted they all attend the show and use Buck's box seats.

"I haven't given up on Sophia," she said. "But life does go on."

❖

Dust stirred up by the horses colored the setting sun a pale gold. The bowl-shaped arena muffled the sounds of the crowd. Gloria waved her four-carat diamond at acquaintances as she walked down the concrete steps to their seats. Her serene smile spoke volumes. She was Mrs. Judge Lamar Overton now.

Mercy settled in a chair, numb. She half-expected to turn and find her sister beside her, breathtakingly beautiful with her high cheekbones and dark eyes, entertaining them with the latest gossip. She realized she had both loved and hated Sophia, and that the horror of her loss had not yet sunk in. Her throat tightened, and she swallowed a sob.

T. Wayne dropped into the seat beside her, drunk again. He whispered that Lieutenant Hollerith was broadening the case, and that he was no longer considered to be the prime suspect. She suspected Detective Able had not been at the meeting. On the barge, he'd seemed ready to slap handcuffs on T. Wayne, and she doubted he would've changed his opinion this quickly.

T. Wayne bumped her shoulder. "I'm making a run to Austin tomorrow," he slurred. "Business trip."

"Oh, no! That sends the message you've given up on Sophia."

"I don't need your fucking permission to leave town."

Her mother pinched her arm. "T. Wayne, darling, I believe they serve wine at the hospitality tent. Why don't you get us a glass?"

He nodded and hustled up the steps toward a red-striped tent, like a Labrador fetching a downed duck. Mercy wondered at what point in the past week her loyalty to T. Wayne had decayed into denial. In fact she was beginning to trust Billy Able more.

"For God's sake, Momma, the last thing he needs is another drink."

"You shouldn't aggravate him."

"Aggravate *him*!"

"Never mind. I wanted to speak to you about Buck."

"I just want you to be happy," she said, unwilling to face another skirmish.

"That's nice, dear. But I wanted to tell you . . . I wanted to admit that despite my comments the other night, I don't believe your sister would be happy about this marriage. After she introduced me to Buck, I think she became a little jealous." She sniffed. "Meeting Buck is the first bit of happiness I've had in years. Now that we're married, my money will buy Buck whatever he needs, and he'll give me what I lost when you father died—an invitation back into society. A woman needs social status and a good man in her life to give her purpose."

"That's not true." Mercy wanted to tell her about her life in Atlanta, where she had friends and supporters—all based on who she was and her talent as a business woman, not her relationship to a powerful man.

"It's true for me," Gloria went on. "I want to be clear. Buck has use of the money to take us wherever he wants. Last night he told me he's being nominated for a seat on the U.S. Circuit Court of Appeals in Cincinnati. If he's appointed, we'll move there. When this nightmare is over, a fresh start will be good for both of us."

"I hate to bring this up, but I'm very concerned about the power of attorney you signed."

"A man like Buck needs to feel he's in control. But don't you worry. I've hired a CPA firm to do regular audits."

"I'm surprised. Pleased, but surprised."

Gloria raised an eyebrow. "I drink, but I'm not an idiot. Buck and I are a good match. We need each other to get what we want."

A group of young riders trotted through the in-gate and circled the ring for a junior equitation class.

"We have a suite at the Peabody tonight," Gloria said. "And tomorrow I'll move some things to Buck's house. By the way, I'd like to put some money into your bakery account. You have a good business head; you'll know what to do with the money. It would have pleased your father."

Mercy was taken aback. "Thanks. A loan could help me expand right now."

"It's not a loan; it's a gift."

As the horses left the arena, T. Wayne returned, huffing like a buffalo and sat back down with two glasses of chardonnay in his hands. "The old boy ride his horse yet?"

"Next class," Gloria said.

He leaned into Mercy's face and whispered. "I'm about out of this family. Soon as I'm cleared, it's adios." He tipped a glass and poured wine down his shirt.

"Shhh, mother will hear you," she whispered back.

How could she have depended on this jerk all these years, she thought.

The announcer's voice boomed. "Here they come, ladies and gentlemen, our Walking Mare and Gelding Amateur Specialty Class. Give them a big welcome."

The Wurlitzer organ struck up skating rink music as fifteen horses, chomping their bits and bobbing their heads, glided through the gate. Buck was the last one through. He sat tall and handsome in his red shirt and navy suit but appeared to be fighting his horse with every step. Lather dripped off Mistress Colette's neck and her hooves tore up the dirt as she hopped rather than walked.

"There's Buck," Gloria said, dragging Mercy to her feet. "Isn't he magnificent?"

"His horse is about to blow up," T. Wayne said, just as the mare delivered a back kick in front of the judge. Overton clenched his teeth as the horses circled at different gaits.

"Go running walk, ladies and gentlemen, running walk," the announcer called.

The horses moved into an extended gait, the riders leaning back in their saddles and encouraging them with clicks and whistles. Mistress Colette picked up the rhythm and settled into a ground-eating gait.

"See," Gloria said. "Buck knows how to handle a woman."

The mare floated over the ground with an elegance the other horses couldn't match. After several passes, the judge lined them up to stand four-squared with heads up and ears perked. Overton frowned and touched his hat brim as the judge passed. First, second, third, places went to other exhibitors. The judge awarded Mistress Collette fourth place.

"He did a beautiful job riding her," Mercy said.

"The judge saw that kick." T. Wayne laughed. "Buck hates to lose. I sure wouldn't want to be that horse."

"It wasn't her fault, Gloria said. "She's high strung, like Sophia. I'm going to the barns to cheer him up."

"It's always mucky back there," Mercy said. "I'll go and tell him how proud you are."

◆

Mercy walked the dim, muddy path between the stables, searching for the Walking Horse barn. Finally she heard Overton's voice from one aisle over.

"The mare's got talent, but she's unpredictable. All the same, I appreciate your stopping by."

Rounding the corner, Mercy glimpsed the head judge as he shook hands with Overton and walked away. Overton stuck his hands in his pockets and stared at his boots. Despite the poor lighting, she could tell he was furious.

"Judge Overton," she said, uncomfortable calling him anything else. "Mother sends her best. Colette was amazing."

"Never had a chance at the blue, not with her temper tantrum."

She nodded, not knowing what else to do. "That's a shame."

Down the hall, a slim man wearing a pink polo shirt backed out of a stall with a lead rope in his hand. "Ready to load," he called to Overton. Overton nodded toward the man.

"That's my trainer, Gary Parson. Gary, this is my new step-daughter, Mercy Snow."

The trainer waved as Colette emerged from the stall, looking more delicate than Mercy had expected. Parson led her toward a tall van with its loading ramp let down.

"We're going back to the barn. I'll catch a ride to the house with Parson," Overton said. "Make sure my bride gets home safely. Don't let T. Wayne drive."

"You're not competing in more classes?"

"Waste of time."

"Sorry for the disappointment. I think Colette is beautiful."

Mercy backtracked toward the arena, picking her way through puddles, when a scream stopped her in her tacks. A sound like a mallet pounding a drum followed then another scream. She visualized Colette walking into the cavernous van. *No!* She sprinted back to the stable where she saw Overton at the end of the aisle, standing at the top of the ramp, silhouetted by the van's interior light. She caught flashes of Parson's pink shirt inside the van and glimpses of Collette striking out with her front hooves.

"Get the vet," Overton yelled and lunged into the van to grab the mare's halter. Colette reared and flung him off his feet. He got up, yelling to Parson, "Get out, she's crazy with pain."

Colette bellowed and charged the front of the van, knocking Parson against the wall. Overton dragged the trainer out and dropped the board over the opening. Both men stumbled down the ramp. Blood spattered Parson's shirt, and Overton breathed heavily.

"You almost got us killed," he yelled at Parson.

"I didn't expect her to go that nuts," Parson mumbled from behind his hand. Blood dripped from his broken nose.

"*Shut up*," Overton barked, glancing in Mercy's direction.

"I only meant—"

Colette kicked the van wall and moaned. Mercy had never heard an animal express so much agony. She fought back tears, trying to follow what Overton and Parson were saying.

"You told me she climbed the hay net," Overton prompted. "You said you heard her cannon bone snap."

Parson nodded. "That's right. She caught her foreleg in the net. She broke her own leg." He gave Mercy a panicked glance then looked back at Overton.

"Have her put down as soon as the vet gets here," Overton ordered. "Get the vet to sign something first. I don't want the insurance company questioning this."

"Won't you have her x-rayed first?" Mercy said.

"Horses don't survive a broken leg." Overton smacked his fist into his palm. "Damn it! The way she was acting up, I figured something like this would happen."

"You blame Colette?" Mercy said, appalled.

"I blame her bitchy temperament. Fortunately, she's insured. Let's go. I don't want you to see anymore of this."

They wound through the dark show barns toward the arena. Word of the accident must have traveled quickly. Grooms and riders fell silent as they walked by. She frowned, thinking about the way Overton had reacted. She caught up with him.

Even in the shadows, she could see a wicked smile on his face.

Chapter Forty-Seven

Thursday 4:18 p.m.

Billy made it onto the Southwest flight out of Little Rock with only minutes to spare. On the phone, Courtney Burdine had told him she had thirty minutes to give him. Her girlfriends were coming over at five that afternoon, and she would be leaving for an extended trip to California early the next morning.

I was right, Billy thought. Dupree was shipping her off, and he'd caught her just in time. Thirty minutes wasn't much time to convince, guilt-trip or intimidate her into realizing that her involvement with Dupree could implicate her in a crime, but it would have to do. He had no leverage in Texas.

Was she victim or villain? He was expecting Courtney to be the doe-eyed type, bowled over by Dupree's money and charisma. That's why he planned to open with "the bastard has taken advantage of you." Then he would offer to extricate her from a disastrous situation in exchange for damaging information about Dupree.

But Courtney could also be hard-edged and guilty as hell, maybe even the instigator of the plot to kill Sophia. He'd dealt with a lot of bad women in his career. A bad woman can outstrip a bad man by a mile. If he got even a whiff of culpability, he'd be all over Courtney with threats of a subpoena to have her hauled before a grand jury.

There was one hitch. Before leaving Memphis he'd called the homicide desk in Austin and asked the sergeant to check the computer for any local warrants on Ms. Burdine. Her sheet came up clean, but the detective had other information to give him that wasn't on file. Everyone in Texas law enforcement knew the Burdine family. Courtney's father was chief legal counsel to the governor, and her mother practiced criminal law with a top Austin firm. Courtney was connected. Any move he made against her would require asbestos gloves.

He arrived at Childress Place. The doorman directed him to the elevator and the tenth floor. Billy knocked on Courtney's door and pulled out his badge wallet. A blonde holding a stack of blue napkins answered. She was slender, attractive, in her mid-thirties with a big Texas hairdo. She wore black slacks with a leopard print top that stretched over her distended belly. She was at least five months pregnant.

Dupree's motive to get rid of Sophia shot up one thousand percent.

"Hi, I'm Courtney," she chirped.

"I'm Detective Able," he said, covering his surprise.

"Sorry, I've got my hands full." She left him standing in the doorway and walked to a cocktail table across the room, where she put down the napkins. She glanced over her shoulder and crinkled her nose. "Come on in, silly."

The room was furnished with antiques and splashy abstract art. Dupree had obviously spent a fortune on the place. Billy joined her with his badge wallet still in his hand.

She gave him a wide smile. "You can put that away, Detective. I know who you are. May I pour you a drink?"

"Thanks, no." He walked to the wall of floor-to-ceiling windows. The afternoon light reflected off the metallic skin of the river below. He turned. "We don't have much time. How about if we sit down and handle this matter before your friends arrive?"

She batted her lashes but didn't move. "What matter?"

Interesting. She was attempting to control the interview right out of the box. "I came to talk about Mr. Dupree's wife."

She crossed her arms over her belly and pouted. "I can tell you T. Wayne would never hurt a living thing, certainly not a woman. And I won't say another word until you tell me why you're after him."

Her parents must have schooled her in cross-examination techniques. She wanted to know what he knew before she would decide whether to cooperate. He forced his shoulders to relax and smiled pleasantly.

"Okay. But first, let's talk about the nature of your relationship with Mr. Dupree."

"You're kidding me, right?" she looked down at her stomach and gave it a pat. "And don't go all preachy about him being married. I don't know what it's like in Tennessee, but all the good men in Texas are taken. If you want a husband you have to use some ingenuity." She indicated his empty ring finger. "I see you're still single."

He gave her an intimidating frown. "This isn't a game, Ms. Burdine."

"It certainly isn't, Detective." She shrugged.

She had him buffaloed. He cleared his throat. "I'll confirm that Dupree was out of the country when his wife disappeared on Friday night." He waved his arm toward a chair, indicating it was time she took a seat.

"So you'll admit that T. Wayne couldn't possibly be the person who hurt his wife?"

He nodded.

"Then I'll be happy to get off my feet." They settled into club chairs, Courtney curling into the loose pillows with her bare feet tucked beneath her. "Now. Tell me about Sophia."

"Why don't you start, and we'll compare notes?" he said, pulling out his pad. "Fair enough?"

"Okay. Let's see, I know that she makes the society page a lot. And they've both been unhappy for years, even worse after their son died." She frowned. "I can't imagine what it's like to lose a child." She tapped her finger against her cheek. "Oh yes. She had a problem with alcohol even before T. married her, and she goes off on drinking sprees for days at a time." She looked at his pad. "Do our notes match?"

"You believe everything your boyfriend tells you?"

She laughed. "Only an idiot would do that. My information comes from friends in Memphis. T. Wayne's made excuses for his wife's emotional problems, but believe me, her escapades are well known in that city."

She had pinpointed Sophia's binge drinking and disappearances, the major weaknesses in his case against Dupree, and she was letting him know she knew it. Courtney was considerably smarter than she let on.

"How long have you known Mr. Dupree?"

"Over a year."

"When are you due?"

Her lips parted in surprise. "Why, Detective, that's a rather personal question. But I'll answer. Late December. It's a boy, by the way." She arched a pink-polished nail at him. "Carrying a baby to term is stressful. More to the point, I find your presence stressful. I'll tell you one more time, then I'll have to ask you to go. T. Wayne wasn't involved."

Billy eased back in his chair. "We don't know *who's* involved. A homicide case can have a lot of participants."

She blinked. "*Corpus delicti.* Why do you call it homicide when you don't have a body? An unhappy woman like Sophia Dupree might be anywhere and with anyone. She could have jumped off the Mississippi Bridge for all you know."

She smoothed her hair and inspected her manicure. Courtney wasn't stressed. She was about as nervous as a jungle cat stretched out on a tree limb. After Sophia's skittishness, her animal vitality must have been attractive to Dupree.

He was getting nowhere. He had to step up the pressure before she kicked him out.

"We haven't discovered a body . . . yet. But even without one, a case can be successfully prosecuted. I'm going to be up front with you. Evidence is stacking up against Mr. Dupree, and eventually you'll be dragged into it. It's going to be hard on you. Tell me what you know now, we'll get an affidavit, and maybe the D.A. in Memphis will let you skip the grand jury appearance. Might even keep the media off your back."

She tilted her head. "That's so sweet; you want to protect me. But I happen to know that if you had a single piece of evidence against T. Wayne, you would have already used it to scare me. I read the Memphis papers. I know the political pressure you're under. T. Wayne isn't the best man I ever met, but he's mine, or will be by the time this baby's born. He promised. He'll be my husband, so you can forget trying to manipulate me into saying something that might help you."

She gave him a sympathetic smile. "Your tail is in a crack, Mr. Detective. The way I see it, you've flown across two state lines hoping for a gusher and you've come up with a dry hole."

Courtney stood and stretched her lower back. "I'm afraid you'll have to leave now. My friends will be here soon. They're throwing a surprise shower for me. Of course, the surprise is on them. I already know about it."

He stood. Courtney had remained calm and controlled the setting, but he had to take one last shot.

"Thanks for your time. I'm sure you're aware the investigation is just getting underway. I haven't begun to dig into your possible involvement. But I will."

She smiled. "You really want to tangle with me? I'll give you my mother's office number." She walked to the door and opened it. "Speak with her if you have any more questions."

◆

Courtney closed the door behind him. Billy heard the click of the lock. That said it all. He'd gotten nothing out of her and wouldn't get anything in the future. She was so completely unchallenged by his threats; he was surprised she hadn't yawned in his face.

He walked down the hall to the elevator. The doors slid open. He moved to let four young women carrying gifts step into the hallway. One winked as she passed. They giggled as he entered the elevator.

"Buh bye, Detective. Ya'll come back now, ya' here?"

The doors slid closed. He had seriously pissed off Hollerith for nothing. In fact, the investigation was going in reverse, except for the one slip Courtney made during her perfectly orchestrated interview—her admission that Dupree had promised to marry her by December.

Chapter Forty-Eight

Friday, 7 a.m.

The next morning, Billy took the milk run flight to Little Rock and drove back to Memphis with the sunrise burning in his face. He decided to stop by the nursing home to see Tutwiler Jackson before going in to face Hollerith. Jackson may very well have been the last person to talk with Lou. If he had information, Billy wanted to get it into the CJC system before Hollerith lowered the boom. If nothing else, Lou's friend might offer a bit of wisdom.

Billy could use some wisdom about now. Courtney had been too smart, too well connected, and too pregnant to be intimidated into implicating Dupree. He'd left Texas without enough juice to approach the D.A. for an indictment or even the hope that leaning on Dupree's buddy in Louisiana would produce information. He'd gambled for nothing.

At the Grimes Nursing Home, Billy parked under a grove of ancient pecan trees. Greek Revival columns lined the porch, where two of the residents sat in their wheelchairs. He said good morning, but they only stared blankly at the traffic on Elvis Presley Boulevard. He noticed the hall leading to the reception desk smelled like rotten strawberries and rubbing alcohol.

A pretty young woman in a blue uniform led him to the back doorway. He watched Jackson, an overweight black man in a wheelchair, roll down the ramp and stop at a patch of marigolds growing in the center of the courtyard. Jackson held onto the wheelchair with one hand and strained over the arm to weed with the other. He wore a white shirt with sleeves rolled to the elbows, a pair of red suspenders with the words "Go Razorbacks" stitched in white, and a Panama hat. The veins on his arms stood out like cord under his skin. Both legs had been amputated below the knee.

The old man looked up from his weeding to watch Billy cross the asphalt courtyard to the patch of orange marigolds. Jackson squinted up at him from under the hat. "You're Able, Lou's partner, aren't you?"

"That's right, Mr. Jackson."

"My friends call me Tut."

Billy squatted. The man's lower lids hung loose and red, and his skin looked ashy. "How's the world been treating you?"

"Not bad. Didn't make Lou's funeral. Felt awful about it."

"Ruby told me you and him were friends from way back."

Tut chuckled. "We've swapped some stories, I'll say that."

"I'm looking for details about the hours before Lou's accident. The sign-in book shows he came by here that day. Anything you can remember would help."

A FedEx plane rumbled on its low approach to the airport. Tut rubbed his hand across his mouth and mumbled something.

"Beg your pardon?"

"I said *why?* Tell me *why* Lou killed hisself?"

Billy wondered if the old boy was losing it until he remembered Jackson had been a cop. Tut wouldn't bring up suicide if he weren't pretty damned sure about it.

"Did Lou talk about suicide?"

"Didn't have to. He always brought a box of dietetic chocolates with him." Tut pointed at his stumps. "I got 'sugar.' That's why they cut my legs off. Saturday he left eight boxes of those chocolates at the desk. Asked the ladies to give me a box every other week. Eight boxes told me he wasn't planning to come back."

"Did he talk about what happened Saturday morning?"

"Said he had a real bad day."

"No shit. What else?"

"He talked about picking up security work for one of those tight-assed corporations. Said he needed to bring in some big bucks. Seemed real blue."

"He's been blue for months."

Tut shook his head. "Ruby destroyed that man. No other woman would do unless it was the ghost of Marilyn Monroe."

"I went by his house. I don't think he even lived there. Maybe he was seeing a woman, a woman with kids."

"I ain't saying a lady didn't catch his interest, but Ruby broke his heart beyond fixing. Damned shame to see it." Tut stared at his hands in his lap. "Wish I had me a cigar. They won't let us smoke here. Or do much a nothin' else."

Billy could see talking about Lou was taking its toll. He changed subjects. "I hear you were a bailiff at the courthouse."

Tut's eyes brightened. "I was the second black Shelby County deputy sheriff hired. Caught hell, but I made it through. Came out of the field and moved to the courthouse. I'll tell you what, some bullshit goes on down there."

"Judge Overton told me about the guy showing up in his courtroom with a grenade."

Tut blinked. "Say what? What you talking about . . . a grenade?"

"Overton said Lou stopped the guy."

Tut rolled his chair back and forth, chuckling. "That Judge. He's still the king bee buzzing around. Must have a reason for floating a whopper like that."

"You're saying it didn't happen?"

224

"No, sir, it didn't. I'd know."

Billy stood. If Overton's debt to Lou never existed, why had he gone to the trouble of lying about why he'd called Lou on Thursday?

"I met Lou at the courthouse," Tut continued. "We been tight ever since. Made good money together, too." He winked.

"How's that?"

Tut hesitated, chewed his lip. "You should know. You're the man's partner. He told you about our deal, right?"

Billy had to think fast. Lou worked Vice back then, handling the strip clubs. "You mean that thing he had going with the clubs?"

"Yeah, them titty clubs." Tut grinned. "We had us a sweet thing going. Lou controlled the number of busts. If one got to court, I'd get the case rescheduled then thrown out. We saved those club owners a shit-pile of money. I can't give you a figure. Lou was the one who kept notes on every payout. He called it insurance." Tut shook his head. "If I had that money now, I'd hire that young thing at the front desk to look after me."

Billy's heart pounded, but he managed to keep his voice even. "I guess Lou put back a nice nest egg."

Tut laughed. "No, sir. That Ruby was a shopping fool. Of course, neither of us thought about the spigot running dry."

"What happened?"

"That pain-in-the-ass Waters got wind of a cocaine deal going down at a club and decided to step in without Lou knowing it. I heard about the bust. Had to pull some strings that night, I'll tell you what. Made sure the bust fell apart. Waters got suspicious. He kicked up enough stink for Lou and me to shut down. I probably should've thanked Waters for closing us down before we got caught." Tut swatted at a fly. "But somehow the mood never hit me."

Speechless, Billy wiped sweat off his face. The kickbacks must've been what Sam had been talking about at The Western.

Tut waved his hand. "Don't mind me. I'm just a senile old fool. They say 'sugar' affects the brain." He smiled. His dentures slipped. He slid them back with his tongue. "New teeth. Can't chew nothing." He leaned over and snatched a few weeds, looking pale under his hat.

Billy laid his hand on Tut's shoulder. "Mr. Jackson, I need to head out. Meeting you has been enlightening."

"There was one thing I forgot that Lou mentioned that day. He said, 'If my partner comes by asking questions, tell him I think he's a hell of a good cop.'"

◆

On his way downtown, Billy stopped at a drive-thru and ordered two bacon and egg biscuits he washed down with a large coffee. Comfort food.

He crumpled the wrappers and tossed them on the floorboard as he drove. When your world's shot to hell, no use keeping up appearances.

Tutwiler Jackson made it clear he and Lou had been on the take. And Sam Waters had backed that up. Lou was a dirty cop. Billy's allegiance to Lou had given him tunnel vision. No telling what else he'd missed.

He wanted to call Jones, but he'd gone to Texas without his charger. His cell was dead. He pulled over to a pay phone and made the call.

"Agent Jones."

"Morning. The great state of Texas sends you greetings."

Jones's voice dropped. "You still in Austin?"

"No, Memphis."

"Did the girlfriend flip on Dupree?"

"I'll explain later. I'm calling to test the waters."

Jones muffled the phone with his hand then came back.

"I'm surrounded here. Where can we meet?"

◆

The sky hung low and chalky over the bench Billy had picked for their meeting on the bluff. The Mississippi flowed by, broad and sluggish. He'd counted on the river's energy to feed him, but that wasn't going to happen today.

Jones strolled up from the parking lot wearing his cool shades and charcoal suit. Pigeons scattered as he sat down and stretched his legs in front of him. "Nice place. I haven't seen the river this close up before. By the way, you look like hell."

"That's what Texas will do for you."

"Right." Jones yawned. "I hope you can wait on divine justice, because you won't see much of the other kind today. I tried calling your cell to warn you."

"Battery's dead. What's up?"

"Troopers pulled over some cracker driving a van with stolen tags outside of Holly Springs. Found a woman he'd snatched tied up in the back. The sheriff sent up his prints, and Hollerith had me run a rap sheet. This guy has a list of warrants long as your arm—assault and battery, auto theft, armed robbery, and they're looking at him for a double homicide."

The news stunned Billy, but he didn't want Jones to see it. "Holly Springs. That's Marshall County Sheriff's Department. Let me use your cell. I want to call them."

Jones didn't reach for his cell. He squinted out across the river. "Here's where it gets strange. Hollerith took over the case. He's in Mississippi right now."

"What the hell . . . he's a desk jockey. Only time he leaves the office anymore is for a damned stats meeting."

"Hollerith made it clear he wanted a private conversation with the guy they arrested. He didn't invite me to tag along."

"Come on, what's he up to?"

"I know what I'd do in his position. Offer the guy a deal to get him to cop to the Dupree abduction. Hollerith closes the case and grabs the credit. It's happened before."

"Did he discuss it with Carey?"

Jones nodded. "I assume they worked out a deal to get a confession. Hollerith left a message for Overton, then he called Mosby and sold this guy as a sure thing for the Dupree abduction. He puffed up his role and said he was taking over the case. He ran the same routine with the mayor. The politicians are really sweating this one."

"Yeah, Overton's sweating too," Billy said. "Noel's considering him for a seat on the U.S. Court of Appeals, which explains why he's so hot to get Dupree cleared. He wants this investigation over before the FBI checks under his hood."

Jones looked stunned. "How did you hear that?"

Billy shrugged. "Girl talk."

"I'm not *even* going to ask."

A young Asian couple, walking hand in hand, wandered near the bench to look at the river. The girl glanced over at them. She spoke in Japanese to the boy, and they hurried away.

"We must look like the bad guys," Billy said.

"Hey, it's hard to tell the difference these days." Jones leaned forward and rested his elbows on his thighs. "I'll tell you something about Hollerith because you need a heads up, but you have to promise you won't act on this."

"You got it."

"There's a big-time, number-crunching pilot project underway for state law enforcement. It's called 'a multi-variable regression analysis.' Major federal money is riding on this."

"What are they after?"

"They're dumping every crime in Memphis for the past seven years into a database using specifics from each case. They're including every weird variable they can think of—weather, the stock market, moon cycles. They want to predict criminal activity down to the week and sector—bank robberies, carjacking, burglaries, even which public events need beefed-up security. I came to Memphis to map gang territories and gather stats. They're looking to significantly raise solve rates. If it works, everybody involved gets a gold star."

"They can't predict human behavior with a mathematical equation."

"Who knows, maybe they can."

"So that's why Hollerith keeps running off to stats meetings," he said. "This project is his dream job."

"The mayor asked Noel to bump Hollerith to the top of the list for project director. No telling why the mayor did it, but I'll bet Overton is involved. I checked out Hollerith's bio. He has a degree in criminology and computer science plus a Masters in statistics. But there's a hitch. They'll have to move him up two grades to meet the requirements."

"That's why he's in Mississippi. He's going to use this case to grandstand for a big promotion."

Jones held up a warning finger. "Not a word about what I just told you."

"So Overton and the mayor pressured Hollerith to close the Dupree investigation. Hollerith finds a fall guy. The story drops out of the news, and Dupree walks on murder charges. Everyone gets what he wants." Billy watched a powerboat slap the water, heading upstream. He felt like he'd been sucker-punched. "Ya' know, I ought to belt Hollerith in the mouth."

Jones cut his eyes over. "Yeah, *that'd* be a smart move. You better calm down and switch gears. Tell me what happened in Austin."

He took a breath. "Courtney Burdine, the Texas Queen. She answered the door, and you'll never guess what she was wearing."

"A thong?"

"A maternity top. She's pregnant with Dupree's kid."

"Holy shit."

"The rat bastard promised a wedding before the baby comes. She didn't realize it, but she gave his motive and deadline for getting rid of Sophia. Otherwise, she didn't give an inch. Did I mention her father is legal counsel to the governor, and her mother is a criminal attorney? The biggest mistake I've made was giving Hollerith an excuse to dump me off the case."

Jones shook his head. "Look. The evidence says Dupree made a move against his wife. The way I see it, if he didn't have her killed, it's only because someone else got to her first."

"Or the guy in custody in Mississippi did it. Maybe I've been too focused on Dupree. Gut feelings can blind you to other options."

"The ship's sailed on this investigation. You've got to let it go. I guarantee the lieutenant is down there cutting a deal. He'll ask the D.A. to combine all counts, including those homicides. They'll offer him no death penalty with time in a federal prison, not some state hellhole. The guy will plead guilty, and the Mississippi A.G. will snap at it to save the state trial costs."

"If that's how it goes, and he's not the perp, we'll never find Sophia." Billy shook his head. "He'll fake a plausible explanation for not producing the body, like he dumped her in a swamp full of gators—case closed. That's going to be hard to live with."

Jones cleared his throat. "I've got one question."

"Take a shot."

"You had a thing going with Mrs. Dupree, right?"

He nodded. "A long time ago."

"Back when her boy died?"

"Just after."

"She left her mark on you, man. She must have been somebody special."

"I loved her. Guess that's worth losing my career over."

Jones blew out a breath. "Don't talk crazy. Hollerith is moving on. He doesn't want to get tied up with your dismissal. It's my understanding you've been suspended on administrative and medical leave. That passes the decision over to Anderson. Make your apologies and show up at the shrink's. You've got to concentrate on getting your swing back."

"Yeah, *right*," Billy scoffed. A week ago getting his swing back would've been enough. Now he was mad enough to knock a ball through a stadium wall. "This whole damned deal makes me sick."

"Face facts," Jones said. "You're off the case, and I'm back with the task force at the governor's request."

"That means Hollerith has the field to himself. By the way, did he mention the color of the van in Holly Springs?"

"I hate to even say it. It's white."

"The alleged van parked beside Sophia's car was blue."

Jones stood to leave. "Who knows? The guy could have a whole fleet of snatch-ass vans."

He stood and shook Jones's hand. "You're a great cop and a good partner. Best of luck."

"Hold on. What's your next move?" Jones searched Billy's face. "I mean today. You going to do something stupid?"

He smiled at Jones's growing alarm. "I'm going to make sure everyone around Dupree knows what he's been up to. They can decide on their own if he's responsible for Sophia's disappearance. But I guarantee, if I see him, I'll string him up like Christmas lights and flip the switch. Later, partner."

Chapter Forty-Nine

Friday, 8:30 a.m.

Mercy rubbed her tired eyes, took a bite of cereal, and glanced out the kitchen window. "Mother and the judge just pulled up to the front door," she said to T. Wayne, who was sitting across from her, sipping coffee and reading the Wall Street Journal.

He slapped down his paper. "What the hell do they want?"

Mercy considered dumping her cereal in his lap. A week of his drunken bullying had been enough. "They're here to pick up some of her things. You got a problem with that?"

He looked away, didn't answer.

She watched out the window as Overton walked around the Mercedes to help her mother, who was struggling, to get out of the car. Lieutenant Hollerith's call last night, informing them that a probable suspect was in custody in Holly Springs, had knocked Mercy and her mother off their feet. Mercy had tossed and turned all night, wondering when they'd hear if the man had confessed. Apparently, the stress of the news had started Gloria's heavy drinking again.

T. Wayne stood and leaned over the table to watch Overton and Gloria climb the front steps. "Damn it. I have a ten-hour drive in front of me. I'm going to slip out the back."

"What! You're leaving?"

"I was a heartbeat away from going to jail because of your sister. I have a place in Austin. If something happens, you can reach me through my office." He gulped his coffee and hurried down the back hall with suitcases he had stashed in the laundry room.

Selfish bastard. Living with him must have been hell for Sophia. Mercy heard the front door open. "I'm in the kitchen," she called, prepared for the ensuing drama when her mother realized T. Wayne had run out the back door to avoid her.

She heard his BMW's engine turn over, and at the same moment saw Billy Able's car turn into the driveway. The BMW flew past the kitchen door and into view, heading straight for Billy's vehicle. Both cars swerved. She closed her eyes and heard the awful *whump* of metal hitting metal.

"What the hell was that?" Overton demanded as he came into the kitchen.

She opened her eyes, felt her stomach drop. "The Mercedes is insured, right?"

◆

Billy had been so focused on the gold Mercedes parked in front of the house he didn't see the BMW barreling straight for him until it was too late.

He yanked the wheel right and slammed to a stop in the flowerbed that lined the drive. He opened his door and saw Dupree already out of his car, muttering as he bent down to examine the damage to the mangled rear bumper of the Mercedes.

Billy strolled over. "Nice work. Been driving long?"

"What are you doing here?" Dupree spat.

"I came to talk with the ladies, but this is even better. You'll see their faces when I explain how you planned to get rid of your wife."

"My car!" Gloria called and ran out of the house with Mercy and Overton following. Crying, Gloria traced her hands over the Mercedes' wrecked fender. Overton pulled her back, all the while glaring at Billy.

Dupree paced, whipping himself up for a fight, while Mercy walked around the Mercedes, studying the damage. She looked like a woman nearing the end of her rope. Billy's first instinct was to get her out of there before things got nasty, but that wasn't going to happen. Might as well play out his hand.

He'd noticed the suitcases on the BMW's backseat. "Driving to Texas?" he said. "Going to visit Courtney?"

Gloria wiped her tears. "Who's Courtney?"

"None of your business," Dupree said.

Mercy turned a cold gaze on Dupree. "What's he talking about."

"Ask him about the new beneficiary of his life insurance," Billy said. "And why he called the Lava Café in Baton Rouge."

"Gotcha, smart-ass," Dupree said. "Mercy, you remember when we were at the Sonic? I told you about Tucker Stans. He owns the Lava Café."

She nodded and looked at Billy, waiting.

"Your pal Stans is mobbed up," Billy said. "Twenty grand is the going rate in Louisiana for a hit, and Tucker's the man who can hook you up."

"I called Tucker because his dad died."

"Yeah, we looked into that. His dad kicked the bucket a year ago."

Dupree looked flustered. "But I just found out."

"So you made a condolence call. What about the second call? And the call to Jazzy's? That's a gangbanger hangout. What's a place like that going to do for you?"

Gloria shrugged off Overton's arm. "Who's this Courtney?"

"That's enough, Detective," Overton broke in. "You're upsetting my wife."

"I want to know what he's talking about," Gloria said.

"Her name is Courtney Burdine," Billy said. "She's been living in Dupree's condo in Austin for the last six months." He let the stunned expression grow on Gloria's face before he delivered his punch line. "She's his fiancée."

"That can't be true," Gloria said. She looked up at Overton. "Tell me that's not true." Overton shrugged. Gloria turned to Mercy. "Did you know about this?"

Mercy's face tightened. "I'm not surprised. I found out he's been married before. He beat up his first wife, and he probably beat Sophia."

"Damn it!" Dupree said, his face reddening. He ran at Billy and shoved him hard in the chest with both palms. Billy stepped back, solid on his feet, waiting. "Get off my property," Dupree hollered and lunged, swinging his right fist.

Billy sidestepped, grabbed a handful of shirt and twisted Dupree's arm behind his back. Then he jerked Dupree around to face Mercy. "Tell them about Courtney. All of it."

"Shit," Dupree panted.

Billy jammed his arm higher.

Dupree grunted against the pain. "It wasn't me. Sophia cheated first. She's a slut."

"Make him shut up," Gloria said and wilted against the judge.

Dupree went on. "She's been sleeping around. She's done it before. After Casey died, she ran off with some guy. Stayed drunk for weeks. I took her back. This is the thanks I get."

"You're lying," Gloria cried.

Dupree laughed. "You and your bitch daughter are nothing but drunks. You made my life hell."

Billy spun Dupree around and bashed him in the mouth with a right cross. Dupree hit the ground, moaning and covering his mouth.

"Get up, you idiot," Overton said. He turned to Billy with a threatening smile. "T. Wayne doesn't have all the facts, but I do. Our detective here was the man Sophia took up with." He jerked a thumb at Billy. "He took advantage of Sophia during her time of grief, then he bailed out."

"*No,*" Mercy cried.

Dupree rolled off the ground and back on his feet, hunkered over with his fists raised. "Motherfucker. I'll get you for that."

"Come on, cowboy; let's see what you got," Billy said, beckoning with both hands.

"Stop it." Mercy stepped between them and faced Billy. "Tell me it's a lie, and I'll believe you." Her eyes pleaded with him.

He put his hands on her shoulders. "Truth is, after Sophia lost Casey, she collapsed. I stepped in."

"You had an affair with my sister? And then you left her?"

"It wasn't like that. She left me."

Mercy shrugged off his hands. "So you were in love with her."

"I was the first person on the scene when Casey was hurt." He shook his head. "Dupree abandoned her."

Overton broke in. "I *told* you Able was out for revenge. It's the reason Hollerith took over the investigation."

Billy felt them all staring, but he spoke only to Mercy. "No matter what you think of me, believe this: Dupree tried to hire a hit man to have your sister murdered. Even if the guy in custody took her life, that doesn't make Dupree innocent. I came here to tell you. You can't trust him."

"Hey," Dupree snapped. "You're the man who can't be trusted. You fucked my wife."

Billy ignored him and focused on Mercy. "My relationship with Sophia ended ten years ago. Since then I've tried to keep her safe. That's all."

Dupree sneered, asking for another punch in the mouth, but Billy kept his gaze on Mercy. "One thing you should know before he walks away. The Texas girlfriend, Courtney Burdine . . . she's five months pregnant."

Chapter Fifty

Friday, 2 p.m.

Dr. Jimmy stood at the Walgreen's checkout with a two-foot tall giraffe tucked under his arm. He'd chosen the giraffe because of its striped vest. He paid, walked out to the parking lot, pulled three one-hundred-dollar bills out of his wallet and folded them into the giraffe's vest pocket. In his wallet was another piece of paper, a current address for Fred and Karen Belleflower, the parents of little Rebecca Jane.

The giraffe was to be a prop in the most twisted mission Dr. Jimmy had ever undertaken.

After his stop at Ruby's house on Wednesday, he'd returned to the farm to find Evie on the sofa, struggling to catch her breath. They spent two days in the hospital clearing fluid from her lungs and adjusting her meds to ease her congestive heart failure. He'd walked the halls, worrying, and at the same time making dead end calls in search of Rebecca Jane's parents. The Belleflowers had done a good job hiding themselves, not only from social services, but the phone company, Memphis Light Gas and Water, Memphis Housing Authority, the school board, even the IRS. On paper they didn't exist.

At noon, he'd driven Evie home from the hospital and given the Belleflowers' names to his grandson. The boy hopped on his computer and found them in fifteen minutes.

Walking to his truck, holding the giraffe, Dr. Jimmy wondered if he'd done the right thing leaving Evie in their daughter's care so soon after coming out of the hospital. And he felt foolish questioning Lou's integrity. But he had to see Rebecca Jane for himself. Until he confirmed the child was safe with her parents, he wouldn't get another night's sleep.

After a couple of wrong turns, Dr. Jimmy found the house and parked his truck across the street. Four children played in the yard of the ratty bungalow, the older boy chasing the two girls with the garden hose. All four looked pasty and underfed, their clothes hanging off their thin frames. A naked toddler collapsed in a puddle and sobbed.

Rebecca Jane wasn't among them.

He noticed a window curtain move inside the house, and in seconds a woman appeared at the door, holding a beer can in one hand and a cigarette in the other, scowling at him. The fact that he could see the beer must have registered because she tucked it behind her back. That meant she thought he was there to check up on the kids. He pulled his digital voice recorder out of the glove compartment. After years of working with the sheriff's department,

234

he knew the value of substantiated evidence. If he uncovered a problem with Rebecca Jane, his next step would be to take the recording downtown to the Sex Crimes Unit. He turned on the recorder, slipped it in his front pocket and a slim, sterling flask into his hip pocket. It was important he create a believable persona—an admirable citizen with an edge of depravity. He got out of the truck with the giraffe and went to stand in the yard in front of the house. Karen Belleflower hung back in the doorway a moment, then stepped out on the porch.

"Afternoon, Mrs. Belleflower. My name is Dr. Jimmy Dale Dexter. I hope you don't mind my dropping by unannounced."

Her feral eyes darted from the children to him. "Somebody say my kids are sick? They're liars; see for yourself."

He held up his free hand. "No, ma'am, no complaints. I don't work for the state of Tennessee. Here are my credentials from Arkansas if you'd like to see them. I have a medical clinic there. And here's my driver's license. Tell you the truth, I'm here on personal business."

"Personal. I see." She came down into the yard and peered at the clinic's certificate, then the picture on his license. She nodded. "Yeah, I seen you interviewed on the five o'clock news. Your clinic sees people who don't have insurance." She drew on the cigarette and tilted her head up to blow the smoke. "You were watching my kids. What do you want?"

He pulled out the picture of Rebecca Jane that Ms. Moore had given him. "Your daughter visited my clinic. I treated her for a pretty severe upper respiratory infection."

The woman squinted, still suspicious. "She's all right now."

"She's had pneumonia. There's a danger of relapse. We follow up with someone like your daughter, but she never came back to the clinic. I was in Memphis today, thought I'd stop by to be sure she recovered."

"Becca ain't here. She's living with relatives." She handed the snapshot back to him. "I never heard of a doctor driving to another state to make a house call. You're showing up with a giraffe and a picture of my kid. Why?"

"She's a special child, an unusually beautiful girl." He nearly choked on the words, but if he was going to test the waters, now was the time.

The kids, who had been standing around listening, grew still. Karen Belleflower's gaze locked in, appraising him. "You telling me you like little girls?"

Dr. Jimmy held two views of pedophilia. The first was grimly pragmatic; as a physician he had stayed current on studies revealing the anomalies found in a pedophile's brain. His second view was emotional; as a father, he'd horsewhip anyone who sexually abused a child. The thought that he was about to step into the role of pedophile made his skin crawl.

"Rebecca Jane brought out something in me that I've ignored in the past."

"I don't understand what you're saying, Doctor."

"I'd like to see your daughter again. Take care of her." That was as far as he could go.

Karen's eyes narrowed. "How do I know you're not fronting for the cops?"

"I don't work for the cops." He took a breath. "I want your daughter, if you understand my meaning."

His misery must have added a convincing element. She grinned. "Yeah, I bet you see lots of little girls at that clinic. Guess you've got a perfect set-up."

He pulled the flask from his hip pocket and took a swig. "I've never done anything like this before. I'm a married man, got kids myself. But there's something about your daughter." He fumbled with the giraffe. "I brought this."

"Guys like you bring toys. I got a house full of them. I need to see more than that if this conversation is to continue."

"The giraffe's holding." He pointed at the bills folded in its vest pocket. "Go get Rebecca Jane and bring her here so I can see her. We'll talk about her future."

"Rebecca Jane's unavailable." Karen put on a sly grin and cocked her head toward the children. "Don't know if you noticed, but she has a couple of good-looking sisters. I'm taking them to a talent agent to get them work in TV commercials. What do you think, Doc?" She waved her arm at the children. "Come on girls, line up so the gentleman can take a look."

Karen Belleflower pushed her daughters forward, straightening their hair, working them like a horse trader offering a pair of ponies for inspection. The girls stood close to each other. The little one peeked up at him through her bangs. She tried to smile. He thought he was going to be sick.

"Doc, you better settle down, you're all red in the face."

"Who's that you're talking to?" a male voice called from inside the house.

"Oh, crap," Karen muttered then shouted over her shoulder. "It's a doctor. He's come to see about Becca."

Fred Belleflower emerged from the gloom of the house onto the porch, skinny and bare-chested, wearing ripped jeans. The tattoos and frazzled braid that hung down his back pegged him as either a Neo-hippie or a biker freak—the kind of guy who believed his lack of hygiene and income represented a valid social statement. Dr. Jimmy saw ten just like him in the morgue every year, dead from knifings, overdoses or gunshot wounds. This guy was a coward and a pretender, not bad enough to be a threat to anyone but his own kids. Fred stepped off the porch and wrapped his big-knuckled hand around his wife's waist. He smelled like dirty bed sheets and pot.

"You kids get inside," he said.

"They're muddy," Karen whined, as the older girl dragged the bawling toddler up the steps.

Fred thrust out his chest. "I protect what's mine. What's this talk about Rebecca Jane?"

Karen pulled the money out of the giraffe's pocket. "He's the doctor from that clinic we seen on TV. He wants to see her is all."

"I want to be sure your daughter has recovered," Dr. Jimmy said.

Fred sneered. "Yeah, right. That's not enough cash to get a look at my daughter. What else you got?"

Dr. Jimmy's hand began to tremble. He was going to have to play along with this piece of road kill to get a look at Rebecca Jane or find out where she was being held. After that he'd come back wearing a police wire to get the kind of evidence that would put these people out of business forever.

He lifted the corners of his mouth in what he hoped looked like a smile. "I'm out of cash. What would you suggest?"

Fred's gaze fell on Dr. Jimmy's belt buckle. "I like the looks of your buckle. Is that brass or gold plate?"

"Gold plate," he lied.

"Good enough. I'll go pick her up so you can take a look. After that, we'll see what we can work out."

Dr. Jimmy drew the leather through his pants loops, calling on all his reserves to keep from whipping the flesh off both these miscreants. He handed over the belt.

"Mighty fine," Fred said, inspecting the sculpted tree. He turned it over. "What's this word on the back?"

"Forever," Dr. Jimmy said, knowing Evie would understand why he had to give it up.

Fred laughed. "I guess this proves it. Nothing lasts . . . forever, I mean."

Chapter Fifty-One

Friday 4:40 p.m.

Billy left the Dupree house too pumped and angry to do anything but drive. He sought the comfort of the Mississippi back roads, driving past his home church and his uncle's roadside restaurant, with its locked doors and boarded-up windows, but his emotions continued to simmer. The sadness he'd seen on Mercy's face when he left was too much.

WEVL 89.9 played a string of Memphis blues artists—Jim Jackson, Furry Lewis and Sleepy John Estes. Billy was into it until they played *Floating Bridge*— a heartbreaker of a song about a drowning man. That made him switch to the Cardinal's game on AM 560. He turned up the volume and let the play-by-play crowd out his mental rehashing of the confrontation with Dupree.

In the bottom of the ninth he noticed the afternoon light slanting across the road and realized he'd been drifting the way Lou used to do. He headed back to Memphis and ended up on Front Street at Lytle's—a bar reborn from the bones of an old cotton broker's warehouse. Lytle's Bar was a hangout for every upwardly-mobile drinker living downtown who'd lost his job, his lover, or his good sense. Today Billy qualified for two out of three of those categories.

He grabbed a seat at the horseshoe-shaped bar and ordered a double shot of Jack with a beer back. After a few swallows, he closed his eyes, savoring the whiskey burn on the back of his throat, and the image of that jackass Dupree thrashing around on the ground. The memory of Overton blindsiding him with Mercy brought him up short. *Damn.* He gulped more whiskey. He could kick himself for not leveling with Mercy sooner. But what was he going to say . . . by the way, Mercy, I slept with your sister?

"Another Jack and keep them coming," he said to the bartender.

And how the hell had Overton found out about the affair? Lou, the only other person who knew about it, had always been tight-lipped. Maybe Lou was drunk when he talked to Overton and let it slip. Hard to believe, but then the Lou he'd discovered this week was a complete stranger.

He knocked back the second Jack and chased it with half the beer. Punching Dupree in the mouth had felt damned good, but it was going to cost him his job. A dismissal by the board would ruin his permanent record and ultimately trash his career. His only choice was to resign and move on to another city with a clean slate. In this line of work, you're not always right, but you recover and make up for lost ground. If you don't, you're done.

Billy watched the after-business crowd drift in, cocky lawyers and stockbrokers with their sleeves rolled up, ending the week early. The bartender bumped up the volume and dropped off another round. Ladies came through the door, moving to the music and shedding their office jackets to reveal low cut dresses. Across the room, the crowd parted for a young woman whose blond hair swung across her shoulders. She waved to a man sitting at the end of the bar. Billy noted the way she touched his hand as they took their seats and how she leaned into his gaze.

Mercy had that same earnest way about her. She made him want to take her into his arms.

He remembered how she'd looked to him for some sanity while she stood next to the wrecked Mercedes. Then Overton had blurted out about the affair. The disappointment on Mercy's face nearly broke him. Protecting the investigation had seemed like a valid reason to hide the affair from Mercy, but his silence had also ruined his chances with the best woman he'd ever known.

If he didn't do something fast, he was going to lose her. He slid off his stool and flipped open his cell. It was dead. He sat back down. Maybe it was best. He was drunk, and he hadn't even tasted the whiskey. When he had a better grip on himself, he would ask her to hear him out.

The activity picked up. On the far side of the bar, a tall guy with salt and pepper hair was talking to the two best-looking women in the room. The guy turned around to set down his glass. It was Sam Waters.

Billy picked up his beer and walked over. Sam saw him coming and held up his drink.

"I hear the Dupree case is a wrap. Congratulations."

"Here's to American Justice, long may she behave." Billy drained his mug, saluted Sam with it, and caught the bartender's attention. "Another round for both of us."

"You look a little worse for wear," Sam said. "Got a problem?"

"It's all good. Hollerith took over the case, and I'm suspended."

"Rumor called it 'medical leave.'"

"Nope. I've been working hard to get my ass kicked off the force."

"Now you're preaching to the choir. If I'm not on probation, I don't know how to handle myself."

Billy nodded. "By the way, I met one of your old buddies this morning . . . Tutwiler Jackson."

"How's Tut doing?"

"He's in a wheelchair. Diabetes took his legs. Said he'd like to have some of that money he and Lou skimmed off the strip clubs so he could hire a private nurse. You know, go out in style."

He glanced over to gauge Sam's reaction. Sam's gaze didn't waiver, but the muscles in his jaw worked.

"If you'll excuse us, ladies," Sam said to the women. They made a show of pouting and left. "Look, Able, in my book reliving history ain't worth much. It generally just pisses people off."

"I've been shoveling Lou's bullshit all week. I need some real answers about Lou."

"That's a big change from the other night."

"I've picked up some wisdom since then."

Sam slapped him on the back. "Yep, and you're still standing."

The room pulsed. Billy leaned against the bar to steady himself. "Tell you what, you talk and I'll listen."

"You won't take a swing at me?"

"I'll hold off."

Sam took a swig of his fresh drink. "Here goes with the history. Lou and I worked together off and on since I joined the force. He knew who to avoid in the department, where the bodies were buried. We partnered in Vice, which included working the topless bars. When I came on the scene Lou already had the players in line. I mean there were the usual underage drinkers, the occasional G-string malfunctions, but overall the clubs ran pretty clean. They were taking in big money in those places. Large money."

Sam paused to wink at a flirty redhead across the bar. He held up his glass and swirled the ice. "Sorry. I got distracted. Before long I noticed most clubs we busted kept their liquor license and opened right back up. And Lou had a lot of cash. He didn't flash it around, but pocket money wasn't an issue."

The bartender dropped off a bowl of popcorn. Sam dug in and tossed back a handful.

"I started asking the dancers questions. They didn't give up much, but enough to make me suspicious. Later, I got wind of a big cocaine delivery, so I got the warrant and set up the bust. I didn't tell Lou. When we showed up at the club, the drugs were gone. I figured that was no coincidence and confronted Lou. We had a knock-down-drag-out. That's the day I told you about—the one where he chased me around the cruiser with a broken beer bottle. I thought about it for a week and then met with Internal Affairs. They told me the FBI had a sting running on the clubs and didn't want local bullshit screwing things up. They told me to back off. I transferred out of Vice. After awhile, Lou moved over to Homicide."

A week ago, Sam's story would've been fighting words. Now it made sense.

The redhead gave Sam a blatant come-hither look. Sam nodded to her and drummed his fingers on the bar. "You remember the other night when I said Lou made some underhanded choices?"

"You said life sucks when you find out Superman's a jerk. I almost slugged you."

"I'll tell you what really sucks . . . when you have good reason to rat on Superman. Got to go, my friend. Duty calls."

Sometime during his talk with Sam, the sun had set. Billy went back to the bar and found a seat. He watched car lights trail electric blue tracers outside the windows, and people on the sidewalk move like jerky cartoon characters. He was good and drunk. Rarified drunk. That didn't stop him from realizing Sam's story had corroborated Tut's version of the graft scheme. But one piece was missing. How did Tut get all those cases dismissed? A bailiff can arrange for a cop to be a "no show" and make a few cases go away, but Tut said this set-up had gone on for a long time. That meant a judge had been in collusion with Tut and Lou.

One phone call would confirm the guilty judge, but Billy already knew the answer. It was the Honorable Buck Overton. If the grenade story was a lie, he now knew the real reason for a relationship between Lou and the judge. It had paid off for both of them.

Billy was too drunk to think anymore. He paid his tab and weaved onto the sidewalk. The fresh air helped keep him on his feet, and the traffic kept him from veering off the sidewalk—real-world stuff a guy could focus on. Something with a bone in it.

He made it to the barge. Somehow the key fit the lock, and he turned on the lamp without knocking it over. He put his cell on the charger and noticed the machine's blinking message light. Probably Hollerith calling to tell Billy he had to go up before the board. Screw it. He went to the galley, poured up the last of a bottle of whiskey, and knocked back half the glass. Definitely hell to pay in the morning after a daylong fuckfest of bad news and more booze in one night than he'd drunk in six months. He plopped onto the sofa with a buzz in his head, and his eyes feeling like they'd been taped open.

Now that he had a fix on Overton's motives, he wanted to hear from Lou. He wanted Lou to explain the graft and why he'd killed himself. Why he left it to his friends to cover for him. The disc with the video of the ballgame sat on top of the TV. He struggled up, switched on the set, and fed it into the player.

"*You ain't hitting the ball hard enough to make a dent in a doughnut,*" he heard Lou grumble. "*And you ain't getting another partner that easy.*"

He watched himself crouch over the plate and swing at a ball, low and inside.

"*Strike two, asshole,*" Lou growled under his breath. "*You're on your way out.*"

"YOU'RE the one on the way out," Billy yelled and threw a book at the screen. Lou thought he was God almighty, the self-righteous bastard. Gave Billy hell for two years—the real rookie treatment.

"*Strike three,*" the ump called over catcalls from the other team.

He watched himself bounce the meat end of the bat in the dirt. The bat flipped out of the frame. Lou zoomed in, picking up his frustration.

"Too bad, bud. How about if we get in the batting cage next week, get you straightened out?" Lou said.

It sounded like the old Lou. No sarcasm, no meanness.

"Great," he heard himself say. *"When?"*

"Line it up for the weekend."

The screen went to black. He sat there a full minute before realizing the show was over.

He slumped back on the sofa, sipping the end of the whiskey. They never made it to the batting cages. Lou's attitude had gone downhill after that game. In fact, from that time on Lou hadn't made much sense at all.

He got up and weaved to the galley for a beer. Why not keep a good buzz going? Couldn't hurt. He found two cans of Bud and hoop cheese wrapped in wax paper. He grabbed all three, managed to set the beer on the counter and fumbled the cheese.

"Butterfingers," he said out loud.

As he bent to pick it up, he heard Lou say, "That's right." He came up slowly, staring at the cans of beer on the counter. Okay, no more booze. Then he heard a splashing sound followed by a squeal that sent him scrambling to the TV.

The screen was all lit up again. "Atta girl, hop in," Lou said.

Billy was looking at Lou's back as he knelt beside a bathtub filled with bubbles. The camera had been positioned above and behind Lou. It wasn't clear if someone was holding it.

"Feels good, Daddy," a child's voice said.

"Let's have that foot, young lady. How did you find a mud puddle in the middle of an asphalt parking lot?"

A child's delicate foot lifted out of the water. Lou took it and began washing between the toes with a sponge. He moved up her leg then started on her other foot. "How about singing a song?"

"Is the camera on?" she said.

"Of course, Miss Monroe." Lou splashed bubbles, making the girl laugh.

In a little girl's voice, she sang Marilyn Monroe's song about diamonds being a girl's best friend. Lou glanced over his shoulder and grinned into the lens, happier than Billy had seen him in a year.

Here, finally, was the answer. Lou must have met someone and taken on the responsibility of her child. For some reason, he'd kept it a secret. He would have needed a lot of money to support Ruby and a secret family. The money pressures might have put Lou under.

"Daddy, I want to go outside and play," the child said with a pout in her voice.

"No, sweetie, it's not safe. That's why you have to stay quiet as a mouse and keep the door locked. The bogeyman might come and steal you away from Daddy. You don't want that do you?"

"No . . . "

"Don't you like our new home in the sky and your clothes and games? And having Daddy come home to you every night?"

"I do." She lowered her voice. "I don't want to go back. I want you to be my daddy always."

"Tell me again what you'll do if Daddy can't come home for a few days."

"I'll draw and play games and practice singing and dancing."

"And you can watch movies. Your movies will always be on."

"And I'll eat Cheerios and peanut butter sandwiches."

"That's right. There's plenty of food. What else?"

"I'll take my Sleeping Beauty pill every morning, and I'll wait right here till you come home. That way the bogeyman won't get me." She splashed the bath water, ending her list with a flourish.

"Smart girl," Lou said. "You've got it down."

Billy frowned. What bogeyman? What the hell was Lou talking about?

"Daddy, get the duck, I want the duck tonight," the child's voice pleaded.

"You think you've been a good girl this week?"

"Yes!"

Lou moved to sit on the edge of the tub. The screen came alive with the face of a beautiful child about six years old, her blond hair piled on her head and secured with a ribbon, her tiny shoulders and chest covered in bubbles. Her smile for Lou was irresistible. Lou stood and walked out of camera range. Billy heard him opening a cabinet in another part of the bathroom.

The child played with the bubbles, making peaks then flattening them. Her fingernails glittered with blue polish, and she wore diamond studs in her ears and a gold and diamond chain around her neck. On a shelf behind the tub, he saw a doll that had Marilyn Monroe's features, a bouffant hairdo and a sparkling evening dress.

Two muffled pops punctuated the sound of her splashing. Lou reappeared carrying what looked like champagne bottles with gold metallic wrappers at the necks. The girl squealed and clapped.

"Cold Duck for my sweetheart," Lou said and upended both bottles into the bath. The child splashed the water with her feet, tilted her head back, and began singing about diamonds again.

Lou knelt beside the tub on one knee, absorbed in the girl's performance. The camera caught them both—she was the actress; he was her adoring fan. Lou's pupils dilated. His mouth went slack.

A chill hit Billy. *No man should look at his child that way.*

The girl sang another song, just like a little Marilyn Monroe. When she'd finished, Lou helped her out of the tub, murmuring to her as he wrapped a towel around her small body and began to rub her all over. She closed her eyes, seeming to relax and enjoy the attention. Lou dropped the towel, picked up the naked child and cradled her in his arms.

"Love you, Daddy," she said.

"I love you too, Rebecca Jane." Then he bent his head and French-kissed the child long and full on the mouth, hugging her tiny body to his chest. When he'd finished, before he turned to leave the room, Lou looked at the camera and winked.

Everything that happened to Billy next was involuntary. The bile rose first. Then all the alcohol he'd drunk flooded his mouth and spewed onto the floor in front of him. He staggered across the room, knocking over the lamp, trying to get to the TV. His foot shattered the screen on the third try. He grabbed the player and flung it across the room. The room was dark now, and he dropped to his knees, sobbing. Everything made horrible, perfect sense.

If he'd known about the girl, he would have killed Lou himself.

◆

Billy opened his eyes. A square of moonlight glowed in front of his face. He was lying on the floor and smelled boozy vomit in the room. He must have passed out. In the shadows, he saw the gutted TV lying beside him. Something horrible had happened, but he couldn't remember what. He sat up. The bathroom scenes from the video tore through him, the details burning into his brain.

My, God. Lou had taped himself molesting a child. Billy's throat closed, keeping the bile down this time. He rubbed his face, trying to clear his mind. He remembered Lou calling her Rebecca Jane.

Hold on. Lou was dead, but what about the girl? Where did she come from? Nothing he'd found in the past week connected Lou to a woman with kids. Was she dead? If Lou had followed the pattern of a lot of tormented males, he killed her on Saturday, and later, drove off the bridge. Or Lou could have left her alive. Billy's heart stopped. *Holy Jesus.* Rebecca Jane could be locked up in what Lou had called their "home in the sky." She could be like the Riley sisters who were left locked up in the basement.

He had to find her.

Billy stumbled to his feet, hitting the wall with his shoulder. He was still very drunk. He turned on the lights. The clock read four in the morning. *Pull it together,* he thought. *Get a plan. Call and see who's on duty in Sex Crimes.* He picked up the receiver and dialed.

"Dispatch, Williams ."

"Billy Able here."

A pause.

"Sergeant Able? That you? Don't sound like you."

"Iss me," Billy slurred. "Gimme Sex Crimes."

"Cut the jokes. You know those geniuses don't work graveyard shift. They're too fucking special. You can call back in three hours, or you can talk to voice mail."

"Never mind."

Frustrated, Billy hung up. He was too drunk to drive and too messed up to get the details swimming around in his brain straight. It made no sense for him to open a file. This belonged to Sex Crimes. He slammed his fist into the doorjamb. Pain shot up his arm.

Lou. His partner, his friend. A pedophile. Lou had been like a father to him.

Billy shook his head. He needed air to clear his mind. *The Jet Ski,* he thought. Speed might help to obliterate the sickening images of Lou abusing the girl. He fumbled around the bowl on the counter for the keys. Out on the deck, strips of clouds raced over the moon. The Jet Ski bumped against the barge in the water's chop. He slid onto the saddle and turned the key. In seconds he looped around the slack water and was out on the river with the Memphis skyline crowding the bank to his right. Everything looked different from this perspective—the bridge, the Pyramid, the soft porch lights of Harbor Town. Everything *was* different. Nothing would be the same again.

He turned downstream, gunned the engine and zipped under the old bridge, skipping from wave to wave as he shot downriver. There was plenty of wind in his face, but it wasn't working. "You son-of-a-bitch," he screamed into the blackness. No life jacket; no one else on the river. Billy was vaguely aware he was pushing the little craft too fast, but didn't give a damn about the risk.

Seeing that video of Lou and the girl had killed something inside him.

He muscled the wheel around into the full force of the current. Now he was running upstream into heavy chop. He cut along the Arkansas bank. Debris forced him to veer toward the center of the channel where he was startled by the silhouette of a massive coal barge almost on top of him. The rig, five barges long and three barges abreast, was pushed by a three-story towboat. He whipped around 180 degrees, so close to the barge his puny wake splashed against the steel wall.

He'd show the bastard. He spun back toward the monstrous wakes being cast shoreward, cutting as close as he could to get behind them. The first almost flipped him backwards. He shifted his weight forward and charged the next one. Suddenly he was over both wakes with the accelerator wide open. "Fuck you, Lou," he shouted at the sky.

The wake thrown off by the towboat hit next—steep, turbulent, created by two giant screws driven by huge diesel engines. The Jet Ski flew straight up into the air. The propeller whined, cutting nothing but air as it flipped. He hit the water. The Jet Ski landed square on his chest, its weight driving him below the surface. Struggling to free himself, he sucked in a lungful of water. Arms flailing, he reached the surface seconds before it was too late. The other side of the wake hit him, tumbling him like a cork.

He surfaced, choking on water and diesel fuel. The towboat was gone. The river was dark. The current was strong. He knew the river's history. No one survives a Mississippi undertow.

He knew it was as good as over, but he swam toward the city lights anyway. His mom and Uncle Kane were in his mind. He let them go. He thought about Mercy. He wished he'd called her tonight. He was sad about Sophia. He hated Lou for what he'd done, but he had to forgive it all. Even himself. He didn't want to die, but he was already losing the fight. The current tugged at his legs, sucking him under.

Then he remembered the girl, Rebecca Jane. What if she were still alive?

He stopped swimming. He was the only person who knew about her. He couldn't give up. He took a deep breath, put his head in the water, and stroked harder.

"Hey buddy," someone shouted. "Grab ahold."

A Styrofoam cooler landed on the water a few yards in front of Billy. Beyond it the hull of a cabin cruiser rose like an iceberg out of the water's chop, and he saw the silhouette of a man waving his arms. Billy grabbed the cooler.

"Look here, Danny, this crazy son-of-a-bitch is trying to swim the river," the voice called. "Give him a hand up. Hey, you ain't a Razorback fan are you?" the voice said as someone grabbed his arm and hauled him upward.

◆

Billy's rescuers introduced themselves as John Payonk and Danny Richardson. They said they were out early on the river to catch some catfish. John wore a long-billed fishing hat. Danny had on a T shirt that read "Twisted Genius." They didn't ask him why he was jumping barge wakes like a suicidal jackass. He appreciated their discretion.

They dropped him off at his barge as the sun broke the horizon. He rushed inside to shower off the river. He couldn't stop the scenes from the video rolling over him like sewage water. That beautiful child. Lou's wink.

He threw on jeans and a shirt. Lou's bizarre behavior was finally coming into perspective—the paranoid outbursts, his exhaustion and secrecy. The school books and Popsicles at the duplex. The overtime hours and push for money. It had all been about Rebecca Jane.

Lou had said, "You never could see what's inside a man." He'd been right. Who looks into the heart of his best friend and expects to see a monster? Lou didn't commit suicide. He executed himself. Even at that, he'd gotten off easy.

Billy went into the living room and ejected the disc from the DVD player. They would need pictures of Rebecca Jane, but the forensic department didn't come in until eight on Saturday. A friend who owned a 24-hour copy store downtown had the right equipment to print the pictures. By the time he had the pictures, the shift with the Sex Crimes would have clocked in.

He was almost out the door when he noticed again the message light blinking from last night. He punched the button.

"Able, this is Johnnie Walker with Sex Crimes. It's seven on Friday night. We have a Dr. Dexter reporting a missing and possibly abused child involving . . . Uh, we've got a real mess on our hands. This looks bad for Lou. Damn it, Able, pick up. Or get back with me as soon as you hear this message."

Billy grabbed his gun and cell and hurried out the door. At least he wouldn't have to explain Lou's crime to Walker.

◆

While the guy at the print shop pulled a photo of the girl, Billy called Detective Johnnie Walker, a teetotaler who happened to have the same name as the whiskey, to get the details Dexter had given the day before. Walker said they were in the process of setting up a sting on the Belleflowers with the doc going in wearing a body wire. Billy told him about the video and said he was on his way with photos of the girl.

Just after seven, Billy pulled up to the CJC and saw Dexter across the street, standing next to his truck. He didn't know how the doctor had learned about Lou and the girl, but he was damned sure going to find out. He whistled through his fingers at Dexter and dodged traffic as he crossed to the parking lot.

Dexter nodded as he walked up. "I wanted to reach you last night, but my wife had a setback with her heart, and we spent the night in the ER. My daughter is with her now."

"Hope she's okay." Billy pulled out the photo of the girl with Lou sitting on the tub's edge. He watched the doctor's reaction as he took the picture and held it by its edges.

"Damn it to hell," Dexter muttered and handed it back. "That's the same girl. Rebecca Jane Belleflower. Where did you get this?"

"Off a DVD I found in Lou's car trunk. Walker said you saw them together a few months back. If you knew something was wrong, why didn't you report it?"

Dexter bristled. "Me! You were his partner. Couldn't you see he'd gone off the deep end?"

Billy almost responded, then took a mental step back. Guilting Dexter wasn't going to help find the girl.

"We both missed the call on Lou. Just tell me what you know about Rebecca Jane."

Dexter nodded. "Lou brought her to my clinic. She was thin, anemic, had a serious respiratory infection."

"Did he explain why he showed up with someone else's sick kid?"

"He said the parents came in as witnesses for a homicide investigation, and the girl was with them. She was sick."

"That didn't happen," Billy said.

"How the hell was *I* supposed to know that?" Dexter said. "He told me the parents were lowlifes, and he was worried she'd get worse if she didn't see a doctor. He was right. In a couple of days she would've developed pneumonia. I prescribed antibiotics and vitamins and said she should be watched."

"What made you think there was more to it?"

"I thought about the way he put his hands on her. It would have been appropriate if she'd been his daughter, but he was supposed to be a stranger. When I called to check on her, Lou said she was fine and back with her family, but something kept bothering me. I confronted him, said I thought he was lying about his relationship with the girl. He called me a dirty-minded fucker and hung up. I let it go. I didn't want to believe my own doubts."

Dexter thumbed sweat off his brow. "After I saw the way Lou died, I couldn't get the girl out of my mind. I stopped at Child Services on the way to the funeral to ask questions. They sent me to LeBonheur Hospital. I got an address, but it was bogus. My wife's condition worsened, and we checked into the hospital. I didn't find Rebecca Jane's parents until yesterday."

He paused and stared down the street, his disgust evident. "When I got there the mother assumed I was a pedophile interested in Rebecca Jane. The father went to pick her up so I could have a look at her. When he came back, it was apparent he had no idea where she was."

"If you'd said something the day of the funeral, I could've helped you," Billy said.

Dexter gave a resigned shrug. "I needed to believe Lou's story. Until I had proof otherwise, anything else was unthinkable."

"Lou was obsessed with the girl. I've heard about men who'll use a daughter as a sexual substitute for a dead or missing wife."

"Surrogate pedophilia. I just didn't connect it with Lou." Dexter looked down at his hand opening and closing on his keys. "I should've had it out with him. I didn't do a damned thing."

An unmarked car swung into the parking lot. The detective leaned out his window. "Ready, Doc?"

Billy clapped Dexter on the shoulder. "You can do something now. Get the parents. I'll find the girl."

◆

After Dexter left, Billy and Walker analyzed the video shot in the bathroom. It was an upscale setting. A window showed the top of a red billboard. Lou had called it their home in the sky. The place must be several floors up and in a commercial district.

The bottles of Cold Duck Lou had used for the Marilyn Monroe act were the same as the ones Stokes had spotted in the box at the duplex. Human nature leans toward familiar territory. The odds were good Lou had bought the Cold Duck at a store where he felt comfortable. It wasn't much, but it was the best lead Billy had.

The third time through the video, revulsion got the best of him. He left Walker and found an empty office to take a breather. He had to get control of his disgust with Lou. Last night his emotions had gotten the upper hand, and he'd nearly paid with his life.

He took out his cell and called Mercy. He wanted to hear her voice, even if she told him to go to hell.

Her voice mail answered.

"It's Billy. I have an urgent matter to handle; otherwise, I'd be at your door. Please don't leave town before we talk."

After he hung up, he closed out with Walker and left by a side door to avoid running into Hollerith. Now wasn't the time to lose his badge and gun. He had one hunch that might lead to Rebecca Jane. After that, he'd be guessing.

◆

He walked into the Sputnik Liquor Store and saw three older men lined up at the counter. They each wore felt hats and clenched stubby cigars between their teeth. Each man gripped a different bottle—T. W. Samuels Whiskey known as "Tough Willy," Burnett Vodka or "Blue Top," and Seagram's Gin or "Bumpy Face," named for the bottle's pebbled texture. He glimpsed the two gray-haired owners standing behind the counter—tiny Flo Spiro, and her taller, sturdy sister, Georgia Blen. Georgia and Flo had shared a passion for major league baseball with Lou. Billy hoped, for Rebecca Jane's sake, that baseball hadn't been their only topic of conversation.

While the sisters rang up sales and bagged the bottles, Billy paced nervously at the back of the store, and glanced at the Friday night's Braves game played on the overhead TV.

The best way to get information was to stand back and let the ladies tell him what he needed to know without their ever realizing it, although that strategy was going to be tough when the clock was ticking on the child's survival.

Georgia followed the last customer to the door and flipped over the "Closed" sign for a temporary lock up.

Flo scooted around the counter and tucked herself next to Georgia. "We saw you pacing in the back. How can we help?"

"There's something I want to ask about Lou," he said.

The sisters glanced at each other. "All we ever talked about with Lou was baseball," Flo said. "The Braves, you know." She blinked from behind her owl eyeglasses and leaned into Georgia in that needful, Southern-lady manner.

"CSU found an empty fifth of Jack in the cab of Lou's truck. I found more bottles hidden under his kitchen sink."

"We didn't encourage Lou to drink," Georgia said, managing to look sympathetic and insulted at the same time.

"I just wondered if you knew when he started again."

"He bought a few bottles last fall. We gave him such a fit about it he quit asking."

"Did he buy anything other than Jack?"

"A few cases of Cold Duck," Flo said. "Wasn't like him to drink that sweet stuff. After that, he stopped coming in."

"When did he start with the Cold Duck?"

"Early spring," Georgia said. Her voice trailed off.

"That's all we can tell you," Flo said. "We weren't privy to Lou's personal life."

Her tone said she was uneasy discussing Lou's weaknesses after he'd passed. There were rules about such things, and these ladies followed them. Unfortunately, he was going to have to be more direct.

He was about to bring up the child when Georgia asked, "I was curious whether Lou's little niece was at the funeral."

"I don't know. What does she look like?" he said, keeping his voice neutral.

"Curly blond hair. About six years old. Lou showed us a picture. Her name was . . . " Georgia frowned. Billy didn't prompt her.

"Rebecca Jane." Flo smiled, pleased with her good memory. "Lou planned a party for her on Easter. He remembered the soda and chips but forgot refreshments for the adults. He called us late on a Saturday night, all stressed out. We drove a case of Cold Duck over to him in West Memphis after we closed."

"Did you see his niece?"

"He met us in the parking lot because the elevator was broken and he didn't want us to walk up all those stairs."

"Do you remember the name of the building?"

A customer rapped his ring against the glass door. Flo glanced at her watch. "We should open. There's a lineup outside."

"Do you remember, Flo?" Georgia said, heading for the door.

"It's something to do with birds," Flo said.

"That sounds right," Georgia called.

"I've got it," Flo said, beaming. "It's The Aviary Condominiums."

Chapter Fifty-Two

Saturday 2:58 p.m.

Billy drove like a madman across the Old Bridge into West Memphis. Had Rebecca Jane shared the same fate as the little Riley girls? He'd despised the cops who failed to save the girls. Now the onus was on him. His tunnel vision had put Rebecca Jane in grave danger.

As an investigator, you put a puzzle together. Sometimes the pieces make a different picture than you expect, because a deviant mind has created it. The components are right, but nothing fits.

He hadn't seen the big picture because he'd been pre-judging the pieces. He couldn't see behind Lou's mask, the same way the Mississippi cops couldn't believe a pillar of their white community had been capable of abducting two black children.

He veered off at the first West Memphis exit and drove to The Aviary, a ten-story building with an iron birdcage fountain at the entrance. The residents, mostly wealthy retired couples who travel abroad, occasionally leased their condos on a short-term basis. Wheeling into the parking lot, he noted the red billboard across the street. This had to be the place.

He turned off the engine, considering what to do next. As an out-of-state cop without a warrant, he had no authority. He could call Walker, but then Walker and his Arkansas counterparts would need time to work through channels. Since Billy didn't know if Lou had used an alias, asking the manager to open up a condo was out of the question.

He noticed a young guy wearing a gray uniform come around the side of the building with a box under one arm and a ladder under the other. He set the ladder under a light fixture, pulled a bulb out of the box and dropped it. The bulb exploded on the concrete. The guy walked to the door, swiped a card through the electronic lock and went inside.

A kid like that might not be trusted with a passkey, but he probably could get his hands on one. Billy folded the picture of Lou and the girl in half so only Lou was visible. Then he went to his trunk, took out a tool and slipped it into his hip pocket. He strode toward the building just as the kid came out carrying a broom and dustpan.

"Hey, buddy." Billy raised his hand. "How's it going?"

The kid shrugged and backed up a step.

Billy flashed his badge then read the kid's nametag. "Pete, I'm Detective Able. I'm looking for a friend of mine, but I don't know his condo number." He held up Lou's picture. "You know him?"

Pete nodded. "Old guy. Kind of a night owl."

"What do you mean?"

"He's only around at night. I haven't seen him lately."

"We were supposed to get together today, but he's not picking up his calls. He may be sleeping one off, or he may be sick. I could sure use your help checking on him." Billy slipped two twenties out of his wallet. Pete's eyes lit up.

"You know his condo number?" Billy said.

"Sure, 724."

"Can you handle the lock with that card?"

Pete eyed him warily, but his gaze kept dropping to the money. "No, but I can get one. You're a cop, so this is legit, right?"

"You got it." He stuck the bills in the kid's shirt pocket. Pete left and quickly returned with the passkey.

On the seventh floor, the elevator doors slid open. Billy flexed his hands and tried to appear calm as they walked to the end of the hall. Pete indicated the door on the right.

Billy knocked. "Lou. Hey, Lou you in there?"

Pete pointed at the lock. "Your buddy installed a deadbolt. If he doesn't open up, this pass key won't get you in."

"I've got it covered." Billy pulled the pick gun from his pocket, inserted the tool and gave it a few clicks. The lock turned.

"Hey, you picked that lock," Pete said, looking nervous.

"It's standard department equipment. Go on, swipe the card."

Pete backed up a step. "I think I should get the manager."

Billy cursed under his breath. He couldn't let a bone-headed teenager get spooked and call someone in to interfere. He grabbed the card and swiped the lock.

"Hey!" Pete said.

"Wait here," Billy ordered and stepped into the entry, sniffing for the odor of death.

"Rebecca Jane?" he called. He recognized the soundtrack of a *Shrek* movie blaring from the living room. In the kitchen to his left, a jumble of cereal boxes, peanut butter jars, a loaf of bread and juice bottles were scattered across the floor. Canned goods and dishes had been taken out of the cabinets and stacked on the counter as if someone had been making a careful search.

Billy pulled his gun from the holster at the small of his back. Whoever did this could still be in the condo.

To his right, a hall closet door stood open. A box of computer supplies had been dumped on the floor. He moved around the corner to the living room, hoping the girl had been watching the movie, heard the door open, and was hiding. She wasn't there, but an adult had been.

The sofa at the other end of the room lay on its back. No six-year-old could have done that. A large, flat-screen TV stood in the midst of jumbo stuffed animals, coloring books and throw pillows. Everything in the bookcase had been taken out and stacked onto the carpet. On the dining table he saw several botanical presses and stacks of binders that appeared to hold dried leaves and flowers. Children's movies on shelves had been rifled through and replaced.

Billy jerked the plug on the TV to shut *Shrek* up. If the girl were alive, she'd be afraid to come out. "Rebecca Jane it's okay, sweetheart."

To his left was a low platform with a blue velvet curtain hanging behind it. Lou had installed track lighting above it, and his camcorder sat on a tripod to the side. Twenty-five or so photos of Rebecca Jane wearing sparkling costumes hung on the wall.

Billy hurried into a large, rose-colored bedroom. On a table beside the canopy bed stood a Sleeping Beauty lamp and a stack of children's books. Someone had flipped the mattress off its frame. Every drawer in the room had been pulled out and turned upside down in the middle of the floor. Whoever did this was looking for something taped underneath the drawers. Billy checked the closet for the girl, finding only dresses and elaborate stage costumes.

With a sinking feeling, he realized Lou would never have taken Rebecca Jane away from this fantasy world.

In an alcove across the room, he saw a counter with a makeup mirror, prescription bottles and a makeup case. *Beyond that was a closed door.* It had to be the bathroom he'd seen in the video.

"Rebecca Jane, your Daddy sent me. Come on out."

He wanted to believe she was hiding in the bathroom, but the jaded cop in him knew better. He went to the door with his gun raised. The knob turned easily. He took a breath to steady himself and flipped on the light.

She lay in a fetal position with her back against the tub. Blood speckled the marble floor. Her eyelids were swollen shut, her face purplish, her lips blue. Blood from a crushed place above her temple laced through her hair and ran down her cheek. Ugly bruises the diameter of a teacup marked her arms and legs. Chunks of the tub's ceramic edge had been knocked out, probably by wild swings of a weapon that had missed her small body.

A row of Cold Duck bottles lined the back ledge of the tub.

Billy turned away, gagging, imagining her attempts to defend herself from the bogeyman Lou had warned about.

Whoever did this was subhuman.

He holstered his gun, knelt beside her and placed two fingers against her carotid artery. He felt a fluttery pulse. His heart jumped with relief. Her upper arm felt clammy. Between the trauma and the head injury, she wouldn't last long.

"Holy shit!" Pete said from behind him. "A kid!"

"Pull blankets off the bed!" Billy said and looked back at Pete still standing in the doorway, too stunned to move. "*Go.*"

While Pete ran for the blankets, Billy called 911 and tried not to yell at the operator as he gave the location and described the girl's condition. Pete returned, and they layered blankets over her. Billy checked her pulse again. It was a little stronger. He called Dexter's service. The operator said Dexter's wife was back in the hospital and promised to have the doctor meet the ambulance at the ER.

Billy hung up, checked his watch. Nothing to do now but wait. He sat on the floor, studying Rebecca Jane's unrecognizable face. Every wrong turn he'd made while investigating Lou may have cost this girl's life. If only he'd watched the entire video sooner.

"I'm so sorry," he said, brushing the girl's hair from her face. "I'll get who did this."

He heard the ambulance siren in the distance, and Pete was behind him again. "God almighty, why would your friend do that to his own kid?"

"He didn't," Billy said. "He's been dead a week."

◈

Billy was tempted to follow the stretcher to the ambulance but shook off his guilt and stayed with the scene. Now that the worst had happened, he was almost supernaturally calm. He called Walker and gave him a report then looked around the condo. The place was small with very little furniture, and it appeared that the attacker had searched every conceivable hiding place. What had he been looking for?

The uniforms arrived followed by Detective Annette Perwalski. She had a slight overbite and wore a navy blue pant suit tailored for curves that would give Pamela Anderson competition. She took a look around the condo then joined him beside the table with the botanical presses and binders.

"Seems to me, Detective, you either have a professional interest in this child or you showed up for personal reasons." Her eyebrows went up.

She was right to question him. Perpetrators like to pretend they've discovered a body then insert themselves into the investigation. Sick bastards. But he wasn't in the mood to be treated like a suspect. Not *this* kind of suspect.

He handed a card to her. "This is Detective Johnnie Walker's number with the Sex Crimes Unit. He opened a case file on the girl yesterday."

"You have her full name?"

"Rebecca Jane Belleflower."

Perwalski's gaze remained fixed on his. She knew he was holding out on something, but Billy wasn't going to immediately spill his guts about Lou to a West Memphis cop he'd never met.

He heard a commotion in the entry as Dexter shouldered his way through the uniforms at the door.

Dexter nodded to Perwalski. "Annette."

"Dr. Jimmy."

"Is she alive?" Billy said.

"Barely. They'll get her stabilized and move her to The Med."

"Did you get a fix on the time of the attack?" Perwalski said.

"Within the last two hours." He turned to Billy. "We picked up her parents, and Walker has them in custody. How the hell did you find the girl so quickly?"

"The Cold Duck in the video reminded me of Lou's connection with the Sputnik. The ladies made a delivery here, at Easter."

"Hold up, gentlemen, this is my case," Perwalski said. "I'd appreciate it if you'd stop talking around me. The leaseholder's name on this condo is Harry Dalton. Who's Lou?"

"Lou Nevers was my partner," Billy said. "He died in the storm last Saturday. Dexter did his autopsy. They were friends."

Her gaze switched back and forth between them. "My condolences. How does your partner tie in with the girl?"

"Lou must have used the name Harry Dalton." Billy unfolded the picture and gave it to her. "He was keeping her here."

Perwalski's mouth tightened as she studied it. She glanced at Billy. "Your partner kept her here for what . . . amusement?"

She knew what Lou had been up to. She wanted to make him say it.

"Lou got a divorce about a year ago. We think he was using her as a surrogate for his former wife. Abusing the girl . . . sexually." Billy told her about the video.

"I see. So you knew this surrogate bullshit was going on."

"Hell, no!" he fired back and swept the binders off the table. "I would've killed Lou *myself* if I'd known about it."

Perwalski stepped back, her eyes narrowed. "Cool down, mister; you're disrupting my crime scene."

Dexter moved between them. "Ease up, Annette. Able didn't know about this. I'm the one. The girl was sick and Lou brought her to my clinic. He fed me a line and I accepted it. I didn't want to believe Lou would . . ." He swallowed hard. "I'm not making excuses, but I'm sure this was the only time Lou ever abused a child."

Billy shook his head. "We don't know that."

"All right, forget about your partner and let's focus on the person who did this," Perwalski said. "Any ideas?"

"Lou was no fool," Dexter said. "He would've kept this place secret. It has to be an inside job. You should start with the tenants and maintenance crew."

She crossed her arms. "Maybe, but I'm still not convinced Able wasn't involved." She looked at Billy, goading him.

"You're right," Billy said. "I'm the first guy you should look at. But talk to the maintenance guy, Pete. We unlocked the door together. And I can account for my last seven hours with witnesses, including Dexter. Lou was my partner. This happened on my watch. I want to nail this guy more than anybody."

She exhaled, taking her time before answering.

"He's right," Dexter said. "If you want a leg up on this, Detective Able's your guy."

She threw up her hands. "All right. Let's see what we've got."

◆

In the bathroom, Billy inspected the damaged tub and fractured wall tiles in the corner. "This tells us about the weapon. Whatever he used may be broken."

"Unless it was metal, like a crowbar," Dexter said.

Perwalski knelt down. "What's that thing under the water glass?"

"Some kind of ring. I found it after the EMTs left," Billy said. "I covered it to protect it."

She clicked off several digital shots, then moved the glass and used her pen to pick up the ring. "It's gold. It's big for a man's ring. I don't see an inscription." She put the ring back.

"You've noticed this guy didn't toss the place. He was careful. He came here looking for something specific."

Dexter looked at his watch. "If you don't need me, I'm heading back to the hospital. Annette, you have my number."

"Right," she said, and looked past Billy to the bedroom. "CSU just walked in. I'll start them dusting for prints in here."

"You won't find his," Billy said. "I'll bet my paycheck he wore gloves."

"He may have been slick enough to wear gloves, but we'll spot him when we review the security tapes. This building has more cameras than a super lockdown."

"Cameras won't help if he lives or works here," Billy said. "If he doesn't, he'll be in disguise."

They moved into the living room. The condo had been the scene of two crimes: Lou's sexual abuse of Rebecca Jane and someone else's attempt to murder her. The assault wasn't random. The attacker had to be connected to Lou. Billy ran through a mental list of Lou's current parolees. It was a stretch to think any of them had followed Lou here and discovered the girl.

"I checked the locks," Perwalski said. "The deadbolt has a thumb latch. She's six-years-old, right? She could have left, but she didn't."

"On Lou's video, she talked about a Sleeping Beauty pill. I saw sleeping meds on the vanity outside of the bathroom. Lou must have stayed up with her at night and given her pills to knock her out during the day. He had her recite a routine to follow any time he didn't come home and reinforced it by telling her a bogeyman would take her away if she didn't."

"Hell of a thing," Perwalski said. "She did what she was told, and the bogeyman got her anyway." She walked the perimeter of the living room, examining the stage, the camcorder, and the girl's photos. "You think your partner was in the kiddie porn business?"

The thought made Billy shudder. That could be the connection to Rebecca Jane's attacker.

"We can look into that," he said, hoping leads wouldn't take them in that direction.

"I'll check the kitchen," Perwalski said. "How about if you pick up those binders you knocked on the floor?"

Chagrined, Billy stacked the binders and flipped through them. They contained only flowers and leaves Rebecca Jane had pressed and labeled. He gathered crayon drawings that had been scattered around the room. Several pictured Lou filming her as she danced in her elaborate costumes. It seemed likely that Lou had filmed a lot of her performances.

Billy laid the drawings next to the binders and walked over to the shelves to look at the videos. He'd noticed the DVD player had a huge disc capacity. It must have been an electronic babysitter, programmed for non-stop movies. The DVDs on the shelf were kid's stuff and old movies, all clearly labeled. The attacker had looked through them, but they were still lined up. Books and stuffed animals took up the rest of the shelf. In between the movies and toys was an empty space.

Perwalski walked into the living room carrying a spindle of DVD discs in one hand and a package of black cases in the other. Perwalski held up the DVDs. "Your partner kept supplies in the closet for making videos. I'm leaning toward porn."

"Take a look at this," Billy said, pointing to the shelf.

She came up beside him. "You mean the gap?"

"I'll bet there were twenty or more DVDs in that space. The attacker left the movies but took the others because it was clear Lou had produced them."

"Excuse me, Detective," a uniformed cop said. "A maintenance guy named Pete found something."

Pete walked in, carrying a doll wearing a sparkling evening dress. "I found it on the stairwell landing."

Perwalski glanced at Billy.

He nodded. "It's Rebecca Jane's doll. I saw it in the video."

They both looked at Pete. His eyes widened. "Don't look at me. I've been fishing the Little Red for the last two days. I clocked in at three. I never seen the kid till I opened the door with you."

"We'll check everyone with access to a key," Perwalski said to Billy. "What do you make of the doll?"

"Either she broke her routine and left this place or she got away when the intruder came in. She made it as far as the stairwell. He caught her, and she dropped the doll. He dragged her back and beat her to shut her up."

"Huh," she said. "This guy's a real freak show. There aren't a lot of bastards that cold walking around."

"We'll get him," Billy said. "You watch."

Chapter Fifty-Three

Saturday, 7:37 p.m.

The weatherman had predicted a storm out of the southwest, but for now the horizon burned ruby and gold, and the river lay flat and empty. Billy slumped in a chair on the aft deck with a beer in his hand, watching the sun drop below the tree line across the water.

Dexter had called to say Rebecca Jane was stable enough to transfer to The Med, but she was in a coma. He promised to get in touch if her condition changed. Perwalski agreed to go over the forensic results with Billy as soon as they came in.

He rubbed his forehead, trying to put Rebecca Jane's beaten body out of his mind. The sun slipped behind the trees. Distant thunder followed. He set his beer on the deck and stood to stretch his legs. His cell rang. It was Mercy.

"Your message said you were handling something urgent. Is it about Sophia?"

"Sorry, no. It was a missing child. We found her alive."

"Oh. I was hoping the man in custody had disclosed . . . well, I'm glad about the girl." Her voice was cool. "I'm going back to Atlanta in the morning. T. Wayne got his car drivable enough to make it to Austin. He's leaving tomorrow, too."

"How's your mother doing?"

"She's in shock. She's letting Overton take charge."

"How do you feel about that?" He knew the answer, but he needed a reason to keep her on the line.

"It's not my decision." She blew out a breath. "The truth is, the man gives me the creeps." She paused. "Seems to be a trend with the men who marry into my family."

"Something happened?"

Billy listened as she told him about Overton's horse.

"I'm sorry. Accidents happen with show horses."

"Yeah, well. I have a bad feeling this 'accident' was planned."

"What?"

"The trainer came out of the van and told Overton that he was surprised the horse went that crazy. They both looked guilty as hell when they realized I'd heard him. I've read about trainers killing their client's horse to collect the insurance. I think that's what happened, and Overton was in on it."

Billy knew about the sleazy tricks some horse trainers pull. Insurance fraud would be a big risk for Overton, but then so was the graft scheme he and Lou had pulled off.

"You think Overton would take a chance like that for money?" he said.

"The horse made him look bad in the show ring. Apparently, Overton can't stand defiance, especially in an animal. After he told the trainer to have her put down, I caught this . . . I don't know, this scary smile on his face."

"Do you feel threatened?" Billy said.

"He doesn't give a damn about me. You're off the case, and I'll be gone soon. He's won."

She went silent. Then he heard a quiet sob. "I came to you for help, then I find out you were sleeping with my sister. What am I supposed to think?"

He closed his eyes. She was right, and she had every right to hang up on him. "I couldn't tell you or anyone else. Hollerith would have taken me off the investigation."

"You knew she was married. You had an affair then hung around for years." Mercy was sobbing hard.

He hated that they were doing this over the phone. "I won't try to justify what I did, but—"

"But you loved her."

The strain in her voice nearly killed him. "We shared a terrible tragedy. Sophia was alone. She might not have survived if I hadn't been there. It's in the past."

"Not for me."

"I'm sorry I hurt you."

"That's not enough." She hung up.

He stared at the dying sun. Mercy believed he'd betrayed her. In his mind, he'd done what was best for everyone at the time. Or had he just been protecting himself? He picked up the empty beer can and crushed it. He couldn't answer that question. He honestly didn't know.

He couldn't repair the damage he'd done to Mercy, so he went inside to work on Rebecca Jane's case. He started with his notes: the ring, the missing DVDs, the doll. Until the forensics came back, he wouldn't know if his speculation about the attacker's prints was right. The locks weren't broken. Did the man have a key or did Rebecca Jane hear him at the door and let him in? Did he go there with the intention of killing her, or was her presence a surprise?

What had been so important to the attacker that he'd risk breaking in to search for it? The possibility of missing DVDs was compelling. Either the attacker wanted videos of the girl, or Lou had downloaded something valuable onto them.

Billy went over everything again. Heavy rain moved in, and wind gusts swept the deck. Lights flickered along the riverfront. The storm brought back the anguish he'd heard in Mercy's voice.

He tipped his head back and stared at the ceiling. What had Lou been thinking when he abandoned the girl and kill himself? Could he not face her? Did he think she'd give up on his ever returning and walk out of the condo? People do crazy things. Madness makes sense from a mad man's point of view.

The phone rang, and he picked up. The line popped, followed by static.

"Damn, that was close," Jones said through the racket. "Lightning. That's some scary shit." The line buzzed and cleared again.

"Where are you?"

"Moon Landing, north of Tunica. A couple of kids spotted a body hung up on a sandbar in the river. The sheriff's department showed up. They have a boat bringing it out now."

"A woman's body?"

Jones paused. "A white woman. Dark hair."

The words blew through Billy's head. He tried to speak. Nothing came out.

"Sorry to give it to you cold. I know what she meant to you," Jones said.

Billy closed his eyes, wanting to shut out everything.

The line crackled. "You there?" Jones said.

"Yeah."

"Mosby asked the medical examiner to come and make an ID in case it's Sophia. We're already covered up with media. This storm's a bitch. Power lines are down all over east Memphis, and I can't reach the Dupree family. I know you don't want Mercy to be ambushed. Maybe you—"

The connection went dead.

Billy dropped the phone, overwhelmed. Everything, even seeking justice, was meaningless compared to the pain that swept over him. He took a breath, fighting for control. He'd already let Mercy down once. The least he could do was spare her from being blind-sided by the media. He tried Dupree's landline, then Mercy's cell. Neither worked.

He ran for the car.

◆

The storm had blown a destructive path through the city. Wind smashed through the center of town, flattened trees and pulled down power lines. The damage reminded Billy of the hundred-mile-an-hour, straight-line wind dubbed "Hurricane Elvis" that had shut down Memphis for weeks. This storm wasn't as destructive, but it looked like thousands of people would be without power for a few days.

He maneuvered around the upended roots of a big oak at the end of Sophia's driveway. His headlights flashed across Mercy's Toyota parked at the foot of the flagstone steps. No reporters yet. He clicked on his Stealth as he took the steps, two at a time, up to the darkened house. The front door stood ajar, so he pushed it open with his shoe. A suitcase sat just inside. The entry glowed with candles on a table next to a vase filled with fresh lilies.

"Who's there?" Mercy called from the landing above him.

Relieved to hear her voice, he directed the flashlight's beam up to where she stood with a candle in her hand and Caesar at her side.

"It's Billy. You all right? Your phones are out."

She started down the steps. "Can you believe this? I heard that big tree go down, and then we lost power."

"Hell of a blow."

"The house was burglarized the last time the power went out. T. Wayne's stomping around with a knife stuck in his belt. He's in his bedroom staying clear of me."

She reached the bottom step and stood in front of Billy, close enough to touch. He swallowed a smartass remark about Dupree going to Austin to be with Courtney. Mercy didn't need to hear it. He was here to deliver the news that a dead woman pulled from the river was most likely her sister. Mercy would always remember he'd been the messenger.

"I'm packing the car. I'm leaving for Atlanta tonight," she said.

He kept his gaze on her. "You should stay in town tonight."

"Why?"

He took her candle and set it on the floor. As gently as he could, he said, "I got a call from Jones. They found a body in the river, a woman with dark hair."

She stilled. "Is it Sophia?"

"There's no ID yet, but you need to be prepared."

Her eyes closed and her knees sagged. He guided her down to sit on the steps. Caesar pushed between them. She sunk her fingers into his coat. "Where?"

"A place called Moon Landing, on the river below Memphis. Detective Jones is there now."

Tears welled up. She tried to speak but couldn't.

"The media is on the scene. I was afraid they'd show up here."

Tears slid down her cheeks. "Does Momma know?"

"The department won't call Overton until it's confirmed."

"I'll tell T. Wayne." She sighed and pressed her hand to her forehead. "God, I never realized he was such a son-of-a-bitch. I don't know whether he'll break down or celebrate. Keep Caesar company, will you?" She picked up his flashlight and walked through the doors into the darkened great room and down the hall.

Billy wanted to be the one to jam the news down Dupree's throat, but he had no rights in this house. He got up and paced with the dog, aware of the scent of lilies on the table and the rain dripping on the porch. He thought about Sophia, not wanting to picture what the catfish had done to her, but he knew. He'd pulled floaters out of the river before.

It wasn't long before the Stealth's beam bounced off the doorjamb, and he heard Dupree's voice growing louder as he came down the hall. Mercy turned the corner, her eyes wide and lips parted in a silent warning as Dupree blustered through the doorway behind her. Billy noticed the dagger wedged under his belt and the nasty gloat on his face. It was clear Dupree had forgotten his earlier humiliation in the driveway. He was working himself up for another round. That was fine. Billy was loading up too.

"What the *hell* are you doing in this house?" Dupree bellowed.

"You'd better go," Mercy said quietly.

Billy shook his head. "I'm not leaving until I know you're safe."

"Safe? Safe from what?" Dupree flung his hand at the door like a bad stage actor. "Get out of my house."

Caesar lowered his head and growled.

"I'm staying until T. Wayne and I identify the body."

Dupree glanced over at her. "I'm not making the ID. I told you I'm out of here."

Her jaw dropped. "But she's your wife."

"Let me spell it out for you. The police have their guy. I'm no longer a suspect. I'll come back for the funeral. That's it."

Dupree thought having the man in custody made him untouchable.

"Think again, bud," Billy said. "That confession was a setup. I'm sticking with it till I get some real answers, and when they lead back to you I'll be a happy man. How long you think Courtney will wait for you—ten, twenty years to life?"

"She won't have to wait. You've got *nothing*. I didn't have my wife killed. But you know, who could blame me for thinking about it? Especially after they get a look at Courtney. She's a beautiful woman, isn't she?"

Dupree's eyes rounded in mock surprise. "Ooh, not what you expected to hear, is it, Detective? She told me about your visit. Sure, I was planning to divorce Sophia. I sold her car, cancelled the cruise. Of course I made Courtney the beneficiary of my insurance; she's carrying my child. I gave Sophia the money to decorate the house so it would sell quicker. It's my bad luck everything I did made me look guilty. And you know what?" He smirked. "You got every bit of it wrong, my friend."

"I got one thing right," Billy said. "You're a bully. You like to hit women. Sophia never had a chance, married to you."

Dupree sneered. "Know what your problem is? You had it bad for Sophia. She suckered you. Truth is, the jerk who killed her did us both a favor." He elbowed Mercy. "Right, Mercy Pie?"

Out of nowhere, Mercy launched a roundhouse swing, landing it on Dupree's jaw. He stumbled back.

"Bitch," he shouted and went for her, shoving her hard with both hands. Mercy fell back, her head striking the wall with a thud.

Caesar flashed past Billy, snarling as he threw himself at Dupree's chest and clamped his teeth on the man's forearm. They crashed together on the floor at Mercy's feet.

"Damn it," Dupree yelled as the dog whipped his head and tore into his arm. Dupree managed to pull his knife and raise it to plunge into the dog's back.

"No! Caesar!" Mercy lunged for the dog just as the knife slashed down.

Billy saw the blade glance off her bicep, and she screamed as it sliced through her flesh. He dropkicked the knife out of Dupree's hand and wrapped his arms around Mercy to haul her to safety.

"Caesar! Back!" she shouted. The dog backed toward her, still snarling. Gasping, she pressed her palm over her arm to stop the flow of blood.

Dupree struggled to sit up. "I'll have that dog shot," he choked out.

Billy released Mercy and pounced on Dupree, his fists landing piston-like blows to the man's face. Dupree's brow split open, and blood streamed down his face onto the marble floor.

"Get off me," Dupree whined, panicked by the sight of his own blood.

Billy stopped the pummeling long enough to lean his knee on Dupree's chest, forcing air out of his diaphragm. "I'm going to ask questions. You'll answer or I'll kick your ribs in."

Dupree tried to suck in air but couldn't. His eyes rolled back in his head. Billy let up on the pressure and slapped him into consciousness.

"No one's going to save your ass this time."

Dupree craned his neck at Mercy. "He's crazy. Call the cops."

She shook her head. "The only cop I need is right here."

"You bought a contract on Sophia with that twenty thousand," Billy said. "Who did you hire?"

"I didn't. I gave Sophia ten thousand. I made a down payment on Courtney's ring with the rest."

"You called your mob buddy in Baton Rouge."

"I told you—"

"Don't give me that shit. Get it right."

"Tucker Stans' dad died."

Billy slapped him so hard blood flew through the air. "We've already discussed the man's dead daddy. I ain't buying it."

"I swear to God . . . "

Billy picked up the dagger and held the point to Dupree's eye. "Quit lying."

"All right." Dupree's voice was hoarse with fear. "Sophia and I had a fight. I got mad. I called Tucker about a hit. He said I was an idiot and wouldn't touch it. That was all, I swear."

"Bullshit. You made a second call confirming the hit."

A spasm of coughs hit Dupree. "You're killing me."

"Quit lying or I'll stick the knife in myself," Mercy yelled.

"I'm telling the truth." Dupree struggled to breathe. "Get off, you're giving me a heart attack."

Billy knew about liars. Dupree was the kind of loudmouth who should crack early, but that wasn't happening. He had to be telling some version of the truth.

Billy straightened with the dagger still in his hand. "So you tried to buy a hit and lost your nerve. You're a piece of crap, you know that? You never admitted your guilt in Casey's death. You stood by for years and watched Sophia fall apart."

Dupree struggled up on one elbow and wiped blood off his face. "You don't know what you're talking about. Sophia was vicious." He pointed to the white line on his forehead. "She gave me this scar. She's sent me to the emergency room twice." He spit blood onto the marble tile. "Fall apart, my ass."

Billy drew a fist back to pound Dupree again.

"Don't, Billy," Mercy said. "You never saw that side of Sophia. I told you I cut my face because I tripped carrying a fish bowl. That wasn't true. Sophia pushed me."

Billy stared at Mercy in the shadows. "But you were just kids. It had to be an accident."

She shook her head. "It wasn't. Sophia smiled when she saw the blood."

◈

The flooded streets had drained by the time Billy drove Mercy to The Med. She sat stiff and quiet, pressing a bloody towel to her upper arm. Caesar rode in the back with his head hung over the seat next to Mercy's shoulder.

Dr. Sangster met them in the hallway. He remembered Billy's snake bite and concussion. Any mention of Dupree's attack with the knife would mean they'd spend the night in a police station filling out paperwork. Mercy didn't want that, so Billy told the doctor she'd been injured during the storm. Sangster took her back immediately, gave her a pain shot and twenty stitches.

Billy slipped his arm around Mercy's waist as they walked to the car. God, she'd been through so much. Tonight a man she'd depended on most of her life had slashed her arm with a knife.

When she'd settled into the passenger seat, Mercy turned to him with the glaze of pain meds half-closing her eyes. "The doctor told me to think of something else while he sewed up my arm, so I came up with a question."

"Shoot," he said, flexing his knuckles, swollen from pounding Dupree.

"Did I hear you come to the conclusion that T. Wayne didn't actually hire someone to kill Sophia?"

"I think he tried but didn't pull it off."

She nodded. "And that other guy, the one they arrested; you don't think he did it either."

"He was going down no matter what. I think he traded up on his jailhouse accommodations in exchange for a confession."

"Can they do that?"

"It happens. Sophia's case is closed, and Hollerith gets the credit. It's a win for everyone except you, me and justice."

Her hands trembled with exhaustion. "I don't want to go the house. I'd rather check into a hotel. Did you bring my suitcase?"

"It's in the back. But the power is out over most of the city. The hotels will be booked."

"Oh." Her eyelids slowly closed.

He sat for a moment in the parking lot with the car windows down, listening to the sound of tree frogs tuning up after the storm.

"Mercy?" he said softly. Her head drooped forward.

He started the car and drove slowly toward the river.

Chapter Fifty-Four

Sunday, 1:00 a.m.

Mercy jerked awake at the sound of a phone ringing in the next room. She sat up in the dark, not recognizing the single, high window and narrow bed. Caesar sat up on the bed beside her and nudged her shoulder with his nose. She reached over to pet him. Pain stabbed her bicep and brought everything back—the fight at the house, the knife slashing her arm. She remembered Billy taking her to the ER. After that things got fuzzy. She looked around. Apparently, he'd brought her to the barge.

A strip of light shone under the door. She tottered over to peek out. Billy was sitting on the sofa, elbows resting on his knees, as he studied a piece of paper in his hands. His sad expression brought everything back with a jolt.

The body in the river. Sophia.

Caesar came off the bed and pushed past her, shoving the door open into the living room. Billy jumped to his feet, grabbed a throw from off the back of the sofa and hurried forward to drape it over her shoulders. "Are you in pain?"

His hair was wet and slicked back, and he stood close enough for her to get a whiff of soap.

"I'm okay. I heard the phone." She rubbed her eyes. "What time is it?"

"A little after one. Let's have a look at your arm." He inspected the bandage for signs of bleeding. "The cut isn't deep. The doctor said it should heal nicely."

Mercy brushed hair from her face. She remembered when she was a kid, and the first doctor who'd stitched up her cheek told her the same thing.

All these years she'd kept the secret: Sophia had hurt her on purpose. Now Billy knew her secret. Up till now, she'd been too ashamed to admit it, as if Sophia's attack had been partly her fault. Victim's guilt. One of the reasons she'd come back to Memphis was to confront Sophia and cut away that unhealthy part of her past. With Sophia gone, that plan was irrelevant.

Billy's gaze moved from the bandage to her cheek. "I'm sorry Sophia hurt you. She had me fooled. It's hard to recognize the truth about the people we love."

Mercy blinked. *The people we love.* Was he referring to *her* feelings about Sophia or *his*? She felt her cheeks flush and looked away, hoping he wouldn't notice.

"It doesn't matter," she said. "It happened a long time ago."

"Of course it matters." He touched her shoulder. "I have something to tell you. That was Jones on the phone. The body they pulled from the river wasn't Sophia. It's a teen-aged girl. Probably a suicide."

"You're telling me Sophia isn't dead?"

"I can't say that. All we know is this woman is definitely not Sophia."

"I'm confused," she said, feeling the room begin to spin.

"That's okay. It's been a rough night. You've had some pain meds."

She put her hand on his arm to steady herself. "I understood what you said; I just don't know how to feel about it. I don't want Sophia to be dead, but I thought this ordeal was over."

He frowned, studying her face. "You're looking a little pale."

"I'm fine."

"Come on, sit down."

He guided her toward the sofa with such care she didn't have the heart to argue. She sat and curled up with the blanket tucked around her legs.

"Maybe a cup of tea would clear my head," she said.

"Sure thing."

Caesar followed him to the galley, leaving her alone for a moment to regroup.

The news that it wasn't Sophia's body they'd found in the river should have been cause to celebrate. Instead, it was a letdown. She wondered if God would forgive her for being disappointed. What if Sophia were never found? Mercy couldn't imagine anything worse, and yet she knew the worst had happened to another family tonight. The police had zipped someone's daughter into a body bag. There would be an autopsy. The family would question themselves for the rest of their lives.

Just a few hours ago she'd been in their place.

Aching down to her bones, needing a distraction, she picked up the paper Billy had been studying earlier. It was a photo of a little girl in a bubble bath with her father sitting on the edge of the tub.

Billy came back from the galley carrying a steaming mug. She held up the picture. "Is this your family?"

He set the mug down and sat beside her. "The man was my partner, Lou Nevers."

She laid the photo on the table. "I'm so sorry. That must be his little girl."

"No."

His expression reflected so much pain it took her breath away.

"Billy, what's the matter?"

His jaw flexed. "That's the child I told you about. Lou had her locked up. No one knew about her. The wrong person found her. Beat her. Left her for dead."

She stared at the photo. "My God. Who could do that to a child?"

He leaned back and locked his hands behind his head. It was a while before he spoke again.

"I've read there's a delay between the time when light strikes your eye and your mind recognizes what it sees. Like when you're in a car accident. Your eye sees the other car coming, but your brain gets smashed before the event registers. You literally never know what hit you."

He lowered his hands. "Lou changed after his divorce. My eyes saw it, but my brain didn't perceive what it meant. Two days ago I found a video Lou made of himself with this little girl. I'm sick every time I think about it. I'd rather have my brain smashed in a car wreck than remember what he did to her. And what's worse, I never saw it coming."

A siren echoed off the river. She didn't know what to say to this man sitting quietly beside her, turned inward with the pain and shame of his partner's actions. Anger hit her. Billy was a good man, yet he was saddling himself with another man's guilt. It wasn't fair.

She shook his arm. "Hey. You didn't see it coming because you believed in Lou. You trusted him with your life. His crime isn't your responsibility any more than Sophia's attack on me was mine." She felt better now, all heated up with indignation. "You were right."

He looked at her. "About what?"

"Lou. T. Wayne and Sophia. You said it's hard when we see the truth about the people we love. It's hard, but we have to deal with it. Sometimes it means walking away."

"You're right. But you didn't walk away from Dupree tonight. You smacked the hell out of him. That was impressive."

"Come on, I'm serious."

"So am I."

He pulled her toward him, or did she move toward him first? She didn't remember, and it didn't matter. Because it was exactly where she wanted to be.

Chapter Fifty-Five

They woke up early, tangled together under the sheets of his narrow bed, naked and safe from the moment they opened their eyes and saw each other. Billy pulled her closer, careful not to hurt her arm. She came to him easily, her breasts nestled against his ribs and her thighs molded to his. Her palm slid up his stomach, and her fingers curled slowly against his skin.

She moved her face close to his. "You have blue eyes."

He kissed her.

She sat up with the sheet looped around her hips, and her hair falling in her face. "I'll make breakfast."

"There's a deli down the street."

"I'll find something in the galley. I'm a chef, you know."

"There's coffee and canned biscuits and not much else."

"I'll make do."

Twenty minutes later they sat propped up in bed with mugs of coffee with chicory and warm cinnamon rolls she'd made by folding biscuits over cream cheese and adding cinnamon and butter. He licked the butter from her fingers and they made love again. Last night had been quick and heated. This morning they took their time exploring each other's bodies in the light. They finished with slow deep kisses, separating only when Caesar hopped up on the bed and licked Billy's toes.

"I'll take him out," he said.

"I love a man who'll walk a dog. When you come back, would you bring in my suitcase? I have something to show you."

By the time he returned from walking the shoreline with Caesar, Mercy had showered and pulled on the police department T shirt he'd left out for her. It pleased him to see her damp hair coiling on the shoulders of his shirt.

An edge of sadness crept into her face. "I woke up knowing that the truth you forced out of T. Wayne last night will help me let go of Sophia." She stepped closer, rested her forehead on his chest. "Knowing *something* is better than knowing nothing."

He touched her hair, wondering how he could protect her from the anguish of an unresolved case. He'd dealt with families who'd spent years searching for their loved ones.

He tilted her face up to meet his gaze. "We don't always learn the whole truth."

"Maybe we never will. But I want to show you something." She opened her suitcase and came up with a green, clothbound book. "I found this tucked behind Sophia's cookbooks."

He flipped through. A diary. The dates ran from two years ago until a few weeks before Sophia disappeared. It read like the ranting of a spoiled, psychotic child. Simple aggravations had triggered paranoid revenge scenarios. This was the nasty side Sophia had managed to keep hidden from him. Several themes stood out. She was absurdly dependent on her mother. She despised Mercy for her independence, and her anger with Dupree ran so deep, it was a miracle she hadn't murdered him in his sleep.

Then the tone changed. A man who made her feel important entered her life. Unlike Dupree, he talked to her about politics and discussed art and architecture with her. They took that secret trip to New Orleans that thrilled her. Now Billy understood the significance of the Commander's Palace swizzle stick hidden under her mattress. She wrote pages about her bizarre sex life with the unnamed lover, identified only as "him" and "he." Billy shook his head, even more aware he'd never known this Sophia at all.

Toward the end, she wrote about wanting more from this man, but her demands had escalated their quarrels into shouting matches and brutal sex. The harder she pushed, the more explosive his anger became. In the final pages, she'd threatened him with a scandal in the press if she didn't get what she wanted.

Billy closed the diary, frustrated that Sophia hadn't given more specifics to identify the man. But she'd given a distinct clue. The man had plenty at stake—family, position, or a reputation he wanted to protect.

"Pretty twisted stuff," Mercy said. "You think this mystery lover had anything to do with her disappearance?"

"It's possible. Her threats infuriated him. If it boiled over, their sex games could've turned lethal, or he could've gotten rid of her because of the blackmail. But . . . there's a small chance it's a fantasy. No telling what kind of mental state Sophia was in when she wrote this."

"Where does that leave us?" Mercy said.

"I'll call Paul Anderson, our department psychologist, at home and ask him to look at this right away. This morning, in fact."

"It's eight-thirty on Sunday."

"I'll drag him out of Sunday school if I have to. If Anderson says this lead is worth pursuing, I'll go after our mystery man."

◆

Anderson's service wouldn't give out his number, but Billy found his home address in a department directory. For a shrink, Paul Anderson was a pretty good guy. Billy was confident he would read the diary right away and have an opinion about whether the man was a fantasy or flesh and blood.

Next, he called Dexter for information about Rebecca Jane. For the girl's safety, the doc said Perwalski had planted a story in the morning paper saying she wasn't expected to live. The truth was, Rebecca Jane was showing signs of coming out of her coma.

They put Caesar in the car and drove to Sophia and T. Wayne's house. Crews had worked through the night to remove tree limbs and restore power. Except for branches scattered around the yard, the house appeared to have come through the storm intact. Billy parked next to Mercy's car and noticed the porch light burning over the front door. The power was back on. He went to look through the sidelight next to the door. Blood from last night's brawl had dried on the floor, and the security panel blinked red, which meant the alarm was armed.

Mercy didn't want to run into Dupree, so Billy went around back and checked to be sure the BMW was gone. He came back and gave her the all clear.

"I have a key and the alarm code," she said. "I want to grab Caesar's blanket and water bowl out of the laundry room. Would you come with me?"

They walked around to the back door, where she let herself in. He waited, thinking about her life in Atlanta. After a week of physical and emotional battering, she might decide to hell with Memphis and never come back. If that happened, he'd go to Atlanta. He wasn't about to lose her without a fight.

Out of cop's habit, he walked over to check out the Acura in the carport. Graphite powder for lifting prints still smudged the door handles and trunk. As he walked around the car, he glanced at the license plate. 266-SVL. He'd seen the number in Sophia's file . . . and somewhere else. He walked back and stood in front of the plate. SVL, LVS.

LVS.

He had it. Lou had written down the plate number in reverse—662-LVS—and the words "pig out" along with the date, which was the same day Overton had called him.

Billy had just connected three facts. One, Overton called Lou on Thursday night. Two, the numbers and letters Lou wrote down were the Acura's license plate number. Three, Overton had been in a unique position to know Sophia was driving the Acura instead of the BMW. The chances someone else had given Lou that number were slim to none.

"Son-of-a-bitch," he said out loud, not noticing Mercy was walking toward him, carrying the blanket and bowl.

"Who's a son-of-a-bitch?"

"Nothing." He took her arm to walk her to her car. He didn't want to involve her in his guesswork until he had answers.

"Wait a minute," she said, slowing down.

"You need to get on the road, sweet thing. Call when you get home and let me know you're safe."

"Don't patronize me, and don't call me 'sweet thing'," Mercy fumed. "I'm not leaving until I know what just happened. It's about the car, isn't it? I'm going back to look. You might as well tell me. I'm not leaving until I know."

"Mercy . . . "

"I mean it."

He didn't want to argue. And she had a stake in this too. "All right, damn it. Let Caesar out of the car, and I'll tell you what's going on."

They settled on the flagstone steps with Caesar at their feet. "My instincts tell me Overton is the man Sophia described in her diary," Billy said. "He's the right personality profile—narcissistic, manipulative, a pathological liar."

"Get out. That would mean Overton and Sophia . . . " Mercy looked bewildered. "Oh my God, my mother married her daughter's lover?"

"Yep."

"You got that from looking at the Acura?"

"Let's walk through it. Lou wrote some numbers and letters on a pad by his phone and dated it the day before Sophia disappeared. I didn't recognize the Acura's plate number until now, because he'd reversed the numbers and letters and stacked everything. It's an old trick. My Uncle Kane used it as a way to keep information confidential.

"While I was investigating Lou's death, I found out that Overton had called Lou on that same Thursday night. When I asked the judge about the call, he fed me a plausible story. Later I learned he'd lied."

Mercy shook her head. "I don't understand what the Acura's license plate has to do with Overton."

"Overton was one of the few people who knew Sophia was driving the Acura last week. Lou would have looked for the blue Mercedes. Overton told him about the Acura. Gave him the plate number."

"Why would *Lou* be looking for Sophia?"

He took a breath. "Because Overton ordered Lou to kill Sophia."

Her jaw dropped. "Whoa. That's a huge leap."

"Not if Overton is the man in the diary. Sophia was threatening to damage his reputation right about the time he learned he was being considered for an appointment to a federal appellate court."

She nodded. "Momma told me about that."

"An ambitious judge doesn't want his name in the press. Every time his name appears, somebody likes him or resents him. Sophia would've ruined Overton's chances with a scandal. I think he's responsible for her disappearance, but I don't have what I need to prove it."

"So." She hesitated, glanced over. "You believe your partner was capable of killing my sister?"

He considered her question. Lou was a pedophile, and Tut's story about the graft was true. But Lou a murderer?

"Lou was desperate for money to keep Rebecca Jane hidden. I don't want to believe it, but…" He needed to change the subject. "How did your mother meet Overton?"

"Sophia introduced them. Momma admitted Sophia was jealous. I guess for once she was on target."

He remembered Gloria talking about the tension in the house. She must have been suspicious about the relationship between Sophia and Overton even though she wanted to deny it.

Billy was getting a clearer picture. Sophia probably told Overton about their affair. He could imagine her taunting Overton about the sex she'd had with a young cop. The judge would have been in a jealous rage.

Billy felt sick down to his soul. After so many years on the force, he thought he was immune to the ugliness of human nature. He'd loved Lou and Sophia. Both had deceived him.

Mercy must have read the anguish on his face. She took his hand and pulled it onto her lap. "I think you're right about this. What happens next?"

"I'm going to Overton's house to surprise him. I don't have the full story, but I want to try and rattle him and make him incriminate himself."

"I'll distract my mother while you trap Overton."

He put his arm around her. "I'm not sure that's a good idea. I have nothing to lose if this plan goes south. You do."

"If you're right, my mother married the man who had her daughter murdered. He could do the same to her. I want to be there when you bring him down."

Billy stood and pulled Mercy to her feet. "All right. Let's go spoil Overton's day."

Chapter Fifty-Six

Sunday, 8:45 a.m.

The answer turned out to be so simple. A wooden gate, a simple latch.

Billy drove to Overton's home with Mercy quiet beside him, giving him a chance to think how he was going to nail this guy. The last time he'd been at the house, Overton had played him like a big-mouth bass. It hadn't occurred to him the judge was capable of non-stop, straight-faced lying. This time would be different.

Problem was, he couldn't walk in and accuse Overton of solicitation of murder. He had no proof the judge and Lou had ever discussed a hit or agreed to a payoff. But he had an edge. He knew about the graft. He had damning details about Overton in the diary, something the judge probably didn't know existed. Then there was Overton's arrogance—the judge would never believe a hick cop could trip him up.

He glanced over at Mercy. The strain of the last twelve hours showed on her face. He wanted to get this right for her. Otherwise, she'd wonder for the rest of her life what had happened to her sister.

Stay calm, he told himself. *Don't lose your temper and blow this.*

Billy pulled into the driveway behind Gloria's Mercedes. As they got out, a beat-up Ford Escort parked next to the trash bins caught Billy's attention. Then he heard Overton's voice coming from behind the backyard fence. He looked at Mercy across the top of the car. "You sure you want to go in with me?"

She nodded. "Let's get him."

He flipped open the latch on the gate. They walked the stone path, crowded with damp beds of tiger lilies, following Overton's voice past the pool house to a lawn surrounded by oaks at the back of the property.

Billy saw her first, wrapped in an over-sized terrycloth robe, standing in the middle of the judge's private croquet court. Shock rolled over him. Mercy gasped.

Sophia.

They watched her grasp a mallet, her bare feet spread apart, and her eyes focused down on the ball in front of her. Overton, wearing a navy blue robe and deck shoes, watched Sophia from farther down the court.

Billy couldn't believe it. He'd given up hope for Sophia, but there she was, straddling her mallet with her hair hanging in chopped clumps around her face. She tapped the ball. It rolled past the wicket and across the lawn toward him. He felt Mercy's hand on his arm.

"I'll be damned," she whispered.

Sophia's head turned at the sound of Mercy's voice, and a glazed smile spread over her face. "My baby sister . . . and Billy."

Billy steadied himself with a deep breath. He thought Dupree had paid to have Sophia murdered. Then he believed Overton coerced Lou into doing it. How did he get it so wrong? He looked across the lawn at the judge. Overton's mouth twitched with satisfaction. He waved his mallet at Billy in a mock salute.

Son-of-a-bitch. The judge *had* set up the hit with Lou, but Sophia must have realized the danger and bolted before either man knew she was gone.

Billy stared at Overton. *You bastard. You think you're off the hook.*

He suppressed his anger and focused on Sophia. "Where've you been?" he said as she approached.

"I left the city for a while. Then I saw Momma's wedding announcement in the paper yesterday and thought I should come home to offer my congratulations." She picked up the ball. "Where's my welcome-home kiss?"

A blown vein in her right eye had left a bloom of red in the corner. Her hair looked like a child chopped it off with scissors. She must have done it herself in a drunken frenzy. The last time he'd seen her in that kind of shape was after Casey's funeral.

"We thought you were dead," Mercy said.

She shrugged. "I'm fine."

"You can see she's fine," Overton called across the court. He drew back his mallet and smacked the ball through the next wicket.

Sophia applauded the shot. The Mercedes charm bracelet jingled on her wrist. She held it up for Mercy to see. "I forgot this when I left town. Momma brought it as a keepsake when she moved in last night. She cried when she gave it back to me."

"What have you done with Momma?" Mercy said. Her voice vibrated with anger.

Sophia's eyes hardened. "What do you mean, 'done with her'? She's asleep. Buck and I stayed up all night talking. We decided it was best to let Momma wake on her own."

"You didn't say where you've been," Billy prompted.

"If you must know, I took a suite at the Alluvian Hotel down in Mississippi. I needed to rethink my marriage, so I cut myself off from the world. Viking has a cooking school next door to the hotel. It took me two whole days to master the soufflé."

"You narcissistic bitch," Mercy snapped.

"Calm down, young lady," Overton said as he walked up. "Your sister left town to consider her divorce options. She was in the hotel's bar last night and saw the TV coverage about the body in the river. They named her as the probable victim. She was afraid the police would charge her with something because of the trouble and expense she's caused, so she drove here to get my advice."

Bullshit, Billy thought. Sophia didn't give a damn about the cops. She saw the announcement in the paper and ran back to re-negotiate her relationship with Overton.

"There's cold juice in the pool house," Sophia said. "And coffee. Billy, let me get you a cup. It's made with chicory, the way you like it."

"Forget the coffee, Sophia. I want the real reason you went into hiding."

Sophia glanced at Overton, frowning, worried. "It was a silly misunderstanding."

"She's back with her family, end of discussion," Overton said. "Now, if you'll excuse me." He strolled to his ball and squatted to sight his next shot.

When he was out of earshot, Sophia leaned toward Billy and Mercy and whispered, "I didn't just run off. I tricked T. Wayne into giving me the money. I bought a used car and parked it at SuperShoppers. Then I drove the Acura over, bought groceries, and put on a disguise so no one would recognize me when I switched cars. I hopped into the Escort and drove to the Alluvian in Mississippi." She crinkled her nose. "It was easy."

She's proud of what she did, Billy thought. *She'd never admit this if she weren't so messed up.* "Tell me how you lost the shoe and purse."

Sophia blinked innocently. "I guess I dropped them when I switched cars."

Like hell. She could've dropped the shoe, but she left the purse where Charles would find it. She wanted everyone to believe she'd been snatched.

"You should've told me what you were up to," he said.

"But I did, sweetie. I mailed your business card to you. I thought you'd understand."

"That's a kidnapper's move. I expected your finger to be delivered in a box the next day."

"Oh. Sorry," she said, and waved away a mosquito.

There wasn't a speck of regret on her face. The uproar she'd caused must have thrilled the drama queen in her. And, she'd gotten to punish Dupree, knowing he'd be suspected.

Billy looked over at Mercy and noticed the blood had risen to her face.

"Let me get this straight," Mercy said. "You came up with this scheme and then invited me here to be part of it."

Sophia's chin went up. "I thought Momma might need a little handholding. Besides, it's time you paid some dues."

"A man in Holly Springs confessed to killing you," Mercy said. "Billy risked his job because of you. Momma could've had a heart attack. You're just plain evil."

Sophia let out a short laugh. "Everything's worked out. Don't be so mean to your big sister."

"Mean to you! Are you kidding? T. Wayne went crazy last night and cut my arm with a knife. That's your fault. Just like this." She pointed at her cheek. "You did this. You scarred me for life."

Sophia seemed to focus on Mercy; then her attention drifted to Overton who was lining up for a long shot. "Isn't Buck amazing?" she murmured. "He's been invited to compete in a national tournament."

Billy pulled Sophia around to face him. "If you want help staying out of trouble with the police, you have to tell me the truth."

"I want to, Billy, I really do, but lately . . . " She pushed her hair out of her face. "I heard T. Wayne calling that Texas woman in the middle of the night." She bit her lip. "I wanted another child. T. Wayne said I was too irresponsible. Then he goes and makes that bitch pregnant. I heard him promising to marry her before the baby comes. He booked that cruise to push me over the rail; I just know it. He wanted to kill me."

They heard the solid whack of Overton's ball hitting the final peg, and they all turned toward the sound.

"Peg out!" Overton shouted and lifted his mallet over his head. Sophia clapped her hands like a child.

Billy looked at Mercy. She shook her head. There wasn't much he could do. Sophia's explanation was credible, and he had nothing solid against the judge. Except . . .

"Sophia, what does 'peg out' mean?" Billy said.

She turned to him, eyes shining. "Game over. Buck's won."

The pieces snapped into place. Lou had written "peg out" on the pad, not "pig out." Overton had used the phrase when he talked to Lou. That was proof enough for Billy, but not enough to take to the D.A.—not with Sophia alive and Lou dead.

Overton scooped up his ball and strode toward them. "Here's the plan," he said, tossing the ball in the air and catching it. "I'll call Mosby. Tomorrow Sophia can go down, give a statement and apologize for wasting the department's time. She committed no crime. There's been no harm." He glanced at Mercy's arm. "No *real* harm."

"There's harm all right," Billy said. "Lou Nevers is dead."

Overton gave him a hard look. "Sophia had nothing to do with Lou's unfortunate . . . "

"Not Sophia. I mean *you*. You gave Lou the Acura's plate number. You told him it was 'peg out' for Sophia—'game over'."

"Lou could have taken down the plate number for himself," Overton said. "Maybe he was stalking Sophia. Everyone on the force knows he was coming unglued."

"You talked to Lou on the phone at the Tuggle's house. Right after that, he threw the chair through a window. He screwed with the evidence in the Acura, and then he killed himself. You had a hand in all of it."

Overton slammed the ball into the ground. "That's enough. Sophia, call 911. I want this crazy son-of-a-bitch off my property."

She turned to go, but Mercy blocked her way. "Hold on. You're not going anywhere."

Billy put a heavy hand on Sophia's shoulder and pulled her around. "Admit it; you thought Overton was going to kill you."

Her eyes widened. "What? No . . . it was T. Wayne. Now let go of me."

He gripped her shoulders and shook her. "You're lying!"

She broke down, started crying. "Stop it. Okay, you're right. I was mad. Buck was going to marry my mother. My *mother!*"

"Shut up," Overton shouted.

She was sobbing now. "I wouldn't go along with his plans. I was afraid he'd—" Her head jerked toward Overton. "But it's okay now, right Buck? You're not angry anymore."

"Don't count on that," Mercy said. "Not after he reads what you wrote about him in your diary." She looked at the judge. "Pretty hot stuff. Jealousy, rage. Abusive sex."

Overton glared at Sophia.

She looked frightened. "I made notes for a story, that's all."

"The diary's just for starters," Billy said. "We've got Tutwiler Jackson and the bribes you took back in the day, Judge. Forget your nomination. The next court you're in, you'll be the defendant."

Sophia got in Billy's face. The blood spot in her eye looked like ruby glass. "Listen," she hissed. "If you make my diary public or anything else about me or Buck public, I'll call you a liar." She backed off, looking like a total stranger to Billy.

Overton pulled a rag out of his pocket and began to wipe down his mallet head. "Game over, Detective. Say one word about this, and I'll slap you with a slander suit you'll never get out from under." He gave Billy a dismissive wave. "Go on now. You're interrupting our game."

It was a stand-off. "This isn't over, Judge."

Overton ignored him, busying himself with stowing his mallet in a leather carrying case. Out the corner of his eye Billy saw Mercy standing to the side, waiting for his cue.

He held out his hand to her. "Let's go."

She nodded. "I'll be right with you." She walked up to Sophia and slapped her hard. Sophia's head jerked back, and her hand went to her cheek.

"As far as I'm concerned, I no longer have a sister," Mercy said. She walked back to Billy. "I'm ready now."

Chapter Fifty-Seven

The wind blew through the tops of the trees as they walked past the pool house and out the gate to the driveway. The car Sophia had used for her getaway caught Billy's attention a second time. He walked over to the curb next to the Escort.

The car had bald tires and a dented side panel. He remembered how Sophia had loved her blue Mercedes—how it had defined her. There was little of the Sophia he remembered in the wreck of a woman he'd just left.

He looked down at a broken bottle that had fallen out of Overton's recycle bin. Shards lay next to the car's back tire. He picked up the pieces and threw them in the bin. Beneath the bottles was a clear plastic bag loaded with what appeared to be black rectangles.

He pushed the bottles aside, opened the bag and pulled out a DVD case with a row of silver, star-shaped stickers running down the spine.

"God almighty," he murmured. He opened the case. Empty. He checked more cases. They were all empty. Adrenaline shot through him.

Mercy joined him. "What is it?"

His mind raced through the connecting web. Overton and Sophia. Sophia and Lou. Lou and Rebecca Jane. Her bruises, the splinters, the ring. The mallets. The judge.

Everything circled back to Overton. He'd taken Lou's DVDs, thrown away the cases, but probably had no time to review the discs. They were in his house right this minute. Why the DVD's? What did Overton risk his entire future to find?

Billy took a deep breath, checked his watch and pulled out his cell. "Don't say anything, just listen," he said to Mercy. He dialed. Perwalski answered.

"I was about to call you," she said. "I ran through the security tapes from the condo entrance and found our guy. You were right. He's wearing a hat and dark glasses—"

"—and he's carrying a leather case about three feet long."

"Shit. How did you know?"

He told her what he'd seen at Overton's house then gave her the Memphis D.A.'s number for her to request a search warrant. Getting a warrant to search the digs of a prominent judge could take time. Somehow he had to stop Overton from dumping the discs and sanitizing the place before the warrant was served.

"Light a fire under the D.A. for the warrant," he said to Perwalski. "I'll figure a way to pin the judge down."

He called Dispatch for a patrol car to meet him at Overton's address. He hung up. Mercy was leaning against the Escort as if all the strength had left her legs.

"You're saying Overton attacked that little girl?"

He nodded. "I'm going back in there. This could get ugly; at least I hope it will. I want you to wait here."

"We had this discussion earlier. I'm coming with you."

He didn't have time to argue. "All right, but watch your back. I don't want you hurt again."

"I'll watch *your* back. I don't want you hurt again, either."

They found Overton standing in the middle of the croquet green, looming over Sophia and talking to her in a menacing tone. She was wide-eyed and shaking her head.

"Answer me," Overton shouted at her and yanked the mallet out of her hand.

"Get away from him," Billy ordered. Sophia scrambled out of Overton's reach.

"What are you doing back here?" the judge growled.

"I kept wondering what you used to coerce Lou. I couldn't put it together. Then I found this." He held up the DVD case. "Look at it, Judge. A twenty-five cent piece of plastic sitting in your trash along with a couple-dozen others. Every case has silver stars on its spine. I noticed them because I'd seen one like it before in Lou's car trunk."

Overton's knuckles whitened on the mallet's shaft. "You need a warrant to go through trash on my property."

"As you well know, the court calls it 'expectation of privacy.' You haven't got it, because the bins are out on the curb. I wouldn't have given them a second look until yesterday when I went to Lou's condo. I found a six-year-old girl who'd been living with him. The disc in his trunk showed him molesting her."

"That's disgusting," Overton spat.

"Damned straight. We assumed he'd made more videos, but they were missing. Whoever took them also tried to beat that little girl to death."

Sophia gasped.

A breeze ruffled Overton's hair. He smoothed it. "I read about it in this morning's paper. They don't expect the girl to live. Damn shame. Now I'm going inside to call Director Mosby and get you off my back."

Before Overton could move, Billy stepped in and stabbed the judge's chest with stiff fingers. "Mercy told me what you did to your horse. You kill animals; you threaten women. You clubbed that little girl nearly to death, but you sure as *hell* can't bully me. Now shut up, and stand there until I'm finished."

"This is ridiculous . . . "

"You thought you could get Lou to murder Sophia. I couldn't understand why," Billy said. "It was like a bone stuck in my throat. Then I got it. Tutwiler talked about the notes Lou made on the strip club payouts. Lou kept them as an insurance policy against you.

"Here's what I'm thinking, Judge. Lou got drunk and desperate, and called you for money. He made the mistake of telling you about Rebecca Jane. You refused to help him; he threatened blackmail. You turned the tables. You said, 'I'll give you the money if you get rid of Sophia.'"

"Listen here—"

"Shut up! I'll tell you when I'm through."

Overton's head jerked, startled.

"Sophia went missing. Then Lou died. Things worked out better than you'd planned until you remembered the notes. I told you I'd found nothing unusual at Lou's house, so you figured the notes had to be at the condo. You went after them."

Billy was ramping up the insults, letting his voice get louder and louder. "The last thing you expected was Rebecca Jane standing at the door."

Sophia's hand covered her mouth. "Oh, Buck."

"She ran. Got past you into the hall. Must have infuriated you. You caught her in the stairwell. We know, because we found her doll there. You dragged her back to the condo, but you couldn't keep her quiet. You were afraid someone might recognize you. You had to shut her up. You snapped."

"You're the one who's snapped . . . "

"You made a big mistake. You left her for dead. I talked to Dexter this morning. She's coming out of the coma. You thought Sophia was dead too, but now she's shown up on your doorstep." Billy shook his head. "You're not doing so well with females, Judge. You kill them but they won't stay dead."

Mercy and Sophia stood motionless in shock.

"You've lost your mind," Overton said. "No one's going to believe—"

"It's over. You're nothing but a fucking joke. All your pretentious bullshit . . . " He pointed at the mallet. "Your toy is what's going to land you in the slammer."

Overton's face went rigid. The mallet came up in an arcing, overhead swing at Billy's skull. Billy caught the shaft as the mallet sliced down, stopping it. They gripped the shaft, fighting to a standstill, the gold fitting between them.

Billy's eyes were riveted on Overton. "I found a gold ring beside the girl's body. It looks like this one. How many mallets you own, Judge?"

"Fuck off," Overton spat.

"Four," Sophia said quietly. "It's a one-of-a-kind set."

"Where's the fourth, Your Honor? Did you break it? Did you throw it in the river?"

"Drop the weapon," a voice shouted from behind Billy.

He turned to see Wheezer Trit and another cop, with their weapons drawn, running into the yard.

Overton dropped the mallet and reeled toward the officers. "Thank God you're here." He pointed at Billy. "This man's trespassing. Get him off my property."

"Detective Able called for back-up. We saw you take a swing at him. Is that how it happened, Detective?"

"You got it," Billy said. "Aggravated assault."

Trit holstered his gun, grabbed Overton's wrist and snapped on a cuff. "We thought you were gonna get your brains bashed in, Sergeant. By the way, you're under arrest, sir." Trit whipped Overton's other wrist behind him and snapped on the second cuff.

"Just a damned minute," Overton blustered.

"Forget the bluff, Judge," Billy said. "A West Memphis detective is going to show up with a search warrant and seize everything relevant. Since you'll be in custody, charged with aggravated assault, you won't have a chance to destroy one damned thing."

And that's exactly what I had in mind, Billy thought, *when I got you to take a swing at me.*

"One last thing," Billy said. "The security camera recorded a man in the building at the time of the attack. He disguised himself so well; we could never have made an ID . . . except for one thing. He carried a mallet case. When the boys in forensics examine the tape, I'll bet that case and the one over there will be the same. Your case, just like your mallets, will be one of a kind."

Billy gripped the mallet, swung at Sophia's ball and smacked it across the green.

"Game over, Judge."

Chapter Fifty-Eight

Thursday, 6:05 a.m.

Billy was up early for a two-mile run on the Riverwalk along Riverside Drive. He didn't need a clock for his new routine. His body pushed him onto the deck while he was still only half awake. His muscles warmed, his heart pumped. The slap of his running shoes on the asphalt cleared his brain. His snake-bit arm was healing, and he was sleeping through the night now. He felt intact, body and soul. Nothing had been taken from him. However, the truth about Lou would remain an inoperable bullet lodged against his spine. He would carry the wound, but he would survive.

So would Rebecca Jane. She was out of the coma, and the doctors felt that with therapy, she would be strong enough to testify against Overton during a trial. Child Services would place her in a good foster home. Maybe her sisters would be with her, too.

Sadly, Dexter was a casualty of last week's events. When Billy called about Rebecca Jane, Dexter said he'd decided to give up his medical license. He'd let his loyalty to Lou override his duties as a doctor. "I let the child down. I need to atone for that." Billy understood why the doc's emotions were running high, but he was too good a man to be sucked under by Lou. He suggested the doc reconsider his decision.

Back from his run, Billy scooped up the paper off the barge ramp and opened to the front page headline:

Memphis Judge Charged with Attempted Murder

The photo taken at the courthouse showed Overton with his shoulders hunched and one arm raised to fend off the cameras. Incarceration had knocked the bluster out of the man. Billy had gone to the courthouse yesterday to see Overton take the perp walk.

He tossed the paper onto the counter, wondering what had caused Overton to betray the public trust. The judge had been like a giant oak with everything going for him—power, position, a great future. Then the mighty oak fell, exposing the rot hidden by his tough exterior.

Crawling into the mind of a petty criminal was child's play compared to penetrating the motives of a man, like Overton, who holds great power.

Billy showered and turned his thoughts to Mercy. He thought about eating pie with her and making love. He thought about her dignity and strength. He hadn't seen her since Sunday. She'd withdrawn a bit since they closed the investigation, almost distancing herself, trying to show him she didn't expect anything. That pissed him off. He didn't intend to let her slip quietly back to Atlanta.

As badly as her mother had treated her, Mercy was staying at Overton's house to support Gloria until the judge was released on bond. The couple of times they'd talked, Mercy's voice had been guarded. He'd about had his fill of the people in his life slipping away from him. Now he had to convince her of that.

Sophia, on the other hand, phoned him several times a day. Dupree had already listed their house for sale and left for Texas. She had no money. Billy gave her the names of two divorce attorneys whom he respected and suggested she ask her mother to open a bank account for her. Last night she'd called him at one in the morning, begging him to come over. He gave her the number of Paul Anderson's psychological group and said he hoped she'd find some peace.

He was about to leave when his cell rang. He checked the ID. It was Jones.

"What's happening, pardner?" Jones said.

"Like the saying goes, I'm hanging loose, admitting nothing."

Jones chuckled. "Healthy attitude. Float on the top. Sophia really pulled one over on us. What's she up to now?"

"She's learning that consequences are a bitch. She had no idea running off would lead to her new step-daddy going to jail."

"You sound sure of your case against him."

"It's Annette Perwalski's case, and it's a lock. She found the DVDs in Overton's study. That puts him at the scene. The gold rings on his mallets tie him to the weapon. Plus we've got something you don't know about—we caught Overton on the surveillance tape wearing a hat and dark glasses and carrying a custom-made croquet mallet case."

"Oh, come on."

"Overton's a fanatic. He never leaves his mallets in the car because the heat might warp the shafts."

"How smart can you be to get caught on camera with the weapon in your hand?"

"It wasn't supposed to be a weapon. He went there for notes Lou had made when they ran a bribe scheme in the eighties. The irony is, I've looked everywhere, even viewed the DVDs. No notes."

"Overton was on the take?"

"Makes you wonder how many more crooks out there are running the show."

"I can name three in Nashville alone," Jones said. "I'm heading back there tomorrow. Some yahoo walked into the state senate chamber with a homemade bomb stuffed down his pants. The governor wants to overhaul security throughout the capitol buildings. He asked me to head up the team."

"Congrats, man. You'll be running the office in a few years. Say, did you hear about Hollerith's appointment as director of the statistics project?"

Jones laughed. "Hollerith is the Teflon Man. All that shit he pulled in Holly Springs slid right off him."

"Yeah, but there's a load coming down that's not going to slide so easy. Terri smells a big story. Hollerith, the mayor, Senator Noel—they're all tied into Overton. The whole crowd may end up looking for new careers."

"So how they treating you at the CJC?"

"Not a word about suspension from Mosby. I take my lieutenant's exam next month. He hinted I may have a shot at being the next shift commander."

"Or you could knock the Mississippi mud off your boots and come to Nashville. We have some interesting jobs opening up. TBI needs good men."

"Thanks. I'll consider it."

He almost heard Jones shaking his head. "You got to work on your lying, man. I can hear you've got something else in mind."

"I'm looking at job postings in Atlanta."

Jones chuckled. "Mercy's a fine lady."

"We're meeting at Court Square. I'm hoping my natural charm will wear her down."

◆

He walked the few blocks up from the river to Court Square, where blue sky sliced through the shade trees and outlined the buildings surrounding them. He could smell biscuits and bacon over at the Blue Plate Café, and the deep fryers heating up for lunch service.

Mercy sat on a bench with her head turned to watch the water spilling down the tiered bronze fountain at the center of the square. She wore jeans and a v-necked blouse with her hair pulled up in a clip, exposing the elegant curve of her neck and the scar on her cheek.

Caesar sat at her feet. He woofed as Billy approached. Mercy stood with a fixed smile. She didn't move toward him, which he took to be a bad sign, because he was holding himself back from running to her. Her right hand came up as he drew near as if she expected to shake hands, but then she slipped it around his neck and hugged him. It felt like a cousin hug.

"You still smell like cinnamon," he said, holding her. She pulled back, and he caught her closed expression.

"Good to see you."

"Good to see you, too," he said in the same formal tone, hoping to make her laugh.

Her tight smile fell apart, and she hugged him close this time. "I really am glad. It's been surreal, dealing with Mother while Overton's been in jail. And the press, God." She shook her head.

"How's the arm?"

She held it up. "Healing. It itches."

Their eyes met for a second, then she glanced away.

"How about if we sit and watch the pigeons until we figure out what we're going to say to each other," he said.

She sat close enough to him on the bench to give him hope that she wasn't about to bolt.

"They moved Rebecca Jane to LeBonheur," she said.

He nodded. "I saw her yesterday. She has several fractures. Some internal injuries. The brain trauma left her weak on her right side. She'll need a lot of therapy, but at least she's alive."

"Thanks to you."

"If I'd seen the video a day earlier . . . " He shook his head.

"You found her in time, that's what's important. I thought you'd be pleased to know Sophia plans to do all she can for Rebecca Jane. She's heading up a fundraiser to cover some medical costs. I imagine Mother will be her biggest donor."

"Who knows, Rebecca Jane may be Sophia's second chance." He remembered Mercy's vow to cut Sophia out of her life. "How did you find out what Sophia's up to? I thought you were done with her."

"She leaves voice mail messages. Mother won't take her calls. I don't know if she'll ever forgive Sophia."

"That's an about-face. Your mom won't speak to her?"

Mercy nodded. "She's angrier with Sophia for sleeping with Overton than with Overton for almost killing Rebecca Jane. Or for plotting to kill Sophia. I thought Mother was in shock, but she's actually pretty clear-eyed. She insists she's going to 'stand by her man.' God forbid I point out that he's guilty."

"Baby, I hate to tell you, but Overton is going down hard. He could get up to twenty-five years."

"Sheesh." Mercy rolled her eyes. "Mother hired Lindsey Baldwin as his attorney. She instructed him to use every possible resource to get Overton acquitted. Thank God she revoked the power of attorney. Overton might've skipped the country with a suitcase full of cash."

"Overton's defense depends on staying in your mother's good graces. That's got to drive him crazy."

"Serves him right, but I've been told Baldwin is the best defense attorney in the business." She frowned. "What if he gets Overton off on a technicality?"

"Even if Rebecca Jane's testimony isn't conclusive, the prosecutors have enough physical evidence to lock him up."

"I'm sure you're right." She got to her feet and looked down at him with that fixed smile he'd seen earlier. "I want you to know how grateful I am for what you've done. For me, for my family. But I think it's time for me to get back to my life."

"Your life's in Atlanta." He came slowly to his feet.

She nodded, frowned. "Overton is out on bond. I couldn't imagine watching him come through the door and touch my mother." She wrapped her arms around her body. "Before I left, I told her that Overton would be convicted. She either had to get an annulment or go through the rest of her life rubbing elbows with the other inmates' spouses on visiting day."

"You said that?"

"I did. She turned her back on me. Acted as if I wasn't in the room." Her voice broke. "I had to give her one last chance. I should have known better."

He reached out, but she held up her palm.

"I'm all right. It's the nicest thing she's ever done for me. I packed my bags. She's my mother, so before I left I told her I loved her and suggested she settle her differences with Sophia. Now it's finished. I drove here to thank you and say goodbye."

Wind gusted up from the river and blew mist from the fountain onto Mercy's hair. He'd never forget how she looked standing here. Vulnerable. Strong. Beautiful. A calm came over him.

"You might want to save that 'Good bye,' you're working up to. I'm making a move out of Memphis. I hear the Atlanta PD has got some unsolved crimes with my name written all over them. Looks like you'll have to put up with me for a long time. That's going to make your goodbye kind of a waste."

She stared at him, absorbing the fact that he meant every word. She turned her head and pretended to watch a child chasing a pigeon on the other side of the fountain. Then she looked back at him.

She held his gaze. "How about we see if I can put up with you for today?"

He nodded. "Today's good."

"You think a girl could get a root beer float around here?"

He shrugged. "I think we can work that out over at the Blue Plate. One scoop or two?"

"Two," she said.

"Two it is."

They walked through the square, the day filled with blue sky and August sunlight. Caesar trailed behind them on his leash, tail wagging. Billy thought about the people in his life—the ones who'd left him. He wished he could tell them everything was going to be all right.

He'd found his way. He'd found Mercy.

◆

Reader Questions

1. At the end Mercy told her mother, "I love you." She told Billy that she'd said the words for herself. Were those the words of an emotionally healthy individual or a woman still straining for her mother's love?

2. Billy's mother walked out on him. Why, instead of hating her, did he seek out and help a woman with similar problems?

3. August weather in the South can be violent. What did the storms represent in the story?

4. How did denial figure in Lou's life? In Billy's life? In Mercy's life?

5. What can happen to a person when, like Lou, their sins force them out of denial?

6. Do you know of a business-like relationship, similar to Gloria's and Overton's marriage, that works? Do you think such an arrangement is cold-blooded or pragmatic?

7. Why did Sophia leave Billy and go back to T. Wayne?

8. What made Overton try to kill Rebecca Jane?

9. What makes a mother, like Gloria Snow, go to such extremes to favor one child over another? Have you ever witnessed it?

10. Are sociopaths a product of nature or nurture?

11. Did you believe that was the first time Lou had ever molested a child? If so, why did he do it?

12. What's your opinion of Gloria's denial of Overton's guilt, and her choice of him over her daughters?

About the Author

Lisa Turner lives in two worlds—the Deep South of her childhood and the wildly beautiful coast of Nova Scotia. When she isn't writing, making jewelry, or cooking for friends, she's sailing the coast of the Maritimes with the love of her life.